THE GRIZZLY EXTINCTION PLOT

THE
GRIZZLY
EXTINCTION PLOT

by

Liam Shay

Kerrera House Press

The Grizzly Extinction Plot—1st Edition
p.   cm.
ISBN 978-0-9859650-5-1

Kerrera House Press
Culver City, CA
www.KerreraHousePress.com

First Printing: 2013
Printed in the United States of America

10 9 8 7 6 5 4 3 2 1

To my father,
who kept alive the tradition of the senachie,
the clan bard of the Highland Scots,
by being the teller of tales, the spinner of yarns
and the master of the absurd story.

No matter how long and storied a team's history, no matter how strong their fans' support, no matter how much their owners deny it, in every fan's heart is a sliver of fear that their beloved sports team will leave—and many have. Dozens of professional teams have abandoned their fans for new arenas, new deals and, if they're lucky, new fans.

For all those who have suffered such a grievous loss, all those who have rooted for their home team and sweated blood at the close games only to have their reason for being move, this story is for you. It may suggest some of the possible nefarious machinations behind such moves in which the cash registers that are many owners' hearts count for far more than honoring the sacred compact between fans and their team, which, when broken, leaves fans with a hole in their heart.

Spring 2001

Chapter 1

In the pre-dawn darkness, Hogarth Roman O'Leary Chevalier grunted as he lifted a black, metal suitcase full of Semtec plastic explosives out of the trunk of his electric car. Peering up and down the street to make sure it was devoid of life, he hurried up the sidewalk in the moonlight lugging his precious, if explosive, load on his way to striking the first blow of the New Luddite Revolution.

He had to move fast because although Blaine, Washington appeared as idyllic as Elysium, Hogarth knew from his extensive pre-revolution research that this tiny town had a crime rate to rival South Central Los Angeles during a blackout. Blaine encompassed three ports of entry from Canada: two by land and one by sea. Therefore, every smuggler, illegal immigrant and felon attempting to sneak, skulk or slip into the Land of the Free and arrested at the border was included in law-abiding Blaine's crime statistics. Every dark cloud having a silver lining, Blaine was patrolled not only by the limited forces of the Blaine Police, but also by deputies of the Whatcom County Sheriff's Office, the Washington State Highway Patrol, Border Patrol personnel, and all manner of INS, DEA, FBI, and ATF agents. The battalions of law enforcers kept the real crime rate in Blaine itself down to the level of a small ghost town, but also greatly increased the chance that Hogarth would run into one of the hordes of guardians of the law who patrolled Blaine. Shaking with excitement and at least a sliver of fear, Hogarth wondered nervously if the ATF covered explosives, since there was no "E" in their acronym. Regardless of the ATF's responsibilities, a rendezvous with a representative of any law enforcement agency, whether it had an E in its acronym or not, was something he definitely desired to avoid as he lugged his bomb up the street.

With relief, Hogarth saw that the Professor had been right. Hogarth spotted his quarry in the driveway of a darkened house: a silver Dodge Omni. The learned scholar had explained that Americans never kept cars in their garages. Garages are for junk. Driveways are for cars. Hogarth would have classified all gas-guzzling vehicles as junk suitable for entombment in a rubbish-filled garage, never to be driven again, but he was relieved that the Professor had been right. Picking the locks on garage doors had never been his forte. His hopes for a successful revolution rising, Hogarth rushed toward the car with his bomb.

Chapter 2

Sebastian LeClerc Gianninni sneaked out of his darkened bed-room, closing the door with nary a sound. A wash and a shave later, he headed for the kitchen downstairs at the back of the house to create a breakfast for the ages. The lead story on the lo-cal radio news from Vancouver, just across the border, was about the NBA's Vancouver Grizzlies, who would put a 16-game win-ning streak on the line that night against the Los Angeles Lakers. As he busied himself making breakfast, Sebastian was impressed by the Grizzly's 92 percent winning percentage, besting the 1995-96 Chicago Bulls' 87.8 percent, which had previously appeared unassailable, at least according to the announcer. As he would have been the first to admit, Sebastian did not follow round ball as ardently as some and certainly not as feverishly as almost ev-eryone now did this early spring of 2001 in Vancouver, home of the aforementioned figuratively, if not literally unbeatable ursines.

After a busy interlude in the kitchen, he poured a precise amount of the finest, Macdonald Canadian maple syrup onto four steaming pieces of French toast. Too much and the toast would be too sweet, too little and the toast would be as dry as a parson's home. Beaming at his culinary creation, Sebastian wiped the con-densation off a tumbler of fresh naval orange juice and placed it on the breakfast tray beside the plate of French toast. He took silverware out of the drawer, buffed it to a shine with a kitchen towel and aligned it carefully on the tray. Inhaling the invigorating vapors deep into his lungs, he poured a cup of fresh-brewed coffee—Peruvian Platinum blend—from the coffee maker and then added a grapefruit (sliced into precise sections) to the tray.

Standing back to admire his breakfast, he thought that Shelley was right, 'Familiar acts are beautiful through love.'

Sebastian removed the cellophane from the single white rose he had purchased the night before. He had hidden the flower in the fridge behind a carton of mushrooms and a bottle of Hunt Country Riesling, which he was saving to imbibe with the teriyaki salmon he planned to prepare Saturday night. After plucking off one sadly prematurely wilted petal, he decided the rose was as perfect as his breakfast feast. All was ready.

He picked up the tray and, walking with the solemn air of a man bearing the Holy Grail, headed upstairs to the master bedroom. Putting on his broadest smile, he gently pushed open the door with his foot.

"'She walks in beauty, like the night / Of cloudless climes and starry skies; And all that's best of dark and bright / Meet in her aspect and her eyes,'" he recited before his eyes adjusted to the semi-darkness of the bedroom and he realized his wife, Elizabeth, was not in bed or even in the room.

Chapter 3

No one can blame Hogarth, his nerves taut, for dropping the suitcase of plastic explosives when two German shepherds across the street detected his scent on the breeze and commenced barking like the hounds of Hell. The heavy case landed on his right foot and, suppressing a scream, Hogarth wheeled to the right and back to escape from the offending case. As he did so, he moved past the end of the Omni and into the field of detection of an automatic light, which clicked on.

Forgetting his numerous vows at various times and in many places to die for the New Luddite Revolution and fearing he had been caught by the authorities, Hogarth threw up his arms and froze. The dogs' cacophony died down. Silence seared Hogarth's ears. Nothing happened. He slowly turned his head and scanned the moonlit street: empty. No house lights clicked on.

Glancing around to make sure no one had seen his *faux pas* of surrendering to a light, albeit an automatic one, Hogarth hitched up his pants, slicked back his long, black hair and stepped back toward his suitcase. Just then the light, not having sensed any movement for a minute, went out. The area behind the Omni was plunged into darkness and because his pupils had contracted in the light, Hogarth lost sight of the suitcase. His right knee slammed into its unforgiving metal side. He toppled over the case and skinned his hand on the pavement as the light, detecting his feet as they kicked out past the Omni, clicked back on and the dogs broke into their second Wagnerian chorus.

Foot throbbing, knee bruised, hand skinned, and ego smarting, Hogarth leapt to his feet and again checked the street: empty. He looked at the houses: still dark.

After waiting for the dogs to calm back down, he took out his lock-pick kit—$49.99 from lockpick.com, $54.99 with express, next-day delivery. No P.O. boxes or personal checks. It was hard to trust the purchaser of a lock-pick kit.

Hogarth took out a mini-flashlight and inspected the Omni's hatchback lock. He rested the flashlight on the edge of the car's rear window but the window was sloped, so the flashlight rolled off. Hogarth only narrowly managed to overtake it as it rolled down the driveway headed straight for the gutter, which held a distressing amount of sludge from a recent rain storm. His mother, if she had been present, would have commented that the sludge was the perfect culture for growing not only botulism, plague and typhus, but also Ebola, Avian flu and smallpox.

Frowning, Hogarth tried propping the recently rescued flashlight on the rear windshield wiper to illuminate the lock, but without success. The beam fell on a fir that lurked nearby. Fearing that time was wasting and dawn fast approaching, he stuck the flashlight in his mouth and managed to light the lock, leaving both hands free for his lock-picking exercise.

Hogarth had flunked fifth grade, been fired as an apprentice paint brush cleaner, and failed in his endeavor to return to, and live off, the land in Tuscany, where he found a profusion of grapes but little else to appease his hunger. Even so, he was adept at one skill: picking locks. Given the bank-account breaking amounts locksmiths charge for house calls, he had learned early in life that the best remedy for losing a key, which he perpetually did given his absentmindedness, was to pick the lock. In less than a minute he had the hatchback open. Thinking the hardest part of the operation was concluded, having found the car and gained access, he could be excused for frowning at what he beheld in the trunk: stacks of paper held in neat batches with thick elastic bands. Upon closer inspection with his mouth-held flashlight, he saw that the papers were novel manuscripts. They filled the trunk. What was a revolutionary to do? Jefferson would have read the manuscripts, while Mao would have burned them, unless they were little and red. Hogarth stared at the manuscripts, willing his mind to function and figure out what he should do: read, burn or do something else entirely?

Chapter 4

"What's that, dear?" Elizabeth's voice came from the en suite.

Sebastian frowned. Elizabeth could not be awake already. It was only 6:20 and she never rose before 6:45. She was nothing if not punctual and predictable in her morning routine.

"I was just…" He stopped mid-sentence when she swept into the room. She wore a suit and was attaching an earring to her left lobe. "I thought…"

"Thanks for getting up," she said as she snatched up her ox-blood leather briefcase off a chair in one smooth motion and headed out the bedroom door with a parting glance back at the breakfast tray. "That French toast smells heavenly. Do you think you'll have time to eat it?"

Sebastian was confounded and considered going back to bed. He could only sputter, "I thought," as he picked up the tray and pursued his wife downstairs.

She was putting her two-inch heels on at the kitchen table as he entered and set the succulent breakfast on the counter.

"We should be going soon," she said, glancing at her watch. "Mind if I snatch a few bites of your French toast? That orange juice looks like God's gift to the parched."

"Of course, my love," Sebastian said, relieved his culinary efforts had not gone completely unnoticed. "I…"

Elizabeth looked at her watch again as she wolfed down two bites of French toast followed by three gulps of orange juice. "We better get going if you're going to have time to drop me off before your first class."

Finally Sebastian remembered; Elizabeth's Mercedes was in the shop. She had dropped it off yesterday. No wonder this morning had seemed like the perfect morning to arise before the first light of dawn to create a romantic breakfast. Somewhere deep in Sebastian's subconscious must have been the thought that he had to get up early anyway to take Elizabeth to work.

With a sigh, Sebastian rushed upstairs, grabbed his battered briefcase and well-worn jacket before returning to the kitchen for a bite of French toast, a section of grapefruit and a gulp of juice before he heeded Elizabeth's impatient stare and followed her out the front door.

Chapter 5

The suitcase would definitely not fit in the trunk with all of the manuscripts inside. Not one to wilt before a challenge, Hogarth lifted two stacks of papers out of the trunk and set them carefully on the dewed driveway in a dry spot under an overhanging fir. The last thing he wanted was to damage the manuscripts. For all he knew they were the writings of the next great naturalist to rival Henry David Thoreau, John Muir or Farley Mowat.

A space made, Hogarth gently and carefully placed the suitcase in the trunk. Breathing around the flashlight, still clenched between his teeth, he placed four manuscripts in a neat row over the suitcase, most effectively hiding it.

Hogarth glanced at the six manuscripts still on the pavement. He jammed two more into the trunk and then, with great reluctance, pulled out several hundred pages from each of the remaining bundles. After his brutal editing, the four now shrunken manuscripts neatly finished filling in the trunk.

Smiling, Hogarth stepped back to admire his handiwork. The movement set off the automatic light. Startled, his arms shot up and he dropped the flashlight, the hundreds of manuscript pages he had been holding and his lock-pick kit. This time, however, as the dogs across the street began their third chorus, he swiftly regained his composure and ran down the driveway to snatch his flashlight just before it reached the gutter and its questionable contents. Turning, he beheld manuscript pages strewn across the driveway like confetti left over from a giant's wedding. He darted to and fro to gather them up, also finding in the process his precious lock-pick kit.

As his arms grew full, the manuscript pages began to evade capture. When he reached for new prey, he dropped pages he had already captured, proving that two chapters in hand are better than one on the driveway. Worse, a breeze carrying the cool salt air of an incoming Pacific storm came up, further complicating his quest to collect all of the manuscript pages by blowing the sheets across the front lawn into some bushes and beyond onto a neighbor's property. Just when he was at the point of giving up, he heard the front door of the house begin to open.

Hogarth had dawdled too long collecting manuscript pages. The sun was peeking over the horizon. He leapt back to the Omni and steeling his nerves, gently lowered the hatchback and heard it reassuringly click shut. Glancing around as he scurried back toward his own car, his arms full of miscellaneous manuscript pages, Hogarth wondered who would have a sane reason to arise at such an ungodly hour. More importantly, he also tried to remember if he had put his car keys in his pocket or if he had left them in the ignition. Luckily, if he had locked himself out of his car, he still had his trusty lock-pick kit.

Chapter 6

Just as Hogarth reached his car and found he had not locked his keys inside, Sebastian and Elizabeth hurried out their front door. As he beheld his silver Omni, as was often the case Sebastian wished he had a romantic car; a Silver Ghost, a Bentley or even (dare he dream?), an Alfa Romeo. Elizabeth had ruled out an Alfa Romeo Sebastian had discovered in the classifieds as merely replacing one perfectly reliable car—the Omni—with another of unknown reliability; the pre-owned Alfa Romeo. Sebastian had pointed out that Elizabeth drove a Mercedes, but to no avail. It was, she counter-pointed-out, a company car. Sebastian had wrung from her the concession that when the Omni finally went to auto purgatory for disassembly into all its resalable parts, he could replace it with a car of his choice. With hopes that the apparently immortal Omni would die some day soon, Sebastian opened Elizabeth's door, stealing a long, appreciative look at her as she slid into the passenger seat.

"'Placed in all thy charms before me, All I forget but to adore thee,'" he recited.

"Thank you," she said. "You could have parked in the garage last night. My car's in the shop. Did you remember? Byron, right?"

"George Noel Gordon. Yes, Lord Byron. I forgot about your car." He closed her door and ambled, head down, around to the driver's side, his failed romantic breakfast heavy on his mind. He opened the door, placed his briefcase on the backseat and slid behind the wheel. Shoulders slumped, eyes drooping, he inserted his key in the ignition and turned to Elizabeth, debating whether to mention his grand romantic plan for an intimate breakfast in bed. Then he saw the rose. She held it before her, admiring its immaculate petals.

"It's truly beautiful, isn't it?" Sebastian asked, smiling that at least a part of his breakfast offering had met with approval.

"Very," Elizabeth agreed and bestowed a kiss upon him. "Thanks for breakfast. It tasted wonderful. Sorry we didn't have time to truly enjoy it."

"There'll be other times," Sebastian said with a smile, his hand on the key. He was about to start the car when someone rapped on his window.

The window rapper was Mrs. Rosalita Turnbell, the Gianninni's neighbor.

Unbuckling his seat belt and slipping out of the car, Sebastian said, "Good morning and what a fine morning it is."

Her face aglow in the dawn's early light, Mrs. Turnbell beamed like a cherub. She clutched a sheet of paper to her bountiful bosom as if it were the recipe for eternal life. Spinning past him with a move that would have done an All-Pro defensive lineman proud, she was between Sebastian and the car before he even knew he was under assault. Her ample derriere slammed the car door shut, leaving a bewildered Elizabeth wondering why her husband was yakking with the neighbors when they were already late.

"What can I do for you, Mrs. Turnbell?" Sebastian adhered like glue to the belief that you should treat others as you wish to be treated.

"Rosa, please," Mrs. Turnbell gushed, still fondling the piece of paper as if it was an aphrodisiac of the gods. "I received your note."

"My note?" Sebastian asked, bewildered.

She looked down at the sheet and read, "'Lord Strongblade took the serving wench, who was, in truth, the Lady Wilhemina, in his strong, tanned arms and kissed her as she had never been kissed before.'"

"That's very nice, Mrs…Rosa, but I don't think I have time right now for a reading." Sebastian stole a glance into his car and was rewarded by a view of Elizabeth tapping her watch with a come-hither-and-get-thee-and-me-to-work look.

"I thought it was especially clever how you used Lord Strongblade and Lady Wilhemina as an analogy to a certain other couple." Mrs. Turnbell leaned toward Sebastian, fluttering her eyes like a nervous butterfly's wings.

Sebastian took an involuntary step back and was stopped by the generous bosom of Destiny Mary-Louise Turnbell, Rosa's teenaged daughter. The romance-novel inspired name Destiny came from her Harlequin-addicted mother. The Mary-Louise came from her sober and serious father.

"Mr. Gianninni," Destiny said breathily, simultaneously pushing him away with mock modesty and clinging to him like an octopus hauling in an especially tasty morsel.

Sun rising, time wasting and wife glaring, Sebastian sidestepped out of the clutches of his newest admirer.

"I found this stuffed into the screen on my window this morning," Destiny said, flourishing a piece of paper as if it was a holy relic. "It's lovely. 'He could not proclaim his love for the young damsel, for that would risk the approbation of her powerful father,'" she read, smiling at Sebastian and leaning toward him like a sapling in a gale.

"I must apologize," a baffled Sebastian said, his head swiveling between Rosa and Destiny as if he was watching a tennis match. "I fear some pages from my novels found their way onto your property. It must have been the wind. 'O wild West Wind, thou breath of Autumn's being, / Thou, from whose unseen presence the leaves' or in this case the pages, 'Are driven, like ghosts from an enchanter fleeing.'"

"I know how the note got into my window screen and it wasn't the wind," Destiny stated, lowering her eyes and fluttering her lashes.

"Is there something in your eyes?" Sebastian asked, concerned about his young neighbor. Then he noticed she was clothed in an extremely short dressing gown of a material that appeared to admit more light than it blocked. He feared the West Wind might blow more than leaves and pages. It might well blow a cold.

Chapter 7

Although Destiny might be risking a cold, Hogarth was risking heart failure. He sat in his car half a block down B Street from Sebastian's driveway wondering if he could withstand his torment a second longer. The good professor and his wife appeared to be determined never to leave. They mooned over a rose, chatted with the neighbors and as he watched, the wife slid out of the car and joined the party. They never would have loitered so long if they had known the trunk contained a bomb.

Suddenly Hogarth's car began to rock and sway. An earthquake? No manner of calamity would surprise him on this calamity filled day. Glancing to the right he saw a neon-yellow wall moving past his car window. Momentarily panicked, he realized that the wall was in fact the jogging suit of a man who was fully as broad as he was tall. The man was attached to a small, black dog with a beard, eyebrows, ear tufts, and a springy gait as jaunty as the King of England must have displayed after he trounced the French at Agincourt in straight sets. Hogarth watched the man pound up the road, surprised he didn't crash through the pavement with each footfall. He was led by a Scottish terrier, who appeared able to roll his front half independent of his rear half. The vast expanse of the man's neon-yellow jacket and pants, probably visible as far as Honolulu, if not Tokyo, served as a beacon for any ship, boat, kayak or canoe entering Blaine's Drayton Harbor four blocks to the west.

Even as Hogarth watched, the worst happened: the jogger and his bearded dog veered across the street and joined the old woman, the young woman, the professor and his wife beside the professor's bomb-laden car. What else could delay the journey of Hogarth's precious explosives? By now he would have hesitated to place a bet against the possibility of a garage band showing up and a block party magically appearing with pajama-clad towns-people joining the general revelry. Frustrated, Hogarth started hitting his forehead repeatedly on the steering wheel as he wondered why he had not become a doctor specializing in wealthy diseases as his parents had wished, instead of an agent on the forefront of the New Luddite Revolution.

Chapter 8

"Sebastian," Mr. Samuel E. Turnbell, ex-Wall Street banker, ex-Golden Gloves amateur boxer, ex-United States Marine, bellowed, his voice like a bullhorn in a cathedral during a funeral mass. Then, his voice softening considerably, he turned to Elizabeth and said, "Mrs. Gianninni, you look beguilingly beautiful this morning."

Rosa and Destiny magically secreted their prized possessions—the romantic notes—within their dressing gowns in the time it took Sam to grasp Elizabeth's hand and bestow a gallant kiss.

Sam winked at Sebastian, who had been tutoring his neighbor in the ways of romance so as to avoid a precipitous decline in the mercury between Mr. and Mrs. Samuel Turnbell, better known as Rosa. Sebastian managed to smile in return at his pupil. Sam, his shoulders twice as broad as Sebastian's, his neck the circumference of Sebastian's waist and his hands like two blocks of granite, instilled a high level of unease in Sebastian. Sam had never said an unkind word to Sebastian, let alone threatened him or done anything that could, even by the most sensitive of neighbors, be construed as an overt act of aggression. Even so, Sebastian felt uneasy around his muscular, if short, neighbor. Worse yet, he did not like the idea of his romance tutoring being used on his own beloved Elizabeth.

"We should be going," Sebastian announced.

"Yes, we must be going," Elizabeth agreed, tapping her watch.

"Just when I arrive to enjoy the pleasure of your company," Sam said, bowing so low to Elizabeth that his sweeping hand grazed the pavement. "What were you all talking about?"

Used to being the center of attention and having had enough of being ignored, Tyrone—Sam's Scottie—reared back on his hind quarters and pawed the air like the boxer his master had once been. The spectacle resulted in the desired behavior: every human eye turned to look at the shadow-boxing terrier, accompanied by appropriately gushed, "Ahs," "Tyrone" and "What a cute dog." Tyrone was a firm believer that idle hands were the devil's play things, and any hands that were not scratching or patting him were idle indeed. He wiggled as hands reached down to scratch, pat and stroke his head, back and flanks.

"Mr. Gianninni was just saying good morning, Sam," Rosa said, taking her husband's sweaty arm, even as she cast an appraising, even predatory eye over Sebastian.

"We really should be going," Elizabeth repeated and climbed back into the car.

With Rosa securely berthed alongside her husband and Destiny momentarily distracted by Tyrone, Sebastian slipped back into the driver's seat.

Chapter 9

Seeing the professor and his wife climb back into the Omni, Hogarth thought his torments were at long last over. Finally, they were leaving. He stopped bouncing his forehead off the steering wheel and, thanking Allah, God, Buddha and his lucky stars, fingered his keys preparatory to starting his car to follow his bomb on its planned, but long-delayed journey north.

Looking back up the street, however, Hogarth's hopes were once again dashed. The small black dog was showing an intense interest in the trunk of the Omni. The more the huge neon-yellow-festooned neighbor pulled the stubborn dog away, the more the little bearded monster fought to thrust his forepaws at the rear bumper and attempted to claw his way through the steel and plastic into the trunk.

Hogarth watched with horror, wondering if the Scottish terrier was as well-endowed in the sniffer department as the German Shepherd that had foiled his attempt to smuggle explosives into Israel to blow up a computer simulation of King David's Temple. For 25 shekels the simulation allowed visitors to take a virtual tour of the temple destroyed thousands of years before by a Roman legion on holiday. A German shepherd named Coco had sniffed out Hogarth's suitcase of C-3 explosives at Tel Aviv airport. Luckily Hogarth had been in the restroom throwing up after a most turbulent flight. Hogarth would never again fly, even if his motion sickness had saved him from several decades in an Israeli prison located on some of the more parched acreage of the Negev desert.

Hogarth took his binoculars out of the glove compartment and focused in on the nose of the terrier in question. He needn't have used the binoculars. The canine's sniffer took up approximately 60 percent of the dog and, Hogarth had no doubt, the terrier could smell a three-day-old French fry left in the bleachers in center field from home plate in Dodger Stadium with the wind at his back.

Hogarth started his car, ready to bolt and abort the entire operation when he spied the owner dragging the dog away from the hatchback, which remained unopened. The neon-yellow-clad man, towing the terrier as if he was landing a prize marlin with plenty of fight still left in it, led the two women across the yard to the neighboring house. The Omni then backed out into the street. Hogarth's ordeal was finally over—or at least the portion restricted to United States' soil.

Chapter 10

"Funny," Sebastian said, glancing at a green electric car parked just down the street from their house.

"What?" Elizabeth asked.

"That man."

"What man?"

"The man in that parked car we just passed. His forehead is as red as a rose."

"Strange."

Mindful of the many police agencies that patrolled Blaine, Sebastian drove precisely at the posted 25 mph.

"I need to pick up some cigarettes, milk and cheese for Bill," Sebastian said as he slowed to turn into a service station/convenience store. Blaine has a plethora of such stores since it sits within a chip shot of the Canadian border. The stores conduct a roaring trade in commodities that the Canadian government in all its wisdom taxes heavily, such as gasoline, cigarettes, milk and cheese, but which the American government in all its wisdom taxes much less heavily. Therefore, if Blaine were to secede from the union and keep all of the taxes, even the lower U.S. taxes, on the supertankers of gasoline, cartons of cigarettes, oceans of milk and mountains of cheese sold to Canadians, it could pave its streets with gold, sidewalks with silver and crosswalks with platinum, if its city council was so inclined.

Elizabeth glanced at her watch. "Can't you stop tomorrow? I don't want to be late."

"Alright," Sebastian said, happy to oblige his lady love.

Passing the store, he turned north into the Peace Arch Park and the Port of Entry. Adhered to the windshield of his car was a PACE sticker that enabled them to cross the border almost as easily as they drove through Blaine. Sebastian had long since forgotten what PACE stood for, but it certainly increased the pace at which they crossed the border as they commuted from Blaine to their jobs in Vancouver, Canada.

Sebastian stayed in the far right lane, which was designated for PACE members. He admired the great white Peace Arch and the view across Boundary Bay as the Omni chugged up the slight rise to the booth at the Canadian inspection station. It was early and business at the border, even in the non-PACE lanes was light. Sebastian stopped and said a cheerful, "Good morning."

Canadian Border Agency Services officer Fawn "Bulldog" Cates glanced at the middle-aged man with the broad grin and managed a brief upturn at the corners of her mouth as she peered at the data about Sebastian Gianninni, his car and his border-crossing habits on her computer. PACE cars were normally just waved through, since the owner and occupants of the vehicle had already been checked by the FBI and RCMP. Bulldog, however, was sniffing around for a major bust to boost her chances of being accepted into the elite Special Investigation Unit (SIU), whose members were armed, unlike Canadian Border Agency Services officers.

Bulldog's eyes locked on the vehicle's weight displayed on the computer. The Omni registered on the sensors under the road as weighing 120 pounds more than it should have based on the manufacturer's weight for that particular make and model combined with the average weight of two adult passengers.

"What's the purpose of your visit to Canada?" Bulldog asked, buying time as she scrolled down to skim the records of the previous crossings by Sebastian LeClerc Gianninni.

"My wife and I are off to earn our daily bread," Sebastian explained, his fingers tapping a joyous tattoo on the steering wheel. He was already plotting another sumptuous surprise breakfast for

Elizabeth. This time it would be on a weekend, so there would be no conflict in early morning scheduling between work and romance.

Bulldog's eyes widened. For years, every time the Omni had crossed the border it had been far above the weight allowance for that type and make of car with the noted number of occupants. That is, unless the occupants were sumo wrestlers. Glancing over, Bulldog judged that Sebastian and Elizabeth were both a few snacks shy of being slim, but they were many feasts away from being fat. Her eyes narrow and suspicions running rampant, Bulldog wondered what this middle-aged couple had been smuggling into Canada all these years and why with the proceeds they had not purchased a nicer car.

Whatever they were smuggling and regardless of what they were doing with the proceeds, it just might be the major bust that would take her out of the ranks of the booth tenders and into the ranks of the SIU. A major bust would surely put her over the top on this, her seventh attempt to join the elite unit, which investigated, infiltrated and imprisoned smugglers and their nefarious gangs who attempted to smuggle cheap milk, cigarettes and gasoline into the Dominion of Canada without paying the Queen's tariffs, taxes and duties.

"Please pull over to your left and park where the sign says, 'Vehicle Inspections,'" Bulldog ordered, forcing a smile to keep her quarry off guard. She pressed the button by her left foot to alert the Armed Response Team—ART to those in the know.

Sebastian was not surprised. The guards had searched his car several times over the years. Once the Canadian Border Agency Services had received a tip from a reliable informant, an R.I., that a man driving a silver Omni was planning to smuggle 25,000 cartons of cigarettes into Canada. Ignoring the fact that an Omni could not hold 25,000 cartons of cigarettes, the guards had searched Sebastian's car from bumper to bumper, roof to tire treads. They found no trace of tobacco, nicotine, tar or any of the other questionable contents of cigarettes the tobacco industry claims are good for toughening up the immune system. Sebastian had enjoyed the whole experience, since it had detained him long enough to miss a faculty meeting. After thanking Sebastian for his patience, the guards had released him and his well-searched car. The reliable informant, R.I., was downgraded to an occasionally unreliable informant, O.U.I.—an oinker to those in the know.

"I hope this won't make you late, dear," Sebastian said as he drove across to the Vehicle Inspections area.

Elizabeth glanced at her watch. "It can't be helped. I'll get some reading done on a proposal for a medical records building in Saskatoon." She pulled a file out of her briefcase and opened it on her lap. Written in Sebastian's hand on a sticky note on the file was penned, "'Grow old with me! The best is yet to be.' Robert Browning." Elizabeth read the note, beamed over at her husband and said, "I'd rather grow old with you, Sebastian."

"Robert Browning's long gone, so you're stuck with me anyway."

Elizabeth smiled and started reviewing her file. Sebastian glanced at the rows of figures, dense text and complex charts and, thinking 'There, but for the grace of God, go I,' turned off the engine. He looked outside and, not seeing any other cars awaiting inspection, remarked, "At least there won't be a wait. Maybe they'll be quick."

Even as the words left his mouth, eight figures in camouflage gear, bullet-proof vests, helmets and black boots touting M-16 assault rifles burst from the building and sprinted toward the Omni.

"I think they may be rather quick, dear," Sebastian commented, as he watched the guards rush to take up positions around the Omni. Bulldog, having quickly found a relief for her booth so she could be in on the bust that would make her career, stalked up to the car. They would hear about this one as far away as the River de Chute station on the Maine-New Brunswick border.

"Please exit the car!" Bulldog barked loud enough to be heard even in the sealed Omni. "Keep your hands in sight at all times!"

Sebastian and Elizabeth froze, staring at the M-16-armed border guards who encircled their car and the muscular, yet feminine woman who shouted orders at them like a nun in an especially strict school for wayward girls.

"We better get out," Sebastian advised as he raised his hands so they would be visible to the guards. Elizabeth dropped her file and followed her husband's example.

Bulldog watched as Sebastian and Elizabeth sat wide-eyed and frozen like last-week's salmon catch.

"Exit the car!" Bulldog bellowed as the ART members fingered their weapons nervously, waiting for the next act in this tense, yet glacially developing international incident.

Having been wrestling with a dilemma adorned with particularly sharp horns, Sebastian had a flash of brilliance. Keeping his hands in sight, he reached slowly for a collection of Shelley's poems wedged between the dashboard and the windshield. As Bulldog and ART tensed at the curious behavior of their quarry, Sebastian used the book to push the window handle down. The window open an inch, Sebastian could now reply without having to yell like an ill-bred sports fan after a questionable officiating call against the home team. "I can't reach to open the door."

"Why not?" Bulldog demanded. "Are you handicapped?"

"No, but thank you for asking." Sebastian smiled out at Bulldog.

"Then what's wrong?"

"I can't reach the door handle without dropping my hand below the window."

"So?!" Bulldog concluded she was dealing with a mule: an unsuspecting courier whom some criminal mastermind had duped into smuggling illegal goods. This one certainly fit the description in both meanings of the word, assuming a mule was closely related to an ass.

"You said to keep my hands in sight, but if I reach for the door handle you'll lose sight of my hand as it goes below the window."

As the ART members kept their weapons on the occupants of the car, Bulldog issued her orders. Two ART members leapt to the car's doors and flung them open.

"Thank you so much," Sebastian said as he exited the car, his hands still raised. A concerned, perturbed and frightened Elizabeth got out her side and hurried around to stand close to her husband. Their cars had been searched before, but never by an armed squad of officers who appeared ready to take on a battalion of North Korea's finest.

"You can put your hands down," Bulldog said. "We'll have to search your car."

"That's quite all right," Sebastian said, relieved to lower his hands. His arms were beginning to ache.

"Please step onto the curb and remain there while we conduct the search."

Sebastian and Elizabeth stepped onto the curb.

"Quite a nice morning," Sebastian remarked as ART searched the car. Two members started in the front, while another tried to open the hatchback, but finding it locked, asked Sebastian for the key.

"Let me open it for you," Sebastian offered, ever ready to provide assistance, as he stepped off the curb.

"Remain where you are!" Bulldog barked as guards swung their M-16s in his direction.

Sebastian jumped back onto the curb. "The keys are in the ignition. Your keep-your-hands-in-sight order didn't give me a chance to remove them."

The ART member searching the driver's side of the front of the car tossed the keys to another member who caught them and inserted them into the hatchback's lock.

Chapter 11

"What's the purpose of your visit to Canada?" a guard asked Hogarth as he sat in his car at the border not 50 meters—he was just inside metric Canada—from Sebastian's ART-surrounded, bomb-laden car. Hogarth's eyes were transfixed on the scene before him: eight armed guards searching the Omni. With mounting horror he saw that one of the guards was about to open the hatchback. All was lost. The operation had turned into a disaster before it had even begun.

"Sir? The purpose of your visit to Canada?" the guard prompted, looking up from Hogarth's passport.

"I'm sorry. I've been up all night."

"You should take a nap at the tourist center just up the road then, or you can get a cup of coffee at the kiosk next to the center," the guard advised, pointing. "May I ask the purpose of your visit?"

"Business."

"Well then," the guard said, handing Hogarth back his passport, "Have a pleasant trip and I hope your business turns out well."

"I don't see how it can," Hogarth mumbled as he eased his car ahead, his eyes focused on the Omni as the guard opened the hatchback. Hogarth accelerated past the unfolding disaster.

Chapter 12

"That's strange," Sebastian remarked.

"What?" Elizabeth asked.

"That man who was parked by our house and had the red forehead," Sebastian said, pointing as a green electric car drove past. "There he is again, but this time he's banging his head on the steering wheel."

"Why doesn't his horn go off?" Elizabeth wondered as they watched Hogarth, his head bouncing off the steering wheel, drive up toward the freeway.

"Pay dirt!" The ART member who had opened the hatchback yelled before Sebastian could answer Elizabeth's question.

As expectant as a dog in a clumsy cook's kitchen, Bulldog scrambled around the car and peered into the hatchback. "Do you have an explanation for this?" she demanded.

Sebastian and Elizabeth took a step forward, then stopped, their toes dangling over the curb.

"Come here!" Bulldog ordered.

"You said to stay on the curb," Sebastian said.

"Come here!"

Sebastian and Elizabeth walked hesitantly past the ART members to the rear of the car where Sebastian said as he looked in the trunk, beaming like a father showing off his favorite son, "That's my life's work."

"What is it all?" Bulldog demanded as she picked up an elastic-band-bound sheaf of papers.

"They are my novel manuscripts."

Bulldog saw her career-making bust disintegrating before her eyes into a farcical incident that would surely reach River de Chute as the funniest border happening since a smuggler packed marijuana around his car's engine. He was far from the brightest smuggler since every drug connoisseur knew that BC marijuana, nicknamed BC Bud, was the finest on earth. Why import whacky weed *into* BC when the local product was vastly superior to all others?

The smuggler's ignorance was further demonstrated when the hot engine set the hashish on fire at the worst possible moment for the smuggler: just as he told the border guard he had nothing to declare. The billowing, white, hallucinogenic smoke engulfed the border crossing, turning the entire border guard contingent into a hallucinating throwback to the most psychedelic hippie days of the 1960s. The smuggler, with long and varied experience operating under the influence of all manner of hallucinogens, ran back into the United States and escaped. The buzzed guards, inexperienced in the use of controlled substances, lost the smuggler in what they thought was a field of 40-foot daisies, but was in reality just a small tulip garden in Peace Arch Park.

"Manuscripts, huh. Do they have any value?" Bulldog asked, grasping at the last possible straw. Maybe she could arrest Sebastian for illegally importing merchandise for sale or distribution.

"Why?" Sebastian asked as he picked up one of his masterpieces. "Do you want to buy one?"

"Why do you keep them in your trunk?" an ART member asked.

"Insurance."

"Insurance?" Bulldog asked, her ears perking up at the possibility of a multinational insurance scam. Her career just might be saved.

"I keep one copy of each novel in my home, one at my office and one in my car. If my house or office burns down, then I'll still have a copy here in my car." Sebastian patted his trusty Omni affectionately, momentarily forgetting his dreams of an Alfa Romeo. "Let me read you a selection."

As the ART members gathered around, Sebastian thumbed through one of his latest works and began to read. Elizabeth, resigned to a long wait, retreated to the Omni's passenger seat to go over her Saskatoon medical records building proposal.

"'Emily Fairweather looked across the crowded room and beheld her first, true love: John Trueblood.'" Sebastian lowered the manuscript for a moment to interject, "This is, of course, at her wedding reception; her wedding to another man, the nefarious and diabolical, yet extremely wealthy and darkly handsome Dr. Eustace Loftgang." Sebastian frowned. "Strange, some pages seem to be missing."

"You write romances?" Bulldog asked.

"Of course. What else would you expect from an Italian-French-Canadian professor of Romantic literature? The French and the Italians invented seduction, love and romance." Sebastian made a dramatic sweeping gesture with his left hand, but the effect of the grand gesture was spoiled when his hand banged against one of the ART members' M-16s and his ring struck the weapon with a metallic clink.

Bulldog's demeanor changed instantly. "I love romances. Have you published any?"

Sebastian glanced at his shoes in sorrow. "I must confess no, but the bias in the romance industry against male writers is of Everest proportions. They refuse to publish a novel by a man and I, standing on principle as every truly artist must, will not submit to publishing my life's work under an assumed name merely to fool the consumer, nay, the reader, into believing that a novel was penned by a woman. Think of the greatest romantic writers of all time, Percy Bysshe Shelley, George Noel Gordon, better known as Lord Byron, William Wordsworth, Thomas Love Peacock and even Coleridge, with 'She is not fair to outward view, As maidens be, Her loveliness I never knew, Until she smiled on me.' As Browning—another man by the way—wrote, 'Love is the energy of life,' for both women and men. Where would we be if no one had ever published romantic poetry written by men for the women they love? I dare say, the worse for it."

"Can I get a copy of one of your books?" Bulldog asked, momentarily forgetting where and who she was. Her home was stuffed full of repeatedly read romances and the thought of a book in manuscript form, pre-publication, was a thrill devoutly to be wished. She could be the first to read a novel hot from the author's passionate imagination.

"I'd like a copy, too," a female member of ART chirped in, shifting her M-16 to her shoulder to raise her hand to attract Sebastian's attention.

"You're far too kind to deign to read my work at this early stage in my career," Sebastian said modestly, inclining his head in a slight bow to acknowledge his new fans.

"A romance writer," another female ART member gushed. Affirmative action had drastically altered the composition, not to mention the interests of ART members. "I'd love a copy, too."

"Me, too," a strapping, broad-shouldered male ART member said. Everyone turned on him with frowns and he hastily added, "For my wife."

"No reason men can't indulge in romances, my good man," Sebastian said, patting the man-mountain on the shoulder. "For all men, at one time or another have beheld, 'upon the night's starred face, Huge cloudy symbols of a high romance.'"

"Did you write that?" Bulldog asked, enthralled.

"No. It's by a minor poet, by the name of Keats, John Keats. Another man, by the way."

"I must have a copy of one of your works," Bulldog insisted. "Can I buy one, please?"

"If you insist, I could be persuaded to part with these copies," Sebastian said, gesturing at the manuscripts in the trunk, "since I have duplicates at home and at work."

"How did you find the time to write so many?" an ART member asked.

"I merely 'filled the papers with the breathings of my heart,' to borrow some fitting words from the sublime Wordsworth."

Still sitting in the car, Elizabeth waved to attract Sebastian's attention and tapped her watch. Medical records nor the buildings that house them wait for no man or woman.

"How much for *Lord Chatterley's Mistress*?" An ART member asked, clutching a manuscript possessively.

"When they're published, I had planned them to be nice, big thick paperbacks in the true romance tradition," Sebastian said, weighing the heft of one of his other masterpieces. "Shall we say, seven dollars?"

"Canadian or American?" Bulldog asked, pulling out her wallet.

"American. Shall we say, 10 dollars Canadian?"

Sales were brisk and in moments the trunk was empty, save for a black suitcase, and Sebastian clutched just shy of $320 in sales in a mix of Canadian and American currency. He thought that if sales continued at the brisk pace of the past five minutes he would be atop the *New York Times* bestseller list by lunchtime. He was drawn out of his dreams of success by the black suitcase. He had never seen it before. Was it Elizabeth's?

"Can we place orders for other copies?" a border guard who had come over to investigate the hubbub asked as she skimmed *1,001 Iroquois Nights*.

"Of course, but I need a pen and some paper."

An ART member ripped a wanted poster off a nearby bulletin board and handed it and a pen emblazoned with the name of an assault rifle manufacturer to Sebastian, who glanced at the rows of wanted rogues on the poster.

"Not the most ruly bunch," he commented as he turned it over.

A growing crowd of ART members, guards and people who had been crossing the border and had parked to investigate the source of the commotion clustered around Sebastian. Word raced through the throng that a writer had been arrested, then that a writer was giving away books and finally that a writer was selling limited first editions. The crowd swelled like a South Carolina congregation after a long, dry sermon on a sweltering summer day gathering for free iced tea and cold watermelon in the cool shade of an ancient weeping willow.

Elizabeth bypassed a row of bulletproof-vest wearing border guards and successfully breached the wall of ART members before emerging from the crowd to stand beside her beloved husband. She opened her mouth to state politely that they had to be going, when her eyes alighted on the wad of currency in Sebastian's right hand. Beautiful green Yankee bills mixed with a profusion of colorful Canadian paper, forming a currency rainbow. Sebastian had only taken one order, for *Out of Asia,* when Elizabeth, her business acumen showing like a comet on a cloudless night, took over. She had the patrons in a queue, cash ready (no CODs) and had set up a book-order file on her laptop as she balanced the computer on the car bumper in a most unladylike crouch in less time than it took Sebastian to wonder if his computer printer would be able to keep up with the demand for his home-printed manuscripts.

"Canada is certainly the land of opportunity," Elizabeth whispered to Sebastian as she added two columns for sales tax, one American and one Canadian, to her spreadsheet, since she was unsure if she was technically in the United States or in Canada.

"You can sit on this while you take our orders," an ART member suggested as he leaned his M-16 against the car and reached for the black, metal suitcase in the Omni's trunk.

Chapter 13

Parked at the Beautiful British Columbia tourist office just up the road from the border, Hogarth sat in his car watching the disaster unfold. As ART searched the Omni, his fingers hovered over the key to start his car and flee at the first sign of the discovery of his explosives, but the border guards did not seem to find the suitcase.

A crowd formed and, through the shifting masses, Hogarth saw manuscripts change hands. He was relieved he had not damaged too many of the precious tomes, since they were evidently much sought after works of great literature.

Still trying to figure out what was happening, he spotted a border guard lifting his explosive suitcase out of the Omni. Discovered. All was lost.

Hogarth turned the key and, checking his car's blind spots—this was no time for an accident, especially in his prized electric car for which he had languished six months on a waiting list to purchase—pulled out and sped up the 99 Freeway toward Vancouver and away from the monumental debacle at the Peace Arch port of entry.

In his mind were the words of his Uncle Shamus O'Leary, "Why don't you become an air traffic controller?" Hogarth had rejected the suggestion at the time. He did not deal well with stress. Right now, however, Hogarth thought that directing 747s with 400 passengers aboard each craft hurtling through the congested skies at 500 miles an hour appeared to be the least stressful of jobs compared to the occupation of international terrorist in the fight for the New Luddite Revolution. Revolutionary was no profession for the faint of heart.

The professor, with his titanium nerves, steel spine and dry-ice-cold visage would know what to do. The professor had the heart, body and soul of a true New Luddite Revolutionary, willing to struggle through any hardship, endure any suffering and, if necessary, even die for the glorious coming revolution.

Chapter 14

Professor Ignatius Villano sat in his office at the City College of Vancouver enraptured by the Wagner emanating from his new Bose CD player, warmed by a snifter of Chambord and enthralled by immortal lines from *Othello*, his newest e-book. He stretched out his six-foot-frame in his Quintano black leather, high-backed chair and marveled at the perfection of the little things in life: Wagner, a plush chair, fine blackberry liqueur, and the Bard. He swished the dark Chambord around in its Waterford snifter and glanced out the window. A perfect spring morning and no class for an hour. Paradise *was* attainable in this world.

His office door burst open. A red-foreheaded Hogarth stood panting at the door like some forlorn Saint Bernard who has scrambled up a mountain on a mission of rescue, only to find the party in supposed trouble picnicking on champagne, crackers and brie.

Dr. Villano carefully put his Chambord down and reached over to turn off Wagner as he gestured at Hogarth to wait. The last thing Villano wanted was an abrupt change from the perfection of Wagner, Chambord and *Othello* to the imperfection of a babbling, intelligence-challenged, Irish-Japanese-French-Moroccan New Luddite Revolutionary. Too abrupt a change, Villano feared, could lead to a heart attack, similar to the effect of soaking in hot springs before plunging into arctic-cold water, which only

Finns, Swedes and similarly Polar-bred people could or should attempt.

Villano leaned back and gestured for Hogarth to enter his sanctum. The young revolutionary closed the door and imparted his news in one rapid sentence. "The border guards seized Dr. Gianninni, his wife, the car and the suitcase!"

"Why is your forehead red?"

"I hit it on the steering wheel."

"Where you in an accident?"

"No, I meant to do it."

Villano closed his eyes, not wishing to venture any further up that particular twisted garden path.

"You're sure the border guards seized the bomb?" Villano asked from behind closed lids.

"Of course. I saw the whole disaster from the tourist office just up the road."

"You must return to Seattle and purchase more explosives," Villano said, opening his eyes. Hogarth paced the office, gingerly wiping sweat from his bruised brow and jostling the ornate teak table that held Villano's prized Chambord. Villano rescued his snifter of liqueur from the teetering table. "You can be back this afternoon in time for the game tonight."

"How do I smuggle it into Canada? The border will be sealed up tight now. They just found the suitcase bomb!"

"I will devise a new plan. Call me after you've procured the explosives in Seattle and I'll tell you how to transport them into Canada."

Hogarth stopped pacing and stood, staring at Villano like a flounder long since out of water.

"Go!" Villano ordered. "Now. Time and tide wait for no man."

Hogarth frowned. "Tide? Should I bring the explosives by boat?"

"No! Go!"

Hogarth spun on his heel to leave but stopped in mid-spin facing the window. His jaw fell open, his eyes widened and the likeness to a flounder surpassed that of the likeness to a Saint Bernard. As Hogarth gawked out the window, Villano wondered if, as he had often feared during the past few weeks, he had allied himself with a mental defective. He rose and stood beside Hogarth to look where Hogarth stared, out his second-floor window. Villano saw below in the college's parking lot a silver Omni. Sebastian was just getting out, leather briefcase in one hand and a substantial bouquet of tulips in the other. Hogarth and Villano watched as he walked jauntily across the lot, swinging his briefcase that even from afar showed 30 years of patina from daily use. Sebastian bounded up the stairs two at a time and entered the building.

"You said," Villano began, his voice dripping with contempt.

"He must have escaped."

"Did he look like a man on the run?"

"No, but…"

"I'll invite him to breakfast. You check the trunk of his car. If the bomb is still there, get it out. We need it, now. If not, report back to me immediately. Understood?"

Hogarth nodded rapidly and repeatedly. "How will you keep Dr. Gianninni occupied?"

"Easy. I'll praise Shakespeare."

Chapter 15

Bulldog sat in her cubicle as she attempted to avert a catastrophic end to her promising career. Calling out ART to search a middle-aged English professor's car only to find a trunk full of manuscripts rarely led to promotion and often to demotion, especially when the search produced a book bazaar atmosphere and a crowd that would have heartened most high school football teams. She had to think of a reason to include in her report to justify the use of ART and the crowd that, when Sebastian announced he would be unable to complete his newest novel, *Strangers and Lovers in the Night*, for several weeks had bordered on a mob.

At a loss for a plausible explanation, she leaned back in her chair and glanced around the office for inspiration. The door at the end of the row of cubicles opened and Officer Christian Labuda emerged from the locker room. Before the door swung closed, Bulldog spotted the buxom, brunette centerfold adorned with a crayon bikini in a Maple Leaf pattern someone had pinned to the bulletin board the previous July 1, Canada's birthday. The commander of the border station had convened a 12-member panel to determine whether the centerfold was sexist, pornographic and demeaning to women or, given her new patriotic attire, was actually a proclamation of Canadian nationalism, female sexuality and the right of the anonymous artist to creative expression. After several weeks of deliberations over many taxpayer funded lunches, the committee concluded the issue required further study—and further lunches. Reports were drafted, reviewed and redrafted before the potential public relations debacle was kicked up the pay scale to Ottawa. The brass in the capital earned the big bucks, so let them tackle the big issues. The brass had yet to rule on the porno versus patriotism issue, so the centerfold with the Canadian-nationalist crayon bikini was still pinned to the bulletin board after almost 10 months for Bulldog to see and provide her with the spark that, she hoped and prayed, would save her budding career.

Inspired, her fingers flew across the keyboard as she wove a story to justify the morning's events. She had, Bulldog typed, been investigating Sebastian LeClerc Gianninni for almost a year. Every time his car crossed the border it had been overweight, but she and her colleagues had decided to observe and monitor the good doctor instead of searching his vehicle immediately. This would explain why she and her associates had missed the fact that the car was overweight every weekday for the past nine years.

Today, she had sprung her trap. She had called out ART to ensure a sufficient show of force so as to forestall any possible armed response from the Sultan of Romantic Aides, as she christened Sebastian. Proclaiming the raid a complete success, she reported the seizure and destruction of 165 pounds of illegally imported "romantic aides." The destruction would explain why she had nothing to show for the raid, especially since she had nothing to show for the raid, except for the five original Gianninni manuscripts she had purchased and there was no way she would ever surrender them to anyone.

She typed that Gianninni had agreed to cease and desist his smuggling and, with a warning, Bulldog had released him. Smuggling of goods valued at less than $500 rarely led to more than a warning for a first offense, so Bulldog felt safe with this aspect of her tall tale. It also would mean that Gianninni could continue to cross the border.

Leaning back and smiling at her creative abilities, Bulldog felt an immense weight shift off her shoulders. She even considered writing a romance novel herself, given her recently discovered creative abilities. Even as she devised a tentative plot, she pressed a key and Sebastian LeClerc Gianninni entered the Canadian Criminal Database, available to border guards, the Royal Canadian Mounted Police, local police, the Immigration Service, the Canadian Security and Intelligence Service, and any journalist owed a favor by any member of the aforementioned services, as a purveyor and smuggler of "romantic aids," in short the Sultan of Romantic Aids.

Bulldog rose to go to lunch. She picked up her copy of *The Undergraduate*, one of Sebastian's early works, hitched up her gunless gun belt—at least until she was promoted to the armed Special Investigation Unit—and picked up a luggage catalogue from her desk. She was off to Venice for a week's vacation next month and she needed new luggage for the trip. As she walked toward the lunch room, she thought the black suitcase Dr. Gianninni had in his trunk would be perfect for her. Bulldog wanted one with compartments inside so that her evening dresses, makeup and lingerie would not get all jumbled and tangled. She was not sure if the one Dr. Gianninni had was compartmentalized, since she had been far more interested in the good doctor's literary output than the interior of his suitcase. Maybe, Bulldog thought, she would be in luck and find a model similar to Gianninni's suitcase with compartments in the catalogue. If not, maybe she would see Gianninni again and she could ask him to let her inspect the inside of his suitcase.

Chapter 16

Hogarth Chevalier galloped out of City College and down the concrete steps to the parking lot. The spring sun was just peeking over the horizon, but the lot already held several cars. His eyes locked on the silver Omni, parked under a weeping willow on the far side of the lot. Maybe, just maybe, Professor Gianninni had somehow managed to slip the bomb across the border past the battalion of guards who had surrounded him.

As Hogarth ran out from between two parked SUVs approximately the sizes of Everest and K2, a taxi, its brakes squealing, bumped into his right thigh. Hogarth was thrown to the pavement and lay there, wondering whether he still lived to pursue the soon-to-be-glorious New Luddite Revolution. Taking stock, he concluded he was bruised, but unbroken. As he opened his eyes, he beheld the cabby looming over him.

"Are you alright?" the beefy driver asked, kneeling down to lift Hogarth's head and shoulders gently, even tenderly, off the pavement. "What the hell were you doing, running out from behind that truck? You shouldn't jog in a parking lot! I could have killed you and you would have deserved it!"

Hogarth was trying to make sense of the concerned, yet belligerent taxi driver when a woman appeared in his field of vision just above the cabby. She looked familiar; Mrs. Gianninni. Hogarth sat up, as if he had been kicked by a muscular mule. "I'm fine.

I've gotta go." As he rose, he glanced at the Omni longingly, like a geeky teenager at his first dance eyeing the head cheerleader.

"My car must have hit your head," the cabby said.

"No, it didn't," Hogarth said.

"But your forehead's red. You must have hit my hood," the cabby said, casting a concerned eye at the hood of his recently washed taxi.

Hogarth said, "No, I hit the steering wheel."

"That's impossible. The windshield's not even cracked."

"It's quite possible."

"How?"

"I did it on purpose."

The cabby whispered to Elizabeth, "He's delirious; must have a concussion."

Hogarth wobbled to his feet as Elizabeth apologized and said she had to be going, adding to the cabby, "Can you call an ambulance?"

"I don't need an ambulance. I...," Hogarth began, but faltered. What could he say?

Elizabeth paid her fare and told the cabby, taking a business card from her briefcase and handing it to him, "I better give you my contact information in case your insurance company requires a witness." Then she took out her keys and said, "I'm sorry, but I'm late for an important meeting. I must go." She started toward the Omni.

Hogarth, his thigh aching, his legs wobbly and his head pounding from its repeated encounters with the steering wheel earlier that morning, started to weep at what he feared was about to happen.

"He's crying," the cabby called after Elizabeth, his concern overcoming his anger at Hogarth's choice of jogging locations.

"The shock must be wearing off." Little did Elizabeth know that Hogarth's shock had been building all morning and was far from wearing off, if anything, it was about to get far, far worse. "You should call an ambulance right away."

The tears rolled down Hogarth's face as Elizabeth got into Sebastian's Omni and drove off. Hogarth fell to his knees crying as the taxi driver, unsure of his victim's sanity, backed toward his cab.

"I'll call an ambulance," the driver said.

"No!" Hogarth wailed. "It won't do any good!"

"Fine, I won't." The cabby climbed into his vehicle and sped away from the scene of what would become one of his better pub stories of the time he almost ran over a lunatic, who, after being bumped by the bumper, thought he had been hit in the forehead by the cab's steering wheel.

Chapter 17

Sebastian strolled through the main City College building swinging his briefcase and carrying his bouquet of yellow tulips. His first stop was the English department office. Lucy Dottweiler, a rotund administrative assistant, stood at the counter filling out an order form for pens, pencils, binder clips and lined pads, legal and regular. After failing to order the supplies on the Internet because she could not figure out how to actually purchase the goods displayed so enticingly on the site, she had resorted to the old order form, which she planned to fax to the company if she could ever fit the words "medium binder clips" in the sliver of space allotted for each order on the form. Lucy was about to give up when she looked up to behold Sebastian, beaming and brandishing his tulips.

"Professor Gianninni," she said, the torment of the form instantly forgotten.

"Sebastian, please." He plucked one of the tulips from his arrangement and presenting it to her with a flourish, said, "For you."

"You're too kind," Lucy gushed, with a blush and a lowering of her dark green eyes beneath fluttering lashes.

Sebastian surveyed the office and, spotting his next quarry, requested admittance. Lucy grandly lifted the counter partition and Sebastian strolled into the inner sanctum of those who actually ran the department. With equal parts enthusiasm and zest, he presented a bright yellow tulip to 63-year-old Mrs. Brumburry, who, after 43 years at the college was called by her last name by everyone up to and including the president, and to 22-year-old Suzanne LaTouche, who was given quite unknowingly to striking male students speechless with her stunning looks.

"You are all the most beautiful women in the world," Sebastian announced, surveying the trio from the center of the office, "excepting, of course, my sublime Elizabeth."

"How can they all be the most beautiful?" Bill Rogers asked from the counter where he had just entered to pick up his grade sheets from Lucy, who, for reasons known only to Bill and Lucy, procured his grade sheets even though he was in the Department of Mathematics.

"Because, Professor-Uncle Bill, they are all the most beautiful in different ways." Professor Rogers also happened to be Sebastian's uncle and, therefore, was Professor-Uncle Bill to him.

"'Farewell!'" Sebastian bid the ladies. "'For in that word— that fatal word—howe'er We promise—hope—believe—their breathes despair.'" Sebastian appeared suitably devastated at the parting.

The ladies looked as if they would wilt from desire and loss.

Sebastian followed Bill out into the hall and whispered, "Lord Byron always leaves them weak in the knees, but in a good way."

As they walked toward their offices, Bill, a weathered, gangly expert on applied statistical probability and mathematics, brought up his favorite subject. "Can you escape this asylum and join me at the track this afternoon?"

"I have a class until two," Sebastian replied as he flipped through his mail, which he had retrieved from his box. He flitted into an office, reappearing a moment later minus another yellow tulip.

"You give flowers to Krumm?" Bill asked, alarmed. "You know her husband is—"

"I give flowers to all the women I know."

"I could never afford to do that. I wouldn't have a dime left for the track, poker or ball games. The track at two then?" Bill asked as they reached the stairwell, which led up to his office.

"I have papers to grade and I need to make some phone calls about...about something I'm planning for Elizabeth. I don't think I can make it."

Bill shook his head. "Whatever happened to the good old days?"

"When you used to come to school and tell the teacher my father had fallen into a vat at the winery?" Sebastian asked. "Worried my teachers something fierce."

"I explained that your father had been in the wine business so long, the dunking did him little harm, merely increasing his blood alcohol level from that of a watery house wine to that of a rather fine rich port with plenty of body."

"Even so, dear old dad desperately wanted to see me," Sebastian said, "so you were forced to pull me out of school to see him."

"Who else could I get to go to the track with me when I was on sabbatical and didn't have any classes?"

"You aren't still taking your statistics classes to the track are you?"

"Where else can you study odds in a realistic setting?"

"Didn't President Kratz talk to you about that years ago?"

"No, he didn't say anything about the track."

"He did tell you to stop playing poker in your classes."

"No, he did not. I demonstrated how odds work in a game of poker and he decided it was an excellent teaching tool," Bill explained as he took out his tobacco pouch and rolling paper. He commenced constructing a cigarette. "Of course, it cost him 30 bucks for me to illustrate the point. Just between you and me, he's far from a fast learner."

"You took 30 dollars off President Kratz playing poker?"

"I merely taught him a lesson about odds, principally about trying to draw to a straight when your opponent has a pair of kings showing."

"Did you at least give him his money back?"

Bill straightened and looked down at his nephew. "Maybe the milkman, if not the paperboy rumors are true. I sometimes wondered about your mother's extravagant gifts for the help. In any case, I thought I raised you better than that." Sebastian still appeared chagrined, so Bill added, "I did invite Kratz to my class at any time for another lesson. Far be it from me to skip out on a game when I'm ahead. You have to give the other gent a chance to win his money back…or to lose some more."

Sebastian shook his head. Uncle Bill finished his attempt at a hand-rolled cigarette, which resembled a snake that had recently eaten an obese rabbit and had not yet had adequate time to digest its meal. Although thumb-wide in the middle and tapering to narrow ends, the shape of his cigarette did nothing to deter Bill from placing one of the creation's severely tapered ends in his mouth and patting the pockets of his rumpled suit for matches. Bill had smoked since he was 12 and was perpetually cloaked in an aroma of well-aged tobacco smoke.

"You know you can't smoke in the building."

"Of course I can." Uncle Bill glanced around to ensure their privacy and, leaning conspiratorially close to his nephew, whispered, "I had Lester drill a set of holes in my office window. I can puff away for hours in there and, with a small fan from Marty down in supply, no one's the wiser."

"Lester, the janitor?"

"Custodial engineer; different union. He's great at acquiring little things for me. He's supposed to be getting me a 60-inch plasma television, cheap."

"A hot television?"

"Only when it's been on for a while," Bill said with a grin, finally finding matches tucked into the top of his right sock, which, incidentally, did not match his left sock. "Bandit on your six," Bill hissed as he snatched the misshapen cigarette out of his mouth and hid it in the palm of his hand in one smooth well-practiced motion. Sebastian turned to see President B. U. Kratz approaching. At six-foot-four he was two inches taller than Uncle Bill and much younger. He never raised his voice, never expressed a negative emotion and he had never been seen to make a public enemy in his life. Everyone, save those who liked a boss to make tough decisions with a modicum of intelligence, loved him. The perfect administrator, he was concerned primarily with a smoothly running school with nothing but good news flowing from the Office of Public Information, the school's propaganda arm, which, if employed by Stalin, Hitler and Pol Pot could have turned them into the three most popular men in history.

"Sebastian, Bill," Kratz greeted them jovially as he collegially patted each on the shoulder. "I hope I'm not intruding on anything."

"We were just arranging a little experiment in statistics for this afternoon," Bill said, smiling. "Two o'clock okay with you, Sebastian?"

"I'll try and make it, but I have to pick up Elizabeth after work."

"Try your best. It won't be the same without you. See you later." Bill turned and sprinted up the stairs toward his office to undoubtedly enjoy his cigarette facsimile in smoky peace and privacy.

"May I speak with you, Sebastian?" Kratz asked.

"Of course." Sebastian opened the door to his office. The second-floor office overlooked the parking lot and had once been a storage closet. As the college grew, so did the need for space. With bookcases, a filing cabinet, desk and chair, the storage closet had been transformed into Sebastian's office. It had not, however, lost all of its former function. In one corner stood a rack of rapiers, cutlasses and broadswords from the theater department down the hall. A box near the door held an assortment of other props, which gave Sebastian's office the appearance of clutter, even though his part of the closet-cum-office was neat and orderly. A bust of Byron sat on the corner of his desk beside a photograph of Elizabeth and a white quill pen. A portrait of Shelley hung on the wall and, although romance novels occupied the lower shelves of the bookcases, the top shelves, visible from the door and to anyone sitting in the visitor's chair, were packed with academic textbooks and journals on the romantics, from Byron to Wordsworth.

"Please sit down," Sebastian said as he set his briefcase on the floor and sat down behind his desk. The move to the new office had coincided with the administration's discovery that Sebastian had published a short story, "To Have and Have More," in a romance magazine. Some of his colleagues had sniffed with a great air of snobbery at Sebastian's choice of publication venues, not to mention his choice of subject matter.

"Is that a new chair?" Kratz asked, peering at Sebastian's high-backed, black leather chair as he settled into the pre-formed plastic chair Sebastian used for students.

"Yes," Sebastian said, patting the soft leather. "Uncle, I mean Professor Bill, I mean Professor Rogers, gave it to me for my last birthday. It's extremely comfortable."

"It looks startlingly like one that went missing from my office two months ago. When was your birthday?"

"About," Sebastian said, then realized it had been about two months ago, "a while ago. Do you have any idea who might have taken your chair?"

"Not that I'm formally accusing anyone, but the custodial engineer, Lester Means, was our prime suspect. We were never able to find any real proof, though."

Sebastian refrained from asking if there was any fake proof. Instead, he just said thoughtfully, "Strange." He wondered if the chair had found its way from President Kratz's office via Lester and Uncle Bill to his closet-cum-office. He wondered about it, but not enough to ask Kratz, who had the power to have his office relocated to the storage shed on the football field. "What did you wish to speak to me about?" he asked, eager to change the topic of discussion away from the possibility that he had received stolen presidential goods.

Kratz continued to peer at the chair as if it were a newly discovered life form.

"President Kratz?" Sebastian prompted, trying to align his head with Kratz's field of vision but failing, since Kratz was leaning past the end of Sebastian's desk, looking at the left side of Sebastian's chair.

"It couldn't be mine," Kratz concluded. "Mine had a coffee stain on the side from when the students occupied my office to demand an end to letter grades. Not a bad idea in and of itself, of course, since it would greatly cut down on paperwork."

"Of course it couldn't be," Sebastian agreed, draping his hand over the right side of his chair, where a dark brown stain marred the fine Corinthian leather. He then leaned to the right, trying to ensure that the stain remained well and truly hidden. He made a mental note to "thank" Uncle Bill and Lester for the chair, after cleaning it ASAP.

"Are you alright?" Kratz asked.

"Yes, why?"

"You seem...bent."

Sebastian tried to straighten, even while keeping his arm and shoulder between Kratz and the damning coffee stain. "I'm in excellent health. You wanted to talk to me about something?"

"I wanted to talk to you about a matter of the utmost importance."

Sebastian leaned forward, his relief showing at the conversation steering away from the subject of chairs, especially the one in which he now reposed.

"We have a psychopathic mind at work in our beloved college and I think you are the man to help catch him," Kratz said gravely, "or her."

"Wouldn't someone from the psychology department be better suited to catching psychopathic minds, or at least the bodies in which such minds reside?"

Kratz frowned for a moment at Sebastian's splitting of semantic hairs and then said, "This psychopathic mind has a literary bent. He has been despoiling college property."

"What property?"

"Restroom walls."

Sebastian frowned, mystified.

"Men's restroom walls to be exact."

"I haven't noticed anything wrong with the walls in the restrooms."

"The stalls' walls."

Sebastian still frowned, not following his president.

"He or she writes graffiti all over the stalls' walls with an indelible marker. We have the devil of a time getting it off."

"Don't the janitors clean it off?"

"Of course. Why?"

"You said, '*We* have the devil of a time getting it off,' so I thought..."

"Merely a figure of speech."

"Oh, and you want me to….?"

"Analyze it. Get into his or her sick head and tell me what sort of a mind we're dealing with."

"A sick one, apparently."

"Yes, I know that, but whose?"

"What about the police?"

"No, I'm sure it's not the police. Much of the graffiti is rather anti-law-and-order."

"No, I meant, why don't you call the police?"

"I did, but they said they were far too busy chasing murderers, rapists and car thieves to bother about our bathroom stalls' walls."

"Rather rude of them, but I guess they do get rather busy in the spring."

"Why in the spring?"

"Nicer weather. I wouldn't even consider stealing a car in the winter. The rain and the cold makes going out at all rather a dismal prospect, let alone to steal a car. The heater might not even work. I bought a used car once and all the heat ducts were taped over. I nearly froze every winter."

"Why didn't you just remove the tape?"

"When I did, exhaust filled the car. Freezing was preferable to asphyxiation, although on some cold mornings it was a near run thing which I preferred."

Kratz frowned, shook his head and returned to the topic he had meant to discuss. "Can you take a look at the graffiti? It's in the men's restrooms on the first, second and third floors of this building."

"Of course, but I'm not sure how much help I can be. The psychology department would be more—"

"I'm sure you'll be able to smoke out just who it is who's despoiling our stalls' walls." Kratz stood, gravely shook hands with Sebastian and was gone, his mission accomplished.

Kratz had barely left when a voice warned from just outside Sebastian's office, "You should be extremely careful."

Chapter 18

Sebastian looked up to see Bill slip into his office. "Couldn't help overhearing," Bill said as he carefully shut Sebastian's door and produced a smoldering cigarette from his weathered suit's jacket pocket.

"Be careful of what? And put that out, please."

"I'm almost finished," Bill said, inhaling a long, powerful drag from his hand-made cigarette. "Kratz shifted responsibility for the graffiti problem to you. If you fail to finger the culprit, then he can blame you and use it as an excuse to transfer you from teaching the Romantics to teaching remedial English in the athletics department."

"Why in the name of Byron would he want to do that?"

"So he never again has to have you and your penchant for penning romance novels besmirching his Department of English."

"But I'm in the English Department."

"Kratz will offer you an office in the gymnasium complex so that you can be closer to your remedial English athletics students."

"I don't believe it."

"Our Machiavellian leader believes his plan is foolproof. Time will provide the proof about whether you're the fool he thinks you are."

"Where do you get this...this story? Wordsworth was thinking of you, when he wrote you find 'a tale in everything.'"

"I have my sources," Bill said, taking a long drag on the remains of his misshapen cigarette. He glanced at his silver pocket watch and with a start announced, "Ah, I must be going or I shall be late for class. I have to place some bets back east first. There's a promising filly running at a little track in the Finger Lakes this afternoon. Care to put your hand in?"

"I'll keep my hands to myself, thanks."

"Your loss."

"No, probably yours," Sebastian countered with a sweet smile.

Looking hurt, Bill rushed off to place his bets.

As Sebastian gathered his notes for his morning lecture, Professor Villano stuck his head through the open doorway and asked, "Sebastian, care for some breakfast? On me."

"A perfectly timed offer," Sebastian said, eager to accept, given the rumblings in his tummy after his skipped romantic gourmet breakfast with Elizabeth. He also took it as a golden opportunity to mend fences with Villano, who had led the assault on Sebastian after the unfortunate "To Have and Have More" incident. Their relationship, never sound given their differences over Shakespeare, Villano's specialty, and the romantic poets, Sebastian's reason for living, was ripe for restructuring over some white eggs and ham.

They ate in the faculty lounge, which was as always almost empty. Designed primarily for fundraisers, it had enough padded chrome and leather chairs for 350 well-attired posteriors, a vaulted ceiling, plush sofas along the walls and a view of the neighboring golf course that developers would have sold their first-, second- and third-borns for in order to convert into luxury, Yuppie condos. The cafeteria was never used to its full capacity by the faculty, who numbered only 247 at full strength. The lounge was only full when crammed with wealthy alumni and potential donors being wined and dined, and then hit upon for sizable contributions by the president and his fund-raising minions. Uncle Bill had often marveled at the skill of Kratz and his hench-persons at separating alumni and so-called friends of the college from their money. It was a skill Bill had only ever seen rivaled by his great Uncle

Slim, who usually used weighted dice, marked cards or an associate named Mouse, whose size completely contradicted his name, to separate people from their money as rapidly as Kratz and his well-polished and always polite young assistants.

"Did you hear the drama department is staging *Hamlet?*" Villano asked as he took a bite of buttered toast.

Sebastian sipped his orange juice and, deciding his own fresh-squeezed juice at home was markedly superior, replied, "I did. I hope they cast him correctly."

"What do you mean?" Villano asked, cutting his bacon into regular squares.

"The queen, Gertrude, states quite clearly in the final scene that Hamlet is 'fat,' yet they always cast him as a thin fellow."

"'Fat'?" Villano exclaimed in disbelief, his fork poised halfway between plate and mouth with its cargo of egg in danger of dripping off.

"She's his mother. She should know."

"Fat in that case, my dear Professor Gianninni, means sweaty. Hamlet is in a duel at the time with Laertes, which tends to lead to a certain level of exertion, especially if one's life is at risk."

"Leave it to Shakespeare to change the meaning of a word," Sebastian said as he savored his bacon, nicely cooked.

"The word had a different meaning in Shakespeare's time."

Sebastian waved off Villano's defense of the Bard and said, "That's the least of the problems with *The Tragedy of the Prince of Denmark.*"

"Such as?"

"Such as, 'Shakespeare's name, you may depend upon it, stands absurdly too high and will go down.'"

"Pray tell, why?"

"If you may be so good to allow me to finish the quote." After a suitable dramatic pause, Sebastian continued, "'He took all his plots from old novels.'"

"So you say."

"So says Lord Byron."

"All authors borrow. Nothing is completely novel."

"That's the least of Shakespeare's offenses."

"Offenses? That seems harsh. Such as?"

"Such as the most indecisive protagonist ever created. What young man would ever hesitate so long if he thought his uncle had murdered his father?"

"But Hamlet is indecisive. It's a central trait of his character."

"And the mistaken killings? Hamlet kills Polonius by mistake because he thinks he's Claudius. Gertrude accidentally drinks the poison Claudius intended for Hamlet. Forgive me, but how much coincidence is an audience supposed to stomach before reaching for the antacids and a book of Shelley's fine poetry?"

And so it went, Villano defending Shakespeare, with an occasional foray against the Romantic poets and Sebastian attacking *Hamlet* specifically and Shakespeare in general, with the occasional defense of his beloved Keats, Shelley and their Romantic brethren. It was just as Sebastian was checking the neo-classical clock on the wall and deciding he should return to his office to gather his notes for his 8:30 lecture when a wiry young man approached their table. His forehead was bruised, his jeans and leather jacket dirty, and he did not fit at all into the well-dressed ambience of the sedate faculty lounge.

"Dr. Villano, she's left," the young man blurted out with nary a good morning.

Villano froze, a piece of jam-covered toast halfway between plate and mouth. "In the car?"

"Yes," Hogarth answered, shaking. He appeared barely able to contain himself at this newest manifestation of the day's rapidly unfolding disasters.

"With the...our belongings still, possibly, in the trunk?" Villano asked as he glanced at the bewildered Sebastian.

"Yes, I was about to get the...uh...our belongings when she arrived, hit me and sped off," Hogarth explained in a cascade of words worthy of an auctioneer in a hurry.

"She hit you?" Villano asked, shocked.

Sebastian listened to this exchange with increasing interest, since it reminded him of one of Uncle Bill's better stories.

"No, the taxi driver did," Hogarth clarified.

"What taxi driver?"

"The driver who brought Mrs——."

"I see, I see," Villano interrupted before Hogarth mentioned Mrs. Gianninni and connected the dots that had already been neatly laid out before Sebastian. Dots which, when connected, could only lead to embarrassing questions that Villano had no intention of ever allowing to be asked, let alone ever answering. "Sebastian," Villano said, rising as he neatly placed his napkin over the remains of his breakfast, "It's been a pleasure, as always. Shall we call it a draw: Shakespeare 3, the Romantics 3?"

"'Twas blow for blow, disputing inch by inch, For one would not retreat, nor t'other flinch,'" Sebastian quoted with glee, energized by their morning debate. "However, 'I am bound to furnish my antagonists with arguments, but not with comprehension.'"

"You had to get in just a couple more quotes. Then pray allow me to conclude with a quote from another of your Romantics, Thomas Moore," Villano said. "'Romantic love is an illusion. Most of us discover this truth at the end of a love affair or else when the sweet emotions of love lead us into marriage and then turn down their flames.'"

"Moore also wrote, 'The heart that has truly loved never forgets / But as truly loves on to the close,'" Sebastian countered, but then added, "Of course, Moore spent more time working for the admiralty in Bermuda and penning ballads than writing poems. He's not really a romantic poet at all."

"Don't tell the Irish that. He is their National Bard."

Brought back to the present situation by a tug on the sleeve by Hogarth, Villano said, "I am sorry, much as I have enjoyed our lively discussion, you must excuse me. My student here is having some trouble, which I must address directly. You understand, of course?"

Sebastian rose and said, "Of course. We'll continue our discussion another time. I have a class in a few minutes anyway." He turned to Hogarth and, the thought growing in his mind that he had seen this scuffed and red-foreheaded young man before, asked, "Have I had the pleasure?"

"No, no, no," Hogarth said, retreating before the mild-mannered professor as if he faced Cerberus at the gates of Hell.

"You've never taken English 203: Irish, Welsh and Scottish Romantic Literature: Better than Shakespeare?"

"No."

"English 441: The Romantic Poets and Romance Today: A Pale Shadow?"

"No," Hogarth said as the adjacent table abruptly halted his retreat from Sebastian. As the professors at that table steadied their dangerously swishing drinks, Villano stepped in to save the day.

"My student is studying engineering," Villano explained.

"Demolitions, actually," Hogarth added helpfully.

Before he could divulge anything more, Villano led Hogarth by the arm out of range of Sebastian's unwelcome questions and increasingly curious ears.

As he watched the duo depart, Sebastian knew he had seen the young man before, but could not place him. He had never excelled at putting names to faces or even faces to names. Yet, he knew he had seen the young man before, but where? Even more intriguingly, what was Villano doing mentoring an engineering student? Engineers were not known for their interest in literature. For their English requirement, most opted to take Art Arnold's creative writing course. Art believed that the best creative writing revealed the soul of the writer, even if the words did not strictly come out in complete sentences or conform strictly, loosely or even remotely to the rules of grammar as set down in Strunk and White's grammatical bible, *The Elements of Style*.

As he pondered the identity of Villano's student, Sebastian strolled back to his office. He collected his notes and walked to his lecture hall to present his most fascinating lecture on one of his favorite topics: Shelley's 'Ode to the West Wind.'

O Wild West Wind, thou breath of Autumn's being

Thou from whose unseen presence the leaves dead

Are driven like ghosts from an enchanter fleeing,...

The thought of such a beautiful, image-evoking poem quickly pushed any thought of Villano's demolition-studying engineering student to the back of Sebastian's mind. Professor Villano and Hogarth Chevalier, however, would ensure such questions did not remain long at the back of Sebastian's mind.

Chapter 19

As Sebastian launched into his favorite lecture, polished from years of loving use, Elizabeth sped down the 99 freeway toward the American border, home and a key file on the medical records building in Saskatoon, which she had left behind that morning. She had decided it would be best not to call and mention this lapse to Sebastian. On several recent occasions she had chastised him for forgetfulness, telling him that it was the first sign of advancing age. It had all been in the nature of a gentle joke on her slightly older spouse, but she now regretted her chiding. Serious, upright and of a very high moral fiber, she did not like being the butt of a joke, even from her loving husband. If he learned that she had forgotten a file, she would undoubtedly be the butt of at least one humorous comment, if not more, depending on how creative Sebastian was feeling. She could, however, drive home, retrieve the file, return the Omni to the college, call a taxi and be back at work with Sebastian none the wiser, especially if she topped off the Omni's gas tank.

Elizabeth beetled up to the PACE booth without even having to wait in line, although the regular border crossing lanes were backed up with Canadians eager to enter, albeit briefly, the land of cheap gasoline, milk and tobacco. The border guard usually just nodded and waved people with PACE stickers through, but this time the officer, after glancing at his computer screen, asked Elizabeth, "Aren't you the one married to the writer?"

'No, the professor,' leapt to Elizabeth's tongue, but then, remembering all too vividly the events of that morning and thinking of another possible manuscript sale, she replied, "Yes, I am."

"I heard about him from my girlfriend. She works over on the other side." At first Elizabeth thought he dated a ghost, but the officer twitched his head northward toward Canada, clarifying his phraseology. The guard waited for a return comment and, after an awkward pause, Elizabeth supplied it.

"How nice," she said, eager to reach home, retrieve her file, buy gas, return the Omni to the college, call a cab and get back to work in time for the medical records building meeting she had been forced to reschedule for later that morning, all for the lack of a file. Because, for want of a file, the medical records building contract would be lost; for want of the medical records building contract, her company's Saskatoon office would be lost; and for want of the Saskatoon office, her company's entire fledgling Saskatchewan operation would be lost, which might very well mean her Christmas bonus would be lost—all for the want of a file.

"Yes, my girlfriend is nice," the guard agreed, glancing up the empty PACE lane. With nothing but time to waste, he asked his captive guest, "Does your husband write a lot?"

"Quite a bit," Elizabeth said, wishing only to leave, but fearing what offending the guard could lead to: a search of her car, a search of her person, loss of the PACE sticker, and all manner of hassles and debasements not at all in keeping with the image of a senior partner in the largest civil engineering firm west of Kamloops.

"I read a few pages of the manuscript Bulldog bought; not Wordsworth or Keats, but not bad."

"Bulldog?"

"My girlfriend, Fawn Cates. Her nickname is Bulldog."

This time Elizabeth let the pause in the conversation mature from childhood through adolescence and into adulthood onto the very verge of old age. She hoped that if she remained silent, the guard would let her pass. The silence mounted like an impending avalanche over a tiny ski village high in the Italian Alps.

"Yeah, it's sort of an odd nickname when you first hear it, but she's got the tenacity of a bulldog," the guard said, carrying the conversation forward on a monologue basis. "Once she gets a hold of something, she doesn't let go."

"Wouldn't that be more like a terrier?" Elizabeth asked, thinking of her neighbor's pride and joy, Tyrone. Even as she said it, she regretted restarting the dialogue.

"What do you mean?"

Elizabeth's hopes of getting across the border rapidly faded as she was forced to continue the conversation. "Terriers are ratters. They were bred to go down holes after rats and vermin. They kill by biting their prey, holding on and shaking the life out of it or breaking its neck. I don't think bulldogs attack in that way."

"Interesting."

Elizabeth was wondering how long this purgatory could continue when the guard looked up from his shallow thoughts about his girlfriend's nickname and spotted another PACE car approaching.

"Well, have a nice day." He gestured that Elizabeth was free at long last to enter the Land of the Free.

Grabbing the file at home was a matter of a few moments and Elizabeth was on her way back out the front door when through the kitchen window she spied two burly men in coveralls lurking in the back garden. Burglars!

Most women, even modern independent professional types would have raced for the telephone to call 911 to summon the police. The daughter of a Western rancher, Elizabeth was made of sterner stuff. She raced upstairs for her great Uncle Deke's .22 rifle. It held a special place in her heart. She still remembered the first time her father had shown her the polished rifle. Her father inherited it after Deke passed on after a rabbit he shot with the .22 turned out to be a grizzly cub with a mother none too far away. The gun's stock still bore a large nick, worn smooth from age and use, from said aggrieved mother.

One of the few times her father had unreservedly praised Elizabeth's skills was when she hit tin cans and the occasional rabbit, after carefully checking that the fluffy form was a rabbit and not a bear cub. Rabbits ate her parents' small kitchen garden's limited produce. Soon, no tin can was safe from Elizabeth's marks-womanship. She did, however, avoid shooting Thumper's relatives unless her father was present to fortify her against the profound sadness she felt over shooting happy, hoppy herbivores. She had no such need for parental support to shoot a burglar.

Advancing downstairs as she loaded the weapon, Elizabeth sped out the side door and around to the garden. The two men wore dark coveralls to better camouflage their nefarious doings, she thought, even though a floral ensemble might have more effectively blended into the flower garden. The men straightened up from their task at the muffled sound of heels racing across the backyard turf. Their shock was evident as Elizabeth aimed the rifle at them. Their arms shot heavenward toward where great Uncle Deke was, even now, probably blasting holes in tin cans, since shooting rabbits was probably frowned upon in heaven.

"Freeze!" Elizabeth ordered, savoring the words she had heard a thousand times in cop movies and on police television dramas. The words hung in the air as the two men, speechless and motionless, stood, arms upraised, staring at the lady in the dark suit and heels toting a small yet menacing rifle. It quickly dawned on Elizabeth that in movies what happened next was that the suspects attempted to run, leading to a chase and then a shootout, or backup arrived in the form of a hundred police cars to arrest the miscreants as the credits rolled. She glanced around and did not see any backup, and the suspects showed no signs of breathing, let alone running.

"Who are you?" Elizabeth finally asked.

"Dan Bogley," one of the men said, his arms still skyward, although fatigue was setting in and his elbows were beginning to bend earthward. "This is Marty Molina," he added with a jerk of his head toward his partner.

Elizabeth took in this information and realized it told her nothing. "But who are you?"

Dan glanced at his partner and, after a brief and bashful hesitation, said, "We're the Blue bird's best friend, the Starling's succor, the Chickadee's confidante. We are Birdie's Bath, Feeders and Accessories."

Elizabeth's eyes strayed from her quarry to a wooden crate on the grass, half open, which revealed a white, stone bird bath. It bore a remarkable resemblance to one she and Sebastian had eyed while out shopping last weekend. One which, on passing, she had mentioned that since childhood she had always desired. The thought of a burbling fountain in the garden with all manner of feathered friends bathing in it had always symbolized to her the soul of gentility, wealth and refinement.

"And who, if I may be so bold, are you?" Dan asked, his arms weary and his hopes growing that he would live to see another bird bath installation.

Elizabeth shouldered her rifle and advanced to shake hands. "I'm Elizabeth Gianninni. The wife of the wonderful man who I presume ordered the bird bath."

They shook hands and Elizabeth was soon admiring her new acquisition. "Do you have the invoice?" she asked, her eye as always on fiscal realities.

Dan pulled out a bill and handed it to the still rifle-toting lady. She peered at the bottom line critically and, after a quick calculation relating to the family's monthly budget, realized it was well within their means, if not their absolute needs. She folded the bill neatly and put it in her pocket.

"Carry on, gentlemen," she said, turning back toward the house with a warm glow for her thoughtful and devoted husband as she unloaded the .22. At the door, she turned back toward the two men, who still watched her warily, and said sheepishly, "Sorry about the rifle. You never know who's sneaking around birdbaths with nefarious thoughts in mind, besides cats, that is."

She stepped inside and closed the door, leaving two extremely nervous bird bath installers to continue their work, which, under the threat of another encounter with the rifle-toting lady, they completed in record time.

Elizabeth replaced the rifle in the master bedroom closet, the shells in the locked bureau and, checking her watch, realized it would be a near-run-thing to make the rescheduled 10:30 am medical records building meeting. Even as she debated whether to call her secretary to reschedule again, the doorbell rang. Thinking it was the bird bath installers with a question, she rushed to the front door and flung it open.

"Oh, Sebast—," Rosa Turnbell began as she rushed in and enveloped Elizabeth in a passionate embrace, only to stop mid-word when she realized the target of her affections was not the one to whom she had been aiming. She retreated in confusion and, apologizing profusely to a startled Elizabeth, dashed for the sanctuary of her home next door.

Her mouth open in amazement, Elizabeth stared out the door like a nun who had just witnessed her first orgy. Her warm feelings for Sebastian from the bird bath incident were now on shakier foundations as she wondered what exactly he did on the days when he did not have a class and stayed home to grade papers, prepare lectures or write romances. Maybe he was romancing more than the computer keyboard.

Recovering enough to close the door, Elizabeth thought the whole thing must be some sort of misunderstanding. She had been married to Sebastian for almost 20 years and in all those years she had never noticed him to take any serious notice of another woman. Sebastian was polite to women, even gallant, but never did anything beyond common courtesy, even if it was a courtesy that had not been in fashion since knights slew dragons to rescue damsels in distress. He could not have strayed.

Grabbing the file she had dropped when Rosa had so warmly assaulted her, Elizabeth was reaching for the door handle to leave when she heard a rap on the back patio door. It must be the bird bath installers this time. She rushed back through the living room to the sliding glass door and, pushing the blinds aside, opened the door in one smooth motion.

They say, like mother, like daughter but Elizabeth thought that this was not what they meant when, whoever they were, said it. Destiny Turnbell burst through the door, arms outstretched for a hug, clutching a piece of paper in one hand, as she sought her quarry and called out, "Sebastian," packing the single word with enough passion to ignite a soggy cord of driftwood. This time Elizabeth was prepared and sidestepped the proffered hug with a move Walter Payton could have used most effectively against the Packers' secondary.

"What are you doing here?" Elizabeth demanded of the startled young lady who, like her mother, had made a similar miscalculation as to the identity, not to mention the sex, of the occupant of the Gianninni house at this particular hour.

"I...I...I," Destiny stammered before she, too, beat a hasty retreat to her home, although not before dropping the sheet of paper she had been clutching.

Elizabeth slid the sliding door closed, locked it and debated whether she would need the .22 to fight her way out of the house past the legion of females who fought to embrace her husband. She turned toward the front door and stepped squarely on Destiny's prized piece of paper. Elizabeth picked it up and, after reading a few lines, realized it was in Sebastian's distinctive romantic style. A love note? To Destiny Turnbell? It could not be. There must be some mistake. She stood and pondered the note, then realized what time it was.

Still ruminating on the note, Elizabeth grabbed her file and exited the front door, after first ascertaining through the peep hole that there were no females waiting to ambush her with yet another attempted passionate embrace. Confused and concerned, Elizabeth sped to the border in Sebastian's trusty Omni and beetled up to the PACE booth to return to Canada and confront her husband about what appeared to be his extramarital romantic activities.

"You're Mrs. Gianninni," the guard said, leaning out of the booth and ignoring the flashing icon on her computer screen, which had appeared after she typed in the Omni's license plate number. If she had clicked on the icon, it would have opened a file chronicling Fawn "Bulldog" (or should it be "Terrier"?) Cates' investigation of Sebastian Gianninni's international smuggling activities as the Sultan of Romantic Aids.

"Is it romantic living with such a man?" the red-headed guard gushed, having already read the first three chapters of *Madam Beau Mary* between border-crossers since she purchased it that morning from Sebastian.

Elizabeth had no time for small talk and especially not about the romantic activities of what she now feared was her lecherously roving husband.

"No, he's not particularly romantic." As soon as she said it, Elizabeth knew it did not ring true. Sebastian sent her brief emails every morning, wishing her a happy day, telling her he was thinking of her and mentioning future plans from the dinner he planned for that night, often including her favorite blackened chicken, Yorkshire puddings with gravy or cheesecake desert, to a movie he wanted to rent to watch with her which he thought she might enjoy, and always ending with a declaration of his love for her. There were the breakfasts in bed, the flowers for no particular occasion, the messages of romantic poetry recitations left on the answering machine, and, most recently, the birdbath. These were all the things that had helped Sebastian win her hand years ago but which had slowly faded from her consciousness as she grew accustomed to such treatment. It was a terrible thing to have happened, but careers and the tasks of maintaining a house, investing a diversified portfolio for retirement and just plain living life had pushed Sebastian's better qualities to the back and then completely out of her mind. Familiarity had bred not contempt, but forgetfulness for what a special, romantic man she had married.

"I wish I could find a man who was romantic," the guard pined wistfully, twirling a rubber band with her long, manicured fingers as she looked off into the distance, apparently picturing a romantic man on a white charger galloping across Peace Arch Park to sweep her off her standard issue, Delta-9, military grade booted feet.

Elizabeth had already found a romantic man: almost 20 years ago.

Wallowing in sadness, the lovelorn guard waved Elizabeth on into the Dominion of Canada. The more Elizabeth pondered her husband, the more divided she became. She knew Sebastian was wonderful, but over the years she had come to take his special qualities for granted. Had her neglect led him to wander? Her heart said never to doubt Sebastian, but her head said prudence was always wise in affairs of the heart. Was he a wolf in sheep's clothing or was he a prince, temporarily and unfairly characterized as a frog, or possibly even a toad?

Chapter 20

"You should have followed her," Professor Villano said. "She was probably going on some errand or possibly just returning home."

"There's no way I'm crossing that border ever again," Hogarth declared as he paced in Villano's office. The young international terrorist was near tears. All his hopes for a New Luddite Revolution appeared to be doomed before the first bomb was even imported, let alone planted. Not even the assistance of Dr. Villano, a brilliant and learned man, seemed destined to snatch the situation back from where it teetered on the brink of disaster.

"Then we must shift to plan C."

Hogarth stopped beside his revolutionary colleague and, frowning, asked, "Plan C? Already? What about plan B?"

"We'll keep plan B as a backup in case plan C runs into trouble," Villano explained and turned to face his young associate. Just then, Hogarth's eyes grew wet and he began to cry. His mouth fell open, his shoulders sagged and he looked like a boy who has lost his pet dog of 17 years, only to discover the dog merely has narcolepsy and was taking an extended nap.

"What's wrong?"

Hogarth could not speak. His vocal cords could not make words, only producing a barely audible gurgle. He raised a pale, shaking hand and pointed out the window.

Villano turned and beheld Sebastian's silver Omni as it pulled into the same parking spot it had occupied earlier that morning. Elizabeth slid out and, depositing her cell phone in her briefcase, stood tapping her foot, waiting. In a few moments, a taxi appeared, she climbed aboard and it whisked her on her way.

"Our suitcase may still be in the trunk," Villano said. "Go find out."

"What if Professor Gianninni comes out to his car?"

"Why would he do that?"

"The way things have been going this morning, I wouldn't be surprised if he decided to come out and rotate his tires on a whim."

"I'll find Sebastian and make sure he doesn't come out to the car, whim or no whim."

Chapter 21

There was no danger of Sebastian going out to his car. After delivering an inspired and well-received lecture on the West Wind, he had two things on his mind: a "hot" leather office chair and restroom stall wall graffiti.

Sebastian spotted Uncle Bill rushing down the hall amid a torrent of students on their way to their next classes.

"Professor Rogers," Sebastian called and trotted after his swiftly vanishing uncle. "Uncle Bill, wait a minute!"

Bill glanced back and, with a look like Eddie Shoemaker contemplating another horse about to pass him on the final turn of the Kentucky Derby, yelled back, "Can't talk now, Sebastian. I'm late for class."

Bill rushed through a door and Sebastian followed, slipping just through before the door swung closed. He found himself in a classroom with the desks pushed together to form 10 tables. About 40 students were settling in; four per table. Sebastian followed Bill to the front of the classroom and whispered gravely, "Uncle Bill, I need to talk to you about my office chair."

"I can't now, Sebastian, I have a class to teach." Bill gestured at the room full of waiting, expectant, even eager students.

Sebastian set his face in a stern manner and Bill, sensing his nephew's increasing anger, added, "You can stay for a bit, if you like. We might fit in a wee chat between games."

Determined to get to the bottom of the origin of the office chair, Sebastian found an unoccupied chair off to one side and sat down, maintaining a steely stare on his uncle.

"Settle down, please," Bill began as a couple of late arrivals rushed into the room and found seats. "Lets get started. We're burning fluorescent light. Today we're studying random distribution models. I hope you all read Chapter 14 of Shavelson and Rinkmeyer."

Grumbles and groans arose from the assembled students.

"I agree, dry as a fine martini, but statistics can't read like a thriller, unless it's Huff's excellent *How to Lie with Statistics*," Bill continued as he sauntered around the classroom among his attentive and adoring pupils. "Did everyone remember their cards today? Mr. Short?"

A young man nodded and waved a deck of playing cards still in their cellophane packaging.

"And plenty of ones and change, I hope," Bill said as the students produced coins and dollar bills—Loonie dollar coins were but a gleam in the Canadian mint's eye in 2001—from pockets and backpacks to set before them. "Good, good. Remember, the point of the exercise is to determine the odds at each point in the game of getting the card or cards you're praying for to achieve the hand you're seeking. If you need a five of spades to complete a full house, I want to see your calculation of the probability of you drawing that card, given the cards you already have and the cards showing on the table."

A student raised her hand.

"Yes, Ms. O'Keeffe?"

"Do we have to work out the probability for each draw or only for one?"

"For each draw, if you would be so kind."

"That'll slow the game down a lot," a tall, red-headed male student whined.

"As you improve your ability to determine the odds, the games should pick up. I expect at least six calculations on my desk by the end of our hour together, and don't forget to put your names on them. Shall we begin?"

Students shuffled cards and dealt as games of five-card, two-draw poker commenced at each table. Pencils flew over pads after the first hands were dealt and fingers danced over calculator buttons as students determined the odds of achieving their sought-after hands.

Smiling like a benevolent monarch, Bill sauntered over to Sebastian and sat on the edge of a desk as he took out his cigarette paper and well worn tobacco pouch to begin rolling a hand-made creation that might, if all went well, masquerade as a cigarette.

"Now, what can I do for you?"

Sebastian glanced around the room, but none of the students were paying them the least attention. They were intent on their games and calculations; not only grades, but money was at stake. "I want to talk about my office chair."

"I'm so glad you like it. It was a real job getting it."

"I'll bet."

"You don't have to thank me again, Sebastian. Nothing's too good for my favorite nephew."

"Favorite nephew? Cousin Terry's in the B.C. Pen for insider trading. Cousin Bruce is somewhere in Thailand making low-budget movies of a questionable sort."

"I'm still amazed the post office delivers those cards he sends."

"Cousin Michael builds leaky condos and cousin Kraig was indicted in that influence peddling scandal in Ottawa."

"You forgot dear cousins Paul and Ken."

"Paul works rousting bums out of a Starbucks, while Ken, well, no one quiet knows what Ken does, not even his boss."

"So it's a weak field, but you're out in front by at least three lengths," Bill said with a smile as he glanced around the room. "Mr. Pearson, you can't raise more than a dollar."

"I can't believe you make your students play poker."

Offended, Bill rose to his full height to peer down with the utmost disdain at his formerly favorite nephew. "I do not force them. It is completely voluntary. Furthermore, they are learning about odds, calculating probabilities and," he leaned down close to Sebastian, "have you ever seen a class so intent on their lesson?"

Bill gestured in a grand sweep at his diligent pupils. The students were certainly absorbed. Bill reached down and picked up the textbook of a student seated nearby. He flipped it open to a random page and read aloud, "'Differences in means may produce a misleading correlation coefficient even if the relationship between the variables is the same in each group (see figure 7-6 a, b and f).' Boring drivel. Or how about," he said as he flipped to another page, "'For a two-tailed test, by convention, a sample mean is likely if it lies no less than two standard errors above or below the population mean.' How can that compare with calculating the odds of winning five bucks if you draw to a straight flush when your opponents are holding what appears to be a full house in the making?"

Sebastian sighed. "My chair—"

"My students do startlingly well in upper level statistics classes after taking this course; a fact I would mention, if I had to defend my teaching methods to a young man, such as yourself, who doesn't respect his elders and, may I say, in the area of teaching, his betters."

"My chair, Uncle Bill, it's President Kratz's."

Bill stopped in mid gaze upon one of the games unfolding before him and sat back down on a desk beside Sebastian. He ran his hand through his thinning gray hair and said, "It *was* President Kratz's."

His worst suspicion confirmed, Sebastian whispered, "You stole the office chair of the president of the college?"

"I did not," Bill said, bolting upright in shock as if he had been accused of rape, murder and, worst of all, cheating at poker.

"Then how did you give me his chair for my birthday?"

Bill pursed his lips, leaned close to Sebastian and whispered, "I was involved in a rather complicated experiment the morning of your birthday."

"What kind of an experiment?" Bill had received tenure 30 years before and had only published an occasional, albeit well received research article in the intervening decades, all on some aspect of gambling.

"Predicting the winner of a harness race out at Abbottsford."

Sebastian shook his head in despair. "How does that relate to the chair?"

"Up until then I'd limited myself to horse racing and the multitude of variables governing the outcomes of races between horses. Harness racing has a whole new set of variables. It's fascinating. Those wheels get tangled up with alarming regularity."

"My chair?"

"Ah, yes," Bill said, searching for and once again finding the track of his previous train of thought. "The experiment turned out rather well."

"My chair, Uncle Bill," Sebastian insisted, beginning to tire of another of his uncle's meandering stories. "I don't want to hear about your experiment. I want to hear about my purloined office chair."

"The experiment has everything to do with the chair."

"How?"

"On your birthday I tested my Grand Unifying Harness Racing Theory." Bill paused for dramatic effect and then added, "I won. A trifecta, no less."

"How much?"

"A tidy $257.36."

"Not bad," Sebastian said, impressed despite his intent to maintain a stern countenance toward his uncle. "But about my chair, Uncle Bill."

"I returned to school and ran into you with my happy news. Before I could fill you in on my latest triumph, you blurted out that Elizabeth had given you some poems for your birthday."

"Not just some poems, a Shelley first edition."

"First edition, third edition, whatever; they all have the same words inside," Bill said, waving aside Sebastian's interruption, before plunging on with his story. "Sadly, I had neglected to procure you a gift and, as you stared at me expectantly, I could only promise to deliver your present later that day. I was rather busy that day: classes, a deathly boring committee meeting on something or other, I never quite figured out what, and, of course, fine tuning my Grand Unifying Harness Racing Theory."

"I thought you won with it."

"I did, but there's nothing in the world that can't stand improvement."

"Like you improved your horse racing theory?"

"It was invalid in wet conditions," Bill said defensively. "Given Vancouver's location in a rain forest, what good was it?"

"It was good when it didn't rain, which would have been enough to make us both rich." Sebastian refrained from pointing out that Bill had won $12,196.32 on a $300 investment and Sebastian $2,439.53 on a $60 investment before Bill tinkered with his theory to take into account a wet track. The change led to a succession of losses totaling $14,636.85, which left them a dollar in the hole. The losses also led to a depression in Bill that resulted in him losing the original theory amid the ocean of papers in his office, much to his—and Sebastian's—financial dismay. With the aid of the theory, Sebastian had dared hope his Alfa Romeo was tantalizingly close to being within his grasp. Now both—theory and car—appeared lost and gone forever.

"That's neither here nor there, the key—scientifically—was to perfect the theory," Bill continued. "The important thing to the issue under current discussion is that after I told you your present would be delivered that day, I ran into Lester."

"This relates to my chair, how?"

"I appraised my old friend Lester of my predicament and, given he was out almost $300 on the loss of some rather fine stereo equipment the police had seized from his van in the belief his ownership of it was in question—he had misfiled the sales receipts in his office—agreed for my $257.36 to procure a suitable gift for an up and coming young professor-nephew."

"Lester stole the president's chair?"

Bill frowned and glanced around the room at his students, but as before no one was listening to the two professors. All were intent on their games of probability.

"I doubt it," Bill whispered. "He's more of a fence than a thief."

"Oh, good, my uncle only deals with a fence, not with the actual thief."

"Oh, I've dealt with my fair share of thieves. Did I ever tell you about the stereo I got for my car?"

"Uncle Bill, we have to give it back."

"The stereo? I can't give it back. Someone stole it from me. Probably the same sneak thief who sold it to me in the first place."

"No, the president's chair."

"Why?"

"Because it was wrong to take it."

"The president reported the chair stolen and now has a $900, 100 percent genuine leather office chair with multi-directional controls, which is as soft as a thoroughbred's well-groomed coat on a spring morning. It even has heating and cooling features for the presidential derriere."

"We've got to give it back."

"I doubt he'd take it back. He has a new, better chair and you have a nice new office chair. Who's the loser?"

"It has a coffee stain, which almost gave me away this morning to President Kratz."

"Lester could get that fixed up right quick, and cheap."

"No more Lester, please," Sebastian begged. "Please get the chair cleaned, today. I've got to go investigate some graffiti."

Chapter 22

It was the middle of a class period, so the second floor men's room was empty as Sebastian peered into the first stall and discerned it was barren of anything save the most commonplace graffiti. There were a few cliché lines with phone numbers, physically impossible sex acts and misspelled swear words. This must not be the recurring mass of defacement that kept President Kratz awake nights.

The second stall, directly under a well-placed light, was an entirely different story. From top to bottom the metal walls on all three sides were covered by a dissertation in thick, black, indelible marker penned in paragraphs, sections and subsections. Sebastian wished his students had such neat handwriting on their exams. It was a penmanship that had not been taught since the war. Sebastian stepped inside and began to read. Akin to the Talmud with its notes and comments in the margin, the two stall walls and the back of the door were covered in notes and citations. He pushed the door closed, which enabled him to refer to the notes as he read the main text.

Sebastian was taken by the fascinating dissertation. It was clear, concise and well argued. Focusing on bureaucracy and how it dehumanized human beings, the writer was eloquent and well read, with references to Kant, Spinoza, Hobbes, Freud, Marx, Berra, Fudd, Smith, and a range of other philosophers from a diverse collection of schools of thought. It was difficult to read the text at the rear of the stall near the toilet, so Sebastian lowered the seat and, crouching precariously on the commode, perused the text in the back corner.

Engrossed in his reading, he did not hear the door to the bathroom open and Dr. Villano push Hogarth into the restroom. Holding up his hand for Hogarth to remain silent, Villano walked down the row of stalls and made sure each was empty. With Sebastian crouched on the toilet in the back corner of his stall, Villano did not see him as he peered under the almost closed door.

Villano returned to the restroom's main door and, leaning against it to ensure their privacy, nodded at Hogarth to tell his story. And so it was that the first words Sebastian heard from his toilet-top perch were, "I got the bomb out of the Professor's Omni and put them in my car."

Sebastian froze as he was wrenched from an especially eloquent argument about the *Gemeinschaft* and *Gesellschaft* of a modern, information-based society into a strange new reality.

"Excellent," Villano said, rubbing his hands together in expectation of his well-laid plan's success. "We can assemble the bomb this afternoon and be at the game on time tonight to plant it as scheduled."

Sebastian straightened at the sound of Villano's voice and, eager to learn the identity of the other party to this most intriguing conversation, stood and risked a peek over the top of the stall. As Villano opened the restroom door to let Hogarth out, Sebastian glimpsed the young student who had appeared at their breakfast table. Then the student was gone, followed closely by Villano.

Sebastian clambered down from his perch. He frowned. Was it a practical joke? Was it some new form of interactive, participatory teaching Villano had adopted? Was it really a plot to blow up some game tonight? Were Villano and his student pranksters or international terrorists? If they were pranksters, their little scene was at least, as Byron had scribbled in *Hints from Horace*, "As good as a play."

Upon reflection, Sebastian concluded he would have to treat what he had overheard as a real terrorist plot, since lives might be at stake. If it was a practical joke, then he would just have to endure being the butt of jokes, laughter and, possibly, derision. To risk knowing about such a plot and doing nothing would be more than he could bear if anyone was hurt, let alone killed.

He knew what he had to do. A straight line to the nearest police station was the most logical and prudent, not to mention safest, course. Only in fiction did characters attempt to deal with terrorists on their own. Whoever did so always ended up in deadly peril. They always seemed to escape at the last millisecond, but Sebastian had no wish to ever be in deadly peril, whether he was saved at the last millisecond or not.

Deciding this was a story best told in person, Sebastian was in the parking lot as swiftly as his legs would convey him. Leaving the college also avoided the possibility of running into Villano. If Villano was violent enough to blow up a game, what would he do if he learned Sebastian had overheard his dastardly plan?

Sebastian could not know that Elizabeth, in the course of the taxi ride back to her office, had decided her first priority was to confront Sebastian about his suspected straying. Canceling her Saskatoon medical office building meeting by cell phone, she had ordered the cabby to execute a U-turn at the next legal opportunity and return to the college where she would confront and, if necessary, fight for her man—if she decided she still wanted the philandering toad, if in fact he was such an amphibian.

So it was that as Sebastian pulled out of the college parking lot just before lunchtime, Elizabeth, glum with worry over what she thought was a looming confrontation with her husband, stared out the taxi's grimy window and beheld him speeding past in his car. Was he off to a secret rendezvous with some buxom student or a tryst with one of the Turnbell neighbors, mother or daughter? Or mother *and* daughter? Elizabeth could only wonder.

Should she follow him? Pursuit in the taxi would cripple her finely calibrated family budget. Even so, she had cancelled her meeting and would get nothing done at work in her current frame of mind. She paid the cabby and decided to discuss the matter with the one man who knew Sebastian better than anyone. The man who, with a clear mind and exquisite sense, could analyze Sebastian's deepest thoughts and motives: Uncle Bill. As Elizabeth had heard Sebastian say of Bill; "In short, there never was a better hearer." She thought it might be from Byron but as she made her way into the college, she concluded it might have been Burke, Blake or Burns, or any of the other great Irish, Welsh or Scottish writers the English habitually claimed as their own.

She found her Svengali exiting his Statistics 201 class, counting a wad of dollar bills.

"Uncle Bill," Elizabeth called as she approached him through the sea of students executing a class change.

Bill stuffed the wad of bills into his pocket and embraced his favorite nephew's wife. "Elizabeth, my dear. What have I done to deserve such a pleasant surprise?"

Elizabeth fell silent, looking down as they walked with Bill toward his office.

"It's about Sebastian," she finally admitted as they climbed the broad stairs up to the third floor, where Bill resided during some of his working hours. Most of his work hours were spent at his statistical laboratory: the track.

Bill opened his office door and Elizabeth had to smile despite her dark mood at her uncle-in-law's lavish lair. The lock on the door, Sebastian had told her, was of a much higher quality than any other lock in the college. This was so because, as Bill had confided to her, only Lester could be trusted in such a place. Bill's office had a mahogany desk, a Ox blood leather office chair, matching leather sofa and over-sized club chair, teak filing cabinets, and several paintings of thoroughbreds on the wall. Each painting, Elizabeth had been told by no less an authority than Wilberforce Higgenbotham, chair of the Department of Art, was worthy of hanging in the finest art galleries in the country and would fetch five figures each, not that Bill would ever sell what he called, "My stable."

As Elizabeth entered, Bill quickly closed the door to avoid the unhappy circumstance of a colleague seeing his palatial digs. Elizabeth was, as always, struck by how comfortable and lived-in Bill could make an office appear that was crammed with such expensive and exquisite furniture, nick nacks and paraphernalia. *Racing Forms*, books, journals, and magazines on horse racing, breeding, training, statistics, and mathematical modeling fought for space with betting slips, ledgers and computer printouts filled with data about every aspect of horse racing, betting, and the art and—as Bill was always adamant to emphasize—science of gambling.

As a young lady dating Sebastian, Elizabeth had visited Bill in his office many times and to her surprise had on several occasions discovered rolls of currency secreted here and there. On her first visit, she had moved a pile of old betting slips to sit on the sofa and found to her great surprise a roll of bills the diameter of a tennis ball. Besides always needing cash handy to place wagers, Bill did not trust banks and kept his winnings hidden in his office, which was another reason why only Lester had a key. Only Lester could be trusted to clean Bill's office and not filch an accidentally discovered roll of currency.

Uncle Bill cleared off the leather club chair for Elizabeth and then rapidly constructed a hand-rolled cigarette as he plunked down in his own luxurious leather throne. He switched on the small fan that would blow the smoke from his creation out the window. Although the window could not be opened, it had a dozen holes drilled in the glass. Elizabeth wondered for a moment what happened when it rained or in the depths of winter, but the thought quickly fled her mind as she realized that Uncle Bill was always equipped and prepared for any eventuality. A little thing like winter would not even rise to the level of a challenge to his agile mind, especially when allied with associates like Lester.

"You wanted to talk about Sebastian?" Bill asked as he lit his misshapen creation and decided he had given Elizabeth enough time to stew.

"I was wondering what Sebastian thought about other women," Elizabeth asked tentatively.

"Other women?" Bill asked, leaning back in his chair and taking a long drag on his hand-rolled cancer stick.

"I mean, is he friendly toward them?"

Bill held the cigarette in his mouth as he laced his long, tobacco-stained fingers over his chest. "You mean, other women such as the secretaries in the English Department?"

Elizabeth nodded.

"He loves them."

Elizabeth suppressed a gasp and asked, "Which one?"

"All of them," Bill said matter-of-factly. "He gave each of them a yellow tulip just this morning."

Elizabeth thought of the secretaries in the English Department and could not imagine her Sebastian romantically involved with any of them. Lucy was not exactly pretty, Mrs. Brumburry was not exactly young, and Suzanne La Touche, while beautiful, was certainly too young for Sebastian. Or was she?

"Even to Suzanne?"

"Yes, I believe he gave her a flower. As a matter of fact, he also presented one to Professor Krumm."

Elizabeth leaned forward in alarm. "You've got to be kidding. Her husband once put a guy in the hospital for seven weeks just for opening a door for her—and the guy was the doorman at Athene's."

"Nonetheless, the brave romantic that our Sebastian is, he did."

Elizabeth tried to fathom her husband's behavior, but failed. Was he having affairs with every female in the English office? "How does he behave toward his students?"

"He loves them," Bill said, trying to figure out Elizabeth's sudden interest in her husband's job, even as he inadvertently hammered another nail into the scaffolding that Elizabeth was building in her mind to hang Sebastian. "And his students love him."

"They do?" Elizabeth asked, her mind racing at the thought of the young, buxom co-eds brimming with raging hormones who crowded university classrooms looking for older, more experienced men to teach them the ways of the world, and of the bedroom.

"Of course," Bill said. He may as well build Sebastian up as a great teacher to his wife. What harm could it do? "He gives them flowers, too."

"All of his students?"

"No, just the girls," Bill said but, seeing Elizabeth's chagrined look and fearing she might have certain progressive views about sexual equality, he quickly added, "He brings bagels and donuts for the whole class, though. He doesn't like to play favorites: boys, girls, he loves them all."

Elizabeth frowned as she tried to assimilate that morsel of information into her rapidly evolving—or devolving—mental image of her husband: boys *and* girls?

"Then there are the poetry readings."

"Poetry readings?"

"Yes. Whenever he reads a poem in class, he picks a suitable young lady to read to. It helps personalize the poem, especially love sonnets. At least, that's what he says."

Elizabeth was appalled. She must be married to the worst philanderer in the Western hemisphere, if not the entire Western world.

"Doesn't he do the same sorts of things for you?" Bill asked as he finished his cigarette. Before it burned his fingers, he tossed the butt in an overflowing ashtray hidden in the top drawer of his desk.

"Of course," Elizabeth answered, thinking of the birdbath, the email messages each morning, the surprise flowers, and the breakfasts in bed. But, she wondered, was all of that just Sebastian being Sebastian or were they the misdirections of a man hiding a harem of mistresses to rival the Sultan of Constantinople at the height of his decadent reign? She must learn the truth.

Chapter 23

"Don't you see," Sebastian said, tapping his watch, "we don't have much time. The bomb is supposed to go off at a game tonight."

Two inspectors sat across the table from him in an interrogation room at the Royal Canadian Mounted Police station on 49th and Fraser near City College. The Mounties had led him into a small, light blue room as soon as he had arrived with his outlandish story. The inspectors, who believed the elderly volunteers manning the front desk were frail of mind, body and soul, had not wanted to upset them. The inspectors did not know the volunteers were hardened vets of the Korean War and were far more interested in bomb plots than their usual routine of filing complaints about missing cats, barking dogs and stolen newspapers. They sorely missed the shot, shell and excitement of their younger days and a bomb plot appeared like a promising possibility, until the inspectors took over just as Sebastian was getting to the meat of his story.

"Why were you in the bathroom?" Inspector Adderly asked as the interrogation entered its second hour. Sebastian had repeated his story 11 times and was starting on a twelfth rendition.

"President Kratz asked me to investigate graffiti in the bathroom stalls."

"Do you normally investigate graffiti?" Inspector Short asked with a frown.

"Of course not. I'm an English professor."

"Specializing in graffiti?" Adderly asked.

"No, romantic poets of the 18th Century."

"Then why did the president ask you to read graffiti in the bathroom?"

Before Sebastian could answer, Short asked, "Was he with you at the time?"

"Who?"

"The president."

"Of course not, or I would have brought him along to corroborate my story."

"That would have been much better," Adderly said. He sighed and said, "I think we've heard enough, Dr. Gianninni. We'll fill out a report and follow it up as resources allow. I should warn you, filing a false police report is a serious crime." He stood, his rotund belly just clearing the edge of the interrogation room's table.

Sebastian knew when he was getting the brush off, but he could not believe the police were as unresponsive as they appeared. "I know what I heard," he said, his ire rising.

Adderly opened the door and, with a haphazard goodbye, left. Short, the softer-hearted of the two and not, as Adderly did, needing to use the bathroom, stopped at the door and said, "It could have been some kids playing a joke."

"It was Dr. Villano—hardly a kid—and a student."

"There you are; a student."

Sebastian was still not satisfied.

"You could have misheard," Short suggested. "There can be all sorts of echoes in a bathroom, with the stall's walls, the water running, dripping faucets and all."

"The faucets at City College do not drip," Sebastian said, leaping to the defense of his school.

"As Adderly said, we'll look into it, but if I were you, I'd go home, get some rest and stay out of bathrooms." Short turned to leave, then turned back to add, "And be careful what you report to the police."

Sebastian, or rather Byron, had the final words. "'If a man proves too clearly and convincingly to himself...that a tiger is an

optical illusion—well, he will find out he is wrong. The tiger will
himself intervene in the discussion, in a manner which will be
in every sense conclusive,'" Sebastian recited. "I fear Villano is a
tiger."

Short's frown deepened as he digested Sebastian's elliptical
prediction and watched the English professor slink, dejected and
emotionally drained from the room.

Even though Sebastian had gotten in the last words, his spirits
were low as he wondered how much trouble he would get into if,
as advised, he did stay out of bathrooms, given he had drunk four
cups of tea during the prolonged interrogation.

Little did he know that the moment he had given his name
to the volunteer at the front desk he had been fighting an up-
hill battle. The volunteer had entered Sebastian's name into the
computer and it spit out a report from Officer Fawn "Bulldog"
Cates of the Canadian Border Services. It revealed that Sebastian
LeClerc Gianninni that very morning had been detained at the
border. Officer Cates had confiscated a considerable number of
"romantic aides" from Gianninni's vehicle before she released the
smut smuggler with a considerable and weighty warning.

When the volunteer handed Adderly the report, the inspector
read it and handed it to Short. Sebastian's chances of being believed then plummeted to zero. Adderly and Short made the short
leap—really just a half-step—to the conclusion that Sebastian was
a peddler of pornographic materials who had been caught at the
border that morning and had decided to get back at the police
that afternoon by filing a false report. Investigating such a report
would waste hundreds of man hours of work. Luckily for Sebastian, neither inspector wanted to deal with the voluminous paperwork involved in filing an arrest for a false report. They were
far more interested in pursuing rapists, murderers and purveyors
of BC Bud. Besides, there was a Grizzlies game that evening that
neither wished to miss a second of.

Even so, neither Adderly or Short wanted to wake up the next
morning and find that some IRA-wannabe bomber had blown up
a "game" somewhere in Vancouver. Within an hour, they had a
rough idea of the parameters of the problem Sebastian, on the
slim chance he was telling the truth, had laid before them. Dr.

Villano had no criminal record. Sebastian had not been able to provide the name of the student he alleged had been an active participant in the conspiratorial conversation in the bathroom, so Short and Adderly hit a dead end pursuing that offshoot of Sebastian's story. They did learn from the RCMP Criminal Database that there were no suspected bombers in Vancouver or anywhere within a reasonable bomb-planting distance.

Even worse for Sebastian, they also learned that on top of Bulldog Cates' report, Sebastian also had a criminal record. He had been held overnight after a raid on an illegal gambling parlor in 1996. Sebastian's explanation, that his uncle had dragged him to the parlor on the pretense of "paying some bills," had not impressed the judge who had fined and released Sebastian and Bill after what, for Sebastian, had been a horrendous night in jail. The night had not been a total loss, at least for Bill, who emerged $447 ahead after an all-night poker game with several of their fellow detainees. Neither Bill's winnings nor Sebastian's explanation appeared in the RCMP database. All it recorded was the arrest and Sebastian's release with a fine and a warning.

After reading Sebastian's record, Short called City College and learned there were four games scheduled for that night at the school: a men's basketball game; an exhibition baseball game; a water polo match; and a badminton tournament, which was already in full swing. Adderly, meanwhile, perused the sports section of the newspaper and found that the New Westminster Salmonbellies lacrosse team, on their quest for another championship, played their arch rivals, the Coquitlam Adanacs, that evening. That particular information left Adderly thinking that it was lucky a team in Canada had taken their country's name spelt backwards as their name and not a team from the United States or they would have been called the Setats Detinu, which sounded more like a disease of the lower intestine than a national champion lacrosse team.

Looking at the paper again, Adderly read that the Vancouver Grizzlies would defend their almost perfect record against the Los Angeles Lakers, while Vancouver's class A baseball team, the Mounties, were playing an exhibition game that evening. Furthermore, there were dozens of amateur events, including a major softball tournament in Abbottsford, a junior lacrosse tournament in Ladner and a multitude of high school games that night in all manner of sports.

"There are more games tonight than we have constables on the force," Adderly said dejectedly as he compared notes with his partner.

Short sighed and said, "There's not much we can do. I guess we could put a man on Villano this evening, just in case."

After another half-hour of discussion, Adderly finally agreed. They presented Short's proposal to the Superintendent, who, with a superior air, vetoed their idea.

"But go see Villano and ask him some probing questions," the Superintendent ordered. "It won't hurt to let him know, if he is indeed up to no good, that the good men of the RCMP are hot on his trail."

"But we aren't," Adderly said. "We barely have a trail, let alone a hot one." He thought for a moment and added, "I wonder why a hot trail would be easier to follow than a cold one, unless you had those cool night vision goggles that pick up infra-red stuff."

"Villano doesn't know that," the Superintendent said, ignoring Adderly's musings on the temperature of trails and its relation to tracking ability.

"We could go see Gianninni again," Short suggested.

"Do we have jurisdiction in Blaine?" Adderly asked.

"Why does he live in Blaine?" the Superintendent asked.

"He said his wife wanted to avoid paying higher Canadian taxes," Short explained.

"A tax dodger, eh?" the Superintendent said, his eyes narrowing as if he had just spotted prey. "Just like the draft dodgers in the 1960s."

Adderly and Short frowned, not following their leader's reasoning.

"And this Gianninni character won't even take responsibility for his tax dodging," the Superintendent continued. "He hides behind his wife. I don't trust him."

"Should we still drop it?" Short asked.

The Superintendent paused. "No, I think we should be prudent here. Go see Villano and see what he has to say. Then drop it."

"Why see him," Short asked, "if we're just going to drop it?"

"We must be completely thorough in our investigations before we drop them," the Superintendent stated. "In fact, we must be more thorough in investigating the cases we know we are going to drop than the ones we are going to pursue. It that clear?"

Chapter 24

Sebastian sat on the hard, stone steps of the RCMP station. Had he heard what he thought he had heard in the restroom? Had it even been Dr. Villano? And who was the young man whom Sebastian knew he had seen before, yet could not match to a name, place, class, exam, paper or presentation? What should he do? He had gone to the police, yet his attempt to do the right thing had come to naught. The police believed Sebastian about as much as he believed in the Easter Bunny, Santa Claus and the government ever requiring adequate study of English romantic literature in high schools.

As Mounties strode in and out of the station past him, he decided to go to the one person who might be able to help him with his problem: Uncle Bill or, as Bill always emphasized to Sebastian, Professor-Uncle Bill. To everyone's surprise, including his own, Bill had been granted tenure and become a full professor at City College years before. No one who spent so much time at the track and, conversely, so little time on academic research had ever been granted tenure. Bill would have been the first to argue his research on horse racing was about as far removed from the academic realm as research could be; it was actually useful, interesting and, if he could perfect it, would benefit the common man more than any scientific invention since television. Bill knew his research had economic value—or would, one day—but he was flattered beyond measure to learn it also had academic value, even if that value had been determined by a bunch of eggheads. For that reason, Bill was inordinately proud of his achievement in the academic world. Although, the truth be told, he would have been far happier and far wealthier if he had perfected his Grand Unifying Theory of Horse Racing instead of achieving the Holy Grail of tenure.

Sebastian climbed into his Omni and sped through Vancouver, across the Burrard Street Bridge and through downtown, Gastown and Chinatown to the grand old confines of Exhibition Park. He parked for free where Uncle Bill had shown him years before, down by the Sasketchewan grain elevator on the waterfront to avoid the $6 fee to park at the track. He lacked Bill's lifetime free parking pass, which Bill had procured from Lester in exchange for what turned out to be a sizzling hot tip on a race almost 13 years ago.

Engrossed in the problem at hand, Sebastian strolled up the hill to the track oblivious to the view. Below, in the harbour, freighters from countries rimming the Pacific were moored to the docks of the grain elevator terminal. Cruise ships were tied up at Canada Place, which sported a soaring white roof that evoked memories of the age of sailing ships. In the distance was forested, 1,000-acre Stanley Park, which guarded the entrance to Burrard Inlet like some dark, green sentinel. Graceful Lions Gate Bridge connected the park to West Vancouver across the harbour's narrow entrance.

Sebastian trudged across the parking lot and on to the fairgrounds of the Pacific National Exhibition, more commonly called the PNE. Each August, the PNE hosted a fair and exhibition with rides, agricultural shows, a lumberjack contest, demolition derby, dream home lottery, and a range of exhibits on everything from the latest kitchen products to the Canadian armed forces, both of which often featured knives, although for somewhat different purposes.

Reaching the track's rust-speckled metal turnstiles, Sebastian pulled out his pass, which Bill had procured for him through Lester, some friend of Lester or some friend of one of Lester's many friends. For a weekday afternoon, the park was busy, especially given the sad, slow decline in horse racing attendance figures over the past few decades. It was a sunny spring day, weather that often brought out some of the less addicted, part-time aficionados of the sport of kings. Sebastian strolled past the paddock area and sauntered down in front of the grandstand as the parade to post sounded over the track's loudspeakers. He looked over toward the dirt track and watched the procession of eight thoroughbreds about to thunder around the track for glory and several thousand dollars. He inhaled the mixture of stale popcorn, beer, hotdogs, dirt, horse sweat, and dung. It smelled like home.

After chatting with a passing acquaintance to gather a morsel of local knowledge, Sebastian scanned the crowd. As they made their final choices, men clutching *Racing Forms* rushed up toward the betting machines under the grandstand. Other groups clustered like flocks of feeding birds as they talked or perused newspapers, programs, notebooks or scraps of paper. Others closely watched the horses as they paraded to post, their eyes as intent as any jeweler's examining a fine diamond that just may be cubic zirconium, glass or—God forbid—possibly even paste.

The more experienced bettors would be under the grandstands at the built-in desks where they could watch the race on monitors as they pored over voluminous notes and statistics on every horse that had ever paraded to post at Exhibition Park or anywhere else in North America and beyond. Although Bill was a veteran, he rarely resided under the grandstands. Bill liked to see the horses in the paddock, talk with the jockeys and trainers, many of whom he had known for decades, get a feel for the upcoming contest and soak in the ambience of his favorite place on earth. Bill's statistical modeling of the day's races had been done long beforehand in his office at the college. When he arrived at the track, he had a crib sheet with his scribbled picks for each race. He also had fall back positions if it began to rain, if a horse was scratched or if several of various and innumerable other eventualities occurred to upset his Grand Unifying Theory's precise, yet unfortunately often slightly off predictions.

Sebastian spotted his uncle and then, surprisingly, Elizabeth peering at a particularly frisky chestnut as it paraded to post. They stood amidst a herd of Bill's racetrack cronies.

"I like him," Elizabeth said, eyeing the chestnut. "He seems so....alive."

"Doesn't matter if he's alive or dead," said Winless Joe, who was experiencing a losing streak stretching back to 1957. "Only matters if he can run faster than every other horse in the field, at least by a nose."

"I think he can," Elizabeth said, only the glimmer of a hint of uncertainty in her voice.

"He's a 20-to-1 long shot, Lizzie," commented Chili Ray, who always called women by diminutives, even though he was a foot shorter than the average woman. His nickname came from his teeth, which were in such poor condition he was almost always just returning from a dentist's appointment with his mouth at least partially, if not entirely frozen. "Equinox hasn't even placed in 14 starts."

"He's going to win," Elizabeth declared with a note of certainty.

"Alright," Bill said, "two dollars on Equinox to win. I'll go put your money down for you."

"Thanks, Bill," Elizabeth said and turned back to watch her favorite, Equinox, prancing toward the gate.

Winless Joe, Chili Ray and Midget Williams, who was not a midget, as one might guess, but of average height, watched the horses as grooms coaxed them into the gate. Williams had no distinguishing features to the extent that he had robbed several banks decades before and avoided identification even in repeated lineups by eagle-eyed witnesses with impeccable memories. Chili Ray had started to call him Willie, after Willie Sutton, who famously replied when asked why he robbed banks, "Because that's where the money is." Their cronies quickly decided that that particular nickname hit a little too close to home, especially when there were racetrack police munching donuts nearby. Midget, however, stuck, probably because Midget always tried, given his bank-robbing past, to keep a low profile.

Elizabeth was still leaning on the rail, intently watching the horses as they were maneuvered into the chutes, when an arm reached around her holding a steaming cappuccino.

"'And to his eye / There was but one beloved face on earth, / And that was shining on him,'" a gentle tenor whispered in her ear.

Elizabeth whirled around, almost upsetting the drink, to come face to face with Sebastian. She had planned to unleash a torrent of accusations at him, but now she hesitated. They were surrounded by Bill's racetrack cronies and there was the cappuccino and, as always when they met, Sebastian's loving smile. Elizabeth was struggling to regain her resolve to have it out with Sebastian right then and there when he added, "With chocolate sprinkles on top, just as you like them."

Elizabeth stared down at the dark chocolate bits swimming on the drink's white, frothy surface. It was not a cold day but spring had not quite sprung. The hot drink looked as inviting as a cool lake on the hottest summer day. As she gazed into the face of her Sebastian, her belief, forming since the double-attempted embraces by the females Turnbell that morning, that her husband was a philandering, womanizing, lying, deceitful lout, faded like the end of a movie. The thoughtful man of the birdbath, surprise breakfasts and cappuccinos with chocolate sprinkles could not be anything but the most devoted of husbands. How could she ever have doubted him?

And, Elizabeth thought as she accepted the proffered drink, she could always be mad at him after she finished her cappuccino with chocolate sprinkles.

After saying hello to Chili, Winless and Midget Williams, Sebastian asked Elizabeth, "What brings you here?" He did not believe that Elizabeth, serious and upright, would ever believe his story, although Bill's racetrack cronies probably would at least would lay odds as to its veracity. To avoid ridicule, Sebastian wanted to ask Bill's advice alone about the bomb plot, so, instead, Sebastian asked Elizabeth, "Didn't you have a medical records building meeting for the Saskatoon office today?"

"I cancelled it."

"That was kind of you. Bill asked me to meet him at the track but I wasn't sure I'd make it, so he called you?"

Elizabeth sipped her steaming drink and Sebastian, assuming an affirmative answer, added, "That was nice of you to come keep an old man company."

"Who's an old man?" Bill demanded as he returned from placing bets for Elizabeth and himself. "And who needs company?" He grinned at his three cronies.

"Certainly not you, Uncle Bill. Who's your favorite?" Sebastian asked, trying to divert Bill's attention from the overheard, unfortunate remark.

"Vancouver Slough," Bill said, then added, still miffed, "and it's Professor-Uncle Bill to you."

"Sucker bet," Winless Joe predicted. "Secretary's gonna take the field."

Winless Joe had been through his father's shipping fortune, his wife's ample department store dowry and the inheritance from an uncle who had invested in Coca Cola stock at $1, IBM at 30 cents and Microsoft at $1.20. Worst of all, he had gone through it all placing $2 bets to win. Winless never bet anything less or more than $2 and never bet a place, show, trifecta, superfecta, exacta or quinella. He always bet to win, yet never did.

The last of the horses was loaded into the gate as Bill checked his betting sheet with its complex scribbled calculations one last time. Sebastian glanced from the horses to Elizabeth, back to the horses and then back to his wife, who was staring at him.

"What?" he asked.

"Nothing," Elizabeth said, as she turned to watch the race and sip her hot brew.

"Come home for me, baby," Winless whispered as he reverently clasped his hands and glanced skyward at the supreme being in whose existence his belief had been sorely tested since 1957; the date of his last, still fondly remembered win.

"They're at the post and…they're off!" the announcer's amplified voice boomed across the track as the horses thundered out of the gate.

Sebastian turned to Bill and whispered, "I need to talk to you."

Bill's attention was focused on Vancouver Slough. He replied without taking his eyes off his chosen steed, "I'll get the chair cleaned. I promise."

"It's Vancouver Slough, Equinox, Northern Prancer, Secretary and Man O' Peace in a tight pack, followed by Parking Ticket—Citation's offspring—, Twirl-away, Near Lap and, six lengths back and fading fast, is Dusselworf."

"It's not about my office chair. It's about a plot to blow up a game tonight."

"Parking Ticket is moving up rapdily on the outside. Vancouver Slough is fading as Northern Prancer, Equinox and Secretary take the lead on the first turn."

Bill winced at Vancouver Slough's slippage in the ranks. His attention had not been entirely on Sebastian and he did not think he had heard right. Furrowing his brow, he asked, "Blow up? No need to get so angry over a simple chair."

"As they make the turn into the backstretch, Vancouver Slough is boxed in most securely alongside Parking Ticket, as Northern Prancer, Equinox and Secretary set the pace."

"I need your advice," Sebastian whispered. "I went to the police."

"Come on, Equinox!" Elizabeth screamed.

"Come on Secretary!" Winless Joe yelled.

"Over an office chair?" Bill asked, turning as suddenly as all his attention was focused on his nephew.

"No, over the plot to blow up a game tonight."

"Equinox has moved up on the far turn with Vancouver Slough and Secretary breaking out of the pack on his hooves."

"What game?" Bill asked, turning back to the race as he tried to pick out Vancouver Slough. The horses galloped around the clubhouse turn.

"It's Vancouver Slough, Equinox and Secretary on the outside coming into the home stretch."

"I don't know," Sebastian said.

"What did you tell the police?" Bill asked, as he and Midget Williams started to jump up and down, urging Vancouver Slough home, even as Elizabeth jumped and screamed for Equinox, Chili Ray for Northern Prancer and Winless Joe for Secretary.

"Northern Prancer is making a desperate charge on the inside, but Vancouver Slough, Equinox and Secretary are a solid line abreast as they sprint for the finish."

"I told them I overheard a plot to blow up a game tonight in the men's room," Sebastian said.

"What game do you play in a men's room?" Bill asked between jumps. "Come on, Vancouver Slough! Come on!"

"Not the game," Sebastian yelled over the crowd's roar as the horses galloped up the straightaway. "I overheard the conversation in the men's room."

"It's Vancouver Slough, Equinox and Secretary. Equinox, Secretary and Vancouver Slough. They're neck and neck and neck, and, at the wire....it's Dusselworf on the outside, coming from last place in a splendid, last-second surge."

"Dusselworf?" Elizabeth, Bill, Winless Joe, Chili Ray and Midget Williams asked in a chorus of disbelief as the black horse galloped across the finish line a nostril ahead of the three equines who had been leading the race for almost a mile and a quarter.

"Who in the name of Lakebiscuit is he?" Midget Williams demanded, confounded and confused.

"A rather splendid colt from Germany," Sebastian said. "Just came over last month."

"Never heard of him," Chili Ray said with disgust as he tore his ticket into confetti.

"Me neither," Winless Joe said, having added to his ever lengthening losing streak. "I would have sworn it was going to be a three-way dead heat."

"Who the hell would bet on a horse called Dusselworf?" Midget Williams cursed as he threw his losing ticket to the ground and stomped on it.

"As luck would have it, I would—and did."

All eyes turned on Sebastian as he retrieved a ticket from his pocket.

"Why in the name of all I've taught you would you bet on a horse called Dusselworf, just over from Germany at," Bill glanced at the big board in the infield, "60 to 1?"

"I bumped into Lester at the paddock on my way in. He was with a trainer acquaintance of his, Jake 'Gordie' Gordon, who mentioned a rumor that there was a new, genetically engineered super horse just over from Dusseldorf, Germany. He didn't know the name, but Dusselworf seemed to fit the bill."

With a satisfied smile, Sebastian turned to saunter off to collect his substantial winnings. "We need to talk, Professor-Uncle Bill," he called over his shoulder at the open-mouthed group of dejected bettors.

"And we need to talk," Elizabeth called, as she raced after Sebastian, Bill close on her heels.

Ten minutes later, the trio sat in the grandstand restaurant snacking on French fries and sipping drinks purchased with a small portion of Sebastian's winnings.

"What do you think about our neighbors?" Elizabeth asked Sebastian.

"The Turnbells?" Sebastian asked, frowning.

"Yes, Rosa and Destiny."

"They're nice." Sebastian turned to Bill and said, "I overheard Dr. Villano and a student in the men's room this afternoon discussing explosives and a game tonight."

Bill took out his tobacco pouch and rolling paper. A waiter, approximately the size of a Percheron or at least a Clydesdale, approached at the sight of the paraphernalia.

"This is a no smoking area," the waiter informed Bill, who nodded and continued the early stages of creating his attempt at a cigarette as the waiter hurried off to tend to another table of hungry patrons.

"What about the students at the college?" Elizabeth asked Sebastian. "The female students?"

"What about them?"

"Do you like them?"

"Of course I do, or why would I teach?" Sebastian turned back to Bill, who was sprinkling tobacco unevenly onto a cigarette paper. "I went to the police and told them what I overheard, but they said there were strange echoes in restrooms."

"Yeah, there often are," Bill agreed as he used his teeth to close the golden string on his tobacco pouch. "Once I swore I heard Lester say to put half a C note on Mayfair Lady but it turned out he'd said to place the half yard on Mayfair Lady." Sebastian stared at Bill, not getting it. "He meant to bet Mayfair Lady to place, not win. After the lady placed a strong second, he tried to get what he would have won from me for months until he won on Serious

Stranger—40 to 1—based on my Grand Unifying Horse Racing Theory. If he hadn't, I'd still be hearing about it."

"What should I do?"

"Never take bets from people in the next stall." Bill jammed his tobacco pouch in his pocket and started to roll his cigarette with due diligence and care.

The waiter loomed over Bill and announced, "No smoking, sir." Then a customer beckoned the waiter away to refresh his dangerously low scotch and soda.

"You should tell me about your relationship with the Turnbells," Elizabeth chimed in.

"The Turnbells?" Sebastian asked, confused. "They're our neighbors."

"Yes, but what about Rosa and Destiny?"

"What about them? They're nice. Destiny is 'A lovely being, scarcely formed or molded, / A rose with all its sweetest leaves yet folded.'"

"What?" Elizabeth demanded, alarmed.

"I thought the quote from Byron's *Don Juan* described her rather well."

"Don Juan?" Elizabeth asked, aghast.

"I don't think you could have heard right," Bill told Sebastian as he mulled over his nephew's story. "Why would Villano blow up anything? He's got tenure." To Bill, tenure meant a guaranteed job for life. They could never fire you. You could say or do whatever you wanted. The only requirement was to lecture a couple of times a week. The rest of your time, your entire summer and a month at Christmas was completely your own. Bill could not fathom anyone giving that up for any other life, except for a job as a professional handicapper or bookie. What possible allure could a life of terrorism hold?

Having not taken a tape recorder, camcorder or camera crew with him into the bathroom, Sebastian had no way to prove what he had overheard. Dejected and frustrated, he jammed his hands into his pockets and sank down into his chair. His right hand felt a piece of paper and, lacking a cigarette to roll like Bill to occupy his idle hands, he pulled it out.

"I wish you had a job where there were no women," Elizabeth announced.

Sebastian frowned. "Why?"

"I don't like you being around women, not when you're married to me."

"'You should not take a fellow eight years old and make him swear to never kiss the girls,'" Sebastian recited airily. Even facing an international terrorist threat, he liked being at the track with Bill. It had an air of easy going, if roguish romance about it. "I don't kiss the girls—well, only you, Elizabeth—but I can't help but notice all the beauty around me."

As Elizabeth fumed unnoticed by Sebastian, who returned to ruminating about bomb plots, he unfolded the crumpled paper he had found in his pocket. It was the wanted poster from the border. Sebastian handed the sheet to Elizabeth and said, "I scribbled a book order on this."

Momentarily distracted by the possibility of a sale, Elizabeth took the sheet and, peering at the scribbles on the crumpled paper, said, "I can't read this."

"No," Sebastian gasped as he stared at the back of the sheet.

"No, I really can't," Elizabeth insisted.

"No," Sebastian repeated and snatched the paper back, flipping it over to show the rows of photographs under the bold WANTED heading. "That's the student Villano was talking with this morning." He jabbed his finger at one of the images. The man in the fuzzy, black-and-white photograph was identified as Hogarth Ramen O'Leary Chevalier, international terrorist, implicated in a conspiracy to blow up a simulation of King David's Temple in Jerusalem, a supercomputer at MIT and a PC store in Kalamazoo.

Bill and Elizabeth leaned over and looked closely at the image.

"You have to go tell the police," Elizabeth said.

"That's where I was most of the morning. They didn't believe a word I said."

"They have to believe you now."

"Why, because I say one of the men I overheard is the same man as in this photograph? It's the same as before; my word against logic and common sense. Why would an international terrorist be at City College with Villano?"

"I'd go to the college and see if Villano's still there," Bill advised as he licked his cigarette paper closed. "Confront him and find out what's what."

"If Villano's involved with terrorists, I don't want you confronting him," Elizabeth told her mate. She did not want him dead, at least not until she was sure he was a philandering amphibian.

"I doubt Villano's there anyway," Sebastian said. "If he has a bomb to plant for a game tonight, he isn't going to sit in his office at the college grading papers."

"The only game worth mentioning tonight is the Grizzlies-Lakers game," Bill said.

"Why?" Sebastian asked.

Astounded, Bill asked, "You are a guy, right?"

"I'm secure enough in my masculinity to admit I don't follow any sporting events, except the occasional snooker, darts and cricket from Britain."

"Whether you follow sports or not—and just to be clear, the three you mentioned are pub passtimes, not sports—you must know the Grizzlies are winning more than 90 percent of their games this season. They are by far the best team in the entire history of the NBA."

"I think I heard something about that this morning on the radio."

The waiter once again approached like a mother bear who has spotted an unsavory character near her impressionable cubs. "Excuse me, sir, but…"

"Stay away from the neighbors, Sebastian," Elizabeth warned her husband. Even if the bomb story was true, she had her marriage to save.

"That would be rude," Sebastian said as the waiter loomed over Bill, now like a tiger over a gangly mouse.

"Even if there is a plot to blow up the Grizzly's game tonight, you'd never be able to get in to stop it anyway," Bill lamented.

"Why?"

"Please, Sebastian," Elizabeth pleaded, seeing her marriage fading as fast as Equinox in the straightaway. "You have to change."

"It's sold out," Bill explained. "Has been for months. Scalpers are asking two and three grand a ticket, and that's only when they can actually get a ticket themselves. Even Lester couldn't get a ticket for a seat they just added to accommodate demand, and its view is obstructed by a dusty rafter and a Division Championship banner from the Canuck's 1974-75 season."

"I…," the waiter tried again but failed to enter the flow of the dueling conversations about basketball and neighbors.

"I can't change who I am," Sebastian told Elizabeth, taking her hand across the table as he shifted focus to that thread of the conversation. "I'm a romantic. You knew that when you married me. Isn't that why you married me?"

"You can't smoke in here, sir," the waiter told Bill as he finally caught a pause in the conversational flow just as the Professor-Uncle placed the cigarette in his mouth.

As Elizabeth thought about Sebastian and realized his romantic bent was, indeed, why she had married him and decided to give him just one more chance, albeit on a much shorter leash, Bill replied to the waiter, "I am not smoking."

"You've got a cigarette in your mouth."

"But I'm not smoking," Bill insisted, which, while technically true, even to the extent of standing up in a court of law, would not stand up in the Turf Club.

The waiter, mindful of Bill's advancing years, picked him up gently but firmly and carried him toward the door. If Bill had been younger, the waiter would have tossed him out the door. In deference to his age, the waiter merely deposited him on his feet just outside the door like a recalcitrant toddler.

"You would never stray, would you Sebastian?" Elizabeth asked when they were finally alone.

"Of course not," Sebastian said. "I don't have time. I've got a bomb plot to foil."

The waiter returned and, glaring at Sebastian and Elizabeth, indicated with unmistakable body language that their patronage was no longer sought nor desired.

"We're not smoking," Sebastian said, biting off the last word he was about to add: 'either.' At certain times, the truth was not the best defense.

The waiter seemed unimpressed by his customer's claim, so Sebastian led Elizabeth past the anti-smoking Goliath outside to find Bill staring morosely down at his crushed cigarette.

"He just snatched it from my mouth and crushed it under his hob-nail boot," Bill reported, downcast. "It was the best one I ever made."

"It was the most cylindrical," Sebastian agreed. "Maybe you can recreate it."

"It took me 58 years to make one that good."

"I could buy you one."

"A mass-produced cancer stick? You must be insane to think I'd stick one of those deadly things in my mouth. God only knows what goes into them."

Turning, Bill pulled out his tobacco pouch and rolling paper as he headed toward the park's exit. Maybe he could recreate another perfect cigarette. Hope sprang eternal, especially at a race track.

Chapter 25

A half hour later, Sebastian and Elizabeth parked at the college and rushed over to Bill, who had beat them back from the track and stood waiting on the steps. Bill knew every shortcut, legal and illegal, used by the finest drivers of police cars, ambulances, taxis, fire engines and get-away-cars in the city and had, therefore, been waiting for quite some time. He did not mind waiting because he had no desire to confront Villano alone. Either the professor was a terrorist and probably well armed or it was all a practical joke and Bill preferred Sebastian be the exclamation point in the punch line. Bill had not let the devil find his hands idle, however. He had spent the time trying to duplicate the perfect cigarette the Turf Club waiter had snatched at such a tender and un-smoked age from Bill's mouth and stomped into the pavement with an ungentlemanly relish.

"Damn," Bill mumbled as Elizabeth and Sebastian arrived. His newest attempt at a hand-rolled cigarette had not even ap-proached his worst previous effort. Dejected, Bill let his newest creation disintegrate and flutter to the ground as he followed his nephew and niece-in-law into the glass and concrete building.

"What if they're armed?" Elizabeth asked as they entered the stairwell and climbed toward the English faculty offices on the second floor.

"They aren't going to shoot someone in a college hallway," Sebastian stated emphatically, tempted to laugh at the very idea.

"Oh, no," Bill said, sarcasm dripping liberally from every word. "They plan to blow up a sold-out basketball game and kill tens of thousands of fans, but they won't shoot a couple of tenured professors and a beautiful young lady in a college hallway."

Sebastian stopped, halting his companions in mid-step, as he considered the danger in the new light cast by Bill.

"The police?" Elizabeth ventured, her concern growing that she might never find out if Sebastian had strayed, especially if he caught a stray or not so stray bullet. "I know they didn't believe you this morning, but we could go with you."

"His wife and uncle supporting his story," Bill said, shaking his head. "They'll lock us all up in Riverview until we can convince a board of shrinks we're sane. No way I'm going to risk that. I never met a shrink who didn't frown on gambling, poker and horse racing as degenerative activities. I might never get out. I, for one, don't ever want to face a board of shrinks again."

"Again?" Elizabeth asked, staring quizzically at Bill as Sebastian led the way upstairs toward his office. "When did you face a board of shrinks, Bill?"

"If we want to make sure we see tomorrow, we need a weapon," Sebastian said, focused on the problem at hand.

Even as Bill was about to answer Elizabeth, Sebastian unlocked the door to his office and was reaching for the object that was the purpose of his visit when Destiny Turnbell jumped up from behind his desk and gushed with a palpable undercurrent of lust, "Sebastian."

The word hung in the air as Destiny spotted Elizabeth behind her intended beau. Even as Destiny froze, Rosa Turnbell stepped from behind the boxes in the corner containing the *Hamlet* impedimenta and screamed, "Destiny, what are you doing here?!"

Sebastian was quite interested in the answer to that question, as well as the identical question he had been about to pose to Rosa. Elizabeth, however, postponed his question and anyone's answers by slapping Sebastian's face, spinning on her heel and tearing back down the stairs gushing a torrent of tears.

Sebastian fought to recover from the recent shocks which his flesh, having just been slapped, and his eyes, having just seen two Turnbells in his office, had been heir to. Momentarily stunned, he finally recovered and yelled, "Elizabeth! 'Think not I am what I appear!'"

"Even if she could hear you, I'd lay off the poetry at a time like this," Bill warned as he drew Sebastian by the arm to the window and pointed out at Elizabeth sprinting across the parking lot below them. "With speed like that, I'd put my money on her this afternoon against the entire field, except for Dusselworf."

Sebastian's world crumbled. It was too late. She had not heard his Byron for the defense. He watched helplessly as Elizabeth wiped tears from her eyes, unlocked the Omni and drove off as quickly as the subcompact would go within the posted speed limit.

Sebastian sat down heavily at his desk, lacking the will to continue.

"What are you doing here?" Rosa demanded of her wayward daughter again as they stood on either side of Sebastian's neatly organized desk.

"I…I came to see Sebast…Dr. Gianninni about a…a school project."

"You're in high school, not college," Rosa said, putting Destiny's destiny in doubt.

"It was an English paper," Destiny whimpered and then, following Elizabeth's stellar example, opened the sluice gates of tears in both her eyes.

As Rosa closed in for the *coup de grace*, Destiny, in full wail, dashed out of the office. Leaning against the wall as he constructed his newest hand-rolled cigarette, Bill gazed out the window. Moments later, he spotted the young lady as she ran across the parking lot to the bus stop where she sat down with a visible, if unheard, thump.

"May I ask why you've come and graced my office with your presence, Mrs. Turnbell?" Sebastian asked, having recovered enough to steel his will and gather his courage to pose the question, even as he wondered what else could occur on this overly eventful day.

"Please, call me Rosa," she said, rolling the "R" in a most seductive manner, which even drew Bill's attention away from his cigarette project.

"Of course, Rosa," Sebastian said graciously, although he avoided even a hint of a turn, let alone a roll, of the "R." "Pray tell me, what are you doing in my office?"

"I needed to see you," she replied, glancing demurely at Bill.

"How did you get in?"

"I told the secretary I was your colleague from Tuktuyaktuk University."

"Ah, Tuk U," Bill said wistfully.

"I still don't see why—" Sebastian began.

"Your love note this morning was so very nice, and I wanted to apologize for…" Her voice faltered and she looked away.

Sebastian, wishing to reach the bottom of this story regardless of how far into his own private hell he had to descend, urged her to continue.

"I ran into Elizabeth this morning," Rosa began.

"I know, but—"

"At your house…"

"Yes, this morning, before we left for work."

"No. After you'd gone to work, she came back home in your car."

"I still don't see," Sebastian said, wondering if Elizabeth's slap had damaged the ability of his brain to follow a story, even if it was a mystery.

Rosa looked up at Bill, who was licking his cigarette closed, for help, but Bill had long since decided to remain as well outside the parameters of this story as possible. Slapping had been involved and slapping did not agree with him, especially if he was the slapee.

Finding no succor in Bill, Rosa plunged on with her story. "I saw your car in front of your house and I thought you had come home. Elizabeth's car wasn't in the driveway, so I thought she was at work. You'd given me such a sweet note this morning"—at this, Sebastian frowned but, now that her story was making at least a scintilla of sense, he decided to let her run with it—"I thought we could," she cast a coquettish glance at Bill, before continuing, "we could spend some time together....alone." She loaded the last word with enough meaning to break even the strong back of Atlas.

Sebastian leaned forward, urging her to continue now that she was making headway toward a climax and the all important denouement of her tale.

"I knocked and Elizabeth answered the door. I hugged her, thinking she was you and then, realizing my momentous mistake, fled back to my house. I'm so sorry, Sebastian. I wanted to apologize and let you know what happened before Elizabeth found out about us."

Sebastian was too gracious to point out there was no "us" nor would there ever be an "us." Concluding another such story would be too much for his heart, mind or soul just now, he decided not to ask whether Rosa had any idea why Destiny had been hiding in his office.

"It's nothing," he found himself saying, even though he feared, given Elizabeth's violent reaction upon her departure, that it was as far from nothing as one could get. He only had a few hours to foil a villain's plot to blow up a sold-out stadium of basketball-rabid fans. At the moment, that mission outweighed everything else, even his unraveling marriage. Lives were at stake at GM Place. He was confident he could suture the rift between Elizabeth and himself, especially since there was really no basis for the whole imbroglio and, he hoped, no time limit to resolving that crisis, unlike Villano's plot, which had an explosive time limit.

"We should go, Professor-Uncle Bill," Sebastian announced.

His creation complete, Bill put his cigarette between his lips, nodded and headed for the door, believing in such situations that silence is golden, as well as being the best way to avoid getting slapped.

"I took a cab, but I don't have enough money to make it back home," Rosa explained, following Sebastian closely out the door. "Can I get a ride?"

"We're not going back to Blaine."

"That's fine. Wherever you're going, Sebastian, I will follow."

Sebastian, his hand on the doorknob to close it, smiled at Rosa. There was no need to be ungracious, regardless of the situation. Then, his mind pulling back from inspecting the brink of the abyss on which he feared his marriage was teetering, he remembered why he had come to his office in the first place. He reached into his den and selected a rapier from the *Hamlet* accoutrements.

"A sword?" Bill asked in disbelief, breaking his short-lived vow of silence.

"It's the best I can do," Sebastian said, having had enough of talk. Words had got him into trouble at the border, in the bathroom, at the police station, and in his office. He wished only to act; to wrap up the whole bomb-plot mess and attend to his crumbling marriage before it was too late. Setting his face in a stern countenance, he ordered, "Let's go."

Chapter 26

As students glanced at him curiously, Sebastian, rapier in hand, led the way through the college's halls to Villano's office. When they reached the professor's door, Bill leaned against the wall and lit his cigarette, figuring if Sebastian could carry a dangerous weapon, he could ignite some dangerous tobacco leaves. Sebastian tried the door. The amorous Rosa stood closer to him than he would have liked, but he focused on the task at hand.

"Locked," Sebastian reported and jiggled the knob, establishing for all that it was, indeed, locked. "He's not here."

"Might be evidence about his plans inside," Bill suggested. Leaning past Sebastian and peering at the lock, he added, "Not as good as mine." He rummaged in his pockets.

"What are you doing?" Sebastian asked as a pair of students walked past, glancing at the lady and the two professors: one rapier-armed, the other smoking what appeared to be a cigarette constructed by the lowest bidder.

"Looking for…," Bill pulled out a key from the depths of his cluttered pockets, "this. Lester got it for me."

"What is it?"

"A skeleton key. We'll be inside before you can say Dusselworf."

With a sense of gravitas, Bill leaned down to insert the key in the lock. Sebastian and Rosa, blocked from seeing the keyhole by

Bill's body, leaned to the right and left, respectively, to watch the lock-pick operation.

"Bloody hell," Bill cursed under his breath and then swiveled his head and apologized to Rosa for his curses.

"Quite understandable, given the situation," Rosa said, although she had no idea what the situation was. In any case, his cursing was nothing compared to what she had heard growing up in a family of actors who specialized in playing witches and warlocks: always casting curses on one producer, director, rival thespian or another.

"Sorry to bother you, Professor-Uncle, but when might we expect admittance?" Sebastian asked, eager to get into the office and search for further clues about Villano's plot.

"Hold your breath and you'll die before this key works." Bill flung the key to the floor before a startled student. "The bloody thing doesn't even fit in the hole."

"Now what?" Sebastian asked.

"I'm going to have a few choice words with Lester," Bill announced and, taking one last, long drag on his cigarette before it flared out and died, stalked off down the hall with murder in his eyes.

Seizing the initiative, Sebastian gently directed Rosa to the side of the doorway. He walked across the hall to the far wall. Lowering his shoulder, he charged across the hall, connected with the door and collapsed in a heap.

"Are you alright?" Rosa asked, kneeling beside Sebastian as he lay crumpled against the door, grasping his shoulder, fearing it might be cracked.

Struggling to his feet again, Sebastian eased Rosa back out of the way. Judging the distance, he gave the door a swift and resounding kick. In movies the door always collapses neatly. In this case, the door remained exactly as it was. Sebastian was the one who collapsed neatly as soon as he put his weight on his kicking foot.

"Sebastian," Rosa gushed, worry in every letter of the word as she leaned down to tend to her Romeo.

Sebastian gasped and, gathering all of his remaining spirit, regained his unsteady feet. "I'm quite alright, Mrs. Turnbell." He peered at the door. "Rather a tough one. They don't make them like that anymore. Fine construction. Very sturdy."

"Not really," Lester said as he appeared in his spotless, pressed white custodial engineer's coveralls. Hands in his pockets, he strolled up to Sebastian and Rosa as if he were taking a Sunday walk in the park on the finest of fine spring days. "You just need the right tools."

"Hello, Lester," Sebastian said, debating whether to mention the incident of the president's chair. Such a discussion might turn ugly, especially since he was armed with a rapier, and there was a lady present. Better, he decided, to let the chair matter simmer for a while on the back burner.

Lester took a ring of keys out of his pocket and, waving Sebastian and Rosa away from the door, fiddled for a moment with the keys.

"There you are," Bill roared as he appeared around the corner down the hall. "I'd like a few words with you, Lester, about the purported usefulness of a certain skeleton key, which you traded me for a peek at my Grand Unifying Horse Racing Theory."

"I assume you tried that key in this lock?" Lester asked, not even bothering to look up as he flipped through his ring of keys.

"You assume correctly, you charlatan," Bill yelled, rearing up to his full, if terribly thin, 6 foot height. "You rogue! You scoundrel, miscreant and, dare I say, rat?"

"If you recall, that key was, as I informed you when we negotiated the transaction, purported to fit all North American locks," Lester said with suave assurance.

"You're bloody well right," Bill said, "and it doesn't even fit in that lock, which, unless I am mistaken, that door, the lock and we are all in North America."

"True."

"Rat."

"Allow me to clarify. The key opens all locks made in North America, not all locks in North America. This particular lock was made in Japan, not that that presents any problem." With a dramatic sweep of his arm, Lester unlocked the door and let it swing slowly open. Smiling, Lester stood back and admitted Sebastian, Rosa and, lastly, a reluctant Bill, who struggled to remember whether Lester had stated at the time of their deal whether the key would open all locks in North America or, as the custodial engineer claimed, all North American locks.

"Thanks, Lester," Sebastian said grudgingly, the stolen presidential chair still on his mind. He flipped through the neat piles of papers and journals on Villano's desk.

Bill spun around, rushed past Lester, flung open the door and to the amazement of several freshmen walking past, skittered around on the floor in the hall. Finding the skeleton key he had so recently discarded, he tucked it carefully back into his sport jacket's pocket. A key for North American locks was better than no key at all. How many locks could Japan supply to North America anyway; they were so busy shipping over millions of cars, televisions, DVD players, cameras, and Playstations?

Reentering the office, Bill found Sebastian sitting, head in hands, in Villano's chair, which was almost as nice as Bill's own chair. Bill glanced suspiciously at Lester. With the skeleton key in mind, Bill feared his relationship with the custodial engineer/fence/all around fixer was more of a common tete-a-tete than the unique, mutually supporting special relationship he had long supposed.

"Nothing incriminating at all," Sebastian reported from behind Villano's desk. "It's as clean as a new car."

Bill took out his tobacco pouch and started constructing yet another creation. Lester leaned against the closed door and Rosa, still in the dark about what was going on but willing to follow Sebastian anywhere, stood mute, waiting as she gazed at the object of her ardent desire.

"Now what?" Bill asked.

"Mind telling me what's going on?" Lester asked, always with both ears open for information that might at some opportune future moment turn a profit.

Bill explained, "Sebastian overheard Villano and a student plotting to plant a bomb at the Grizzlies-Lakers game tonight."

"Not necessarily the Grizzlies game," Sebastian corrected, his uncertainty growing. "Just at a game. That's why we came here; to try to find information about Villano's plans."

"Grizzlies-Lakers is the only game worth mentioning tonight, especially considering this." Lester stepped aside and pointed at a Grizzlies' schedule poster taped to the back of the office door. His finger hovered over something that held the attention of Sebastian and Bill like a pair of cobras focused on a bobbing snake charmer, someone had pencilled a circle around the Grizzlies-Lakers game scheduled for that very night. Although the circle had been erased, the evidence was there for all to see with their own eyes, except Bill, at least until he took out his reading glasses to be able to see the incriminating circle of partially-erased graphite.

"My God," Sebastian blurted out and for the first time truly, completely and unreservedly believed his own story. "It's not a joke."

"There'll be 20,000 people at the game!" Bill dropped his half-finished cigarette on the floor in shock.

"Actually only 19,193," Lester said. The others stared at him. "If it's sold out." Still the focus of questioning stares, he added, "I won a bet once about the number of seat bottoms left in the down position after a Canuck's playoff game at GM Place. It was helpful to find out exactly how many seats there are in the arena."

Sebastian shook his head to refocus and said, "So Villano and that Hogarth character plan to blow up GM Place."

"What?" Rosa exclaimed, learning of the dire situation for the first time. It was as if she had come into a movie in the final three minutes as the villain was revealing his dastardly plot to the hero, who at that very moment was tied to a log headed down a sluice into the path of a six-foot buzz saw spinning at full speed.

Sebastian explained, "Villano and an international terrorist named Hogarth are planning to blow up GM Place tonight when it's filled to capacity for the Grizzlies-Lakers game."

"We can't let that happen," Lester said, his dark eyes wide. "I've got money on that game."

"What happens if the game is called on account of an explosion?" Bill asked. "Maybe I should include that possibility in my Grand Unifying Horse Racing Theory. If a basketball arena can be the target of a terrorist attack, God forbid, why not a racetrack?"

"If that happens," Lester said, "everyone in the arena loses."

"Let's go," Sebastian said as he picked up his rapier from where he had laid it across Villano's desk.

"Just one thing," Bill asked, holding up a tobacco-stained hand. "How are we going to find a bomb in GM Place? It's a tad larger than a bread box."

"The bomb's going to be on the bus," Sebastian said.

"What?"

"The Grizzly team bus."

"How could you possibly know that?" Bill asked, something Lester was also wondering. Rosa, who believed Sebastian capable of anything, thought it was just another example of his brilliant, yet romantic mind at work.

"Wordsworth was right," Sebastian said. "'Wisdom is oft times nearer when we stoop than when we soar!'" He stooped down, picked up a brochure from out of Villano's trashcan and read, "'The Briar Rabbit Coach Company: Official bus line of the Vancouver Grizzlies basketball team.'"

"Never heard of it," Bill said.

"They have offices coast to coast, in Vancouver, Hope, Spuzzum, Medicine Hat, Sioux Lookout, Moosonee, Timmons and Antigonish," Sebastian read.

"Where's Spuzzum?" Rosa asked.

"Beyond Hope," Bill answered, displaying his knowledge of every city, town and village in Canada. He had spent a brief portion of his youth working for the CNR, the Canadian National Railway. At least he had until his boss realized he was spending more time riding the rails on his company pass to get to racetracks from coast to coast than inspecting the state of rail spikes on the line, as he had been hired to do. For Bill, rail spikes could never hold a candle to horse races in terms of fascination.

With Spuzzum's geographic location established, Sebastian, rapier in hand, led the way out the door. He and his posse charged out the college's front doors like bats out of a cave, down the stairs and across the parking lot. Then Sebastian stopped so suddenly that Rosa and Bill bumped into him.

"Why are you stopping?" Bill demanded, panting as if he was a thoroughbred who has just run a 30 furlong stakes race.

"Elizabeth took my car," Sebastian said, his heart breaking at what ill thoughts he feared she was thinking about him at that very moment.

"My car's over there," Bill said, pointing toward his prized, Big Bird-yellow 1959 Cadillac Eldorado convertible with fins that would have done an orca proud. Lester had procured the mammoth vehicle for Bill from an ex-dancer at the Bird Cage Restaurant, Bar and Strip Club. In a complex negotiation that would have boggled the minds of Harvard MBAs, veteran corporate raiders and Wall Street tycoons, Lester had invested a mere $396.43, but emerged from the deal with the Cadillac, 45,321 Coho salmon, 12,453 bottles of McDonald Whiskey and four police dogs, all soon turned over at tidy profits in other, only slightly less complex deals. Sebastian never understood how or why Bill ended up with the Cadillac, 160 Coho salmon and a case of whiskey, although with none of the rather fine canines. Sebastian had too little time in his life to listen to another one of Bill's epic explanations if he could avoid such an experience, so he had never asked.

Bill led the way to his car. They piled into the cavernous automobile, one of the finest Detroit ever made, and Bill brought the huge engine to life, after four or five stuttering, smoke-belching false starts.

"You should really take it to Omar to get it tuned up regularly," Lester advised.

"No time, no time," Bill said.

"Unless Omar has a branch station at the track," Sebastian said.

"We're off!" Bill yelled, ignoring his nephew's comment as he swung out of his reserved double parking space, also procured by Lester, and cruised out of the lot.

"There's Destiny," Rosa said, pointing at her dejected daughter, slouched and forlorn on the bus stop bench near the parking lot entrance. A puddle of tears had formed at her feet on the sidewalk.

"This could be dangerous," Sebastian warned Rosa as Bill slowed to pick up the distressed damsel.

"We'll be safe with you, Sebastian," Rosa stated as she shifted closer to her much sought-after love in the back seat, pressing him against one of the car's padded leather doors.

Bill stopped the Caddy as Sebastian apologized and slipped over Rosa to take advantage of the 12 feet of open back seat on the other side of his enamored neighbor. As he executed his tactical relocation, he said, "I'll make some room for Destiny."

Her eyes red from tears of embarrassment and despair, Destiny moped around the car and climbed into the back seat. Sebastian, however, had committed a grave tactical blunder: he was now between the Turnbells. In a pair of amorous heartbeats, Destiny and Rosa had Sebastian wedged between them, like three peas in a sun-shriveled pod.

"My dear ladies," Sebastian said, "would you mind shifting over a wee bit. I can't get my seat belt on."

"That's alright," Rosa cooed. "I'm sure your uncle is an excellent driver."

As Bill took a corner at 60 miles an hour, Destiny slid against Sebastian, who slid against Rosa, forming an intimate tri-person sandwich. Turning to his backseat passengers, Bill announced proudly, "Only had one reported accident in all my years of driving. My secret, I always carry this."

Bill leaned over, taking his eyes off the road for at least half a block, opened the glove compartment, which was large enough to hold a giant's boxing gloves, and withdrew a roll of currency that would have made an excellent doorstop for the main gate of Edinburgh Castle. Bill displayed the money with a grin.

"What's that for?" Sebastian asked, eager to keep the attention of Destiny and Rosa on anything other than himself.

"Whenever I hit somebody, I offer them a small gift like this and the whole thing's forgotten. I have a spotless driving record."

"And his insurance premiums stay low," Lester added as he lounged in the passenger side of the front seat, his long legs stretched out as if he was on his sofa at home. In fact, he had more room than at home; his sofa at home was a foot shorter than the Cadillac's front seat.

"I still have my safe driver deduction," Bill boasted, his gray hair blowing in the wind from his open window as he ran a red light to a cacophony of horns, curses and squealing brakes.

As the Cadillac left the pavement for a moment at the crest of a hill, Destiny and Rosa squealed and clasped onto Sebastian's arms like two limpets on an especially choice boulder. Ever the gallant, Sebastian could not even attempt to free himself given the ladies' agitated state at Bill's offensive driving, so he smiled bravely at his companions. His gallantry did not prevent him from praying Bill would soon deliver them to GM Place so he could extricate himself from the unsought, unwanted and unrequited lust-filled attentions of the mother and daughter Turnbell.

Bill finally stopped at a light, having missed the yellow by a margin even he considered too great to run. Inspectors Short and Adderly sat in their unmarked sedan across the intersection waiting to turn left on their way to City College for their hoped for chat with Dr. Villano about overheard restroom conversations, games and bombs.

"Isn't that Gianninni over there in the yellow Caddy?" Short asked, squinting across the intersection.

Adderly, who was driving, looked over and nodded, "Yeah, I think that's the Sultan of Romantic Aids. I wonder where he's off to."

Short glanced at his watch. "They're headed downtown," he said, then added, thinking out loud, "toward GM Place."

"The Grizzlies play tonight," Adderly commented.

Short mused, "I doubt Villano's even at the college."

"Gianninni did say the plot was to blow up a game."

"What bigger game is there tonight than the Grizzlies-Lakers?"

"It's been sold out all season," Adderly commented, glancing hopefully at his partner. "It would be by-the-book procedure to follow Gianninni. We have him in sight, not Villano."

"And he's headed for 'a game.'"

Needing no further hints, Adderly turned left, roared up the street half a block and executed a tight U-turn without even slowing down, while Short kept an eye on the yellow Cadillac as it crossed the intersection and roared toward downtown. His task was far from difficult given Bill's driving, which consisted of weaving back and forth within and between lanes and around other cars like a drunken slalom skier on speed.

"We could pull him over for a few dozen traffic violations," Short suggested as they cruised up behind the Caddy.

"And miss the game?"

"If that's even where they're headed," Short said, afraid to get his hopes up.

"They're turning down that alley."

"Where are they going? The arena's straight ahead," Short moaned, seeing his dream of actually seeing a Grizzly game vanishing as the Big Bird yellow Cadillac disappeared down the narrow alley.

Chapter 27

The reason Sebastian and his entourage had found Dr. Villano's office empty was because, although he was at the college that afternoon, the villainous Villano had not even visited his office. If he had known about the events that had transpired within the confines of his academic lair he would have boxed Hogarth's ears, for the young New Luddite had been the one who, in a fit of bravado, had taped the Grizzly's schedule on the back of Villano's office door. To make matters worse, he had then circled the date of their secret operation. Upon seeing the circle on the schedule, Villano had lost his temper with his accomplice and, after a few words that would have reddened the face of a waterfront barroom bouncer, had done his best to erase the incriminating circle. Even erased, the line left by the penciled circle on the glossy poster was still clear to see to all save a shortsighted mole. Furious, Villano's hand had been on the incriminating poster poised to tear it down, when he noticed the image of a snarling grizzly bear and the artist's name in the bottom corner: I.M. Good, a distant relation of the famous, Louvre architect, I.M. Pei. I.M. Good's works graced the walls of the homes of only the most snobbish Canadians. The poster must stay. Besides, Villano thought, who would even notice the faint circle, let alone discern its import? Furthermore, it would help keep his imbecilic accomplice focused on the task at hand and remind him of the correct date for their operation.

That incident had been weeks ago and now, on the day of their planned bombing, Villano found himself in an empty chemistry lab at the college with Hogarth and his suitcase. The door was locked with a chair wedged against the handle for good measure.

"How long?" Villano asked. The game was only a little more than three hours away.

Hogarth lifted the suitcase and laid it on one of the high, black lab tables. "About 20 minutes. I already have the detonator wired to the receiver. I just need to wire the explosives to the detonator and check that the transmitter is operating at peak efficiency."

"Hopefully you'll check the transmitter before you wire the detonator to the explosives," Villano advised from his perch on a lab stool near the door.

The professor took out a Cuban cigarette, the importation of which from their Caribbean home via Canada and hence, into the United States, had been one of his early attempts to make a fortune, and lit it. Unfortunately, he had failed to realize that while Cuban cigars were of an uncommon and much sought-after quality, Cuban cigarettes were used as kindling in the homes of destitute Cubans. His venture was a financial bust, although it left him with 499,997 Cuban cigarettes. He had managed to sell three. There had been no repeat customers. Not even a trader of Lester's skills could unload such merchandise without paying a sizable hazardous waste disposal fee.

"You aren't allowed to smoke in here," Hogarth said, gesturing at a No Smoking sign near the door.

"We're about to blow up an entire basketball team. If we're caught, I doubt smoking will add even an hour to my sentence."

"Smoking is frowned upon pretty seriously nowadays," Hogarth commented as he pressed the latches on the suitcase. "Besides, you're harming the environment and everything that lives in it." He frowned and, checking the four numbered dials on the top of the case, pressed the latches again: nothing happened. He stepped back and stared at the case, his chin on his hand in unintended imitation of *The Thinker*.

"What are you doing?" Villano asked through a cloud of Cuban hazardous smoke.

"Thinking, but nothing's happening."

Unbidden, lines from Shelley leapt into Villano's mind; 'It is better to keep your mouth shut and appear stupid than to open it and remove all doubt.' He didn't mention this snippet of wisdom to Hogarth, in part because he needed the young revolutionary, but also because Villano loathed the Romantics in general and Sebastian's beloved Shelley in particular. Villano shook his head to banish the hated poet's words. Then he closed his eyes, wishing with every neuron in his brain that he was having a nightmare and would awaken to find himself sitting on a sandy beach in the Seychelles, sipping an iced drink beside an exotic island beauty with a wonderland of a body. He opened his eyes: the nightmare continued.

Villano asked, "What's wrong?"

"I forgot the combination to the suitcase," Hogarth admitted, still staring at the lock, as if by force of wishful thinking he could unlock it.

"Break it open."

"Normally that would be a good idea."

"Normally?" Villano asked, fearing nothing involving Hogarth ever could be deemed normal.

"I wired the lock to the explosives inside, so if someone tries to open the suitcase without the correct combination…."

"They'd be standing in a rather deep crater?"

"I don't think they'd actually be *standing* in the crater. They'd be in little pieces," Hogarth said, his attempt at thinking finally paying dividends, if not in any thoughts related to solving the problem at hand.

"What's the bloody combination?" Villano demanded as he stalked over to the suitcase.

"I can't remember," Hogarth said sheepishly, as if he had forgotten something of little import, such as how to spell fiasco.

"Remember, for God's sake," Villano ordered, turning on his erstwhile accomplice.

"It had something to do with our plot. Something to do with the number of….of…."

"The game's at 7 tonight. Try 7-0-0."

"It's four digits."

"Today's date?"

"That would be eight digits, with the year."

"Try the date and the month."

"Oh, that's clever." Hogarth tried it. "Nope."

Villano stalked around the room. "Four digits? The number of seats on the bus, 48: no. Number of seats in GM Place, 20,000: no. Number of wins the Grizzlies have. No, that's only two digits. Four digits? I can't think of a blasted thing that has four digits related to tonight."

Needless to say the gifted Dr. Villano was not at his creative best stalking around a lab puffing a Cuban cigarette while, every few seconds, glaring at a suitcase filled with explosives and then at an international terrorist who would have been a much more effective bombee than bomber.

"I've got it," Hogarth said as he leapt toward the suitcase. "Five!"

Villano stopped, jaw slack, as he attempted to process what he had just heard and make some semblance of sense out of it. "Five?"

"Yes, five," Hogarth repeated as he spun the tumblers and flung the suitcase open with a dramatic flare worthy of the Vaudevillian stage.

Villano controlled his rising temper and, even though he felt he was suffering through a spring nightmare and not a midsummer night's dream, in slow, measured tones he mumbled, "'Lord, what fools these mortals be.'" Forcing a calmness he did not feel into his voice, he said, "Five is one digit, Hogarth."

"I know that."

"Then how can five be the combination to a four-digit lock?"

"Simple: five, five, five, five," Hogarth explained as he lifted the miniature transmitter and receiver out of the suitcase.

Villano sat back on the stool near the door and, wondering whether a premature detonation of the bomb right now would not be the kindest thing for all concerned, asked, "What does five have to do with the game tonight?"

"The number of players on the Grizzlies."

"There are 12 men on a basketball team."

"No, there aren't. There are five."

"There are five men on the court, but they aren't the entire team," Villano said, as if explaining calculus to a kindergartner who has been twice held back. "Twelve men compose a basketball team."

Hogarth froze and looked over at the cloud of Cuban smog from which the professor's voice emanated. "We're going to kill 12 men on the bus tonight, not five?"

"More than that. There'll be trainers, coaches, sports psychologists, physiotherapists, a doctor, ball boys, girlfriends, possibly boyfriends, reporters, and various hangers on aboard, too."

Hogarth frowned and, hesitating, went back to his explosive work.

"What's wrong?" came a voice from the Cuban fog.

"I thought we'd just be killing five basketball players."

"Five, 50, 150, what difference does it make in the great struggle between technology and mother earth? We're striking a blow for the New Luddite Revolution."

"Could you explain to me again how all of it is going to work?"

"Only if you keep working on the bomb." Hogarth nodded and Villano continued. "The Vancouver Grizzlies are the finest team in basketball history. They are undefeated at home in GM Place. The building is a marvel of modern engineering and represents the epitome of modern mass entertainment beamed via high-tech satellites into homes around the world. Just like the gladiatorial games of Rome in the Coliseum and bear bating in England in the 1800s, basketball, like all sporting events, is the opiate of the masses in our technology mad society."

Villano took a long drag on his Cuban cigarette as he twisted his mind around the next steps in his fantastic—fantasy being the root word—story. He appeared to be making an argument to blow up GM Place, not the team and their bus, but Hogarth would never notice the distinction. "An explosion engulfing the Grizzlies will be heard around the world and especially in the technological West. The Grizzlies, as representatives of the mass marketing of everything from sports to soap, fast food to motion pictures, and plastic containers to plastic surgery, must be destroyed. The death of the team will make people understand that the sports gods they watch on television are only men made of flesh, blood and bone. The fans will learn athletes don't deserve their loyalty, identification, time or money."

"I especially don't like 'Dead-eye' Polotnik's advertisements for Dead-eye Rifles," Hogarth said.

"I haven't seen them."

"I think they're only shown in the States."

"Oh," Villano said, hoping Hogarth would finish the bomb soon so he could cease spinning his tall tale, since even his train of thought had long since not only jumped the rails but lost sight of them. "As soon as the bus is blown up and the team killed, we will send our demands to the media."

"Which are?" Hogarth asked as he put the finishing touches on the bomb.

Villano drew on his cigarette as he thought back to the last time he had spun an epic yarn for Hogarth. Finally he remembered the finer points of his oft-told story. "We will call on our friends, Luddites and countrymen to demand the turning off and destruction of all computers in the world, the opening of the sluice gates of all hydro-electric dams, the grounding of all airplanes, and the conversion of all vehicles to electricity, propane, methane, solar or wind power. The revolution will be complete. People will have to get off their sofas and quit watching television, staring at computer screens or listening to loud, unnatural music. They will actually have to get out into nature and experience the world in real life, not via a plasma screen or monitor. And, of course, our revolution will end all televised sports."

"I like that," Hogarth said with a hopeful, childlike grin. "I used to love going to baseball games with my dad back in Atlanta. Now if you go to a game, there are so many breaks for television ads with the players standing around spitting tobacco juice or blowing bubbles while the fans check their text messages or snooze, that you forget why you're even at the stadium."

"I thought you were born in Dublin."

"I was, but I don't remember it much. We only spent a few months in Atlanta, but I remember it particularly fondly of all the places we lived."

"How many places did you live growing up?"

"Dozens. Dad never liked to stay in one country, let alone one city too long. We always had to leave on short notice, but we always got to play act when we left."

"Play act?"

"We got to play at being someone else. We used someone else's passport when we left each country."

"Oh," Villano said, debating whether to ask anything further, although this line of discussion had saved him from wading farther into the murky quagmire of his description of the fast approaching New Luddite Revolution.

"That's where I learned all about travelling as someone else. It really helps if you're a New Luddite revolutionary on the run from the authorities. Dad taught me everything he knew. Of course, I never travel with the blonde."

"The blonde?"

"Dad always called the young lady he brought along, 'the Blonde,' whatever the color of her hair."

"Why did you have to travel so much, and why so suddenly?" Villano asked, forgetting his cardinal rule never to encourage Hogarth to talk. Doing so was always a grave error.

"I don't know why, but Dad always liked travel and everything foreign. In fact, he liked to supplement his income by dating secretaries from foreign embassies or consulates."

"He made money dating embassy secretaries?" Villano asked, struggling to figure out the riddle of Hogarth's early life.

"Dad always said it was very profitable, although I tried it once with an under assistant undersecretary with the Latvian delegation in Budapest. All it did was cost me a bouquet of flowers, dinner and a movie. I didn't make a forint."

Villano said, "I have it. Your father obtained classified information from the secretaries at foreign embassies, which he then sold to other nations. When he was found out, he would quickly leave the country with the young lady who had supplied him the secret information. Then he would dump her to find a new embassy secretary in a new country from whom to gather secret information to sell to yet another foreign power."

There was a crash and Villano rushed out of his Cuban cloud to find Hogarth, ashen-faced, staring down at the transmitter, smashed, on the floor.

"What happened?!" Villano demanded.

"My father did that?"

Seeing the horror on Hogarth's face, Villano quickly changed course and said, "It's merely a bored English professor's creative take on some bare-bones facts. Obviously, there are any number of other, far more plausible explanations that fit the facts. For example, as you said, your father was a romantic man who loved travel, so he loved to date women from foreign lands, who would naturally work at foreign embassies. The profit he was speaking of was of a spiritual and cultural kind, the kind one gets from interacting with other cultures. Being a romantic, I am sure he loved to take his girlfriends on foreign trips and what better way to give a gift, then as a surprise. There would be no time to make sure the lady in question had a passport, so it would be easiest to borrow someone else's passport and then—surprise—you could all go jetting off to some new, exotic foreign land."

"Like Atlanta?"

"Like Atlanta."

Hogarth's face, blood flowing back into it, gradually returned to a more healthy color as this shaky theory sank into his solid brain. "Of course, of course. I sometimes wondered about Dad's activities, but I never came up with anything as wild and outlandish as your first explanation, Professor. I wish I had your creative mind."

"Merely the musings of a bored, lonely college professor," Villano said, relieved he had calmed his high spirited bomb-maker. "Who doesn't dream their father is an international spy."

"What did your father do?"

"He was the first male stewardess on Air America. What about the transmitter?"

Hogarth bent down and picked up the palm-sized device from where he had dropped it, setting it gingerly on the lab table. He used a small Phillip's screwdriver to remove the back of the black case and started checking connections, tapping silicon chips and generally fiddling around as far as Villano could tell. Villano puffed nervously on another Cuban cigarette as if he was a small train with a load of lead ascending the Andes. Finally, after what seemed to Villano an eternity encompassing his consumption of three more of his seemingly endless supply of Cuban cigarettes, Hogarth straightened up from the lab table and announced, "Finished."

"Fixed?" Villano asked expectantly.

"No, completely ruined."

Villano took a few deep breaths as an alternative to Hogarthicide and asked, "What do we do now?"

"We'll have to use the timer I bought as a backup. I thought something might go wrong. Something usually does."

"Undoubtedly."

"We can set the timer for when we're sure the team will be on the bus."

"Good," Villano said with a confidence that had left him long ago; about a minute after first meeting his young accomplice.

Hogarth fiddled with the explosives for a few minutes and then started to close the suitcase again. Villano's hand intercepted the lid just before it closed.

Villano asked, "Is the bomb linked to the lock this time?" He had no faith Hogarth could ever open the suitcase again. Hogarth had in all likelihood changed the combination.

"No. The timer is though. We set the time when we want the bomb to explode by setting the combination lock on the suitcase. Neat, huh?"

"Neat." Villano let Hogarth close and lock the suitcase. "You're sure it'll work?"

"Trust me. I learned everything I know from my brother. He was the finest bomb maker the IRA ever had."

"*Was?*"

Hogarth picked up the suitcase and walked toward the door. Villano stamped out his cigarette on the floor with his heel, making an environmentally and, probably, janitorially unfriendly mess, and yelled, "Was?! How did he die?"

Hogarth stopped and, without turning, said, "He blew himself up, but I learned a lot from his mistakes."

"'Mistakes'? Plural? He blew himself up more than once?!"

"It's the best way to learn, really."

Resigned to his fate and the pact he had made with the stupidest devil on the planet, Villano mumbled, "'Oh, I am fortune's fool,'" hung his head and followed Hogarth out the door.

Chapter 28

After Lester and Bill insisted on stopping to place some well-planned wagers at a betting parlor down an alley near the arena, Sebastian and his crew were late for the tip-off and had to park six blocks away from GM Place. As they approached the arena, the sell-out crowd roared every few seconds; probably every time a Grizzly touched the ball. The Grizzlies had enjoyed sell outs all season, ever since they made five key acquisitions; the sharp-shooting guards, Phil "Dead-eye" Polotnik and Eddie "3-Point" Anderson; the dominating, Towering Twin forwards, Jack and Gill Hill, who came to Vancouver from Indiana because they liked the colorful Canadian money over the drab U.S. currency; and the English-born, seven-foot, two-inch center, Bertram Reginald "Roddy" Windsor, who first saw a basketball at the age of 21 when he immigrated to Osoyoos, British Columbia, to pick apples, saving the orchard owner a fortune in ladders. Despite their disparate backgrounds, in a single season the five newcomers had melded into an unstoppable basket-scoring powerhouse with a defense the Roman army could well have used against the Visigoths. Last season's 10-72 record had been turned on its head. This year they were besting a 90 percent winning percentage and at home in the now incredibly friendly—at least for the Grizzlies—confines of their Vancouver den, they were undefeated.

Waves of sound rippled out of the arena as Sebastian, rapier in hand, led the way toward the car-filled parking lot that surrounded GM Place like a gigantic, multi-colored apron. At an entrance to the lot, Sebastian stopped at a booth. Huddled inside was a bored young man in a bright yellow traffic-safety vest reading *Hamlet.*

"Game's sold out," the youth said and returned to his play.

"I know," Sebastian said. "I need to know where the Grizzlies' team bus is parked."

The youth finished reading his scene even as his unwilling spectators grew increasingly annoyed. Reading is far from a spectator sport. Finally, he looked up.

"I can't tell you that," he said, smiling at Destiny, resplendent in a tight, V-necked black sweater, which she had specially selected for her planned, yet ill-fated rendezvous with Sebastian.

"You have to tell us," Sebastian urged, "this is important."

The youth shook his head.

Sebastian was at a loss as to what to do next, save searching the acres of parking lot around the arena for the bus. Lester, however, elbowed his way past his colleagues to stand before the youth.

"Is Johnny on tonight?" he inquired, still in his spotless custodial engineer's coveralls.

"Johnny who?" the youth asked with more than a trace of lip.

"Johnny Ching."

"Yeah. You know him?"

"We go way back. Get him on that thing, will ya?" Lester gestured at a walkie-talkie perched on a plywood shelf in the booth.

The youth hesitated.

"Hamlet didn't debate this long," Sebastian whispered to Bill.

"Get Johnny on that thing or he'll have you sweeping out every level of the grandstands til noon tomorrow," Lester warned.

The youth decided prudence was the wisest course and, picking up the walkie- talkie, called Johnny.

"Far more decisive than Hamlet," Bill whispered to Sebastian.

As Sebastian and his fellow plot foilers waited for Johnny Ching to appear, Short watched them from behind a minivan across the street.

"What are they doing?" Adderly asked as he leaned against the minivan.

As Adderley's hand touched the van, its alarm sounded, shattering the night's calm. Adderly leapt away from the van, only to be dragged back by Short, who wanted to make certain no one in Sebastian's crew, all of whom were now staring over at the van, spotted his partner. The officers froze in a tight embrace until the alarm stopped. They manfully disengaged themselves and then, while Adderly carefully stood three feet from the minivan, Short peered around the vehicle, careful not to touch it.

"They're talking to a parking attendant," Short reported. "Maybe they're looking for a particular car with a bomb in it."

"There must be 10,000 cars here tonight. No way are they gonna find one specific car, even if the attendant helps them. And if Gianninni knew which car had a bomb in it, why didn't he just tell us this afternoon?" Adderly was about to rest his hand against the van, but hastily withdrew it as if the vehicle was an angry porcupine.

Another roar rumbled out of the arena like a dragon rousing itself after a long winter's nap that has been interrupted by a knight requesting battle at the point of a rather irritatingly pointy lance. Short glanced at his watch. "Must be midway through the first quarter by now."

"Yeah," Adderly said, his shoulder's drooping. So close to five basketball gods and yet so far. "I wonder how they're doing."

"Winning, of course."

They stared at each other, both desperate to be inside but knowing they had a job to do: to protect and serve, even during the final weeks of a basketball season that would go down in history and be remembered forever, especially by those who had actually witnessed a game.

"Somebody's coming," Short reported, watching the gathering at the parking booth.

Without thinking Adderly leaned against the minivan, triggering the alarm again. Short yanked his partner back from the vehicle and they waited for the alarm once again to stop its bleating.

Johnny Ching sauntered up to the parking booth in a foul mood at having been yanked out of the epicenter of the sporting universe to a cold parking booth. His mood was not improved by the irritating car alarm across the street. Prepared to smash the walkie-talkie of the offending parking attendant and demote him to the man in charge of scrubbing out all the deep fryers in the arena's 36 concession stands, Johnny stopped in his tracks as he came around an SUV.

"Lester!" he yelled, rushing forward to embrace the custodial engineer like a long-lost brother just returned from a 30-year sojourn in Nepal.

"Johnny," Lester cried warmly, patting the supervisor's broad back.

"Been too long, Lester. I still owe you for the hot tip on that Lions-Stampeders game. Don't you ever think for a second I've forgotten. I still have the Mercedes I bought with that little pay out. It runs like a gazelle."

Lester threw a grin at Sebastian like a cat about to eat a canary with sweet sauce. Turning back to Johnny, Lester said, "Consider us even. I just have one minor favor to ask."

"The Grizzlies' bus is all the way around on the other side," Johnny Ching told Lester, as another roar erupted from the arena. Johnny looked longingly over at the arena. "I should really be getting back inside, if that's okay."

"Yeah, fine," Lester said. "Thanks for the skinny."

"We're even, right?"

"Flat," Lester agreed, and Johnny was off at a fast trot across the lot and up the stairs to a door leading back into the hottest ticket in town, a ticket he was paid to attend. How sweet life could be.

"Which way?" Bill asked, grimly contemplating the long trek around the arena and the possible date with deadly terrorists on the other side.

"I doubt it matters," Sebastian said. "About the same distance either way."

"Maybe we should split up," Lester suggested, glancing up at the arena as it rumbled with excitement, like an enormous living thing.

"Good idea. We'll attack from both sides," Sebastian said, swishing the rapier with a heroic swoosh. "I'll go this way," he said, indicating the south side of the arena, which bordered Pacific Boulevard and, just beyond, the calm waters of False Creek.

"So will I," Rosa said, as she stepped closer to Sebastian than anyone except his wife should ever be.

"Me, too," Destiny chimed in, eager not to be left out of any excursion involving Sebastian.

"I think I'll go this way," Bill said, gesturing around the north side, which was better lit, more open and seemed, at least to Bill, safer.

"Me, too," Lester said.

Destiny and Rosa, staying as close to Sebastian as smoke to flame, followed him a few steps before he halted. The thought of heading off into the moonlight with two women, neither his wife, terrified him, especially with Elizabeth already close to tallying up all their worldly possessions for a permanent division. "Maybe, given that I have a weapon, you lovely ladies should go with Bill and Lester."

"Quantity has a quality all its own," Bill agreed. He smiled at his nephew's predicament of fending off the amorous females, but was happy to throw him a life preserver. After all, Sebastian was his favorite nephew, even if it was a weak field.

"Good point." Tucking his rapier under his belt, Sebastian took Destiny and Rosa by their arms and, as graciously as the finest of southern gentlemen, escorted them over to Bill and Lester.

As Lester, with Destiny in tow, and Bill, with Rosa on his arm, set off around the arena's north side, Sebastian, relieved of his entourage and feeling rather courageous and daring with his rapier, trotted off alone around the arena's south side.

Fifty yards away, Adderly and Short stood beside a pickup, watching the group divide and go their separate ways.

"Now what do we do?" Adderly asked, wishing their shift was over so they could call for backup and let someone else handle what was in all probability a futile surveillance exercise. Worst of all, it was a surveillance exercise only 100 yards from the sold-out Grizzlies-Lakers game.

"Did you see which way Gianninni went?" Short asked, yet added before his partner could answer, "Because if you didn't, then we could always assume, as any reasonable, well-trained RCMP inspector would, that he entered the arena."

"As any responsable, well-trained RCMP inspector would," Adderly repeated, grinning with mischief dancing in his eyes. "Then, as any responsible, well-trained inspector would, we could flash our badges and, hopefully, get into the arena to conduct a thorough by-the-book search for the suspect."

After a brief pause, Short, attempting to send a negative answer to Adderly telepathically, asked, "Did you see which way he went?"

Telepathy worked. Adderly shook his head emphatically no.

"Then into GM Place we must go."

"We must."

The inspectors took the stairs three at a time up to the arena. A sour-faced usher appeared after they had rattled a door for three and a half minutes.

"Tickets?" the usher asked, eager to return to his clandestine observation of the game on the sliver of court he could see from the concourse down an entryway opposite his assigned post.

Adderly and Short flipped open their wallets to display their badges.

"RCMP," Short said. "We're pursuing a suspect and we have reason to believe he entered this building."

"We need to search for him," Adderly added as he peered over the usher's shoulder and caught a glimpse down an entryway of a Bertram Windsor slam dunk.

"Just the two of you are going to search for one guy in a sold-out arena?"

"That's our job," Short said, assuming a confident, yet put upon air, as if entering GM Place was the last thing he wanted to do.

"I can't let you in," the usher declared, glancing around for a supervisor to assume the responsibility of dealing with the Mounties.

"You have to or we'll be back with a search warrant," Short bluffed. "How would you like to explain to 20,000 screaming fans, and the Grizzly and Lakers players that we had to stop the game so we could check the identity of every single person in the arena and it was all your fault?"

"You can't stop the game. There'd be a riot."

"All your fault."

The usher thought for a second. He glanced up and down the concourse, which was devoid of life since no one wanted to miss a second of the Grizzlies incredible season for any reason, let alone to buy a beer and hot dog that cost roughly the price of a third-round draft pick. What no one saw, no one could fire him for, so the usher waved the inspectors inside. What were two more fans among 20,000 anyway?

Their bluff successful, Adderly and Short rushed into GM Place and across the concourse. As they hurried down the entryway and the noise volume increased, Adderly asked, "What if there really is a bomb in this place?"

"Then we'll die happy," Short replied with a broad grin as they reached the end of the entryway and flashed their badges to another usher, who, not having been told not to let police officers in, let them pass and returned to watching the game.

The arena rose around them on all sides, every seat filled, every eye ball on the 10 men playing a game with an orange-and-black ball below. The noise washed over the inspectors in waves. Their spines vibrated. Their souls soared.

"Besides," Short leaned over to yell in Adderly's ear, "maybe we'll find Gianninni and a bomb in here in time to defuse it."

"Then maybe they'd give us playoff tickets," Adderly said with a smile he had not displayed since his sixth birthday, when he discovered a child-sized Mounties hat among his presents.

"Let's keep moving," Short said, "never know when someone will start asking us too many questions." Short suddenly felt like one of the criminals they regularly sought. He led the way along a walkway around the arena, his eyes locked on the game as one of the Grizzly's guards, Eddie "3-Point" Anderson, lived up to his name and sank a long, arcing 3 pointer from out in the flats.

Outside, an entirely different kind of guard could have used the inspectors' assistance. The young man in question, Homer, was only working nights as a guard to pay for laser corrective eye surgery. He hoped the surgery would allow him to discard his glasses and emerge from behind his introverted, shy personality to become an extroverted Casanova. Waiting for that happy day of transformation, he sat on his gray metal chair at the gate through the chain link fence that enclosed the team buses and the doors to the dressing rooms on the south side of GM Place.

At 5' 7", Homer was not exactly the Arnold Schwarzenegger of security guards, but he was far from the 95-pound weakling of the oft-told story; He was 120 pounds. Worse in terms of security, however, was his lack of a gun; after all, it was peaceful, sedate Canada, a nation in which even the border guards did not carry firearms. Homer relied for authority on his dark-blue uniform, which was rather sharp, his riot baton, which was rather heavy, and the walkie-talkie, which was rather prone to picking up earfuls of static. If the other guards who had pulled seniority to take the coveted assignments within the arena and, hence, within sight of the game were able to hear him over the din inside and the static, he could use the walkie-talkie to summon backup.

There was no one in sight, since all the fans had either filtered inside or given up trying to make deals with the few scalpers who had tickets and rushed off to watch the game at nearby pubs. Daydreaming about his future without glasses, Homer looked up at the sound of footsteps to behold an odd sight. A middle-aged man in a dark suit was striding toward him. It was not every day Homer saw a fan in a suit at a basketball game, but that was not the odd part.

Following behind the suited gentleman was a young man about Homer's age, trotting to keep pace with the taller gentleman. The young man was carrying a black, metal suitcase. It was only the second time Homer had seen someone bring a suitcase to a basketball game. The first had been Susan "Sugar-pants" McCall, an exotic entertainer whom one of the basketball players had hired for another player's birthday. The player involved had offered Homer an envelope full of money not to mention her visit to the press, which he had had no intention of doing, money or no money. The player, however, had thrust the money into Homer's hand and vanished before the guard could explain his views on the personal privacy of athletes. The money would cover the cost of laser surgery for one eye. Deciding his decision to do the right thing had been promptly and generously rewarded, Homer had put the money in his pocket and, sitting back on his gray, metal chair, considered how he would look in a monocle.

The odd thing about the approaching duo, however, was neither the suit nor the suitcase, but the incongruity between the man in the prim and proper suit, and the way he carried a hot dog and soda in a cardboard tray before him, as if he was an English butler about to serve tea and scones on the House of Windsor's finest China to the Queen on a terrace at Sandringham.

"Excuse me, young man," Villano—the suited man with the butler persona—said, assuming his most friendly manner, but only succeeding in striking Homer as pompous. "The management requested I bring this down to you to serve as your evening meal."

Homer frowned and stared at the tray. "The management?"

Villano glanced at the patch on Homer's uniform and said, "Yes, the President and CEO of Terrier Security."

"Who?" Homer asked as he stood, trying to figure out who would send him such a thing, especially conveyed by such an unlikely waiter.

"Your boss…," Villano said, snapping his fingers as if he were trying to recall a name that was, at that very moment, forming on the tip of his tongue. In reality, he had not the slightest idea who headed Terrier Security.

"Fat Tony?"

"Yes, yes, Fat Tony," Villano said, with a chuckle. "He wanted me to let you know that he was reassured to have such a fine young man guarding this crucial, even vital spot and that he was sorry you were stuck out here when the game was, well, in there." Villano nodded toward the arena as a rumble shook the building's walls.

"Fat Tony sent me food?"

"Indeed," Villano said, offering the tray and wishing the youth would just take the blasted eats.

"Fat Tony sent me a hot dog?"

"Yes."

"Fat Tony, who's 300 pounds and never let a pea roll off his plate without recovering it to eat no matter how far it rolled, let alone what it had rolled through?"

"Yes, one and the same."

Frowning, Homer glanced back at Hogarth, who stood, suitcase in hand, just behind Villano.

"Please, take it," Villano urged, thrusting the hot dog and soda toward Homer.

"I can't," Homer said, crushing the nefarious hopes of Villano and Hogarth in two brief words, albeit one a contraction.

"Why in heaven's name not?" Villano asked, seeing his foolproof plan floundering on the rocks of the only male anorexic guard on earth.

"I'm diabetic," Homer confided. "I can't drink the soda."

Relief appearing on the horizon like a golden ray of sunshine on a stormy day, Villano smiled a grin befitting Saint Nicholas. "That's no problem at all. Take the hot dog and we shall return with some water for you. Bottled or sparkling?"

"Bottled, please," Homer said, finally accepting the proffered, by now, warm dog.

As Villano and Hogarth trundled back the way they had come, Homer sat down on his metal chair and started in on his free warm dog.

"Thank God the Grizzlies were so pathetic last year," Villano seethed as he and Hogarth made their way around the arena to the one outdoor concession stand they had found still open, left over from a radio station's pre-game tailgate party.

"What do you mean?" Hogarth asked, transferring the suitcase from his right hand to his left. The bomb was beginning to feel like it was made out of lead, not plastic, explosives.

"Last year the Grizzlies couldn't get enough people to their games to form a decent conga line, so their security guards were minimum-wage, elementary school dropouts who couldn't be trusted to guard a sewage treatment plant. They probably had orders to let anyone break in to the arena who wanted to so at least the team would double their attendance."

"I still don't understand."

Villano was far from surprised to hear Hogarth say that. In fact, Villano was surprised Hogarth did not continually make such an admission. "They obviously haven't replaced that stellar force with new guards this year, even as the Grizzlies' fortunes have ascended and they can afford to hire competent guards."

"Ascended?"

"Risen, improved, gone into the bloody stratosphere."

"Stratosphere?"

Villano stopped abruptly and, controlling his temper, said evenly through clenched teeth, "Forget it."

After a lengthy pause for his mind to change subjects, Hogarth asked, "Now what are we gonna do?"

"Stop talking would be a promising start."

"No, I mean," Hogarth began, gesturing at the concession stand, "it's closed."

"So?" Villano asked, regretting ever choosing a life of international terrorism.

"How will we get the guard the bottled water you promised him?"

"We could just steal it from inside the tent. It's not exactly the Canadian mint."

"Steal it? How would stealing some small businessman's bottled water strike a blow for the New Luddite Revolution against the technological, mass-market, media-saturated West?"

"It *is* bottled in a factory somewhere."

"No, I think the brand they had comes from a spring in the Rockies."

"The picture on the bottles is of a spring in the Rockies," Villano said, "but I read in *Consumer Reports* that the water comes straight out of a city tap in Calgary."

"Why were you reading *Consumer Reports*? It just promotes the decadent consumerist society."

"They do criticize their fair share of products," Villano said. Hogarth was still clearly concerned about his choice of reading material, so Villano added, "In truth, it was research to know the enemy. You have to learn about the consumer society in order to destroy it."

"I still don't think we should steal the water."

"Don't worry, we don't have to." Villano checked his watch and, turning on his heel, led the way back the way they had come.

Hogarth hurried under his bomb burden to keep up. As they approached the fenced area again, Hogarth whispered, "What are you going to tell the guard when he asks for his water?"

Villano did not answer until he stopped at Homer, who was slumped in his chair. A snore rumbled up from his inert head, which lolled forward on his chest.

"I don't think he'll ask."

"You drugged the hot dog?" Hogarth asked in amazement.

"Of course."

"The plan was to drug just the soda."

"The plan was not to leave the bomb in the back of Gianninni's car as his wife took it on a joy ride back across the border," Villano raged, losing his temper. "The plan was not to forget the suitcase's combination. The plan was not to drop the transmitter. The plan was not to ally myself with a complete ignoramus."

Villano pushed open the metal gate and led the way into the fenced area where the Grizzly's Briar Rabbit Coach Line bus was parked. Seeing his plan nearing fruition and pushing thoughts of Hogarth from his mind, Villano sang happily to himself *sotto voce*, "'By the pricking of my thumbs, Something wicked this way comes,'" as he approached the bus. "Macbeth had nothing on me," he said with gloating satisfaction as a malevolent grin spread across his face.

Then, realizing he was leading a party of one, sans bomb, he turned and stalked back to the entrance where Hogarth stood, immobile and head hung low in a state of darkest dejection.

"There's no need to call people names," Hogarth whimpered, his eyes puffy as tears began to form. "Let alone calling me a dinosaur."

"A dinosaur?"

"An ignoramus."

Villano once again shut his eyes and fervently wished he would awaken from his nightmare and find himself on the sandy beach he had often imagined in the Seychelles, sipping an iced drink beside a tanned blonde, brunette or even a redhead. What did it matter, given the alternative? Once again, it was not to be. All he saw when he opened his eyes was a pouting Irish-Moroccan-Japanese-French New-Luddite revolutionary terrorist on the verge of tears, holding a suitcase packed with enough explosives to transform a bus into a giant cheese grater.

"I'm sorry, Hogarth," Villano said, putting his hand on his accomplice's shoulder. "I'm under a great deal of pressure, what with executing the plan, composing the message to the media, making sure the police don't catch us, and…."

"Midterms," Hogarth said as he snuffled back a sob.

Hogarth bit back a sarcastic comment and said, "Yes, and midterms. Shall we do our job and then we can get on with our lives and the revolution?"

"Of course. I'm sorry for my unprofessional behavior."

"As am I." Villano glanced at the guard as Homer chuffled and shifted in his chair. "He'll be awake soon. Shall we be off?"

The two villains rushed toward their target, bomb in hand or at least in one of their hands.

Chapter 29

Like the villains, Sebastian was also on the move, trotting around the rumbling arena. As he puffed along, Sebastian regretted not having synchronized watches so he and his posse would all arrive at the Grizzly's team bus at the same time. Unbeknownst to him, he should have been worried, for his accomplices were falling by the wayside and their numerical superiority over Villano and Hogarth was rapidly diminishing.

Lester was the first to veer from their agreed-upon course. As soon as Lester arrived at the arena he had decided the threat of a bomb in a bus held scant interest compared to a game between the Grizzlies, undefeated at home, and the Lakers who, although boasting a respectable 56-10 record, were in a very distant second place behind the dominating Grizzlies. The Lakers, however, were the best the league could offer the stupendous ursines. Lester had almost asked Johnny Ching to get him inside, but had felt it would have been unseemly to bail out on Dr. Gianninni's escapade at the first opportunity, even if he had never formally been invited along. It did not mean Lester did not keep both eyes wide open for a second opportunity.

Lester carefully eyed each usher as he and his three companions trekked around GM Place. It did not take long before he spotted what he was looking for: an usher who was an old friend. He had been confident it would only be a matter of a brief span of time before he spotted someone he knew. Born and raised in Vancouver, Lester had started working at the age of seven. Since he was often fired for his propensity for making a personal profit above and beyond his wage during working hours by means the law frowned upon, if not entirely forbade, he had worked in his capacity as custodial engineer in more buildings, schools, theaters, warehouses, factories, hospitals, ships, yachts, planes, trains, stadiums, arenas, and racetracks than anyone, except he, could remember. Besides remembering all the many and sundry locations where he had labored, his memory for the names, faces, personalities, likes and dislikes of everyone he had ever met was phenomenal. He could run into someone he had met only once 25 years before and flatter them beyond reason by remembering their name, as well as the name of everyone in their family, including their pets, their hobbies, likes and dislikes, and all of their dreams in ranked order.

"I'm sorry, but I should go," Lester announced as he stopped opposite the usher whom he had recognized from 75 paces even in the dim light of the promenade.

Bill would have none of it. "You're going into the game," he told his old friend, sounding as if the custodial engineer was guilty of conning senior citizens out of money with which they had planned to purchase Christmas presents for crippled orphans.

"It's not like that, Bill. I know the guy who manages the Grizzlies' locker room," Lester explained. "I used to work with him at Empire Stadium before they tore it down, shame that it was."

"I used to like going to Lion's games there," Rosa recalled. "Nothing like it on a warm fall evening with the view of the harbour and the mountains."

"So?" Bill said sternly, ignoring Rosa's reminiscences and refusing to be taken in even one millimeter by Lester's evolving explanation.

"So, I'll go in, find the manager and make sure the team doesn't get on their bus so you guys can stop Villano."

"And if we don't?"

"At least the Grizzlies will be safe."

"You're not scratching yourself from this race, Lester," Bill warned. "My nephew is heading for that bus with only a thin rapier between him and a pair of international terrorists, and I'm about to put my life on the line for the team. Don't fold on us."

"I won't dally a second. I'll get every security guard in the place out to that bus faster than Dusselworf ran today."

"How? The cops didn't believe Sebastian's story. Why should the guards?"

"Oh, Bill, please," Lester said with a sardonic grin and a guffaw. "I'm just a tad more creative than our good Dr. Gianninni."

Lester still waited, not wanting to ruin his friendship with Bill, let alone lose access to the ever evolving and hopefully ever improving Grand Unifying Theory of Horse Racing. He did not want to be left out of the profits on that glorious eureka day when Bill finally perfected the theory and struck the mother of all lodes.

"Alright," Bill finally relented, "but don't go wasting a second watching the game. The Grizzlies are going to maul the Lakers whether or not you watch."

Free at last, Lester rushed off toward his old acquaintance, the usher, and entrance into the most coveted ticket in town.

Upon bidding Lester a reluctant God speed, Bill thought that at least Rosa and Destiny would be stalwart allies in the coming adventure. He counted on their loyalty—or was it lust?—to Sebastian to keep Bill and his nephew well supported in the coming confrontation with the international terrorists, if in fact Sebastian's outlandish story was true. It was not to be, however, for Destiny had a date with Homer, or more eloquently, Homer had a date with Destiny.

As they rounded the arena and spotted the chain-link fence that enclosed the team busses, Bill had serious doubts about whether his nephew's information had been correct. Maybe Sebastian had just mistaken the image on the wanted poster for the student he had seen with Villano at breakfast. For, the truth be told, the photographs on the poster appeared to have been taken with the same type of camera they used to photograph the Loch Ness monster, Bigfoot and UFOs: a black-and-white camera with a special fuzzy lens. Bill knew monster and UFO fanatics lacked funding, but why couldn't the government spring for a color camera with a nice, sharp lens to photograph international terrorists and other ner' do wells?

Even as doubts about the veracity of Sebastian's story bubbled up in Bill's mind, they were squelched once and for all by the sight of a guard lying on the ground at the entrance to the fenced area. The terrorists had murdered a guard!

Peering into the darkness beyond the light cast by the arena for terrorists hiding in the shadows, Bill warily approached the prone guard. Rosa and Destiny, fear enveloping their romantic minds, clung to Bill's arms like well-dressed anchors.

"He's not...," Destiny whispered as Bill knelt at the guard's side.

"Dead?" Rosa completed the question even as Bill reached for one of the guard's wrists.

A melodious snore reached their ears. Shaking his head as his fear receded like a tsunami, Bill gently rolled the guard over.

"He's asleep on duty," Bill said disgustedly, masking his profound relief. "Dereliction of duty, if I ever saw it."

"He didn't even finish his dinner," Rosa said, gesturing at a half-eaten hotdog that had fallen, bun and condiments all, onto the pavement beside the guard's overturned chair, which had toppled over when the guard had done the same.

Bill reached over and picked up the cold dog, which had once been hot. Even as Rosa made a face at his deplorable behavior, Bill sniffed the frankfurter.

"I can't tell for sure, but I'd say this boy's been drugged," he said, as he helped Destiny prop Homer into a sitting position against the chain-link fence.

"He looks so content," Destiny said, cradling the young, bespectacled guard in her arms as she sat beside him.

Homer groaned and his head lolled over onto Destiny's ample bosom.

"He's coming out of it," Bill said. "You better stay with him, Destiny. Use his walkie-talkie to call for help."

"What do I say?" Destiny asked, as she reached for Homer's walkie-talkie, which was clipped to the groggy guard's belt.

"Tell them," Bill started, hesitated and then, inspired, said, "Tell them a mob of wild, female basketball groupies are besieging the locker room entrance."

"But that's not true," Destiny said, eyeing Rosa. There was no time like the present to prove to her mother that, contrary to what might have been implied by her practice of hiding in professor's offices, she was an honest and upstanding young lady.

"Desperate times call for desperate measures, including all shades of lies, and it'll get every male guard within 10 miles here on the double, if not the triple," Bill said as he led Rosa through the open gate.

Destiny keyed the walkie-talkie and told her tale. The effect was not, however, what Bill had predicted because Villano, foreseeing just such an eventuality—maybe not the groupie angle, but the unconscious Homer being discovered—had removed the batteries from the walkie-talkie.

Encouraged by the mistaken belief that well-armed reinforcements were on their way with lust-driven alacrity, Bill led Rosa toward the Briar Rabbit Coach Line bus. The turquoise and black motorcoach, the Grizzly's colors, was dark, parked in silent vigil as it awaited the near-certain victory of the winningest team in professional basketball. The Lakers' bus, a run-of-the-mill Vancouver Coach, Moving and Storage Company rental, sat on the other side of the enclosure, also dark and empty. There appeared to be no one near either bus, but Bill and Rosa could only see the near side of the Grizzly's palatial transport.

Still clinging to Bill's arm, Rosa dug in her three-inch heels and whispered, "There's nobody here. Sebastian must have changed his mind. Let's go."

Bill was on the point of agreeing with her, his concern for his favorite nephew only going so far in the courage department, when they heard a clunk. It sounded like metal striking metal and echoed between the bus and the momentarily quiet arena.

"There's someone on the other side of the bus," Bill whispered.

They stood there, both hoping the other would take charge and make a decision: biologists call it fight or flight. In this case, it was more accurately: curiosity or run for your life. Both leaned toward the later instinct. Neither wanted to confirm that the detrimental effects of curiosity applied not only to felines, but also to humans.

Then they heard a slam, like that of a door closing, followed by a click.

"Come on," Bill said. His favorite nephew was worth at least a quick, careful and discreet peek at the other side of the bus to determine who or what was making the noises.

Rosa decided it was better to stay with Bill than risk being alone in an area where there was already a drugged guard and the possibility of international terrorists lurking in every shadow. She stayed securely moored to her aged companion's arm.

Bill crept up to the bus and then, his back against the vehicle, shuffle-stepped toward the rear. He quickly started lifting his feet to stop the shuffling noise. Then Rosa, once again, dug her spiked heels into the blacktop.

"What?" Bill hissed, aggravated at the delay when he had only just succeeded in steeling his nerves to peer around the end the bus. A delay risked turning his steeled nerves into molten rubber.

Scared mute, Rosa pointed toward the ground. Frowning, Bill thought she had lost an earring and was silently pleading for him to scramble around and search for the lost accouterment at this most inopportune moment.

"We don't have time," Bill whispered, his mind focused on maintaining his courage to stave off the vulcanization of his spine.

Bill took a step, only to be stopped by the anchor that was Rosa.

"Mrs. Turnbell, if you do not wish to accompany me, then please go rejoin your daughter," Bill whispered. "Impeding my progress will only drag out the proceedings unnecessarily."

"Why don't we look under the bus?" Rosa suggested, having finally regained her power of speech.

Bill stopped and smiled at his accomplice. She was not all makeup, big hair and *au couture* knock-off outfits. She had brains. He knelt. With Rosa still attached to his arm, he peered under the bus. Even a short-sighted guard who had not had the advantage of corrective laser eye surgery could have seen the two pairs of legs and shoes on the other side of the bus. One pair of legs was encased in suit material bottomed by black dress shoes, while the other wore faded blue jeans and running shoes.

"Now what?" Rosa whispered in Bill's ear. The words startled Bill, sending fear coursing through his shaking body. A similar sensation would have caused even the bravest of Jason's Argonauts to reconsider their passage on the *Argo* and book passage on some other ship, possibly the *Mediterranean Princess*, complete with shuffleboard, a pool and cocktails starting promptly at four every afternoon on the Lido deck.

"Probably a Grizzly executive and his son waiting for the team." Bill hoped he was right, although he wondered when Sebastian and his rapier, fulfilling the role of the cavalry in their little drama, would arrive. "Come on," Bill said, deciding it was best to seize the tiger by the tail and find out if indeed it was a tiger or, in reality, a docile bovine.

Stealing his courage, Bill led the way around the end of the bus with a confident, even jaunty air. Sebastian's tale could not be true. Turning the corner, Bill stood face-to-face with a surprised Dr. Villano and Hogarth.

"My dear, Professor Rogers," Villano said smoothly, as if it was an everyday occurrence for two professors to meet while skulking around a basketball team's bus on a fine spring evening. "Are you attending the game?"

"No," Bill replied automatically. "My scalpers crapped out. You?"

"I tried only legal means and, unfortunately, also came up shy a seat. Well, it was nice chatting with you, but I think we will return home. Good evening."

His young accomplice in tow, Villano walked toward the front of the bus.

"Hogarth," Bill called out. He had instantly noticed the striking resemblance between Villano's young friend and the international terrorist pictured, however fuzzily, in the border patrol's wanted poster.

Without a thought, Hogarth turned and the game was up. Rosa opened her mouth to scream. Bill was about to attempt to relive his high school rugby days by tackling Hogarth, who, being on a wanted poster, appeared to be a more pressing threat than Villano. The good doctor—Villano, not Bill—put an end to both their plans by drawing a revolver from his suit pocket and saying, "Don't move, please."

Bill and Rosa froze. Hogarth looked around like a fox who was in the middle of selecting his entrée in a hen house when a shotgun-totting farmer appears at the door.

"Move," Villano ordered.

Maneuvering around Bill and Rosa, Villano gestured toward the front of the bus. With Rosa once again attached to his arm, Bill strode with a courage he did not feel toward the front of the bus. Bill realized neither terrorist had a bag, pack or suitcase, so the bomb must already be on the bus. The Grizzlies would soon be roasted bear meat unless he did something. Glancing behind him, Bill saw that Hogarth appeared to be unarmed, although you could never count on an international terrorist to play fair and show all his cards on the game's first draw.

Villano was an entirely different proposition. Even though the English professor had a gun, Bill was not afraid of him. Bill had been in far more dangerous positions before. From an extensive catalogue of possible examples, he recalled the time Big Louie Anderson had appeared to demand payment on a small debt Bill owed Hong Kong Louie. Needless to say, Bill lacked the cash to give Big Louie for his Hong Kong namesake. Bill had offered to cut a deck of cards for double or nothing, but Big Louie had heard every possible excuse and scheme to avoid paying before; he wanted his paymaster's money. On his way to class at the time of his unscheduled and unforeseen meeting with Big Louie, Bill had seized the opportunity presented by a class of underachieving freshmen. Bill had auctioned off grades like the liveliest of Sotheby's auctioneers. In less than five minutes he had raised the money and bid Big Louie Anderson a heartfelt good riddance. Within a week, Bill had won back all of the auctioned promises of As and Bs like so many IOUs in a series of poker games in which he had outdone even his great Uncle Slim's flare for producing just the right card at just the right moment. He had even done it all without once resorting to any of the many slight-of-hand moves Slim had taught Bill as a boy to produce just the right card at just the right moment—well, almost no such moves.

Realizing dangerous situations were well within his ken, Bill settled on his plan. There was an oil spot five feet in front of him as they rounded the front of the bus. The bus was nine feet from the oil spot and Bill's hand, unseen by Villano, clutched a book of matches. Rosa's high heels would provide the final element in Bill's daring plan to hoist Villano on his own gun. It would have been more poetic if Villano had been armed with a petard, but one must make do with whatever situation one finds oneself in.

Bill was about to spring into action and unleash his plan when who should step out from the far side of the bus than Sebastian, rapier in hand. With a dramatic flourish of his stage weapon, Sebastian yelled, "Halt!"

"Professor Gianninni," Villano said, recovering from his surprise at the sight of his colleague sporting such an uncolleagial visage, not to mention a weapon. "'Is this a dagger I see before me'?"

"It's a rapier, not a dagger, but you are as evil as Macbeth, and just as doomed," Sebastian said, recognizing the quote.

"I doubt it. You're no Macduff, but enough clever repartee." Gesturing with his revolver and assuming a cold, emotionless tone, Villano ordered, "Drop that ridiculous sword and fall in with your uncle and his girlfriend."

His choice of words could not have been worse. Rosa, appalled at the suggestion that she was Bill's girlfriend, especially in front of the current focus of all of her desires, Professor Gianninni, spun around and slammed a stiletto heel into Villano's right toe as she spat out, "I am *not* his girlfriend."

Villano dropped his revolver as he hopped on his left foot in the belief that such a move would ease the pain coursing through his right big toe and shooting up his leg like a river of fire, such as flows from Mount Kileau with alarming regularity.

Being equidistant from the fallen revolver, Bill and Hogarth both lunged for the weapon where it lay bereft, alone and unclaimed on the blacktop. Their heads collided like two billiard balls on the break. Both men sat down from their unintended meeting of minds, their vision blurry, limbs tingling and the seats of their pants now soiled with oil from their poor choice of locations to repose. Sebastian watched as Rosa strode toward him like a goddess as her worshippers, Bill and Hogarth, fell to the ground on either side of her as if in the depths of devout prayer, and Villano, with bowed head in apparent supplication, hopped around like a one-legged jack rabbit behind her.

"Sebastian," Rosa gushed. "You've come to rescue me."

It appeared no rescuing was required, although there was still the question of the revolver. Since Bill and Hogarth were temporarily on the injured reserve list and Villano was opting out of the game to contemplate his big toe, Sebastian decided it was an excellent time to, as they say in Latin, *carpe gunem*.

Rapier still in hand since a rapier in the hand was worth a revolver on the pavement, Sebastian rushed toward the gun. He saw his way clear: past Rosa, around the hopping Dr. Villano and then between the prone Uncle Bill and Hogarth to where the revolver would be his for the picking up. Little did he know he would not even complete the first leg of his planned itinerary.

As Sebastian went to weave past Rosa, her arm shot out like an NFL lineman executing his best clothesline tackle. Sebastian caught his neck on her forearm with the full force of his appreciable forward motion. It felt similar, he thought, to what it must feel like to have a silken rope—for Rosa's arm was remarkably smooth—tied around one's neck, with the other end tied to a wooden beam and the floor dropped out from under one. Not a feeling devoutly to be wished for.

As Sebastian crouched on the pavement and struggled to regain the use of his windpipe, Rosa embraced him and inundated his ears with words of sympathy and apology for her inadvertent block. Hogarth and Bill, their minds and eyes cleared sufficiently to discern once again the revolver lying between them, once again lunged for the unclaimed weapon. This time the impact mimicked that of two bighorn sheep during rutting season with just one comely doe left unclaimed. The resounding crack would have been heard throughout the arena if Eddie "Three-point" Anderson had not just sunk one of his patented, mid-court "Moon Shots." The roar of the crowd proved just sufficient to drown out the crack made by the skulls of Bill and Hogarth. Lacking the benefit of six inches of horn between their adversary's brain case and their own, this time both were knocked out. They lay on either side of the revolver like two reclining Greek statues, although neither was missing any arms, as is the Greek style.

As Sebastian extricated himself from Rosa's romantic and rather strong embrace without offending her feelings, Villano concluded his big toe was not actually perforated like a piece of paper after an encounter with a hole punch and lunged for his fallen weapon. Unlike on the attempts by Bill and Hogarth, there was no rival for the revolver's attentions. Villano's hand felt metal and, once again, he was lord of the situation.

"Freeze!" he yelled.

The words were completely lost on Bill and Hogarth who were, with no urging from anyone else, frozen in place already. Having finally broken free of his neighbor's un-neighborly embrace, the rapier-armed Sebastian had been charging toward the revolver. Seeing that Villano would reach the firearm first, Sebastian raised his rapier and, going in for a crippling wound aimed at Villano's left thigh, raced toward the professor-cum-terrorist. As Villano raised the revolver and issued his command to halt, the two—rapier and revolver—met like lovers; Sebastian's rapier slid into the muzzle of Villano's revolver with a sound reminiscent of long fingernails on dry chalkboard. Villano, Rosa and Sebastian winced at the ear-tingling screech.

Sebastian and Villano were locked in a bizarre, although not inelegant, symbiotic relationship via their weapons. Shocked and bewildered by the sight of the two English professors and their odd embrace, Rosa stood and watched like a child at a freak show. Sebastian, his rapier held in the barrel of Villano's revolver, tried to whip his weapon free. Unwilling to relinquish his gun, Villano hung on as the rapier flicked the revolver first this way, then that way. As Sebastian paused to consider his next move, Villano jerked his gun, first back, then to one side and finally to the other side. As with Sebastian's attempts to free his rapier, it was to no avail; Villano's revolver was securely and snugly wedded to Sebastian's rapier.

"Let go of my gun," Villano ordered.

"Let go of my rapier," Sebastian countered.

They glared at each other a moment and then, both deciding further negotiations would only prolong their current impasse, continued their potentially macabre dance as each tried desperately to free his weapon from its clinging rival.

The twangs and wails of the rapier as it bent first one way and then the other reached the ears of Destiny where she sat against the chain link fence 50 yards away cradling Homer who, although now fully conscious, had no intention of moving from the bosom of such a beautiful young girl. Even his sedative-addled mind reasoned she might be an actual, real-life potential girlfriend.

"Nice music," Destiny said with a smile as she tenderly played with Homer's forelocks.

"Very techno," Homer agreed with a smile up at his savior, nurse and potential main—and only—squeeze. "I like it."

The same could not by any stretch of the imagination be said of Sebastian and Villano. Their anger increased as they danced their dance, pulling, pushing, twisting, shimmying, corkscrewing, waggling, and wiggling to free their weapons; all to no avail.

The dance could have gone on indefinitely, but the oil slick, which had formed such a fundamental and integral part of Bill's unexecuted plan, finally came into play. As Sebastian parried a tug from Villano, his right foot slipped in the oil and, to steady himself and save his pants from an oily end, he shot his arms up and out. The sudden, uncalculated movement did what all of Sebastian's previous calculated movements failed to do: the weapons remained fused, but Villano lost his grip and let go of his weapon.

Unfortunately for Sebastian, the upward and outward motion of his hand did not end when Villano lost his grip on the revolver. As Sebastian's right hand continued its flail in his attempt to keep his balance and the seat of his pants oil free, the rapier continued its rapid ascent. The revolver, stuck on the end of the rapier, also continued its even more rapid ascent. When Sebastian's hand stopped, his balance maintained and his pants saved an oiling, the rapier also stopped or, more precisely, the handle stopped. The blade, that thin, fine piece of steel that had all the resiliency and spring of the youngest of willow trees, yet all the strength of an oak, continued on its way, streaking skyward as it acted like a yard-long sling shot. The blade flung the revolver up and out at a speed many a tennis star would have envied for a service. The speed of the revolver-rapier combination accomplished what the combined strength of Sebastian and Villano had been unable to do; end the coupling of the two weapons. The revolver, finally freed from the rapier, arced up into the night sky like a comet, sans tail.

Sebastian, Villano and Rosa watched enthralled as the revolver sailed up over the chain link fence, still gaining altitude. It caught a strong south-westerly breeze, soared over a middle-aged fir and above Pacific Boulevard before it reached the apex of its freedom flight. As the trio watched, the firearm descended in a gentle arc across the four-lane boulevard, just clearing a chain link fence on the far side to plummet into the calm waters of False Creek with a splash.

"Now you halt!" Sebastian ordered, leveling his newly freed rapier at the unarmed Villano's heart. It now appeared the evening belonged to Sebastian, but anyone who has played poker, watched a horse race or played roulette knows how quickly Fortune's wheel can turn 180 degrees.

Chapter 30

Villano raised his hands in surrender. Hogarth, still snoozing in the arms of Morpheus, rolled over. In so doing, his pant lag was pushed up, revealing just above his ankle a tasteful leather holster containing a small pistol.

Villano and Sebastian spotted the weapon at the same instant. Sebastian was closer. Even so, Villano lunged for the gun. Desperate, he might have been faster than Sebastian, but he had not counted on Sebastian's rapier. Villano pulled up just in time to avoid impaling himself on his adversary's blade. With Villano finally at bay, Sebastian removed the pistol from Hogarth's leg holster and wondered why the terrorist had not used the weapon instead of twice butting heads with Bill over Villano's revolver. Little could Sebastian know that Hogarth had forgotten to which leg he had attached his pistol. In the heat of the melee with Bill and Sebastian, Hogarth had feared making a *faux pas* by reaching for his weapon only to reveal an argyle sock.

Once again securely in control of the situation and now doubly-armed, Sebastian told Rosa, "If you would be so kind, please go summon the police."

"I wouldn't do that if I were you," advised Villano with a calmness that appeared completely at odds with his current situation.

"Luckily I am not you," Sebastian countered. "Please, Rosa," he told the confused Rosa as she glanced from Sebastian, with a worshiping look, to Villano, with a look of fear and loathing.

"The bomb is hidden nearby and will explode rather soon," Villano said, taking joy in the devastating effect of his words.

Sebastian's confident expression vanished and Rosa appeared about to fly. Only a reassuring glance at her heroic defender stayed her high-heeled feet.

"I believe it would be wise to let the police in on Dr. Villano's little secret," Sebastian told Rosa. "Please, my dear, go."

Rosa took a step before Villano froze her in her high-heeled tracks with the words, "If you turn me in to the police, I won't tell them where the bomb is planted and many people, including possibly both of you, will die."

"The bomb's on the bus." Sebastian took great pleasure in trumping Villano.

"It might be or it might not." Villano looked far from trumped. "Maybe I changed my mind and hid it in a garbage can in the locker room, in those shrubs by the locker room door or in a car nearby. Even if it is on the bus, do you want to risk the time to discover exactly where? It might be under a seat, in the lavatory, the engine, a cargo bay or maybe even under the bus or on the roof. If you don't call the police, I'll tell you exactly where it is."

"With enough time to defuse it?"

"It can't be defused by the likes of you, but you'll have time to move it to a location where no one will be injured."

"I'm supposed to trust you?"

"If you wait long enough, neither of us will have to trust any-one ever again." Villano cocked his head and managed a look at his watch on his arm, both of which still pointed star-ward. "The game will be over in a few minutes. Thousands of fans will soon be streaming out of the arena. Many of them will stroll past this very spot without a care in the world after their team's victory, until a bomb blows them to smithereens."

Always a stickler for language, Sebastian was about to point out that smithereen was from the Gaelic, *smidirin* meaning small, but not necessarily bloody, pieces, but, thinking it was neither the time nor place to discuss etymology, made his decision and said,

"Alright. Rosa will leave now to get the police. You tell me where the bomb is and I will allow you to escape. That way, if you double-cross me, she'll be safe and will be able to tell the authorities the identity of the mad bomber."

"Mad bomber," Villano repeated, hurt. "I am far from mad, as my personal physician can readily attest, and I didn't actually procure, assemble or plant the bomb. He did." Villano pointed at the slumbering Hogarth.

"In any case, Rosa will leave. Then you will tell me where the bomb is, and then I will let you go on your nefarious way."

"Why should I be any more willing to trust you than you are to trust me?"

"Because I am the good guy," Sebastian said, standing straight and upright, denoting, he believed, goodness.

Villano laughed. When he had regained his composure, he said, "Good and evil are opposing views of what is right."

"Moral relativism doesn't apply in the case of blowing up basketball teams."

"You should read Twain's *The Mysterious Stranger* on the subject of good and evil. Often what appears an evil deed has good effects, and what appears to be a good deed only leads to pain, suffering and damnation."

Sebastian wondered if Villano had forgotten a bomb was close-by ticking down toward boom. Villano might be bluffing. Such a conclusion would explain his apparent lack of concern at engaging in lengthy philosophical conversations at such a time and place. In either case, it was too great a risk to gamble the lives of Rosa, Bill, himself and, in a matter of minutes, the lives of thousands of Grizzly fans on his guess as to the existence, true state and actual location of Villano's bomb. "Do you agree to my proposal?"

"Should you choose to break your word for what you consider to be just ends, at least give me a sporting chance," Villano said. "Your Ms. Rosa will depart, then I will walk out of the enclosure and, standing on the other side of the fence, I will tell you where the bomb is located. You can then retrieve the bomb while I make good my escape."

"How would that help you if I choose to make capturing you justify breaking my word?"

"I assume you're not an accomplished marksman, so I hope the increased range between us, especially at night and with a fence between us, will greatly increase my chances of a successful flight should you start shooting at me."

"Why do you assume I am not an expert marksman?"

"Because the safety is on," Villano said, gesturing at the pistol. "Either you're an extremely safety conscious marksman or a complete neophyte with firearms."

Sebastian peered at the pistol and flicked the safety off. "Why didn't you run when you could see the safety was on?"

"I value my life highly, and you still had the rapier. Besides, you're far closer to the entrance than I am."

Sebastian nodded to Rosa. With a quick peck on Sebastian's cheek, she rushed out of the enclosure. As she hurried past Destiny, she ordered her daughter and her new friend to get away from the bus but, engrossed in their own world of newfound teenage love, they did not hear her. Teetering on her heels, Rosa scrambled up the stairs toward the nearest arena door, having failed to notice that her warning had gone unheeded.

"Now your turn," Sebastian told Villano.

As Villano moved toward the entrance, he cautioned Sebastian, "Even after I escape and you've defused the bomb, I wouldn't mention any of this to the police."

"Why in the name of Keats, not?"

"Because the bomb was smuggled across the border in the trunk of your car," Villano said, with the desired devastating effect on Sebastian.

"What?!"

"The black suitcase in the back of you Omni."

"You blackguard! You used me as your smuggler?"

"With some difficulty. I will also swear that I have observed you in the company of an international terrorist, Mr. Chevalier," Villano said, gesturing with his raised right hand toward Hogarth. "The police will conclude it was your bomb and you 'discovered' it only for the resulting publicity. I fear that it would not go well for you, my learned colleague."

Chastened by that new information, Sebastian kept the pistol leveled at Villano as the terrorist/professor strode out the gate, past Destiny and Homer, and along the fence a short distance before stopping and facing Sebastian through the fence.

"The bomb?" Sebastian demanded, determined to salvage at least some modicum of success from the night's inglorious events.

"It's in the last cargo bay of the bus. I fear I can't say, 'Parting is such sweet sorrow,' but 'good night, good night!'" Turning, Villano sprinted into the parking lot, quickly lost amidst the cars, trucks and SUVs that carpeted the lot from end to end.

Already wishing he had not trusted the villain, Sebastian spun on his heel and ran back to the rear of the bus. He flung open the last cargo bay door and peered inside. His heart stopped: empty. Fear rose in him. Would he feel anything if the bomb went off or would he just cease to exist between one heroic, yet romantic thought and the next? He spun around and could just see Villano racing across Pacific Boulevard and along False Creek toward the Sky Train station opposite the geodesic dome that housed Science World.

"Damn," Sebastian cursed. He yelled, "Destiny! Destiny! Get the guard away from here! There's a bomb on the bus!" as he ran around the bus to the other side.

Destiny and Homer, finally jarred out of their romantic reverie and discussion of what to spend Homer's savings on, since Destiny thought his glasses made him look intellectual, helped each other to their feet. Arm in arm and shoulder to shoulder, they rushed away from the bus enclosure and, Sebastian hoped, out of bomb-explosion range.

Sebastian flung open the rearmost cargo bay on the other side of the bus and peered inside with a devout prayer. It did no good. The bay was stuffed full of basketballs. He was on the verge of dragging the unconscious Professor-Uncle Bill out of the enclosure and at a minimum saving themselves—Hogarth was on his own—when the arena's doors burst open discharging the vanguard of tens of thousands of fans. He must find the bomb or thousands would die.

He stepped up to the next bay, lifted the latch and flung open the door: nothing. The next two bays on that side proved equally barren of bombs or even basketballs. Frustrated, he spotted joyous fans celebrating the Grizzly win as they strolled down the stairs and straight past the bus enclosure on their way to the parking lot and the Sky Train station. The carnage would be indescribable, even to a gifted horror writer, if a bomb exploded in the next few minutes.

Sebastian ran around the bus and tried the front-most bay on that side of the bus: nothing save air. The next two bays were equally devoid of explosives, bombs or anything even flammable. He pulled up short, relieved to see Destiny and the guard far away, yet would it be far enough if Villano had planted the mother of all bombs?

Racing around the bus, Sebastian started pulling the basketballs out of the rearmost cargo bay. It was the only bay with anything in it. The official NBA basketballs rolled and bounced around the enclosure, attracting the attention of passing fans. As Sebastian burrowed into the cargo bay, only his rear end, legs and rapier, which was stuck in his belt, protruded from the bay. Even as he dug, some adventurous and some greedy fans filtered into the enclosure through the unguarded entrance to retrieve the basketballs, which now roamed free.

With a feeling not far different from that of Columbus upon spying land after far too many days at sea and having wondered whether the Earth was indeed flat, Sebastian hit pay dirt: a black, metal suitcase in the farthest recesses of the cargo bay. He'd found it!

Now to dispose of the bomb. Hauling the suitcase bomb out of the bay, Sebastian was confronted by hundreds of fans grappling, wrestling and battling over the dozens of basketballs he had released from their cargo-bay nursery. Although Canadian units made the deepest advance of any of the Allied forces on D-Day against the Germany army, which enjoyed a home-field advantage at the time even though the match was played in France, Canadians are not noted for their combativeness. Even so, the Grizzlies' fans, fresh from seeing their newly beloved team wallop the visiting Lakers, were full of fight. A battalion of them now battled over what they thought were souvenir Grizzly basketballs.

Sebastian hoisted the heavy metal suitcase bomb above his head and yelled, "Clear the way! I've got a bomb!"

The struggles over the balls enjoyed a five-second timeout as all eyes fell on the middle-aged, short but slim man who had yelled in his loudest professorial voice above the general hubbub. He wore a Navy blue sport jacket, gray slacks and a sweater under his jacket. The most striking parts of his ensemble were the rapier rakishly stuck into his leather belt and the black suitcase he carried above his head. Almost all of those wrestling over the balls promptly concluded the strangely attired man was attempting to distract them while he or his as yet unseen accomplices snuck away with a bear's share of the prized Grizzly's souvenir basketballs. Therefore, even as Sebastian seized the moment and started to run, bomb over his head, toward the enclosure entrance, the general melee resumed with renewed vigor.

What had begun for Sebastian as a sprint between frozen fans degenerated into a hazard-filled journey through an increasingly violent and confused battle. With his center of gravity dangerously high given the suitcase above his head, Sebastian had grave difficulty negotiating the challenging course set by the ever-shifting basketball combatants. He quickly realized why running backs keep the football cradled in their gut while smashing through opposing tacklers in a low crouch. It was exponentially easier than carrying a ball, or in his case a suitcase, above one's head and attempting to run with it through an opposing team. Walter Payton, Jim Brown and Barry Sanders would have been hard pressed to set one record between them if they had been required to run in the posture Sebastian was forced to adopt with the bomb. Even so, Sebastian high stepped over an errant basketball, spun around a sumo match between a short, squat lady and a tall, thin man with a ball as the prize between them, and then ricocheted off a man who was bent double in his pursuit of a bouncing baby basketball.

Sebastian spotted the entrance and realized he had only completed the warm-up portion of his race for open country. The entrance was jammed with empty-handed fans on their way into the enclosure and basketball-clutching fans on their way out. In comparison, the George Massey Tunnel between Vancouver and

Richmond during rush hour was as clear as the Saskatchewan prairie.

Sebastian bobbed past a child clutching a prized basketball but, as he sidestepped an oncoming man the width of a passenger train, he miscalculated his course and slammed into the chain-link fence beside the entrance. As he hit the fence, the suitcase, held high above his head, flew out of his sweat-slick hands. It struck the top of the fence and teetered on end like a drunken tightrope walker sans the long skinny bar such strollers carry for balance. Then the same south-westerly that had helped the revolver sail clear of Pacific Boulevard aided the suitcase on its way, toppling it over the fence. The suitcase plummeted straight down and struck the blacktop beside a startled Lakers fan. Disgusted with his team's performance that evening to the point of calling them the Laker Girls or even the Fakers, the fan decided the suitcase near miss was just one more sign from God that it was not his night. He hurried on his way home to snuggle up in bed as far under the covers as he could manage and yet still breath until this most unlucky of days passed into yesterday.

As the suitcase fell, Sebastian bounced off the fence and hit the pavement. He skinned his hands and narrowly avoided skinning his nose. Then the train-sized man who had just entered the enclosure stepped on Sebastian's back in his pursuit of an earring-adorned teenager with a Grizzlies basketball. Expecting to be blown into small, jagged and rather scattered pieces at any moment, Sebastian did not hold the shoe in the back against the train-sized man. He covered his head and prepared for the worst the bomb could deliver. Seconds passed and Sebastian, realizing his body was still in one relatively solid piece, slowly lifted his head and peered through the fence at the black suitcase, which had landed on the other side amid a stream of spectators on their way home. It, too, was still in one relatively solid piece.

Sebastian picked himself up, dusted off his clothes, and headed through the enclosure entrance. After a plethora of phrases, including, "Pardon me, sir," "Excuse me, madam" and "I did not touch your wife *there*, sir," Sebastian wiggled his way through the entrance like a salmon fighting its way upstream to spawn, with bears fishing from every overhanging rock along the way. He hoped the analogy would not prove to be accurate, since salmon died after they reached their spawning ground.

Sebastian dodged along the fence passing fans, some clutching prized basketballs, and reached the suitcase without further mishap. Reaching the ominous *noir* suitcase, he surveyed the area and decided this was the last place to hold a bomb-detonation party. He quickly looked toward the arena, up and down the street, and then across Pacific Boulevard at False Creek. 'Perfect,' he thought as he reached down, grabbed the suitcase and, once again hoisting it above his head like a religious icon, sprinted through the crowd toward the fake creek.

Unlike in the restricted confines of the bus enclosure, Sebastian made good time as he raced across the parking lot around and between fans on their way to their cars or the Sky Train station. Unlike in the entrance to the enclosure, this time he was going with the flow: the salmon, miraculously still alive, was now heading downstream.

Although he was gratified by his rapid progress, the thought was growing in his mind that either the bomb would explode before he could safely dispose of it or the suitcase did not, in fact, contain explosives. Was all this just some monstrous practical joke? He could not believe that Uncle Bill, Rosa and Destiny Turnbell, his dear Elizabeth, the GM Place guard, Lester, Villano, Hogarth and so many others could possibly all be in on such a grand scheme to make him the victim of a momentously complex practical joke. It could not be. Or could it?

He stopped at Pacific Boulevard, looked both ways as his mother had taught him and, waiting for an opportune break in the traffic, sprinted across the street. Reaching the other side, he stopped at the chain-link fence separating the road from the chill waters of False Creek, so named because the first European explorers had erred in concluding that the waters that entered the Pacific at that point were a creek when, in actuality, it was merely a narrow arm of the ocean intruding upon the land.

Deciding he had to know what the suitcase contained, Sebastian set the suitcase down on the sidewalk even as Grizzly fans streamed past with curious glances at the man who had brought a suitcase to the game. Just as Sebastian realized the case was locked, a hand appeared at his side, offering him a fist-sized rock. Turning, Sebastian was greeted by the broad and inviting smile of Rosa Turnbell.

"I called the police," she said, "but they said it'd be a while before they could get any units through all the game traffic."

"Thanks for trying," Sebastian said as he accepted the proffered rock.

Inspecting the catches on the metal suitcase, Sebastian lined up the rock with care. As he reached back to strike the first blow, Rosa's soft hand stopped his arm.

"Should we do this?" she asked.

Sebastian stayed his rock-laden hand and looked up at his smitten neighbor.

"Maybe not," he reluctantly agreed, taking in the stream of fans still flowing past like a mighty river. "Wouldn't do just now to make a crater in the sidewalk at this particular spot, let alone with us in it."

He dropped the rock and picked up the suitcase. He looked to the left toward a marina and to the right toward the Burrard Street Bridge. Straight ahead was open water that appeared to be the choicest location for an explosion. Twirling the suitcase around his torso in a great arc like a Scottish hammer, in the process clearing a tranquil island in the river of fans flowing past on the sidewalk, he let go and flung the case high over the chain-link fence toward the water.

Even as Sebastian held his arms high in a classic, hammer-throw finish, Short arrived, snapped handcuffs on him and said, "You're under arrest."

"You, too, madam," Adderly added, snapping handcuffs on a surprised Rosa.

They all paused to watch the suitcase sail through the air. It caught the same south-westerly that had helped the revolver on its maiden flight.

"Good height," Adderly commented.

Indeed, passing Grizzly fans stopped to watch as the suitcase plummeted into the inlet masquerading as a creek, skipped twice and continued its forward motion for a good 10 meters. Then, with a gurgle, the suitcase settled into the water and sank from view.

"Why am I under arrest?" Sebastian asked, all the participants' attention having now returned to dry land.

"Jaywalking and littering," Short replied.

"Jaywalking?" Rosa asked.

"You crossed the street, just like he did," Adderly shot back.

"As he did," Sebastian corrected. "Or, if I said it, 'as I did.'"

"There, he admits it."

"And littering?" Sebastian asked, confused as to the origin of that charge.

"Several hundred people just saw you hurl a suitcase into False Creek," Short said. "It's a clear violation of the Law of the Sea's International Pollution and Dumping Strictures, the Canadian Environmental Preservation Act, the British Columbia Friends of the Sea Act, and the City of Vancouver Municipal Code. You're a criminal on every level: international, national, provincial and city."

"The suitcase had a bomb in it," Rosa blurted out.

"Sticking to that story, are you Gianninni?" Short asked, his voice dripping with condescension.

"If it was a bomb," Adderly said, "why didn't it explode when it hit the water?"

"It was not fused to go off then," Sebastian said, as if explaining Shelley to a Shakespeare groupie, and not really expecting to make much, if any headway.

"If you knew when it was fused to explode, you must have built it," Adderly reasoned with a triumphant smile.

"I didn't build it, Doctor...., " Sebastian began, but then Villano's warning flashed through his mind. If the police recovered the moist remains of the suitcase, the whole battalion of border guards who had purchased his romance novel manuscripts could certainly identify it as the one that had been in Sebastian's car. Worse, Sebastian's fingerprints were now all over it. Short and Adderly had seen the suitcase bomb in Sebastian's possession and, possession being nine-tenths of the law, the frame around Sebastian was about as well and truly constructed as if it had been fashioned by a master carpenter with a perfectionist bent.

"Nothing," Sebastian finished lamely. He cast a pleading look at Rosa to please, at all costs and in exchange for anything, exercise her right to remain silent.

"But you said Doctor—," Rosa began, choosing to exercise her right to free speech instead.

"I think," Sebastian interrupted her, "we should admit all this was just a poorly conceived, if well executed practical joke."

Rosa followed her beau's lead, much to the consternation of the inspectors, who urged her to continue spilling the story she had already precariously began to pour. Rosa, however, remained silent, if one did not count her affectionate and aggressive body language directed toward Sebastian. Giving up on the long shot of an on-the-spot confession, Short and Adderly led the handcuffed Sebastian and Rosa back toward their car through the gawking crowd.

Chapter 31

As the Mounties escorted their charges off to jail, Bill, still in the bus enclosure, shook his head as he attempted to clear the fuzzy edges from his vision. His head felt like a clumsy Clydesdale had stepped on it repeatedly and, as his vision cleared, he thought he had finally contracted full-blown schizophrenia. There were several dozen people in the bus enclosure, many wrestling over basketballs as if they were the crown jewels. Security guards herded the fans, both with and without basketballs, out of the enclosure. All of this was occurring, at least to Bill, on a vertical plane, since he lay on the blacktop, his head parallel to the cold, hard surface.

"Come on, buddy," a voice above and behind him urged. "Why don't you crawl home and sleep it off?"

A strong hand grasped Bill's left arm and lifted him to his feet, which formed an unstable platform for the rest of his lanky frame. Turning his head, which produced a sharp pain just behind his eyes as if someone had plunged a frozen climbing pick precisely between the sockets, Bill discerned that a security guard was brusquely helping him toward the enclosure's entrance.

Joining the procession out the gate, Bill stumbled out the opening and, turning abruptly right, prevented himself from collapsing by hanging onto the chain-link fence like a spider clinging to its web. As his mind cleared, he remembered all that had happened since he had awoken that morning eager to see the outcome of the third race at Exhibition Park, to put a fifty on the fight in Las Vegas or as Lester called it, Lost Wages, and to introduce his second-year class to the intricacies of the statistical analysis of two-draw poker. Yet all of that had paled compared to what had occurred: Sebastian and suitcase bombs, Dr. Villano, Hogarth and....Hogarth Ramen O'Leary Chevalier! Bill forced his mind to focus and his eyes to zero in on the blacktop near where he had so recently been snoozing. He remembered through the mists of recent time butting heads with the international terrorist, but now he could see neither jeans nor hair of the young threat to Western high-tech civilization. Where was he?

"Bill!" Lester strolled toward Bill as if he was out for a Sunday stroll on the Stanley Park seawall without a worry in the world.

"Where have you been?" Bill demanded, remembering Lester's publicly stated plan to find the cavalry and bring them at the gallop.

"I'm sorry, Bill. It took a while to find Tony."

"Tony?"

"Tony Chambers. He manages the locker rooms. Anyway, it took a while to find him because he wasn't down in the locker rooms. He was upstairs watching the game, like everyone else. Did you catch any of it?"

"Catch any of it?" Bill asked, his aggravation mounting. "I was battling international terrorists."

"Interesting," Lester said, glancing at his watch, "Love to hear your story, but I must be off. I'm meeting some friends at Jack Lonsdale's for a pint."

Bill stepped forward, steadied himself with a hand on the fence since his head was still throbbing from its encounter with Hogarth's boney melon, and said, "You're not going anywhere until you explain why you didn't bring a battalion of security guards to the rescue on the triple."

"I tried, Bill, I truly tried." Lester looked hurt that his declaration did not meet with immediate belief. "I found Tony, gave him the skinny, and he called Joe Cain and he—"

"Joe Cain?"

"Head of arena security. He and I go way back. I worked the Orpheum in those days and he was just a beat cop, but we hit it off. He needed tickets to the opera for his wife and, well, I knew some people."

"So you talked with the head of security," Bill said, his head not improving under the onslaught of Lester's opening argument for the defense in the case of Bill Rogers vs. Lester Means, re: lack of promised support against international terrorists.

"Joe listened to my story," Lester said. "Well, in truth, he listened with one ear, while with his other ear he listened to the game, and both his eyes were locked on the court. Anyway, despite my best efforts Joe didn't believe my story, at least until the game was over. But here they are." Lester nodded toward the security guards clearing the bus enclosure of fans, many of whom toted souvenir basketballs.

The phrase, too little, too late, sprang to Bill's bruised mind, but he just lowered his head. He wished he had just listened to Sebastian's story at the track and then bid him *bon chance*, while remaining at Exhibition Park to make a few well thought out investments on some finely bred equines. Life was so full of choices and it seemed so often you made the wrong one, especially when horses, betting or nephews were involved. "Have you seen the villain on the wanted poster?"

"Not a hair. I better get going. Isn't that Sebastian and his girlfriend?"

Bill looked at where Lester pointed. He spotted two men leading Sebastian and Rosa in handcuffs across the parking lot.

"Come on," Bill ordered.

"I have to get to Jack Lonsdale's. They're expecting me."

With a steel edge in his voice that Lester decided was better not to contradict, Bill said, "Their expectations are going to remain unfulfilled."

Chapter 32

Sebastian sat in jail contemplating the suitcase now resting in the mud at the bottom of False Creek. Had it contained a bomb? Had Villano and his terrorist sidekick planted a dud or had it all been a joke in the baddest of bad taste?

Unbeknownst to Sebastian, his heroic suitcase run from the Grizzly's Briar Rabbit Coach Line bus to False Creek had not been in vain. The suitcase had indeed contained enough explosives to rip the bus and all of its tall occupants, assuming the Grizzlies were aboard, into their constituent molecules. There was, however, little threat of the bomb going off any time soon for Hogarth had made a slight error in setting the timer. He had been crouched with a flashlight in the cargo bay of the bus surrounded by basketballs trying to set the bomb's timer via the tumblers on the suitcase, when Villano whispered, "Someone's coming."

Bill and Rosa had been approaching, startling Hogarth into alacrity, which far from suited his nervous temperament, especially at a time when accuracy was of the utmost importance.

"Hurry," Villano urged, standing just outside the bay holding two net bags full of basketballs, which they had discovered in the rear-most bay of the bus.

His hands trembling, Hogarth had tried to remember the exact time to which Villano had told him to set the timer. Villano had carefully calculated the perfect time to ensure the Grizzlies would be aboard the bus when the bomb blew. The only problem was that as soon as Villano hissed at Hogarth to hurry, the numbers, which Villano had carefully told Hogarth 17 times, jumbled around in the New Luddite terrorist's brain like dry bread crumbs in a blender set on puree.

"What time—," Hogarth began.

Before he could finish asking the crucial question, Villano ordered, "Just set it and get out of there!"

Hogarth did not try to ask Villano again given that the professor appeared to be in a rush and Hogarth had far from forgotten Villano's recent rudeness. Hogarth set the tumblers as best he could remember and slid back out of the bay. Villano gently thrust the basketballs into the bay to hide the suitcase as he quoted the Bard's Richard III, "'And thus I clothe my naked villainy.'" He had closed the bay door just in time to greet Bill and Rosa as they came around the corner of the bus.

Hogarth may have done his best, but the number that jumped into his head at the fateful moment was not 02:30, as Villano had ordered. Such a setting would have allowed ample time for the game to end and the Grizzlies to shower, dress and board the bus. Hogarth had set the tumblers to the combination he had used when he had secreted the suitcase in Sebastian's Omni in Blaine. Although he had been unable to recall without great mental effort the combination when he had been in the lab at the college even with the memory aid that it was the number of men on a basketball team, at least according to him, the number sprang to his mind like a young springbok as he crouched in the cargo bay of the bus. Therefore, when Sebastian made his dash with the suitcase, there was no chance it would explode anytime soon. In fact, it would not explode for just shy of 55 hours and 55 minutes.

Also unbeknownst to Sebastian, the bomb did not explode upon impact with the real water of the false creek because it was not an impact model. Impact models cost more than standard models, and Villano and Hogarth were funding a revolution out of their own shallow pockets. Corners had to be cut. It was always that way in the early stages of a revolution until the bandwagon effect kicks in.

The bomb did, in fact, explode two nights later—or more precisely, the very early morning of the third day after Sebastian's run. The explosion carved a crater in the muddy bottom of False Creek and erupted upward with a force powerful enough to prove that the name of a party boat passing overhead was invalid: the *Unsinkable Molly Brown*. Molly Brown may have survived the sinking of the *Titanic* to earn her sobriquet, but her namesake had a little less luck. The party boat sank. On that night, the Attorney's Orphan Society had rented the mis-christened *Unsinkable Molly*. Luckily for all concerned there were no orphans aboard that night, just a couple of firms' worth of attorneys. The explosion broke *Molly's* back and she sank in three minutes. Like their brethren the shark, however, all of the lawyers could swim, so no one drowned.

Sebastian knew nothing of this forthcoming event as he sat in jail the night of his arrest. He was worried about two things: the state of his marriage, and the whereabouts of Dr. Villano and Hogarth Ramen O'Leary Chevalier.

"Gianninni," a constable barked.

The officer opened the cell door, let Sebastian out and led the exhausted professor to a bank of telephones in a hall next to the holding cell. Reciting something he had said a thousand times, the constable explained, "You get one call; that means one completed call. Answering machines count, as do wrong numbers, calls to friends and relatives who don't have or who can't or won't provide bail. Good luck."

Sebastian glanced at the men using the other telephones. Their heads were bowed as they stared at the chipped and stained linoleum floor whispering arguments in defense of their recent behavior to whoever they hoped would bail them out. Sebastian kept his head high, for he had done nothing wrong. True, he had jaywalked, but only as a means of disposing of the suitcase bomb as promptly as possible. Ditto littering in False Creek. Where else was one to dispose of a bomb in the crowded confines of Vancouver, especially just after GM Place has emptied the contents of nearly 20,000 seats onto the neighboring streets, parking lots and sidewalks?

Sebastian picked up the phone as the man next to him, whom Sebastian could not fail to notice, finished his conversation.

"But I did it all for you," the man wailed.

Most of the other men in the tank wore clothes that appeared to have been recently slept or fallen down in. Not the man beside Sebastian. He was attired in an immaculate suit, right down to an exquisite red boutonniere. The detainee was small, barely 100 pounds, and Asian, with the groomed appearance of someone who has just stepped out of the Raffles Hotel in Singapore after a pink gin and a sedate game of gin rummy.

Sebastian's heart went out to the poor man, but evidently he had failed to arouse similar sympathy in the recipient of his telephone call.

"What am I supposed to do?" the man asked. "I've used my one and only phone call."

The other party apparently offered no sound advice. Defeated and dejected, the man hung up and an RCMP constable escorted him back to his cell to be held until....until when?

Sebastian now realized the gravity of the decision before him. If he called the wrong person, he might end up in jail until his court date. Given he had broken an international agreement, he might have to await a court date at the International Court of Justice at The Hague, which was especially busy at the moment trying all sorts of war criminals from that most recent fracas in the Balkans, not to mention the many and sordid troubles all over the world, save Antarctica. When would his little littering at sea and infringement of the Law of Sea Convention fit into the court's busy schedule? 2066? 2096?

The constable returned from the cells and Sebastian, curious and wishing to delay having to decide whom to call, asked, "Whom did that gentleman call?"

"Gentleman?" the constable asked, never having heard the word applied to any of his brood.

"The man you just escorted back to the holding cell."

"Oh, him. He called his bail bondsman."

Sebastian frowned. "But he told whomever he called that he committed the crime for him."

"For her, you mean. He's the Red Fly."

Sebastian frowned. He did not recognize the sobriquet.

"The Red Fly is the finest second-story man China ever produced. He came over here to try his luck in the materialistic West and did pretty well, until he got caught."

"'A thirst for gold, / The beggar's vice, / which can but overwhelm / The meanest hearts.'"

"Huh?"

"Byron."

"Had a Byron in here once; caught him scratching graffiti on a courthouse column. Said something about having done it at Sounion, why not here? Don't know what it has to do with the Red Fly, though."

"He did the crime, so he had to do the time, as they say," Sebastian said, shaking his head at the old story of crime not paying particularly well in the long run. "And now, barely out of prison, he's in the thick of it again, facing an even longer stretch on the inside; a three-time loser."

"Nope, his lawyer is the best. He's never been inside more than an hour. He used Sandy O'Rourke's Bail Bond Service. He got one look at Sandy's black hair, dark eyes and that body and the Red Fly couldn't stop thinking about her."

"So he tried to go straight, but couldn't stay on the straight and narrow," Sebastian said, again shaking his head at the old story of the career criminal trying to go straight for the love of a good woman and failing.

"Nope, he kept working as a thief—Sandy didn't care, she's used to associating with that element—but he couldn't get a date with Sandy, so he started letting himself get arrested so Sandy would come down and bail him out. It wasn't a date, but at least he got to see her. He even started dressing for the occasion."

"That explains the suit and the boutonniere."

"Yeah, we found him in a tux a few weeks ago sitting on the ledge of the thirteenth floor of the O'Keeffe building downtown singing *Danny Boy* and spinning a necklace he'd recently acquired from a jewelry store vault on the sixth floor. We confiscated the necklace, but he got real upset when we tried to confiscate a diamond ring he had in his pocket. Turned out he had a receipt for it, not to mention the little velvet box you only get when you buy a ring."

"He actually bought a ring instead of stealing one?"

The jailor nodded. "We checked. He was planning to ask Sandy to marry him. Unfortunately for the Fly, she doesn't reciprocate his feelings, but he's such a good client, Sandy said she'd think about it."

"Sounds like she's finished thinking," Sebastian said sadly. "She turned him down for bail."

"That's gonna hurt Sandy's business, not to mention make it a damn sight harder for us to catch the Red Fly."

The concerned constable went on his way, leaving Sebastian once again facing the difficult choice of whom to contact. He thought of Bill, last seen lying in the bus enclosure. Sebastian hoped that by now someone had found and helped the elderly professor as he lay in the oil alongside the Grizzly bus. At the least, the bus driver must have rolled Bill out of the way to avoid driving over him, but Sebastian could not be certain and worried about the fate of his favorite uncle. In any case, Bill was probably in no condition to answer the phone, although he did always have ample cash around to cover Sebastian's bail, even if Sebastian faced city, provincial, federal and international charges.

Sebastian then thought of Elizabeth, but feared she would hang up on him upon hearing his first words, even if they were, "Let me explain." Who else was there? Lester's whereabouts were unknown and Rosa had been arrested with Sebastian, although she languished in a separate cell for women somewhere else in the labyrinthine Vancouver lockup.

Sebastian decided. He would have to rely on the woman who knew him best, the woman who had always forgiven him his minor transgressions and, he devoutly prayed, the woman who would categorize jaywalking and littering at sea as nothing more than high-spirited high jinx.

The phone rang and rang. Was she even at home? Had she already concluded from the presence of two women in his office that he was a debauched adulterer and left him?

"Hello?"

"Elizabeth. It's me, Sebastian. I got rid of the bomb."

His declaration of success was met by a buzzing silence.

"Elizabeth?"

"We need to talk, Sebastian. Where are you?"

"I'm actually somewhat detained at the moment."

"Too detained to try to save our marriage?"

"Well, in point of fact, yes. I'm in jail."

"What?!"

"I hurled the bomb into False Creek and the police arrested me for jaywalking and littering at sea."

"Didn't you explain?"

"I didn't think that was wise. Do you remember the suitcase that was in the back of my car this morning at the border?"

"The one I sat on to take orders for your novels?"

"That's the one. The bomb was in it. Villano used me to smuggle it into Canada, so if I try to explain it all to the police, they might put two and two together and conclude I smuggled the bomb across the border only to appear to save the day—or night—at the arena."

"Did it explode?"

"No, not that I know of," Sebastian said, still puzzled by that development or lack thereof.

"When will you be home? We need to talk."

"I know, but I need someone to post bail."

Trying to decide once again whether Sebastian was true to her or truly despicable, Elizabeth decided that at the very least he did not deserve to rot in jail amongst the riff-raff, ruffians and rogues that she feared inhabited lockups.

An hour later, she was at the booking desk, checkbook in hand as a warder brought Sebastian out of the holding cell. Sebastian went to hug her, but she sidestepped the hug with a move a franchise NFL running back would have envied.

"Can we bail out Mrs. Turnbell, too?" Sebastian asked as he reached for the envelope from the booking sergeant filled with what had been in his pockets when he was arrested.

Elizabeth froze, her pen half way through the bond figure as she wrote her check. Her voice like ice, she asked, "Rosa Turnbell was arrested *with* you?"

"Yes, she was helping me dispose of the bomb."

Elizabeth's anger and sense of betrayal returned with full force. "You got arrested with that woman? The woman who hugged me this morning, thinking I was you? The woman who was in your office to give you a surprise this afternoon in the company of yet another woman?"

"They are our neighbors, dear."

"And you decided to get arrested with her. Or is that just a neighborly thing to do?"

"You don't really decide to get arrested. The police make the decision for you. I had the suitcase and Rosa met me…"

"You had a suitcase all packed to meet her and fly off to some romantic destination, did you?"

"No, no, I…."

"First, she's at the front door hugging me because she thinks I'm you," Elizabeth ranted, attracting the attention of every constable, corporal, staff sergeant, inspector, and felon in the station, "then her daughter is at the back door hugging me because she thinks I'm you, home for a mid-morning *manage a trois*."

"There was no *trois*, not even a *duex*."

"Only because you were at work. They saw your car in the driveway and thought you were home for your regular romantic morning with the Turnbell duo. It's sickening. Then they both pop up in your office this afternoon. Did I spoil your morning tryst at home, so you rescheduled for the afternoon at your office?"

Dumbfounded, shocked and appalled, Sebastian stood, open mouthed, staring at his beloved wife as he tried to pick a place to begin his case for the defense.

"Well?" Elizabeth spat, snapping shut her checkbook and thrusting it back into her purse. "You may as well just spend the night here with your neighbor, Ms. Turnbell. And is Destiny here too?"

"You aren't going to post bail?" the booking sergeant asked, still holding the envelope with Sebastian's belongings inches from Sebastian's outstretched hand.

"For all I care, the philanderer and his hussy can rot in here forever."

"Elizabeth—," Sebastian began to plead.

"Our marriage is over. I'm leaving you, which should make you happy. You'll be free to have affairs with every woman on the planet, not that a wife appears to have slowed you down any."

"Elizabeth—"

"I'll find a nice, boring man without a romantic thought in his head. At least then I'll be able to trust him with my love." With that, Elizabeth spun on her heel and stalked out the door.

Devastated, Sebastian watched with disbelieving eyes as the booking sergeant pulled back the envelope containing Sebastian's meager belongings and gestured at the corporal. Escorted back to his cell, Sebastian sat between two rather portly, smelly gentlemen and pondered the state of his marriage.

"Gianninni," the sergeant called.

Puzzled, Sebastian emerged from the holding cell once again, like a drowning man on his second gasp for air, and followed the non-commissioned officer to the booking desk. This time, Bill and Lester awaited him. Sebastian was relieved to see Bill up, alive and walking.

"I saw Elizabeth heading out as I came in," Bill said in lieu of a greeting. "If I were you, I wouldn't be in any rush to get home. She looked a tad angry."

"Unless you want a few weeks off," Lester added, "in traction."

"It's all a terrible misunderstanding," Sebastian said, eager to get home, crawl into bed, and die a prompt and painless death as soon as he explained everything to Elizabeth.

"That's what I always tell my wife, 'It's a misunderstanding,'" Lester said, shaking his head. "I'd suggest an entirely different approach in these situations."

"These situations?" Sebastian asked, as the booking sergeant handed him the envelope containing the former contents of his pockets.

"Women, not your wife, appearing at home and in offices; bombs on buses; lively sporting events; arrest and a night in jail," Lester rattled off the litany. "Pretty routine."

Sebastian took his watch, wallet, keys and change out of the envelope. "Do your evenings usually include fights with international terrorists?"

"Not generally," Lester admitted. "Although I did lose a fortune on the Red Army hockey team back in their heyday; an international battle, so to speak."

"Why would you ever bet against the Big Red Machine?" Bill asked, always interested in betting strategies.

"Patriotism," Lester admitted ruefully. "I could never pass up the chance to put a few hundred on Team Canada against the Ruskies."

"You can never let emotion get in the way of placing an objective, scientific bet," Bill advised in the tone he usually reserved for his most learned statements in his statistics classes about poker, horse racing or craps.

"Don't I know it. Back in the eighties, I even sent some money to the Contras in Nicaragua to try and undermine that bloody Red Army team. No one was more relieved than me when the Soviets cashed in their chips."

"I'm sorry to interrupt this discussion on a subject dear to both your hearts and minds," Sebastian said, "but did you also pay Mrs. Turnbell's bail?"

"I didn't even pay yours," Bill said with a grin.

Sebastian did not follow.

"Sergeant V.J. Singh, here," Bill said, gesturing at the grinning desk sergeant, "is a regular at the cricket matches at Stanley Park on Sundays."

Sebastian debated whether to inquire further into this potential quagmire of a story but decided that after the day he had experienced one more story could do no further harm to his battered mind, body and soul.

Bill leaned in close to Sebastian and whispered, "Sergeant Singh placed a rather substantial bet with Lester a few Sundays ago and, shall we say, the wicket was rather sticky for his chosen team."

Sebastian turned to Lester. "You reveal newfound depth, Lester. I wasn't aware you were a cricket aficionado."

"It's about the only game in town on Sunday morning this time of year. I tried getting a line on the boccie games at Stanley Park, but there just aren't enough spectators to get a good book going."

"And Mrs. Turnbell?" Sebastian struggled to return by the direct route to the issue at hand.

"I would've been glad to exercise my influence with Sergeant Singh on her behalf, but her husband has already been here to provide for her release."

Sebastian had no doubt that Mr. Turnbell had actually paid the bail, unlike Lester's more unconventional approach to the issue.

"I assume I'll owe you something for this favor," Sebastian told Lester as the trio made their way out of the stationhouse to Bill's Cadillac.

"As luck would have it, it appears it is I who should be begging your forgiveness and asking if I owe you anything further," Lester replied gallantly.

They climbed into Bill's spacious car and Sebastian, too tired to follow Lester's line of thought, merely frowned, trying to clear his mind and relax his body.

"It appears the birthday gift I procured for your uncle to give to you was, shall we say, damaged goods," Lester explained.

"You mean the stolen office chair?" Sebastian asked as he reclined in the back seat. Lester stretched out beside Bill in the front.

"The chair was merely borrowed," Lester explained, "until the president could procure a model more suited to his exalted station."

"Then you're not sorry you stole his chair?"

"Of course not; he ended up with a better chair. A very fine model. And I did not actually steal it."

"Then why do you owe me anything?"

"Bill informed me the chair was stained. I should have cleaned it before passing it along to your uncle to give to you. I offer you a full apology and ask if you'll be kind enough to consider us even after my small favor to you tonight?"

"Lester," Sebastian said as he closed his eyes, "I don't think you are even with anyone in this entire province, let alone in this city. Either you owe them a favor or they owe you. I would be happy to consider us even, but I fear it will never be true."

Chapter 33

The Cadillac stopped and Sebastian was awakened by the gentle rocking of the suspension. He sat up and realized he was still far from home.

"'O sleep!'" Sebastian exclaimed, blearily. "'It is a gentle thing, / Beloved from pole to pole!' Coleridge might have found it from pole to pole, but I can't find it anywhere. Where are we?"

"Le Crab," Lester announced. "I'm meeting some people for a late snack. I was detained from making it to Jack Lonsdale's, my usual post-game spot, but Le Crab's open all night."

Bill said, "I thought it best if you gave Elizabeth a little time to cool off."

"I really want to talk to her," Sebastian said as he reluctantly climbed out of the back seat.

"Ah, Sebastian," Lester said. "'Fly not yet, 'tis just the hour / When pleasure, like the midnight flower / That scorns the eye of vulgar light, / Begins to bloom for sons of night.'"

Sebastian stopped, dumbfounded. "Lester, you know Thomas Moore?"

"Just a few apt quotations from Moore, Keats and some other wordsmiths. In fact, I live by Browning's, 'And gain is gain, however small.'"

"How did you ever learn those quotations?"

"I found it helped in my line of work, so I got a book of quotations from a friend of a friend and spent some time reading up on pertinent entries," Lester said as he led the way inside the restaurant. "I find it helps impress a certain class of people who might otherwise look down on a custodial engineer, let alone do business with one."

"I'm impressed," Sebastian admitted.

Inside the small, exclusive restaurant, the *maitre de* greeted Lester with a hug and a kiss on each cheek as if he was a son who had been reported killed in the wars a decade before only to reappear on the doorstep late one stormy night. Lester stood in the entry, his eyes wide with joy, nose inhaling the aroma of fine cuisine.

"'And gazed around them to the left and right / With the prophetic eye of appetite,'" Sebastian recited.

"That's a good one," Lester said. "Who scribbled that?"

"Scribbled?" Sebastian demanded, barely believing his ears.

"Wrote, penned, authored; whatever you want to call it."

"Took down word for word from the mouth of God, you mean?"

"If you like."

"Byron, from *Don Juan.*"

Lester nodded and scanned the diners in the room, but came up empty.

"Is Tony Lonegon here?" he asked.

The *maitre de*, in coat and tails as if he had stepped out of a Victorian club in the heart of London in 1876, shook his head: no.

Lester rattled off a bewildering list of names to which, at the mention of each, the *maitre de* shook his head sadly: no.

"I guess it'll be a table for three then," the disappointment clear in Lester's voice. He was not a man used to dining with a measly pair of acquaintances.

"But of course, Mr. Means," the *maitre de* said, as he led the way through the restaurant.

As he trailed Bill, who trailed Lester, who trailed the *maitre de*, Sebastian hoped there would be no free tables. He really just wanted Bill to take him home or, barring that, he considered calling a cab, although he did not know if he could convince a driver to cross the border to Blaine. Did they issue international taxi driver licenses? As they threaded past table after table of nattily dressed diners, his hopes rose that there would be no free table and, therefore, a free Bill to perform chauffeur duties.

The *maitre de* stopped at a long table with a dozen empty chairs next to a picture window looking out on a small, yet tasteful, garden lit by a dozen soft lights. The linen was an immaculate white, the silverware sparkled and subtly aromatic candles flickered along the center of the table. It reminded Sebastian of Coleridge, 'In Xanadu did Kubla Khan, A stately pleasure-dome decree.'

"I expect your party will grow," the *maitre de* told Lester, visibly reinvigorating the custodial engineer's spirits.

"You're too kind," Lester said, slipping the *maitre de* a tip, which the man refused as if the very thought of a tip gave offense.

"No, no, no, Mr. Means, I still owe you for that help with my daughter's wedding. I will be forever in your debt, as will my children and my children's children unto the tenth generation."

"Nonsense, Ildefonso," Lester said, pressing the $20 bill into the *maitre de*'s hand.

"I cannot accept it, Mr. Means."

"Send over a bottle of wine and we'll both be satisfied."

"But of course. You always know how to settle a minor disagreement between friends."

The *maitre de* retired, leaving Bill, Sebastian and Lester to sit at the end of the long table like squatters in a ghost town, while around them the restaurant bustled with activity and sparkling conversations.

"You helped him with his daughter's wedding?" Bill asked, starting to construct yet another hand-rolled cigarette.

"It was nothing," Lester said, picking up a menu and perusing its culinary wonders.

"Nothing for you usually means you arranged for her to be married by the Archbishop of Canterbury in St. Paul's Cathedral with Prince Philip as best man and the Prince of Wales as ring bearer," Sebastian said. As his mind started working again after his nap in the back of the Caddy, he realized he was still rather miffed that Lester had deserted them and left Bill, Rosa, Destiny and himself to face the international terrorists alone.

"Actually his daughter had been divorced and it meant a great deal to her mother that she be married the second time in the church," Lester explained. "I just called a bishop I'm acquainted with in passing and the thing was done. Nothing really, just a phone call."

"What Lester is far too modest to mention," Bill said as he added tobacco from his pouch to his creation, "is that Ildefonso's daughter married her lover in the church. A charming, young lady...her lover, that is."

"I think you could call a few friends and produce world peace by morning," Sebastian said, drinking mineral water from his Waterford crystal goblet as the *maitre de* returned with a bottle of wine.

"It's from Tuscany and although it's a tad young—1876—the bouquet, the body and the flavor, I've been assured, are all of a markedly superior quality," the *maitre de* extolled as he handed Lester the cork and poured a small amount for tasting.

Lester sniffed the cork to ensure the wine had aged as advertised and not, through some horrific accident, turned to vinegar. After first inhaling its bouquet, he sampled a taste of the proffered ambrosia.

"I shall die happy if I'm felled this instant," Lester announced, beaming, his eyes mere slits.

Smiling in return, the *maitre de* poured them all wine and said, "Before you order, would you and your friends care to inspect our secret kitchen?"

"I'd like to stay here and keep an eye out for some friends I'm expecting, but I'm sure my close friends Bill and Sebastian would be more than happy to accept your exceedingly kind offer."

Still exhausted even after his nap, Sebastian did not feel like accepting any offer except that of sleep.

"Come on, Sebastian," Bill said, sounding like a little boy calling for his best friend to come see the circus. "Le Crab is world famous for its secret kitchen. Only a handful of people have ever seen it."

"I'd rather not. Thanks anyway."

"You have to come," Bill urged, coming over to his nephew's chair and pulling it out from under him.

"Bill—"

"Professor-Uncle Bill to you. This is a once-in-a-lifetime opportunity. Come on, young man."

They were beginning to make a scene, so Sebastian reluctantly followed Bill, as they trailed the *maitre de* to the rear of the restaurant.

"Michelin just came out," the *maitre de* whispered. "We earned five stars for the fourth year in a row. Not that I'd ever mention it."

"Of course not," Bill agreed. He gave up his effort to roll a cigarette while he walked and dumped the failed attempt on the tray of a waiter who was headed back to the kitchen after clearing a table. At least, that was the direction Bill hoped the waiter was headed or he had just garnished some diner's meal with tobacco and rolling paper.

"'And nearer as they came, a genial savour / Of certain stews and roast-meats, and pilaus,'" Sebastian recited, his spirits reviving at the aroma. "'Things which in hungry mortals' eyes find favour.'"

The *maitre de* opened a swinging door and led Bill and Sebastian into a narrow room. It was nondescript save for a row of silver serving doors on the left wall. Pressed against the right wall beside Bill and Ildefonso, Sebastian realized the metal serving doors opened into the kitchen. He could see no regular door into the kitchen, but there had to be one, unless the chef lived in his secret kitchen.

"The doors ensure the secrecy of Chef Bob's secret recipes," Ildefonso explained proudly. "As the waiters take the food, the serving door closes on the kitchen side, so no one can peek into the secret kitchen. That way, no one can steal his secrets."

"Can we meet Chef Bob?" Bill pleaded.

Bill, Sebastian realized, was far more interested than Sebsatian in the secret kitchen and Chef Bob. Lester had probably sparked Bill's interest with some outlandish story of Chef Bob whipping up a dinner for the Prime Minister of Canada one night and high tea for the Queen of England the next day, between snacks for

Lester and the Sultan of Brunei after Mr. Means had put in a hard day of wheeling and dealing with the occasional spot of janitorial duties at the college.

"I think we might be able to arrange a meeting," Ildefonso said, "for close friends of Mr. Means."

Instead of leading Bill and Sebastian through a hidden door into the secret kitchen, however, Ildefonso darted between an incoming and an outgoing waiter. He lifted one of the silver serving doors half way. By bending down and peering through the hatch he could see into the secret kitchen.

"Chef Bob," Ildefonso called sweetly. "Mr. Means would like you to meet two of his close friends."

Ildefonso gestured for Bill and Sebastian to approach the tiny window into the hallowed kitchen. Bill made it safely between two swiftly moving waiters but Sebastian, slowed by the day's taxing events, clipped a waiter's tray on his journey across the narrow room. The tray and its fresh load of Chef Bob's English-Hungarian fusion food—corned-beef goulash with bangers and chips—crashed to the floor with an ear-splitting cacophony. Shocked, Sebastian jumped back as the waiter spun on his heel and, instead of turning on Sebastian, roared at Ildefonso in some foreign tongue, possibly Cockney.

Ildefonso gave as good as he got and Sebastian understood the gist of the lively conversation from their impressive and accomplished body language. The waiter questioned Ildefonso's decision to bring customers into the sacred, if small, serving room, while Ildefonso, in no uncertain words, defended his decision. Sebastian was prevented from retreating entirely from the room only by the mess on the floor left by the waiter's fumbled tray.

After two other waiters had mopped up the worst of the debris, Sebastian was about to flee when Ildefonso unilaterally declared victory and, turning his back on the still gesticulating waiter whom Sebastian had clipped, returned to his mission of introducing Bill and Sebastian to Chef Bob.

The introductions did not go well. With Chef Bob in the kitchen and Bill and Sebastian in the narrow room, each tried to raise the service door higher to get a better view of the other as Ildefonso performed the introductions. Bill lost his grip on the small door he was holding and it slammed down with a crash on his side as Chef Bob, the resistance gone, flipped up his side.

Bill reached over to the next service door and lifted it up halfway for a peek. He had barely bent over to take his much sought-after look into the secret kitchen when two things happened: Chef Bob saw one of the service doors into his secret kitchen rise half way. Someone was sneaking a look at his rare, imported ingredients, personally designed kitchen implements and unique cooking style. He could not countenance a spy. He reached over and jerked the serving door up to seal off his kitchen from the prying eyes of the would-be peeping gourmet. Just as the chef acted to defend his domain, a waiter reached around Bill for a tray in the serving well. Bill extricated his hand in time but the waiter, reaching deep into the same well, was not so lucky. As Chef Bob jerked up, the stainless steel door slammed down and caught the waiter's fingers. The waiter screamed, reeled back and collided with another waiter as he went by, spilling his tray right beside where the other two waiters had just completed their mop job on the food from the first dropped tray.

Two more waiters piled in through the swinging door, knocking one of the mop-wielding waiters off balance as he stood to admire his just completed clean-up job, only to see it ruined by a new mess. The waiter fell forward into Ildefonso, who only managed to avoid knocking Bill over when the Professor-Uncle executed a sprightly jump over the crouching waiter with the crushed fingers.

Pressed against the wall, Sebastian watched the carnage like a Roman emperor at a lions versus Christians matinee. In this case, however, the carnage was more of a culinary than bloody variety. The waiters verbally fell upon one another as they blamed each other with equal vigor for the various messes and injuries each had, or had nearly, sustained. After apologizing profusely to the waiter with the bruised fingers, Bill snuck past Sebastian and, with a whispered, "I'm going to the head," flitted out of the disaster-plagued room.

Seeing Ildefonso engulfed in an argument with several waiters and deciding the secret kitchen was not worth quite this much trouble, Sebastian slipped out and returned to Lester, who now sat at a full table with only two spare chairs: those for Bill and Sebastian.

After a round of introductions that failed to lodge any names anywhere in Sebastian's exhausted brain, Lester asked, "Did you see the secret kitchen?"

"No, not really," Sebastian said.

Lester looked around. "Where's Bill?"

"We ran into some trouble," Sebastian admitted, glancing around with a hunted expression. "Bill tried to look a little too closely into the secret kitchen and Chef Bob took offense. He and Bill got into an argument and in his anger Bill slammed one of the serving doors down on a waiter's finger."

Shocked and undoubtedly fearing the demise of his cozy and tasty relationship with Le Crab and its internationally renowned chef, Lester exclaimed, "My God! Is the waiter alright?"

Just then the waiter, a white towel stained with a bright red splotch of Chef Bob's secret seafood salad sauce wrapped around his fingers, strode past.

Rising, Lester called, "I'm so sorry, Gilbért. Please, forgive me and my acquaintances!"

Sebastian did not fail to note his demotion from close friend a few minutes before to mere acquaintance in Lester's pantheon of relations.

"It's just part of the restaurant business," Gilbért replied, with a cheery wave of his wounded and apparently bleeding hand.

"'For he on honey-dew hath fed, And drunk the milk of paradise' here at Le Crab," Sebastian told Lester, savoring the moment. "But 'nevermore, quoth the raven, nevermore.'"

Lester sat down heavily. "Where's Bill?" he asked, the enormity of the situation sinking in with devastating effect. His culinary future appeared as a desert: dry and tasteless, at least in relation to Le Crab.

"They're holding him in the kitchen," Sebastian said with a worried glance toward the swinging door that led to the narrow room with the serving doors. The waiters and Ildefonso, still waging the War of Assigning Blame for the Tray Disasters, still could be heard arguing within. "I barely got out without a beating myself."

Appalled, Lester demanded, "How could you abandon your uncle like that?"

Lester's friends at the table, listening with rapt attention, all turned on Sebastian as if he was the worst form of human being since Attila led his Hun on a Roman holiday and set civilization back a few centuries.

"Easy," Sebastian said, taking a sip of water to prolong the juicy moment, "the same way you left him, and me, at GM Place to face international terrorists alone."

Sebastian stared at Lester with a wicked grin. Lester sat in deep, disbelieving shock as the entire table fell silent.

"What's everyone having?" Bill asked, breaking the silence upon his return from the restroom and resuming his seat at the now full table.

Lester gawked at the uninjured Bill.

Recalling Thomas Moore, Sebastian recited, "'Oh, colder than the wind that freezes / Founts, that but now in sunshine play'd, / Is that congealing pang which seizes / The trusting bosom, when betrayed.'"

Chapter 34

An hour later, after much urging from Sebastian, Bill was driving his nephew home with Lester sprawled out in the front seat.

"Maybe we should try going to the police again," Sebastian suggested, lounging in the back of the Caddy.

"They sure believed your tale last time," Lester said contentedly, recovered from Sebastian's joke and pleasantly plump from their meal at Le Crab.

"I'm sure Villano is getting out of the country as fast as his credit card can buy a ticket," Bill predicted.

"I hope so," Sebastian said, fighting to keep his eyes open after his long day and even longer night, and lulled by the rhythmic hum of the Cadillac's powerful engine. He only sought 'to sleep, perchance to dream.' He was even tired enough to use quotes from *Hamlet*.

They reached the border, which was almost deserted at this late hour. The white Peace Arch was lit, creating a stunning spectacle as they drove at 15 mph through the park and across the border. Bill stopped and waited for the single car ahead of them to be admitted to the land of the free and the home of the brave or was it the land of the brave and home of the free—and what difference did it really make?

"Good evening, good sir," Bill said with a grin as he stopped at the US border inspection booth.

The bored guard looked up at the grinning Canadian in the Big Bird yellow Cadillac. "How long are planning to stay in the United States?"

"About 10 minutes."

"Ten minutes? What are going to do in 10 minutes?"

"Drop off my nephew," Bill replied, gesturing at Sebastian in the back seat, "and buy some cheap gas and tobacco."

"Is this a bachelor party prank or something?" the guard asked, remembering the morning he found a stripper and a naked soon-to-be-ex-groom (as soon as his soon-to-be-ex-bride heard about it) handcuffed to the gates of the Peace Arch. The guard would have preferred a nude stripper and a clothed groom, but the reverse still made for an eventful morning, especially when the guards had difficulty cutting the handcuffs off the couple. The five busloads of school children from Point Roberts who arrived to see the sights in the park certainly saw some sights.

"No party," Bill said. "He's been married 19 years."

"I doubt I'll make 20," Sebastian moaned as he considered his imminent meeting with Elizabeth, if she had not fled from their marital home forever.

The guard leaned into the car and peered back at Sebastian. "Aren't you that romance writer?"

"Sort of." With Elizabeth heavy on his mind, Sebastian asked what she would have asked, "Would you like to buy a book?"

"No thanks, I bought some this morning, but my wife would love your autograph. She loves romances. Has so many I used some for kindling last winter and she didn't even notice any were missing."

The guard handed a pen and pad back to Sebastian, who debated how to take the compliment of being asked for an autograph by a man who burned books, and romances no less. Bowing to his desire to get home as soon as international travel would allow, he asked, "What's your wife's name?"

"We aren't supposed to give out any personal information, sir."

Sebastian suppressed a sigh. "To whom should I address the autograph?"

"Oh, Marjorie Sinkweather-Smith."

Balancing the pad on his knee, Sebastian wrote, "To Marjorie Sinkweather-Smith, With all my love and passion, Sebastian LeClerc Gianninni." It was what he thought an internationally famous romance writer would write to an admiring fan. It was, he had to admit, his first autograph, so he was rather new at such endeavors.

The guard took the pad and read it. A look of confusion, followed by suspicion crept over his face. "Do you know my wife?"

"I can't say I've ever had the undoubted pleasure."

The guard peered back at Sebastian again, his hand on his gun holster. "Do you work nights?"

"No, he's a professor," Bill said, tiring of the exchange. He wanted to get home in time to change and get out to the Abbotsford track for an early meeting he had arranged with the country's top harness-racing trainer. He hoped the trainer would have some suggestions for adding crucial but apparently missing variables in order to perfect his Grand Unifying Theory of Harness Racing. It still did not work as well as some early versions of his Grand Unifying Theory of Horse Racing.

"A professor, huh," the guard said. "Does he teach all day?"

"All day?" Lester asked with a chuckle, still smarting from Sebastian's prank at Le Crab. "Both these guys are profs and they could hold down another full-time job without breaking a sweat."

"So he could find time for some visiting during the day?"

Sebastian thought he knew where the guard was headed. His wife would probably love a visit from a romance writer. "Yes, I could arrange to meet your wife on some mutually agreed upon afternoon."

"I knew it," the guard roared. "You're the bastard Marjorie's been messing around with!"

"I have never even met your wife, sir," Sebastian countered, shocked and appalled at the accusation.

"I think we may have to inspect your car, sir," the guard said, his face as hard as flint. "Every nut and every bolt."

"I give you my word as a gentleman, I have never even met your wife."

"I'm supposed to believe a philandering womanizer?"

"Strange, those were exactly the words his wife used today," Lester whispered *sotto voce* to Bill.

"Please pull over to the inspection area, sir. Now!"

Even though Lester had been enjoying Sebastian's discomfort, the gravity of the situation now struck him like an anvil dropped from a stepladder onto his chest. What had been an opportunity to get back at Sebastian for the Le Crab episode had now assumed dire, even grave significance. Lester needed to get home for an early morning appointment with a first mate about a hold full of salmon. Lester needed the fish to repay the manager of the Queen Elizabeth theatre for a dozen dress-circle seats to the season's operas. He needed the opera tickets to trade to four strippers who dated four different concert promoters who could get Lester front-row floor seats to the next four major rock concerts in Vancouver. A simple deal, but worth a small fortune in transaction fees to Lester, not to mention a potential fortune in favors paid and owed. Lester motioned for the guard to journey over to his side of the car. The officer hesitated, then after three more come-hither gestures from Lester, undertook the journey around the Cadillac's massive hood, approximately the distance from Vancouver to Toronto via California and Florida.

"Officer Smith," Lester began.

"I'm Officer Sinkweather."

Sebastian opened his mouth to ask if it was not tradition for women to go first but decided it might not be prudent to ask. Possibly such etiquette did not apply to the merging of last names upon marriage.

Swiftly adjusting to the name change, Lester said, "Officer Sinkweather, if I may be so bold, I would put it to you that Sebastian could not have dallied with your wife."

"Why not?" the guard demanded, giving the impression he would not believe any excuse save the possibility that Sebastian was actually the Pope in disguise.

Lester and the guard held a brief whispered conference. Sebastian and Bill wondered what they were talking about, especially when the guard cast several curious and then somewhat concerned looks at Sebastian. A few moments later, the guard stepped back, staring at Sebastian and ordered, "Proceed." He waved Bill forward as if he was getting rid of a car filled with bubonic plague victims in their most contagious state.

"Never fear," Sebastian called out to the guard as Bill eased the car forward. "Whomever she may or may not be involved with, give your wife another chance! People make mistakes. Try some romance! I'm sure she still loves you!"

Bill grabbed the back of Sebastian's jacket as he leaned out the window shouting to the guard and hauled his nephew back into the car. "Get back in here. We're lucky to get out of there with my Nancy in one piece." Nancy was Bill's nickname for his beloved car. "Thanks for getting us out of there, Lester."

"No problem."

"I think it's time you two shook hands and called a truce," Bill said, menace in his words.

Sebastian glared at Lester, but then reconsidered and gallantly offered his hand to Lester. "I apologize for the prank at Le Crab."

Lester relented and shook Sebastian's hand. "Sorry about watching a few seconds of the Grizzly game before getting the guards to rush on over to the bus. I've always had a slight betting problem."

"Says the man who bets on which rain drop will reach the bottom of the window first," Sebastian said.

"There's nothing else to do when Exhibition Park is rained out," Lester countered indignantly.

"There's car roulette," Bill suggested.

"Car roulette?" Sebastian asked.

"Betting which color car will come around the corner next," Lester explained. "I always bet white, since white cars are by far the most common cars."

"How sporting of you."

"Always wise to research the particulars of a bet before you put your money down," Bill advised "What did you tell the border guard to get us out of there?" Bill asked, hoping to calm the simmering war between Lester and Sebastian as he turned up B Street toward Sebastian's house.

"I told him Sebastian was a mathematical autistic savant degenerative; MASD for short."

"MASD?" Sebastian asked in disbelief.

"I said the college hired you as a mathematician, because it is the one area where you're a genius. Other than that, I told him you're a slobbering, imbecilic nut who eats cereal boxes for breakfast instead of the cereal."

"Thanks, Lester, and I was leaning out the window yelling marriage counseling advice to him. They'll never let me cross the border again."

"I think that probably lent some credence to my story," Lester said with a self-satisfied grin.

"That's strange," Bill said as they drove along Sebastian's block. "The lights are on at your house."

"Elizabeth is probably packing her things to leave me," Sebastian said, too dejected at the prospect to even look.

"I don't think so," Bill said, slowing down.

The front door of Sebastian's house was wide open. Every few seconds objects sailed out the doorway like grapeshot from a double-shotted cannon.

"Unless she has a very strange way of packing."

Chapter 35

"What's going on?" Sebastian asked, his curiosity piqued as he tried to get a better view.

"Looks like Elizabeth is forcibly evicting you," Lester observed as they approached the house.

"Or it's the world's messiest thief," Bill said in wonder as he watched projectiles hurtle out the front door. "I didn't think you could throw a filing cabinet drawer that far."

"She'll probably meet me at the door with her great uncle's .22 leveled at my belly," Sebastian said.

"As long as she isn't aiming any lower," Lester said with a wry grin.

"At least she isn't your great Uncle Jimmy," Bill said as he stopped the car in front of the house and took out his tobacco pouch and rolling paper.

"Great Uncle Jimmy?" Sebastian asked, happy to delay what he expected would be a short, but loud and possibly bruising confrontation with Elizabeth.

"He and Mary were not the happiest of couples," Bill explained as he sprinkled tobacco from his pouch in an uneven row onto a paper. "They were poor and couldn't afford a divorce, let alone pay for houses for each of them to live in separately. So great Uncle Jimmy sawed the house in half."

"You mean physically sawed it?" Sebastian asked as he watched his belongings bounce, thud and roll across his front lawn in the moonlight.

"Yeah," Bill said. "That was the Rogers side of the family. Stubborn as a mule crossed with a donkey and with a memory that'd do a herd of elephants proud, especially of an offense against their person, pride or beliefs."

"So they lived in different parts of the house?" Lester asked.

"She had the rear half, including the kitchen, and he had the front room. They each had a bedroom upstairs, but he had to get to his by climbing a ladder outside, since the stairs fell under her domain."

"How long did that go on?"

"Not long," Bill said, licking the rolling paper to seal his newest misshapen creation. "About 34 years. By then, Jimmy was 94, so he couldn't handle the ladder anymore, especially in the winter. Alberta isn't exactly the tropics. He'd taken to sleeping in the front room. The gale that blew through the gap between the halves of the house was starting to get to him too, so he and Mary decided to at least patch up the division in the house, if not the division in their marriage."

Sebastian decided the time had come to attempt to patch the division in his marriage. As Byron had penned in *Don Juan*, "Adversity is the first path to truth: He who hath proved war, storm or women's rage, / Whether his winters be eighteen or eighty, / Has won experience which is deem'd so weighty." It was time to face a woman's rage and gain some weighty experience, just as long as something weighty did not hit him in the head. He climbed out of the car, thanked Bill for the ride, bid Lester farewell and headed toward his house.

As soon as he came within range of the front door, Sebastian had to dodge books, duck shoes and avoid incoming CDs. He worked his way in fits and starts between salvos up to a protected position behind a fir. The next advance was going to be far more dangerous. He had not yet been hit, but the remaining 40 feet to the front door offered no cover. It was as barren as no man's land on the Western Front after four years of war. Worse, whereas many objects barely reached the fir, as soon as Sebastian left his friend the tree's protection and advanced, he would be well within the killing range of anything thrown from the front door. The projectiles ranged from hardcover books to utensils and what looked to be small but rather hard, kitchen appliances.

"Elizabeth!" Sebastian called. A truce was preferable to running the gauntlet of flying objects to the door only to be met in all probability by an irate, .22-totting wife.

There was a pause in the barrage. Sebastian stuck his head around the tree and called, "We need to talk, Elizabeth! Please, dearest!"

He waited as the pause stretched into what appeared to be a cease-fire. Straightening his jacket, he cast a sorrowful eye at his copy of *The Anthology of the Poetry of the Romantics, Major and Minor Poets*, laying, its back broken, on the lawn. He stepped out from behind the tree and advanced toward his open and hopefully undefended front door.

He did not even see the manuscript that struck him squarely in the chest. The impact knocked him back a step, which actually allowed him to move beyond the range of a Calphalon 12-inch skillet that Elizabeth hurled as an addendum to the manuscript. Sebastian retreated behind his favorite fir and caught his breath. As objects thudded and ricocheted off the other side of the tree, he looked over at the manuscript that had knocked the wind out of him; *Lady Chatterley's Husband*, one of his early works. A bit derivative, Sebastian would be the first to admit, but certainly a ripping good yarn. Peeking quickly and cautiously around the fir between salvos, he noted that Elizabeth appeared to have hit the portion of her stockpile of missiles composed of his book manuscripts.

His anguish rising at the sight of his babies being hurled with abandon into the night, he yelled, "Elizabeth, please don't ruin my manuscripts!"

Thud! Thud! Thud!

Two manuscripts scored direct hits in the center of the fir's trunk, while a third, a little short, almost decapitated a garden gnome who had survived four winters and three run-ins with the neighborhood kids, including one Halloween encounter involving cherry bombs.

"Elizabeth!" Sebastian called, taking another tack. "We already have orders for those manuscripts! Paid in full!"

The words struck the cash register that occupied a favored position in Elizabeth's heart. The salvos ceased and the house fell silent. Wary of being ambushed again, Sebastian removed his jacket and waved it out in the open beside the fir in a life-like manner.

No hostile fire.

Crouching so as to present as small a target as possible, Sebastian darted out from behind his savior fir and sprinted in a zigzag up the garden path to the front door. Before he knew it, he was inside and pulled up just shy of the wood stove in the corner of the living room. Breathing hard, he turned and faced Elizabeth. Even in her agitated and somewhat winded state, she was a vision of beauty. She had dark hair, which was straight and cascaded down to her shoulders like the darkest silk. Her almost black eyes were afire; they blazed out of her golden skin, which gave her the appearance of having a permanent tan. A thin layer of sweat glistened on her forehead like morning dew on a just awakened forest nymph. She reminded him in every way of why he had first asked her out so many years before. She was beautiful. Stunning. Exquisite.

He was greatly relieved to see she was not armed with anything resembling a .22 rifle. She was, in fact, armed with a book manuscript in each hand. Even as he leaned toward her to hold her close and give her a kiss—for what lies could withstand the truth of a kiss when, as Shelley penned, 'soul meets soul on lovers' lips'?—she looked at him and the fire in her eyes was not of passion, but of anger, nay, even hatred.

"Get out, you philanderer," she ordered, her voice as cold as an executioner's heart.

Sebastian opened his mouth to begin what he hoped would be an eloquent case for the defense, even if the jury appeared to have already returned a verdict of guilty with the punishment of transportation far from Elizabeth's stunning shores, when the doorbell rang. It was past 3 a.m. and, although the lights were on, it was not normally a time for solicitors to ply their trade, except possibly for flashlight salesmen.

Evidently considering the house her domain even before all of Sebastian's belongings were actually out the door, Elizabeth stalked past him to the front door. The open door framed a cha-grined Destiny and Rosa Turnbell and, just behind them, like a shepherd herding his flock, loomed—if a man a hair above five feet can loom—the imposing breadth of Sam Turnbell. Sebas-tian also spotted Tyrone, the feisty terrier, sniffing, snorting and pawing Sebastian's belongings on the front lawn. For a moment silence reigned, save for crickets in the yard, Tyrone's snuffling investigations and the distant rumble of trucks gearing down as they approached the Pacific Truck Crossing into Canada four blocks away.

Sam finally broke the standoff. "As you told me, Sebastian, 'Wives in their husbands' absences grow subtler, / And daughters sometimes run off with the butler' or do other some such damn fool things."

"I can't take credit for those words. They were penned by my good Lord Byron."

"Well, whoever penned them," Sam said, looking at Elizabeth. "Rosa and Destiny have something to tell you, Mrs. Gianninni."

"Would you like some coffee?" Elizabeth asked. "Or break-fast?"

Before Elizabeth could reach a decision regarding the proper food and drinks to serve 3 a.m. guests, with a prod and a forceful glare, Sam succeeded in convincing Rosa to blurt out her story.

"I found a love note scrunched into our front door this morn-ing," Rosa said in a cascade of words worthy of Victoria Falls. "I thought it was from Sebastian, so I came over to thank him. But you were with him in the car, so I waited until later in the morn-ing, when I saw his car in the driveway. I thought he'd be home but it was you, Elizabeth. I realized I'd ruined the whole thing, so I went to Sebastian's office to apologize."

"And ran into me again," Elizabeth said, the bitter wine of betrayal dripping from every word.

"Destiny did the same fool thing," Sam said, prodding his daughter forward, her head bowed in shame. "Been sobbing about it all night. No one was getting any sleep, even Tyrone, and all because of Sebastian."

"Well, you can have him for all I care. I'm kicking the rogue out."

"Don't do it," Destiny exclaimed at the sight of Sebastian about to be tossed out on his ear, even if the fall would be cushioned by many of his worldly belongings and, depending on where he landed, a small black dog.

"You're losing a fine, romantic gentleman," Rosa warned.

Rosa and Destiny, however, in attempting to rescue Sebastian from his marital woes, were only succeeding in digging a grave to the appropriate depth of six feet that would accommodate him most snugly in Elizabeth's eyes.

Rosa gushed, "He's the most romantic of men."

"You should know," Elizabeth countered, her anger and despair erupting to the surface. "He's been romancing every woman between 18 and 80 within a hundred miles."

"That's not true," Sebastian said. "Other women are, to quote Thomas Moore, 'Like Dead Sea fruit that tempts the eye, / But turns to ashes on the lips.'"

"So you kiss other women, do you, on the lips?"

"Of course not. I've always romanced you and only you since the first day we met."

"But you certainly have more than enough romance to go around, don't you?"

"I think you misunderstand, Mrs. Gianninni," Sam said. "My women here, they mistook pages from your husband's novels for love notes. He didn't write the notes to them. Here, look."

Sam thrust two crumpled sheets of paper at Elizabeth. As she scanned the pages, Sam maneuvered inside and, taking a manuscript from the haphazard, forlorn pile remaining on the floor, flipped through the pages.

"Here's one of the pages in Sebastian's house copy," Sam said, handing the manuscript to Elizabeth. She could not deny the fact that the page that had set Destiny's heart aflutter had been from *Love's Play Lost*. Sebastian was happy to note that Sam had remembered at least some of the writing in his novels, which Sebastian had loaned to Sam to aid in the romancing of Mrs. Turnbell.

Sam soon found Rosa's prized page in *Gone with the Typhoon*. Tears rolling down her face, Elizabeth thanked the Turnbells three as they made further apologies and departed, Tyrone with an especially interesting shoe he had discovered on the lawn as a souvenir of the visit.

Alone again, Elizabeth turned and faced her husband. She threw herself at him, sobbing. He held her tight.

"I'm sorry, Sebastian," she bawled, agitated beyond measure. "I'm so sorry. How could I ever have doubted you?"

"'Alas! how light a cause may move Dissension between hearts that love! Hearts that the world in vain had tried, And sorrow but more closely tied; That stood the storm when waves were rough, Yet in a sunny hour fall off.'"

"You're the romantic one. I'm the one who's been too busy to pay attention to you or," she said, kissing him hard on the lips, "to…to…to thank you for the breakfast this morning."

"I didn't think you noticed."

"Or to thank you for the birdbath, although you should have told me. I almost shot the birds' best friends. You are the sweetest, most romantic of men. Can we try again? Start life anew?"

"'There is a budding morrow in midnight.' We missed midnight, but, Keats was right, it *is* a new day." Smothered in kisses, Sebastian decided to forego asking about the possible shooting of the birds' best friends.

Tears marked Elizabeth's face as she realized they just might have a second chance.

"'So bright the tears in Beauty's eye, Love half regrets to kiss it dry.'" Even so, Sebastian kissed Elizabeth's tears away and then took his beloved by the hand and from habit began to lead her upstairs to bed.

"No, let's stay down here. We could start on the sofa and see what develops, just like we used to when we were first dating. I want to recapture our romance. How can we do that, Sebastian?"

"I don't really know."

"Sebastian, please. I'm open to any and all suggestions."

"I guess we could slow down a bit. Hold hands and hug a little more. Maybe turn off the television when we go to bed. Kiss a little, slow dance a little, and not just rush into bed to make love. There's always time. I used to love undressing you."

"Feel free, anytime. Starting now…."

"'Her gentle limbs did she undress, And lay down in her love-liness.'"

"Only if you lie down with me."

"Me and Coleridge?"

"No, I want you all to myself tonight, and forever."

Chapter 36

Sebastian awoke on the sofa covered by a quilt Elizabeth must have laid over him sometime during the night. He stretched and glanced at the clock on the mantle: 7:30 a.m. He could hear birds chirping and singing outside. Lines from his favorite Shelley poem sprang into his mind: "Hail to thee blithe Spirit! Bird thou never wert, That from Heaven, or near it, Pourest thy full heart In profuse strains of unpremeditated art."

It was Saturday. Elizabeth would be sleeping in. The perfect opportunity to create a romantic breakfast *par excellence*. He dressed in his clothes of the previous night which, he noticed with a wry, contented smile, were strewn around the room just where Elizabeth had tossed them as she had figuratively and, in the case of his now button-less shirt, literally, torn his clothes off. Remembering the night before, Sebastian agreed with Coleridge; "Blest hour! It was a luxury—to be!"

He stepped over his books, manuscripts and other belongings that Elizabeth must have collected from the front lawn, driveway and sidewalk at some point after their lustful time last night and stacked neatly in the living room, minus Tyrone's trophy shoe. She was always very considerate of his things. She was the one, he recalled fondly, who had bought the earthquake putty to attach his grandfather's retirement clock to the bookcase. If there ever was a 8.0 earthquake in Blaine, the first in history, the clock would be safe. Sebastian was relieved Elizabeth had not included the clock in her previous night's ammunition.

Sebastian entered the kitchen to prepare breakfast and he soon outdid himself. Even the finest of gourmets, gourmands and gluttons would have been impressed by his repertoire. The *piece de resistance* were the German pancakes. Baked in the oven, this particular breed of pancakes rears up out of the pan on all sides like four tidal waves threatening to break in the center. The light, fluffy result is a melt-in-your-mouth delicacy that, Sebastian liked to think, was reserved by royal decree in the days of the Kaiser for only the most refined of the aristocracy. He dappled the finest Canadian Maple syrup—'And lucent syrops, tinct with cinnamon'—over his pancake creation. The syrup was collected, refined and bottled by a reclusive brotherhood of monks in Northern Quebec. It was rumored that St. Sweetum of Badmolar Maple Syrup had been so coveted by a certain pope of the last century, he elevated a monk of the brotherhood to be a cardinal without the formality of ever having been a priest, prelate or bishop.

Around the succulent pancakes, Sebastian arranged a mug of coffee ground by his own hands from beans a friend of Lester's had smuggled in from Columbia. The beans, Lester claimed, were sold only to the elite corps of professional chefs around the world who were members of the Golden Order of the Tall White Hat. Sebastian acquired some of the precious beans in exchange for looking the other way when Lester borrowed one of Uncle Bill's ledgers on horse racing. Next to the steaming java, Sebastian placed a mix of berries—blue, black, rasp and straw—covered in just enough fresh whipped cream to bring out their flavor while not threatening to impinge, let alone smother their taste in the least. Finally, there was fresh squeezed orange juice without even a hint of rind, as Elizabeth craved it, and toast made from Sebastian's own home-made wheat bread.

His creation complete, Sebastian arranged the feast carefully on an oak breakfast tray, adorned it with a brilliant, plate-sized rose from the garden and, after a pit stop in the bathroom to make himself, he hoped, look half as good as the breakfast, proceeded upstairs to the master bedroom.

Balancing the tray in one hand, Sebastian opened the door slowly and silently. He walked over to Elizabeth's bedside table, where he set the tray down. Without making a sound, he walked over to the window and opened the blinds a crack so as to allow his breakfast to be seen in all of its glory. Turning back to his creation and his lovely wife, he stopped dead. The bed was empty. He peered into the en suite: empty.

"Elizabeth," he called tentatively and then again, louder, "Elizabeth!"

Nothing.

He searched the house; empty. He looked out the windows and still saw no wifely vision of loveliness. Finally, the pancakes upstairs wilting like fresh-cut flowers in a sauna, he sat down heavily on a stool at the breakfast bar by the kitchen. Had Elizabeth decided regardless of his explanation, which he had gone through four times the night before as they writhed on the sofa, floor and in the overstuffed chair, that he was indeed a philanderer? Had she left him after all? Had she used him for one last night of passion for old time's sake before discarding him like the first draft of a second-rate poem?

He closed his eyes, praying that she, in all her beauty, would descend the stairs and say good morning with the comfortable, loving familiarity almost 20 years of marriage had spawned. He held his breath, but there were no foot falls on the stairs, no cheery good morning and no Elizabeth. Facing a future alone, he agreed with Byron, 'The worst of woes that wait on age' was certainly 'to be alone on earth as I am now.'

Despairing what to do, his eyes fell on the notepad beside the telephone. He read:

"I loved last night. Even after so many years, you still make my toes tingle. Please forgive me for my groundless suspicions. From now on, you'll have your hands full romancing me and only me. From now on I'll never ignore, overlook or take for granted any of your romantic attentions, starting with the romantic trip I suspect you have planned. I noticed the black suitcase in your car and the matching one in my car. It was so sweet of you to get us matching suitcases for a romantic trip to....anywhere with you would be romantic. See you for breakfast. Love and lust, your Elizabeth."

Matching suitcases? There were two bombs! That was why Villano had accepted defeat so readily at the Grizzly team bus. He could forfeit one bomb because he had another suitcase up his sleeve or, more accurately, in the trunk of Elizabeth's car. But where was she now? The note apparently had been written last night, after he had fallen asleep and before she went up to bed. The bed upstairs had been slept in, but where was she now? Her car was at the garage. Where could she go?

Then he remembered. Elizabeth had persuaded the garage to deliver her car early Saturday morning. She had wanted the car back so she could go in and do some work at the office late Saturday morning. Sebastian rushed to the window and flung back the blinds. Her car was gone. But she never would have gone to work before breakfast with him, especially not after last night's passion, let alone after writing the note mentioning breakfast together. Wherever she was, Villano must be at the bottom of it. Sebastian dashed upstairs to get dressed so he could rescue his beloved.

Dressed in record time, Sebastian bounded down the stairs. Then, realizing he was on his way to confront a violent terrorist who only the evening before had threatened him with a revolver, he bounded back up the stairs to the closet. He found Elizabeth's prized .22 rifle and, stuffing his pockets to the brim with enough rounds to make Swiss cheese out of 150 professors-cum-terrorists, bounded back down the stairs three at a time.

His hand grasped the doorknob as he had a second thought: he would never be allowed to cross the border carrying a .22 and several pocket's full of ammunition. Canada frowned on armed Americans entering her sovereign dominion, even if the purveyor of the weapon stated he was on his way to rescue his wife and, as an incidental benefit, to foil the nefarious plans of an international terrorist bent on permanently eliminating a professional basketball team, which had brought unrivalled glory to Canada, from the NBA championships. With a rapid about face, Sebastian redeposited the ammunition in Elizabeth's metal ammunition safe behind her jewelry in the back of the bureau, the rifle back in the closet behind her pink-chiffon matron-of-honor dress, and sprinted back to the front door.

Sebastian leapt into his car, started the engine and, releasing the brake, slammed it into reverse as he hit the gas. The engine revved like a dragster in the chocks, but the car did not budge. Just as Sebastian was reaching the conclusion that the doohickey connecting the engine to the wheels was broke, the car rolled back a few yards. The wheels felt as if he was driving through a deep layer of lemon meringue topped liberally with buckets of Elmer's glue. He turned off the engine, got out and started to stride toward the front of the car. He knew next to nothing about cars, apart from where the gasoline was input, but he, as did all men, believed that a thorough visual inspection of the engine would do a world of good. And, if such an inspection did not result in a sudden and vast improvement in the car's ability to move, it would at least make Sebastian feel as if he had looked things over and confirmed that an expert was required.

He had stepped around the open door and taken two steps before his foot caught on something. There was a loud, albeit melodious twang and Sebastian found himself hurtling toward the pavement. He caught himself a second before the impact of his prominent, aquiline nose with the pavement, but did scuff his hands in the process, reopening the scrapes of the night before. The twang was still ringing in the morning air as he stood, brushed off his hands and trousers, and looked down at the cause of his stumble. A glistening rapier protruded from his car's left front tire. The tire, now flat, held the rapier so that it stuck out horizontally three inches above the pavement; the perfect height to snag unwary feet.

"Villano," Sebastian spat out the name like a curse.

Not one to let a little thing like a rapier in the tire deter him from his chosen path, Sebastian stalked back to the trunk for the spare. Only the fact that he was keeping his head high in what he hoped was a manner denoting confidence in case anyone should be watching kept him from seeing a second rapier impaled in an identical fashion to the first in the rear driver's side tire. This weapon caught his shoe, sending him once more toward the pavement. This time, all his weight landed on his already scuffed right hand.

His left hand, wisely being slightly slower to be thrust forward, avoided the brunt of the impact with the unyielding pavement.

His anger rising, Sebastian wrenched the rapier out of the rear flat tire and was greeted with a merry twang as the weapon whipped back and forth like a giant's metronome in his hand.

"Villano," Sebastian cursed again.

Many would say Sebastian could be fooled once, even twice but never a third time, and they would be right. Rapier in hand, he crept around the end of the car and, as he had suspected, spotted identical tire-killers stuck into the two passenger-side tires. He straightened and, tapping the rapier he held against his leg, thought through the problem. The math was far from difficult—one spare and four flats: his car was immobilized.

Not one to let a little thing like four rapier-impaled tires slow him down, he raced back inside and called Uncle Bill.

"I need a ride," he said as soon as his uncle answered. "Villano's kidnapped Elizabeth, rapiered my car's tires and has another suitcase for the Grizzlies."

"Villano's giving luggage to the Grizzlies?" Bill asked. "Is he trying to make amends for trying to blow up their bus?"

"No. He's got another suitcase like the first, and he's got Elizabeth."

"He's giving Elizabeth a suitcase. How kind."

"Uncle Bill!"

"That's Professor-Uncle, to you."

"Pay attention, please!"

"I'm a little busy, Sebastian." Bill was at Abbotsford racetrack discussing the finer points of harness racing with the top trainer with whom he had, after six months of wooing, wining and dining, convinced to agree to an early morning meeting. Bill had only answered his cell phone because he thought Lester might be calling about his cut of the salmon deal. The sometime custodial engineer had promised to set aside a few choice kings of the sea for Bill in exchange for future consideration. Bill nodded at the dour trainer who was tapping his foot as he waited for Bill to get off the phone.

"Listen," Sebastian said. "Elizabeth wrote me a note and said she found a suitcase in the trunk of her car, identical to the one in my car's trunk. Villano had two suitcase bombs. I threw one into False Creek last night, but he must have the other suitcase bomb right now."

"And Elizabeth?" Bill asked between puffs on a misshapen, hand-rolled cigarette.

"I woke this morning and she was gone. If the bomb was in her car's trunk, then I fear he's got her car, the bomb and her."

"What are you doing yacking on the phone then?"

"That's where the rapiers come in."

"Rapiers?"

"Swords. Villano punctured all the tires on my car with rapiers. I'm stuck."

"Call a cab."

"I don't think they'll go across the border."

"You should call the police."

"They didn't believe me yesterday and there's no way I'm staking Elizabeth's life on them believing me today."

"Where do you want to go then?"

"To school to search Villano's office."

"I doubt he's got Elizabeth trussed up under his desk while he grades papers and awaits your arrival during office hours."

"Me neither, but where else can I look? If he's not there or if we don't find anything, we can try his house."

"I don't know where he lives."

"I'm sure one of the secretaries can dig up his address for me. I need a ride."

Bill looked longingly after the impatient trainer who had returned to his work and was leading a horse out of its paddock toward a sulky that was missing its equine form of locomotion.

"Uncle Bill?" Sebastian asked, after a pregnant pause.

"That's Professor-Uncle Bill to you," Bill said, trying to stave off the imminent direct question that would, he feared, derail his primer on the finer points of harness racing.

"Can you come pick me up, please?"

"Sounds dangerous."

"'They never fail who die In a great cause.'"

"Quoting Blake, Shelley or any of that lot won't help persuade me."

"It's Byron. Uncle Bill, please?"

"Women," Bill huffed. "What was that quote of Byron's you dislike…uh, 'There is a tide in the affairs of women, Which, taken at the flood, leads—God knows where.'"

"Even Byron had it wrong once in a while. I have to save Elizabeth and I need your help, Uncle Bill."

"I'm sorta busy right now." Bill walked toward the trainer. "I have dozens of questions to ask a trainer I've finally arranged to meet so I can perfect my Grand Unifying Theory of Harness Racing into a parsimonious, not to mention profitable model."

"Meet him some other time."

"Took me six months of wining and dining to setup this meeting."

"Elizabeth is in danger."

Bill thought about his niece-in-law. She was rather pretty, good natured and, he had to admit, was willing to provide a loan to a cash-strapped professor-uncle-in-law who had found his Grand Unifying Theories slightly wanting on certain race days.

"Professor-Uncle Bill? Please?"

"Don't whine, Sebastian, it's unbecoming of a professor at a prestigious university."

"We teach at a city college, Professor-Uncle."

"We beat Simon Fraser University last week in basketball and swept them in football last fall," Bill said as he stood watching the trainer, assisted by a groom, harness the horse to the sulky. The trainer had so much knowledge, Bill could almost feel it emanating from the man's great melon-shaped head.

"Can you come pick me up? I know you're only up at Abbotsford. You could be here in 20 minutes."

"Fifteen, the way I drive. If I come, you owe me a substantial favor."

"Anything. Name it."

"You accompany me to the track at least four times next month."

Unseen by Bill, Sebastian grinned. He would have been glad to go to the track 31 times next month with his favorite uncle. Then his smile turned melancholy as he realized he had allowed other, less important and certainly less fun things get in the way of something he loved to do: going to the track with his uncle.

"Deal."

Chapter 37

Fourteen minutes after Sebastian hung up, Bill's yellow Cadillac swung into Sebastian's driveway. Sebastian stood holding the four rapiers, still glaring at the deflated tires on his immobile Omni.

"Get in!" Bill yelled, caught up in the excitement of the impending chase to rescue Elizabeth, his harness trainer connection, at least for the moment, forgotten.

Sebastian tossed the rapiers into the back seat and climbed into the front.

"Careful of the leather upholstery with those things," Bill chastised him, eyeing the rapiers before stomping on the accelerator and hurtling backwards out of the driveway. "I would have been here in 12 minutes, but there was some lunkhead ahead of me chatting with the border guard and passing wads of paper back and forth."

Sebastian feared his novel manuscripts were enjoying a brisk resale market or worse, a photocopied market that would depress future sales. Elizabeth would be sad to hear it, although, Sebastian knew, she would figure out a way to remedy the situation when they rescued her. Engulfed by fear, he realized it should be if they rescued her, not when.

"There's someone following us," Bill said as he spun around a corner to rocket north toward the border.

Sebastian turned and looked back. "I only see a red sedan back there."

"He pulled out just as we left your place and he's been following us all the way through Blaine," Bill said as he entered the PACE lane into Canada.

"All the way through the megalopolis of Blaine? No?! How long was that, four blocks?" Sebastian laughed. "You're just paranoid after yesterday."

"There's no cause for sarcasm, young man. We'll lose him at the border anyway. He doesn't have a PACE sticker."

"Looks like a rental car." Sebastian thought he saw a license plate frame with a rental car company logo emblazoned upon it. "I haven't seen the car before in Blaine, but maybe he's just some guy visiting his parents or something."

"Maybe," Bill said, unconvinced, as he pulled up to the PACE booth.

"What's the purpose of your visit to Canada," the bored guard asked as he stared at the computer screen before him. Luckily it displayed no criminal information on Sebastian, the Sultan of Romantic Aides, since the guard had entered Bill's license plate number.

Sebastian was about to say 'to rescue my wife from the grips of an international terrorist,' but recalled his previous trouble at the border. Coleridge's admonition, 'Silence is a friend who will never betray,' leapt to mind

"To work," Bill said, hoping to keep the interview short. He had little experience in the rescuing trade, but he believed time was of some import.

"Alright, proceed," the guard said, glancing up and only then spotting the armory in the back seat. "Halt! Hold on, there."

The words froze Bill's piston-like foot over the accelerator.

"What's that in the back seat?" the guard asked, peering into the cavernous car.

"My nephew here," Bill said, indicating Sebastian, "is an English professor. The rapiers are to add some realism to a class production of *Hamlet*."

The Canadian guard nodded. He sat back on his stool and was once again on the cusp of letting the Cadillac and its doctored occupants enter his nation, when his eyes locked on Sebastian. "Isn't he that math savant degenerate genius guy?" The guard's hands flew over his computer keyboard. "Yeah, here it is. Last night you crossed into the States and reported you had a mathematical autistic savant degenerate with you. A math genius, but an eater of cardboard cereal boxes."

"How did you ever get that information?" Bill asked.

"The Yanks send us all sorts of worthless stuff. They love to make reports. It covers them when things go wrong. Of course, we send them endless reports too. Unfortunately, there are far more of them than there are of us, so they end up sending us a dozen reports for every one we send them."

"Just create 10 or 20 copies of all your reports with a slightly different title, mix them up and send them all to the Yanks," Bill suggested, ever helpful and a strong supporter of the adage, 'Be not unkind to strangers, for they may be angels in disguise,' even if they wore the uniform of a border guard. "If you send enough reports, they'll never match any two as being duplicates, let alone any three as triplicates."

The guard grinned with a mischievous glint in his eyes at this newfound strategy in the Great North American Border Report War. Thanks to Bill's suggestion, the secure email lines between the American and Canadian border patrol services were about to be deluged by even more reports about people whose greatest threat to national security was adding a zero to their charitable donations on their tax returns.

"Nice talking with you," Bill said with a big grin and a wave. "Have a nice day."

"You too," the guard said with a nod. "Hold it! You said he was an English professor. The report said that last night you told the Americans a man fitting his description was a math genius. We were informed he was incapable of anything else, even eating a balanced breakfast by himself. How can he be an English professor?"

Before Bill or Sebastian could attempt to explain, the guard's attention was drawn back to the rapiers. "What are those dark stains on the swords?"

"Tire rubber," Bill said, for lack of anything better, or worse, to say.

"Tire rubber?" The guard emerged from his booth, reached into the back seat and picked up one of the rapiers. He peered at the blade and, after a cautious sniff, said, "It *is* rubber."

"Tire rubber. Someone impaled my nephew's tires with rapiers this morning," Bill replied, realizing that truth was indeed stranger than fiction.

The guard returned to his booth and, his fingers flying over the keyboard, pulled up the file listing all substances, produce and merchandise that could not be legally imported into Canada. After a quick perusal, he reported that it was not illegal to import four rapiers into Canada, even if stained with tire rubber.

"Anything in the trunk?" the guard asked.

Bill hesitated, wondering if, as his mother had taught him, he should always tell the truth or, as his father had taught him after many an illicit day at the track, he should bend the truth for the benefit of all. "Nothing," he said. He was secure in the belief that piles of old *Racing Forms*, ledgers on his Grand Unifying Theory of Horse Racing, a few carefully secreted rolls of currency, several tobacco pouches, packets of rolling paper, and the various and sundry debris of his life were not worth the attentions of a busy Canadian border guard.

The officer clearly did not believe Bill. He leaned out of his booth and peered at the trunk of the Cadillac, which was approximately the length of a sofa and the width of a Ping-Pong table. Realizing how long it would take to search such a cavernous trunk and that his breakfast break was fast approaching, the guard said, "Have a nice day," and waved the yellow Caddy and its strange occupants through into the Dominion of Canada.

Bill hit the gas with the greatest alacrity. As they sped up the 99 freeway into Canada, Bill and Sebastian breathed sighs of relief.

"On to rescue our fair Elizabeth," Bill proclaimed, leaning forward to urge the car onward as he weaved his way through the early morning traffic.

It was only a matter of a few miles—or kilometers, in keeping with Canada's metric system—that flashing lights and a siren forced Bill to pull over. A policeman in a turbo-charged Mustang coupe strode up to the passenger-side window of Bill's vehicle. Modified by the finest mechanics in Vancouver, the Mustang was the RCMP's answer to new, faster cars and racing motorcycles that had enabled adventurous speeders to outrun the older, slower police cruisers. The Mounties, long ago having given up their love of horses, save for the black beauties of their famed musical ride, now vied with each other to ride the fastest police cars on the road: the souped-up Mustangs. Bill had, unfortunately, run afoul of just such a vehicle, not that the Mustang needed even half its horsepower to catch the ancient Cadillac.

"Good morning, officer," Bill said in his cheeriest voice as he leaned past his nephew to chat with the figure of governmental authority.

"Good morning, sir," the RCMP corporal said, visually checking the interior of the car, taking in Bill, Sebastian and, with a curious expression, the rapiers in the back seat. "Do you know how fast you were going?"

"I believe I was going 90, sir," Bill said earnestly, stating the correct speed in kilometers per hour as specified by the speed limit signs they had sped past at 123 kilometers per hour.

"I clocked you going just over 120."

"Oh, my God," Bill exclaimed, as if he had just learned the Virgin Mary had not, in fact, been a virgin before giving birth to the son of the aforementioned God.

"You were not aware of your speed?" the corporal asked, cocking an eyebrow to emphasize his skepticism.

"No, sir," Bill said, sounding as sincere as the most honest of three year olds attesting to their good behavior as they asked Santa for a new computer game for Christmas. "Thank you so much, officer, for giving me this warning. I'm sure my speedometer must be malfunctioning. I'll have it inspected by a certified mechanic this very day."

The Mountie, nonplussed, hesitated just long enough for Bill to wish him a merry, "Have a delightful day," start his Caddy and pull back into the flow of traffic.

The policeman chuckled and closed his ticket book as a rented red sedan drove past. It had caught up to the Cadillac after its driver had lost the yellow eyesore at the border when he had to wait to go through a normal non-PACE border-crossing lane.

The remainder of the cruise to the college was uneventful, except for Bill announcing 27 times that a red sedan was following them and Sebastian replying 27 times that the red sedan was merely heading into Vancouver, the same as 10,000 other cars. When they reached the college, Bill parked as Sebastian, rapiers in hand, darted out of the car and sprinted for the front door. Bill tried to keep up, but his first-hand smoker's lungs were no match for Sebastian's younger, second-hand smoker's lungs.

Coughing and hacking as he reached Villano's office, Bill heard Sebastian yell, "'O villain, villain, smiling damned villain,'" and then demand, "I want Elizabeth back, unharmed!"

Bill heard Villano reply, "You, the great defender of the Romantics quoting Hamlet? I'm shocked. Sit down and relax. In three hours she'll be released unharmed, if you do nothing rash."

"I'm supposed to believe you?"

"This should provide proof I have your wife and, if anything should happen to me, she'll never have to suffer through another of your infernal Shelley recitals ever again."

Bill reached the door just as Villano dropped a teddy bear pendant onto his desk beside the three rapiers that, Bill concluded, Sebastian had dropped there. The fourth weapon was in Sebastian's hand aimed in Villano's general direction. Sebastian snatched the pendant off the desk. Bill knew that it was Elizabeth's most prized possession. Sebastian had given it to her when they were first dating and she had treasured it ever since, wearing it every day.

Bill took in the entire startling tableau in the office. Lester, rigid with attention, sat on the leather sofa in the corner like a spectator at a tied football game heading into the final seconds of the fourth quarter. Sebastian, perspiring and panting like a dog just back from a good squirrel chase, ursine pendant in one hand, rapier in the other, collapsed, entirely deflated, into the chair opposite Villano's massive desk. The most surprising aspect of the scene for Bill, however, was the presence of Villano sorting papers at his desk. As he sorted, the English professor cum international terrorist tossed some papers into the trash can, others onto a pile on his desk and a precious few he carefully placed in his leather briefcase. Villano showed no sign of alarm, none of guilt and appeared to be in the mood to invite Lester and Sebastian out for a coffee at the faculty lounge or maybe even for a pint at the Queen's Cross.

Bill stood at the open door with a questioning expression that Villano answered. "Your nephew has interrupted my packing."

"I assume you're off to foreign shores," Bill said, striding into the office and leaning against a bookcase as he took out his tobacco pouch and rolling paper to attempt, yet again, the construction of the perfect cigarette.

"I am, but not for the reasons you think." Villano dropped a thick file of old grades into the waste paper basket with a resounding thud.

"And what do you think I think?" Bill asked.

"The same as I did," Sebastian said. "That he's fleeing the country after we foiled his plans last night."

"He's not fleeing the country?" Bill asked, his tobacco pouch poised above a cigarette paper.

"More of an extended vacation," Villano replied with a grin. "A major network is picking up the tab for me to spend the remainder of my life reading Shakespeare, sipping old brandy and seducing young women."

"A network?" Sebastian asked, more confused than he ever liked to be, save trying to follow one of Bill's more convoluted stories after six rounds in a pub.

"You thought you had all the pieces," Villano said, "but you don't even know the shape of the puzzle."

"I thought he was skedadling for all the wrong reasons, too," Lester commented.

"And the right reasons are?" Sebastian asked.

"The right reasons are that a television network has paid piles of money for the right to broadcast the upcoming NBA playoffs," Villano explained, placing a file containing his pension information in his briefcase. Even with the generous paycheck he was earning from his current bomb plot, you could never have enough money and his pension would pay for a nice bottle of wine once in a great while. "The network execs were worried about the rather astounding performance of the Grizzlies."

"Why?"

"They had rather pessimistic hopes for the Grizzly's ability to draw an audience," Villano said, dropping another file bloated with lectures he would never give again into the trashcan with a thud and a smile.

"They sell out every game," Lester exclaimed.

"The network believed that although people in other cities would watch an almost perfect team play against their home-town team, they were unlikely to tune in to playoffs between Vancouver and whatever unfortunate team ends up facing them in the playoffs, let alone in the finals. The network feared no one would watch the Grizzlies play in, let alone win, the championship. Memories of that Super Bowl a few years ago was fresh in their mind; who watched Tennessee and Seattle?"

"I did, and won a small wager on the outcome," Lester recalled. "Didn't pay much though. The pool was tiny; lack of interest."

"So the network paid you to blow up the Grizzlies?" Sebastian asked, grasping the enormity of Villano's plot.

"Dead basketball players don't play in championships," Villano said, dropping yet another file, this time the minutes from various dreary faculty meetings, into the garbage can: thud.

"What's to say another team will draw any better than Vancouver?" Sebastian asked.

"Not all of them will, but the big city teams have a built-in fan base that's larger than smaller Vancouver could ever provide," Villano said. "Besides, Canadians watch hockey, not basketball."

"So the network wants the Lakers, Nicks or Bulls in the playoffs," Lester said, catching on to the horrific, yet logical and for certain parties, highly profitable, plot. "If I'd known, I could have made a fortune."

"Even Miami or Boston is larger than Vancouver," Bill observed.

"Almost all of the American cities with NBA teams are larger than Vancouver and have a built-in fan base to watch the playoffs if their team makes it in," Villano explained. "And there's the na-

tionalist angle. What American wants to see a Canadian team beat
a bunch of Americans at basketball?"

"A Canadian did invent the game," Lester said.

"But few play it now," Bill said.

"Why did the network ever choose you to do such a thing?"
Sebastian asked. "You're a professor, not an international terrorist. How did you ever get connected with network television ex-
ecutives anyway?"

"Lester introduced us." Villano tossed still more files into the
trash in his cleaning out process before his imminent departure
from academic life.

"Lester?" Sebastian exclaimed.

"Lester," Bill said, turning with a dark visage on his old friend,
a lit match posed above his newest, misshapen creation.

"I don't even have an inkling of what he's talking about," Lester said, hands up, palms out in his best innocent pose. He had
been perfecting the pose since his first deal in kindergarten to
pool all of the students' lunch money, buy pizzas wholesale and
distribute them to the kids while pocketing 80 percent of the difference in price. The school principal discovered the plan when
the cafeteria soon faced bankruptcy because none of the students
were buying cafeteria food anymore. Citing a school district rule
against students conducting business on the schoolyard, the principal nixed the plan, even as Lester pled his innocence. Lester was
left locked into a contract to buy 750 pizzas a day for the rest of
the school year. Needless to say, even at that age, Lester found a
profitable way to dispose of the pizzas. He had been perfecting
his innocent look ever since.

"Come now, Lester," Villano said, "we can tell our colleagues,
especially now that the final buzzer is about to buzz."

"What's he talking about, Lester?" Sebastian demanded.

"Tell us," Bill ordered, looming over his old friend.

"Okay, okay. A certain friend of a friend of an acquaintance
was in hawk for some money to a private equity lender."

"To a loan shark," Bill interpreted.

"If you want to put it so crassly. Anyway, this friend of a
friend of an acquaintance, the one who owed the money, has a
brother whose a big shot network suit in the States."

"The same network that has bankrolled my extended vacation," Villano said with glee.

"So my friend of a friend of an acquaintance who owed the money and had a great fear about the future health of his knees, called his brother for a loan. The network brother knew his little brother had been to college a few times."

"Been to prison," Bill interpreted.

"Yeah, so the network brother told his little brother he'd loan him the money if he'd find somebody to do a little job for the network for a pile of money. That made it easy: money attracts the best."

"He's the best at blowing up basketball teams?" Sebastian asked, casting a skeptical gaze at Villano.

"No, but my friend of a friend of an acquaintance ended up running into two loan officers before he could connect his network brother with a pro. The loan officers—"

"Thugs," Bill clarified.

"The loan officers," Lester repeated, "were a little hasty and they snapped the little brother's knees before he could tell them he had the money. It's rather rare for their customers to have the money to repay their loan at the stage in the negotiations when they become involved."

"Wouldn't that be the first topic of conversation for your friend of a friend's acquaintance to raise with the loan officers?" Sebastian asked.

"He tends to stutter when he gets nervous," Lester said.

"And I'm sure the loan officers made him nervous," Bill said.

"Very. Anyway, the loan officers felt bad having given him a reminder—"

"Breaking his legs," Bill interpreted.

"When he already had the money to repay the loan," Lester continued. "Money, incidentally from his network brother."

"His brother gave him the money even before he'd arranged a meeting with a pro?" Bill asked in disbelief.

"Yeah, he has no experience with business deals."

"But he's a network executive," Sebastian said, frowning.

"Yeah, but he's just a lawyer with an MBA in charge of negotiating the network's domestic development deals. No experience in how deals are made in real life. Anyway, so my friend of a friend's acquaintance is in the hospital with two broken legs and the loan officers are begging him not to let it get around that they roughed him up when he had the money to cover the loan."

"Why did they care?" Sebastian asked, wishing the story would end so he could get to the more relevant topic on his mind: the health and whereabouts of Elizabeth.

"It wouldn't help business if other borrowers thought they would have their legs broke even if they paid," Bill said, understanding the intricacies of low finance far better than Sebastian. "If you got your legs bust whether you paid or not, who would pay?"

"How did all this get the network suit, I mean, executive, linked up with Villano?" Sebastian asked, desperate to reach a conclusion to the story.

"The loan officers offered to pay the loan back themselves if my friend of a friend's acquaintance kept quiet. He did, so he didn't need his network brother's money after all—at least to repay that loan. After he tried to use the money to place a bet but was refused because his bookie wouldn't take such a large wager, he gave the money back, minus his 10% pain-and-suffering fee. This left his brother in the lurch without any hired help."

"And Villano?" Sebastian asked, despairing of ever reaching the end of this twisted underworld saga.

"One day I was bemoaning the state of my finances," Villano said, picking up the story, "and Lester mentioned he'd heard a certain network suit was willing to pay top dollar for a minor job."

"*You* set all this in motion, Lester?" Sebastian asked, his anger rising as he glared at the custodial engineer.

"I didn't mean to."

"Indeed, he did not," Villano confirmed. "I had to pester him for several weeks before he'd reveal the name of the needy, if generous, executive. Then it took several more weeks to convince the executive I could do the job."

"And your henchman, the international terrorist?" Sebastian asked, refocusing his anger from Lester to the true villain of the drama across the desk from him.

"He was taking my pastoral poetry class," Villano said. "Some sort of anti-technology freak."

"He was willing to blow up a basketball team for a television network?" Sebastian asked, once more as confused as he was when Elizabeth discussed the costs and benefits of different forms of depreciation.

Villano said, "A little creative storytelling about a New Luddite Revolution and the need to end the broadcasting of professional sports to the masses as a symbol of the Western, high-tech world was enough to get Hogarth on board. He's not exactly the sharpest pencil in the drawer."

Sebastian stared down at the teddy bear pendant, fighting the temptation to leap across the desk and throttle his colleague. "You'll release Elizabeth after your second bomb goes off sometime today?"

"Very good," Villano said. "I didn't think you'd realize I had two bombs until I was sipping an iced drink on a warm, foreign shore sitting next to a luscious native girl."

"You'll release Elizabeth?"

"Yes, I will release her as soon as the Grizzlies are extinct. But, right now, if you will excuse me, I have a bomb to plant."

"Remember Villano," Sebastian warned, "'From the body of one guilty deed a thousand ghostly fears and haunting thoughts proceed.'"

"I am no Macbeth to lose sleep over a few deaths, no matter how tall the corpses."

"That's Wordsworth, not Shakespeare."

"I'll study both when all this is over and I have thousands of dollars for every second spent on this particular guilty deed."

"Remember too, that 'Those who plot the destruction of others often perish in the attempt.'"

"I think your beloved Thomas Moore is wrong in this case. But, whatever the case, I'd love to continue listening to your recital of quotes, but time and basketball teams wait for no man." Villano snapped closed the catches on his briefcase, glanced around the office and picked up an old, heavy, worn volume. "A gift, for you," he said handing it to Sebastian. "I never thought anyone would detect even a whiff of my plot until I was across the seas. Well done, but not quite well done enough. 'When shall we three'—or in this case, four—'meet again?' Never again." He smiled, then he was gone.

Sebastian flipped open the cover of the book, *A Tragic History of Hamlet Prince of Denmark*.

"Bloody hell," he said, furious, as he hurled the hardbound book through the office window.

The broken glass was still tinkling as Lester and Bill inspected the damage.

"I can get you a deal on a new pane, cheap," Lester offered.

"There's that guy in the rented red sedan who was following us," Bill said as he looked out the now open window at the parking lot below.

"If you ever make a deal again," Sebastian threatened Lester, ignoring Bill's observation, "I'll see to it the next deal you make is for passage across the River Styx."

Lester was only saved from fisticuffs with the advancing Sebastian, who had dropped his rapier and decided his fists, albeit rarely, if ever used, would suffice to thrash Lester, by a tentative knock at the open door.

Lester, Bill and Sebastian turned to behold Hogarth Ramen O'Leary Chevalier, wanted international terrorist of the New Luddite Revolution, at the door. He looked like a lost sheep, hoping to find a welcome mat laid out at the ancestral pasture, or at least a warm look from the rest of the flock.

"You have Elizabeth," Sebastian accused the New Luddite, heading around the desk to do battle with Hogarth, whom, Sebastian concluded upon second thought, deserved a thrashing even more than Lester.

"No," Hogarth said quietly. "I don't."

It was said with such honest simplicity that Sebastian believed the terrorist even as his clenched fists searched for a target to vent his frustration and anger, not to mention his growing fear that he would never see Elizabeth again. He chose as his target a plaster bust of Shakespeare, which Villano had left behind. Sebastian immediately regretted the choice. As Sebastian cradled his bruised knuckles, Hogarth edged into the office.

"Villano hired two thugs from New Hampshire to kidnap your wife, Dr. Gianninni," Hogarth said. "They have her."

"New Hampshire?" Lester asked. "Don't you mean, New York or New Jersey?"

"No, New Hampshire. Laconia has some pretty mean streets."

"Where do they have her?" Sebastian demanded, eager to finally pursue a lead that did not rely on a story involving Bill, Lester or their extensive friends, relations, acquaintances and associates.

"On Dr. Villano's sailboat."

"Villano has a sailboat?" Sebastian asked, wondering if they made knuckle prostheses, given the appalling pain in his hand. "He doesn't seem the type."

"He has a 45 footer moored at Coal Harbour."

"He told me once he wanted to sail with his wife to the South Seas," Lester said, "but she went out once, got sea sick and that was that."

"What's the name of his boat?" Sebastian asked, anxious to avoid another of Lester's stories, even if he was curious about why Villano and the janitor would ever be chatting about yachts, wives and cruises to tropical isles.

"I don't know," Hogarth said. He saw that Sebastian did not believe him, so he quickly added, "Dr. Villano said it would be better for security if I didn't know. I only overheard he was keeping her on his boat because the thugs left a message on his phone's voicemail that I overheard this morning when he checked his messages. He was using the speaker phone."

"His boat's name is the *Jana*," Lester said with disdain, as if such information should be known by all.

"I've got to get to Coal Harbour," Sebastian said as he picked up two of the rapiers from Villano's desk.

"Wait a minute," Bill said, and asked Hogarth, "Where's the other bomb?"

"I put it in a basketball for Villano, but he said he'd plant it this time," Hogarth said, miffed. "I should have been the one to plant it. I put it in Mrs. Dr. Giannini's trunk. I made it. I set it. It's mine."

"A basketball?" Sebastian asked, unsure he had heard correctly.

"A regulation NBA basketball. I spent three weeks finding the right ball. Dr. Villano was very picky."

"I could have got you one," Lester said. "How much did you pay for it?"

Sebastian and Bill glared at Lester, silencing him as effectively as if they had inserted a large cork in his mouth.

Sebastian said, "I wonder where the Grizzlies are now."

"They'll be practicing at GM Place this afternoon," Lester said, checking his Rolex Submariner.

"Their practices are secret," Bill said, turning on Lester with a look of disbelief. "No one knows when or even where they practice."

"I know," Lester said. "I used to scalp tickets for the practices before the team decided they were in need of some privacy, but I still have a friend who's privy to their schedule."

"Villano's going to kill the team with the basketball bomb at the practice this afternoon," Sebastian declared.

"We've got to get over there and stop him," Bill said.

"*We?* What are you talking about?" Lester asked. "Call the police."

"You remember how much trouble you had convincing the rent-a-cops at GM Place to help us foil Villano's first bomb plot?" Sebastian asked. "That's nothing compared to trying to convince the police. I told them about the plot before anything happened and what did it get me? Nothing. I'll go rescue Elizabeth. You and Professor-Uncle Bill go dispose of the bomb before we're minus the finest basketball team in history."

Sebastian, two rapiers in hand, sped toward the door. But, as he passed Hogarth, he paused to ask, "Why did you tell us all this?"

"I overheard Villano tell you he'd made a deal with a television network. That wasn't the plan. He said we were striking a blow for the New Luddite Revolution. Basketball on television is a big business. If we can destroy a symbol of mass-market sports, then people will no longer sit at home glued to their televisions watching sports. They'll get out and enjoy life, experiencing nature and participating in democracy. Worse, the two thugs Villano hired drive a gas-guzzling SUV; not eco-friendly at all."

"You were upset that Villano lied to you about the true purpose of the bombing," Sebastian said, "yet you were going to kill an entire basketball team with your bomb?"

"I was raised right. I don't lie and I don't associate with people who do, but I hate television. I miss watching baseball games like they used to be when I went with my dad, with no stupid breaks for television ads."

"I hate that," Lester said. "You sit there for three minutes staring at a bunch of guys on the field inspecting the stitching on their gloves while the fans at home are informed about how to clean the grout in their shower stall."

"If you missed old-style baseball, why didn't you blow up a baseball game?" Sebastian asked.

"And scorch all that innocent grass?"

"Thanks," Sebastian said, deciding this was a fine time to terminate the conversation and then, rapiers in hand, he was gone.

Sebastian had not been gone a minute when a dark-haired man who had arrived at the college in the rented, red sedan peeked in the open doorway.

"Is Dr. Gianninni in?" he asked.

"You just missed him," Bill said.

"He's off to Coal Harbour Marina," Lester chipped in, ever helpful.

"Thanks," and the man was gone.

"Why'd you tell him that?" Bill asked Lester. "He could've been one of Villano's henchmen."

"He seemed nice," Lester said, "and Sebastian is armed."

Chapter 38

As Bill and Lester sped in Bill's Cadillac toward GM Place to find the basketball bomb, Sebastian called a cab, since his deflated and immobile Omni was still resting peacefully back in Blaine.

"What are those?" the cabby asked as Sebastian piled into the back of the taxi.

"Rapiers. Please take me to the marina at Coal Harbour. Speed is of the utmost importance, so please hurry."

The cabby, wondering if he should pass on this particular rapier-armed fare, decided a fare in the back was better than one on the radio. Speed was requested and speed was achieved. After a tour of alleys, side streets and the occasional sidewalk, the taxi screeched to a halt at the entrance to the Coal Harbour Marina. Sebastian paid the fare and, rapiers in hand, sprinted down the ramp toward the rows of speedboats, yachts and cabin cruisers bobbing in the marina's many sheltered slips.

By nature, Sebastian was a lover of the sea. He had grown up in Vancouver with its beautiful harbour cradled amid fir-covered mountains and its ocean views. Sebastian was a romantic and had courted Elizabeth with walks along Spanish Banks, dinner at the Salmon House in West Vancouver overlooking the harbour, and drives up the rugged coast, which reminded many a visitor of the fjords of Norway and Sweden, although a few dozen degrees warmer. With his native city in mind, he often thought of Wordsworth's words albeit about another setting; 'Two voices are there; one is of the sea, One of the mountains: each a mighty voice.'

Unfortunately, this love of the ocean did not translate into a love of being on, let alone in the ocean. Sebastian could not swim and being aboard boats made him ill. Saying Sebastian was prone to seasickness, however, was like saying Everest is a mole hill, the Nile a creek and the North American prairies a meadow.

Thrusting his fear of being on the sea firmly behind him in the interest of rescuing his beloved Elizabeth, Sebastian raced out onto the wharf. The central part of the floating structure was relatively stable and, being well within the protected confines of Coal Harbour, barely rocked, bobbed or swayed at all. Unfortunately, unlike city streets, Sebastian soon realized that slips and boats are not clearly marked for ease of identification. The name was only on the stern of each boat, which meant that to find a particular craft would require running up and down each and every digit of the multi-fingered wharf. It could take an hour to find the *Jana* and by then....he feared even to contemplate what the New Hampshire thugs might do to his Elizabeth during that length of time. Then he spotted a man rinsing off his mistress of the sea.

"Excuse me," Sebastian asked, careful to stay well back from the edge of the wharf and the dreaded water, "can you tell me where the *Jana* is moored?"

"The *Jana*," the man said, tilting his weathered captain's hat back on his head and pondering the question as if he had been asked the riddle of the Sphinx, given the traditional answer, and been met with a vigorous negative shake of the feline's human head.

"A sailboat," Sebastian prompted, setting his feet farther apart as a cabin cruiser motored past, setting the wharf gently in motion, a motion Sebastian felt was similar to that of an earthquake registering a 57 on the Richter scale.

"Can't say I know her," the man said, scratching his gray whiskers.

"It belongs to Dr. Villano."

"Oh, you must mean the *Jana Villano*. She's just heading out, right there," he said, pointing at a graceful sailboat, its sails furled, putt-putting out of the harbour.

Sebastian's mouth sagged open like a recently landed flounder. "Are you sure?"

"Sure as this boat's the *Juliet Capulet.*"

Sebastian glanced down at the stern and realized he was conversing with a man who had named his speedboat after Shakespeare's tragic heroine. Was there no getting away from the blasted Sweet Swan of Avon?

"I need your boat," Sebastian said, eyeing the *Juliet*'s rakish lines and evidently powerful engines, even while he attempted to ignore her name.

"No one gets their hands on *Juliet*, except Romeo."

"Who's Romeo?"

"The marina's mechanic."

"I'll pay you." Sebastian pulled out his wallet, glanced longingly at the slowly departing *Jana*, and pulled out all of the currency. "Here's….eighty-four dollars. Take it all."

"No way." The man folded his arms with a stern look that did not bode well for the success of Sebastian's negotiation, let alone for his rescue plans.

"Take one of my credit cards. Buy anything you want. I need your boat."

"You're climbing the wrong rigging, young man. They rent boats over there," the old salt said, pointing across the bay, "beside the Yacht Club."

Sebastian looked at the *Jana* as she started to round Stanley Park. Soon she would be gone. "I don't have time. I need a boat. Now."

"Not this one," the man insisted, stepping to the edge of the dock between Sebastian and *Juliet*, prepared to repel boarders.

Sebastian considered using his rapiers to force the issue but decided piracy, even in the pursuit of thugs holding his wife, was unwarranted. Besides, even if he took the *Juliet* by force of arms, how would he operate her? He had never helmed a boat in his life. He stuffed his wallet back into his pocket and dejected, frustrated and queasy from the swaying wharf, steeled himself for a run around the harbour to the yacht club.

"Why are you so desperate for *Juliet*, anyway?"

"Two thugs kidnapped my wife and they're taking her some-where on the *Jana*," Sebastian said, sure the aged captain would be as likely to believe him as the police had been about the suitcase-bomb plot, but too dejected and short on time to devise a more plausible story.

The captain turned to look at the receding *Jana* and, setting his jaw as many a Royal Navy captain must have done upon spy-ing a fat Spanish galleon loaded with gold on the Spanish Main, exclaimed, "Hell, I don't know if you're spinning me a yarn, but I'm game to catch her. Permission to come aboard!"

With hope restored, Sebastian leapt aboard and instantly re-gretted the rash move. *Juliet* rocked and swayed. Sebastian's stom-ach churned and gurgled. While the captain cast off, Sebastian collapsed to the bottom of the stern well of the cabin cruiser. He heard the engine roar to life and the stern settle as the prop dug into the water.

"We'll have to keep it slow until we're clear of the harbour, then we'll catch 'em," the captain promised above the gentle rum-ble of the finely tuned engines as he guided *Juliet* out of her slip and between two rows of yachts. "You alright?"

Sebastian managed to look up.

"You don't thrive at sea, do you?"

"No, sir," Sebastian gasped, agreeing with Byron that 'these vicissitudes come best in youth'—or, even better, not at all.

A rented red sedan parked in the marina's lot and, as the *Juliet* cruised out of her slip, the dark-haired driver rushed down onto the wharf. He arrived just in time to see Sebastian, crouched in the stern of the *Juliet*, heading out to sea. The man despaired of ever catching the wily professor, but the man had a job to do and he was a professional. He could not let a little thing like a constantly moving professor foil him. He would just have to persevere. He returned to his car to plot his next move to catch Dr. Sebastian Gianninni and complete his assignment.

The captain turned *Juliet* into the main channel and gradually in-creased speed as they cleared the marina.

"Stand up here beside me," the captain ordered, as he glanced down at Sebastian huddled on the deck. "The blast of cold air will keep you healthy and my mistress clean."

Sebastian swallowed the bile in his throat and, with thoughts of Elizabeth to fight off his fear and queasy stomach, staggered to his feet. He grabbed the low windscreen in front of the wheel, where the captain stood at *Juliet's* helm. He recalled Byron's advice in *Don Juan*, 'The best of remedies is a beefsteak / Against sea-sickness; try it, sir, before You sneer, and I assure you this is true, / For I have found it answer—so may you.' Unfortunately, Sebastian did not have any sort of steak, let alone a beefsteak with which to verify Byron's counsel.

"That better?"

Sebastian felt somewhat better as the cold, salt air slammed into his face, burning his cheeks and whipping back his hair. The sight ahead, void of any sign of the *Jana*, however, disheartened him.

"I'm Nelson," the captain said, extending his hand, "Nelson Fish."

Sebastian shook hands. "Captain Nelson?" Shouldn't you be an Admiral Lord Nelson?

"No, I'm just Captain Fish, but you can call me Nelson."

"Sebastian Gianninni. Can you catch her?"

"Of course," Nelson said with disdain. "She's just a sailboat. *Juliet* has two 3,500 horsepower engines. She could overtake the *Jana* with only one engine at quarter throttle."

"We are like Cato and Hortensius," Sebastian remarked, trying to keep his mind off the sea and his threatening stomach.

"Who?"

Sebastian cleared his throat of bile and recited, "'Heroic, stoic Cato, the sententious, / Who lent his lady to his friend Hortensius.' It's from *Don Juan* by Lord Byron."

"I think I'll stick to my own name, thanks. If it was good enough for old Admiral Lord Horatio, it's good enough for me."

Sebastian clung with a white-knuckled grip to the windscreen as they cruised out of the marina. Once clear of the marina, Nelson pushed the twin throttles to the chocks. They sped around Stanley Park toward the entrance to Burrard Inlet and, hopefully,

the *Jana*. The cold air helped Sebastian's constitution immeasur-
ably. By the time they spotted the *Jana* putt-putting out of the
harbour under graceful Lions' Gate Bridge headed for English
Bay and the open sea, he was feeling more like his usual self. The
presence of so much water all around him, however, did not make
him feel quite on top of the world.

"'Water, water, everywhere, / And all the boards did shrink,'"
Sebastian recited.

"I certainly hope not," Nelson interrupted. "I just finished
sealing her decks."

"'Water, water everywhere, nor any drop to drink.'"

"I never drink during the week," Nelson confided.

"'The very deep did rot: O Christ! That ever this should be!'"
Sebastian exclaimed as he surveyed the harbour and the deep,
dark sea.

"I love it," Nelson countered.

Sebastian far from loved anything to do with the sea, nor did
the fact that two thugs had kidnapped his wife help his mental
outlook. There was also one other small problem: a freighter.

The *Jana* was slowly overtaking the huge man-of-trade, which
had shipping containers stacked six high on her deck. The *Juliet*
would soon lose sight of the *Jana* behind the freighter's bulk.

Nelson had noted Sebastian's concern and yelled, "We'll catch
her in a minute. That freighter won't hurt matters any."

Nelson was correct. The *Juliet* swiftly gained on the *Jana* and,
as Nelson guided his craft around the stern of the slow-moving
freighter, they were close enough to see two men standing at *Jana*'s
stern; one at the wheel, the other staring up at the mammoth
freighter.

"Now what?" Nelson asked.

The truth be told, imbued with his romantic quest to rescue
his lady, Sebastian had been dwelling not on the intricate mechanics of a rescue at sea, but on some of the most sublime lines
Byron had ever scratched on parchment for his "Apostrophe to
the Ocean": "Roll on, thou deep and dark blue Ocean—roll! Ten
thousand fleets sweep over thee. Man marks the earth with ruin—
his control stops with the shore." Sebastian also felt as if his control stopped with the shore as he realized he had not given this

part of the plan much thought, not that he had given any part of his plan much thought. He did not have a clue how to proceed. As he fingered his rapiers, the image of buccaneers leaping aboard a gold-laden Spanish galleon sprang to mind. Although the thought of leaping over water was the last thing he would have liked to do on a bracing, yet bright spring afternoon, he turned to Nelson and said, "Just get me alongside. I'll do the rest."

It was not to be as easy as Sebastian imagined. One of the men on the *Jana*, whom Sebastian could now see had the square jaw, broad shoulders and dark suit of a thug, turned and watched with malevolent eyes the approaching *Juliet*. Nelson matched the *Jana*'s speed and course as he edged closer to the teak-decked sailboat.

"Get yourself up the port side and prepare to board her," Nelson advised Sebastian as the *Juliet* slowed. The pounding of the waves on the hull slackened even as the *Juliet* slid in beside the *Jana*.

"Port?"

"Left."

Leaving one of his rapiers on the deck and clutching the other tighter, Sebastian edged along the windscreen toward the port side. He peered nervously at the water as it rushed past below in a churning, green and white mass. Timing his step between wave crests, he placed his left foot on the gunwale. The ledge appeared suicidally narrow and the frothing water far too near as he swung out. He kept his eyes locked on the cabin's white bulkhead inches in front of his face as he edged along the *Juliet*'s port side facing in. He had never wanted to be so close to a lady, save for Elizabeth.

Even as his stomach began to rebel and the world swung erratically before him, he forced himself to risk a glance over his shoulder at the *Jana*. The sight froze him in place, even stilling his seasick tummy, as he saw the larger thug, who was evidently related to the lowland gorilla, aim a handgun at him. Even as Sebastian watched, the thug pulled the trigger. The sound of the shot pierced the air above the throb of *Juliet*'s engines and Sebastian felt something pass his left cheek at a velocity that should be reserved for light photons. A jagged hole appeared in the bulkhead mere inches before his eyes.

Surprising even himself, Sebastian was back crouched in the *Juliet*'s cockpit in an instant, well before the gorilla-related thug could fire another salvo. Deterred from approaching the *Jana* by the threat of another shot, Nelson swung the *Juliet* to starboard with a violent wrench away from the well-defended sailboat.

Sebastian huddled in the cockpit as the *mal du mare* struck him with full force. Sweat covered his body from hair to toes.

"Maybe you should stay back here," Nelson advised. Nelson quickly maneuvered his craft so they had the bulletproof protection of the freighter between the *Juliet* and the lead-spitting *Jana*.

"I'm sorry about the bullet hole," Sebastian gasped, his head over the stern to try to avoid ruining his clothes if—or as bad as he felt, when—his stomach succeeded in its rebellion.

"Get up here before you lose your lunch!" Nelson ordered. He reached down and with surprising strength for a senior citizen who might have been a cabin boy on the *Nina*, grabbed Sebastian's arm and hauled him to his feet. Sebastian grabbed the windscreen and, with the cold wind supplemented by the occasional sea spray smacking his face, his condition rapidly improved. A color at least somewhat related to a color found amongst the human race returned to his face and, with his stomach deciding to postpone its rebellion, he was able once again to direct his attention to the rescue of his wife. "Get me close again."

"Are you nuts?" Nelson asked, content to keep the freighter between him and the inhospitable *Jana*. "We should call the Harbour Police. They shot at us!"

"Like Keats, 'Love is my religion—I could die for it.'"

"That just might happen."

"I told you they were wife-nappers. You try and raise the police, but get me close again."

Nelson looked skeptical as he reached for the radio next to the wheel. "Hang on!" With a surge of power and one hand on the wheel, he guided the *Juliet* so she was barely ahead of the freighter's churning and boiling bow wave. He executed a tight turn right under the massive overhanging bow of the onrushing freight-hauler, even as he tuned the radio with his free hand.

Sebastian gulped as he glanced up at the metal behemoth bearing down on them like a barnacle-encrusted, steel avalanche.

Swallowing his fear and queasiness, he once again edged out onto *Juliet*'s port side. This time he stayed in a crouch, hoping to present as tiny a target as possible. The chill wind snatched at his coat, whipped his hair and threatened to snatch him off the narrow ledge.

After shuffling along the gunwale almost to the bow, Sebastian, hanging on with white knuckles, stole a look ahead and was shocked to see the *Jana* less than 20 feet ahead. Nelson was not slowing down this time. Heading straight for the oncoming *Jana*'s prow, the *Juliet* offered a narrow, difficult target as the thug in the stern of the *Jana* attempted to aim over *Jana*'s high bow at the onrushing cabin cruiser. Sebastian heard a shot. This time he could see no damage to the *Juliet*. She raced the last few yards right at the oncoming *Jana*.

'She beats her down majestically near, Speed on her prow,' Sebastian thought, recalling Byron's *The Corsair* in an attempt to calm his terror.

With lightening reflexes, Nelson slammed the throttles into full reverse at the last second. *Juliet*'s sudden deceleration sent Sebastian hurtling off his perch near the prow. Tumbling through the air like a poorly thrown football, he landed in a bruised heap on the bow of the *Jana*, even as the thug at the *Jana*'s helm spun her wheel hard over to avoid the onrushing *Juliet*. The two ships missed a fiberglass- and teak-crunching rendezvous by the width of a halibut.

Helpfully stopped by *Jana*'s mast, Sebastian threw out his arms and hugged the cold, metal cylinder. His terror of ending up in the ocean subsided as he realized he was once again on dry deck. He peered around the mast. The *Juliet* had sped away with Nelson at the helm. Looking toward *Jana*'s stern, Sebastian saw that his uninvited boarding of the vessel was not a welcome one: the gorilla-related thug was advancing up the port side brandishing his gun. Only the mast shielded Sebastian from being shot where he lay.

Sebastian looked around for an escape route or for a weapon. His rapier, having made the unscheduled trip from the *Juliet* with him, had rolled against a hatch cover five feet from where he crouched. Even though he had experience in rapier versus revolver duels and had survived his last bout, even emerging the victor, he did not relish a rematch with a professional contender in a heavier weight division. Even so, a rapier was better than nothing at all, so he lunged across the deck and grabbed his theatrical weapon.

As the thug reached the open foredeck, he beheld a middle-aged man in a Navy sport jacket, Argyll sweater, gray slacks and loafers, swishing a rapier back and forth like Errol Flynn in some black-and-white swashbuckler movie. The thug leveled his handgun at Sebastian and, frowning, demanded, "Who are you?"

"I'm the husband of the woman you kidnapped, you cad!"

With a diabolical smile, the thug aimed his pistol right at Sebastian's heart. He would have killed the rapier-armed English professor if not for the sudden intervention of the thug's accomplice at the *Jana*'s wheel. The veer to port moments before to avoid the *Juliet* had set the *Jana* on a collision course with the freighter. Although the container ship would barely have registered the *Jana* as a speed bump if they had met, such a rendezvous would have been fatal to the *Jana* and all aboard her. The thug at the wheel realized a change of course was urgently required. It was, however, a most inopportune time for a course change in terms of the situation developing on the fore deck—at least for the home team.

The sudden shift in the sailboat's course angled the deck hard over. The thug facing Sebastian stumbled dangerously close to the deck's edge and the deep blue sea beyond. The thug's stumble would have proved a boon to Sebastian if he had kept his footing. Sebastian, however, had the sea legs of a newborn fawn. In trying to keep his balance and avoid going over the starboard side, Sebastian stumbled toward the port edge and toppled over the side like the proverbial drunken sailor. Luckily, his jacket caught on a deck stanchion, halting his fall just as the soles of his shoes touched the water.

Still clutching his rapier, Sebastian stared across the water at the freighter, chugging on its serene way toward the harbour entrance, oblivious to the drama unfolding just off its starboard side. Sebastian looked down at the water. Each wave crest slapped his shoes sternward as the *Jana* putt-putted toward the open ocean.

Strangely, inches from a dunking, Sebastian did not feel the least bit seasick. He did, however, feel in about the most hopeless and dangerous situation in which he had ever been. He heard the New Hampshire thug on the deck above walking toward him.

The thug disdained the course that would result in a body floating in the harbour with a bullet in it, which according to every crime drama on TV could be traced. Besides, he did not have orders to kill boarders. He set his gun on the deck and, crouching, started to work the collar of Sebastian's Navy sport jacket free of the stanchion. The harbour's frigid water would kill Sebastian as surely as a bullet, if not quite as swiftly. He could not have known his victim could not swim, which would only hasten Sebastian's demise.

Sebastian felt his precarious attachment to *Jana* slipping and prepared himself for a drowning. Apart from the *Jana*, where his reception upon attempting to return would be far from warm, the nearest dry object was the freighter. The impossibility of scaling the sheer sides of that leviathan of the sea made that avenue to safety appear hopeless. The shore was at least 500 yards or, in keeping with the naval setting, a tenth of a league away. In any case, Sebastian knew that as soon as he hit the water, he would be fighting just to keep his head above water, let alone struggling to try to make any progress toward dry land. 'I die,' he thought, recalling Byron, 'but first I have possess'd, And come what may, I have been bless'd' by my dear Elizabeth. Was this the end?

Facing the prospect of a liquid grave, Sebastian reminded himself of his favorite Lord Byron quote, 'Brave men are all vertebrates; they have their softness on the surface and their toughness in the middle.' Praying the quote applied to him, Sebastian decided he still had some fight left in him. Live or die, he would fight until he could no longer do battle. The rapier still glinted in his hand. He swung the sword above his head with all the strength he could muster in his awkward position. Although he could not be considered by even the kindest of critics to be anywhere close to the classic position to employ a rapier, the narrow blade found its mark. It was, however, not the mark for which Sebastian had been aiming: the thug's cranium. The rapier connected instead with a line secured to a stanchion. Although a prop, the rapier was sharp, given the play director's passion for realism, and sliced the line clean through. Although the line was merely a secondary one holding the furled spinnaker in place, there was enough tension on the line to send the end of it whipping into the thug's right eye as he looked up at the sound of the whoosh of the rapier.

The thug screamed. He pressed both hands to his injured eye. Reeling in fright and pain, he lost his footing and pitched off the deck. Sebastian scrunched up his shoulders, trying to make himself as small as possible as the huge body tumbled past him into the water with an orca-sized splash.

Greatly relieved but far from out of danger, Sebastian reached up with his left hand and grabbed the edge of the polished, teak deck. No sooner had he gained a four-finger hold than the remaining New Hampshire thug at the *Jana*'s wheel, spying his accomplice splashing around just astern and Sebastian hanging around near the bow, slammed the wheel hard to port. The *Jana* heeled hard over and Sebastian was dunked into the cold water up to his chest. His sport coat, luckily, was most securely snared on the stanchion.

The thug at the wheel spun the wheel hard to starboard. As the *Jana* heeled over in the opposite direction, Sebastian was hauled out of the water. As he lay against the exposed hull above the water line, water draining from every pocket, pant leg and sleeve, he realized he had been given a slim chance at life. Dropping the rapier, which fell into the water but freed his other hand, he struggled to slip out of his jacket. If he could, then he could swing back aboard the *Jana*, or so he fervently prayed. No sooner had he got one arm free than the thug at the wheel spun the helm back hard to port. Sebastian was dumped back into the water. Attached to the *Jana* by a sleeve, he was terrified that he was about to be keelhauled, but he remained in the sleeve of his jacket and the jacket remained ensnared on the stanchion. He made a mental note, if he lived, to write a glowing letter of recommendation to his tailor for the jacket's sturdy, yet handsome, stitching.

The *Jana* returned to an even keel. Sebastian once again hung with waves slapping the soles of his shoes. He grabbed the deck again with his left hand. Wriggling his other arm free of his jacket, he grabbed the deck with his right hand. Hauling himself up, he was finally back on dry deck. As he sat up to get his bearings and blink the salt water out of his eyes, not to mention calm his thumping heart, he perceived the second, smaller New Hampshire thug standing right in front of him. Having abandoned the wheel to determine if his unwanted visitor had been unceremoniously piped overboard, the thug had arrived just as Sebastian regained the deck.

As Sebastian wished he had somehow retained his rapier, the thug—like his colleague, not wishing to leave a traceable lead sample in a corpse—lowered his suit-clad shoulder and hit Sebastian like an NFL linebacker attempting to force a running back out of bounds. Disoriented from his recent washing, Sebastian did not have a chance. He tumbled back into the water and went under. Fear reached out and seized his heart with all 10 icy fingers. He could not swim and now he was in the middle of Burrard Inlet under four feet of water. Filled with terror, he flailed his arms like the drowning man he was.

Sebastian had saltwater in his mouth. All he saw before his wide-open eyes was a swirling, green-and-white kaleidoscope of bubbles, water and the occasional light from above, which he feared was God calling him home, but in reality was merely sunlight filtered through several feet of water as he tumbled and spun around in the nearby freighter's turbulent wake. Righting himself, he clawed for the surface. His hand struck the *Jana*'s hull and, overjoyed there was something solid still within reach, he flailed with both hands. He scratched. He clawed. He grabbed for any hold he could find on the smooth, slick hull. Even as he burst to the surface beside the *Jana* and gulped down air, he kicked like an Olympic sprinter. All he found with his desperately grasping hands, however, was smooth fiberglass as the *Jana* putt-putted serenely past, oblivious to the man drowning alongside her.

A wave crashed over Sebastian's head and, he feared, he had lost his last chance at survival. The hull was suddenly gone, having passed him by. Unable to swim and far from shore, he knew he was a dead man with a long-term reservation for a compartment in Davy Jones' locker. He thought of Elizabeth, hoping their rapprochement of the night before was still fresh in her mind. He hoped she would remember him for the good times: the trip to

Chateau Lake Louise in the Rockies; their trips to Venice, the Scottish Highlands and Santorini; the surprise breakfasts; the bird bath; the daily, morning romantic emails; and the thousands of other things that had been symbols of their life together and of their love. Then he realized that Elizabeth, if indeed a prisoner aboard the *Jana*, may not be much longer for this life than he would be. He could not allow that to happen. He might die, but she must not cast off her rather fine mortal coil.

Knowing he must rescue her, he kicked desperately back toward where he thought the *Jana* must be. His right hand struck something hard: the ladder on the *Jana*'s stern. In an instant, he had both hands on a metal rung. Having gazed into a liquid grave and realized it was not yet time to cast off his mortal coil, with a burst of energy he scrambled up the ladder and collapsed into the *Jana*'s cockpit.

He had survived.

But for how long? The other thug was still aboard, had a gun and would not take kindly to Sebastian once again arriving uninvited, unannounced and unwanted. Worse, Sebastian's trusty rapier, which he had used to best the revolver-armed Dr. Villano and the first New Hampshire thug, now lay somewhere at the bottom of Burrard Inlet.

Ignoring the shivers wracking his body from the drenching in the harbour's icy waters, he scrambled to his feet and found himself at the untended wheel. He spotted the remaining thug making his way along the narrow ledge on the *Jana*'s starboard side. The thug had not yet looked astern and was unaware Sebastian had emerged from the sea, like one of those Icelandic, volcanic islands that are created every once in a geologic while.

Sebastian grabbed the wheel and spun it hard to starboard. The sudden movement surprised the thug, who only avoided a fate similar to Sebastian's recent dunking by grabbing a safety line running around the edge of the cabin's roof. Unfortunately, the sudden shift to starboard and the bobbing of the boat was making Sebastian queasier by the second. Focused on his task, he ignored his churning stomach and spun the wheel as fast as he could to port, then starboard and back to port. The thug clung to the safety line with both hands like a limpet on a choice rock.

Back and forth Sebastian spun the wheel. Feeling like he must soon succumb to the *mal du mare*, he stood up straight, sticking his head above the windscreen so the sea breeze hit him squarely in his sweat-soaked face. The breeze helped, but the constant heeling over of the *Jana*, first left, then right, then left again, only worsened his condition. The alternative was to allow the thug to abandon the defensive and go on what undoubtedly would be a rather deadly offensive, at least where Sebastian was concerned.

The thug, however, was not to be kept on the defensive no matter how vigorously Sebastian performed his imitation of a roulette wheel. Clinging to the line with one hand, the thug reached into his coat. He withdrew a .45 and aimed it right between Sebastian's startled, if somewhat seasick, eyes.

Sebastian ducked just as the thug fired. The bullet missed. From the safety of a crouch behind the cabin, Sebastian spun the wheel back and forth even as his sea sickness engulfed him. As the world spun before his eyes, Sebastian stuck his head above the cabin again so the breeze would keep his nausea at bay. The thug, having grabbed the safety line again with both hands, albeit with the gun still in one hand, spotted his target. He shot again, but this time quickly, barely aiming, as he rushed to get his gun hand back onto the safety line. Sebastian, ducking again, spun the wheel hard to port.

The game went on for what seemed to Sebastian like a nauseous eternity. He would crouch, heeling the *Jana* over to starboard, then to port, then back to starboard, trying to dislodge the pesky thug or, at least, keeping both his hands occupied. *Jana's* motion in the ocean made Sebastian nauseous and green, forcing him to raise his head above the windscreen into the breeze to avoid vomiting and losing control of the boat. The thug, clinging to the safety line, snapped off a shot at Sebastian's bobbing head like a target in a shooting gallery every time Sebastian stuck his head above the windscreen. The thug would then grab the safety line again with both hands as Sebastian ducked and spun the wheel hard over.

It appeared as if the game would continue until the *Jana* crossed the immense Pacific and ran aground on some Japanese beach. But then Sebastian ducked again as the thug let go of the line with his gun hand to take another shot. Above the gentle throb of the *Jana*'s small engine and the rush of water beneath the keel, Sebastian heard the unmistakable click of a dry fire. The .45 was empty. Japan would play no part in this maritime saga.

Sebastian stood. The thug glared at him and, if looks could kill, Sebastian would have been buried at sea. Not being a basilisk or a medusa, the thug's glare did nothing but spur Sebastian on. As he spun the wheel right and left, no longer fearing the *mal du mare* with the blast of cold sea air hitting him square in the mug, Sebastian grabbed the safety line that went around the edge of the cabin roof.

The thug stuffed his gun into a pocket and dug a new magazine out from an inside pocket of his suit. He now faced the problem of inserting the new magazine into his gun with one hand, while keeping his other hand on the lifeline. As soon as he spotted what Sebastian was up to, however, the thug grabbed the line with both hands. Sebastian yanked and pulled the line, trying to make the thug lose his grip. Unfortunately, the line had little play in it and the thug's two-handed grip acted the same as a pair of vices.

"Ahoy!"

Sebastian had been so focused on the battle at hand he had not even noticed the *Juliet* coming alongside. He stole a glance over at Nelson, his captain's hat at a jaunty angle as he stood at the *Juliet*'s wheel. Nelson waved Sebastian's other rapier, looking all the world like a modern-day pirate. "Can you use this?"

"Aye, aye! Throw it to me!" Sebastian yelled as he spun the *Jana*'s wheel to port to keep the thug's hands occupied in endeavors other than reloading.

The *Jana* and the *Juliet* moved apart. Sebastian spun the wheel back to starboard and as the two boats raced back together, Nelson threw the rapier across the intervening chasm of water. Sebastian meant to catch the weapon, but he dared not pause his spinning of the wheel and the rapier clattered to the deck behind him. The thug, seeing what was happening, took two shuffling steps toward the stern. He was within five feet of Sebastian as the English professor spun the wheel hard to port and, reaching out with his soggy shoe, drew the rapier toward him across the deck. Two more spins of the wheel to keep the thug occupied and Sebastian had the rapier atop his shoe. Reaching down with one hand while keeping his other hand on the wheel and raising his foot carefully, he grabbed the rapier. In one smooth motion, he swung it up, over and down on the safety line. The rapier cut the line. The thug, his lifeline suddenly slack, tumbled over backward into the water. As the new captain of the sailboat, Sebastian watched the thug thrash and curse in the water as the *Jana* cruised past in stately formation with the *Juliet*.

Once satisfied that the thug was far astern and would not be making a return appearance on the *Jana*, Sebastian flung open the cabin hatch and leapt down the three narrow steps. Bundled under a rough blanket was a form Sebastian could never fail to recognize; his Elizabeth.

"'Cooped in their'—or her—'winged sea-gift citadel,'" Sebastian exclaimed.

He flung the blanket back to reveal...three pillows.

Staring, mouth open, Sebastian tried to comprehend what he was seeing. He quickly searched the rest of the cabin, but there was little to search and he found no wife. Seized with a dark and abiding fear, he stood in the middle of the cabin contemplating the fact that the New Hampshire thugs may have already disposed of Elizabeth in a burial at sea.

Filled with despair, his tear-glazed eyes fell on a table in the galley on which sat a log. He rushed over and, poring over the ledger and an accompanying chart, learned that the two New Hampshire thugs had been planning to sail the *Jana* around Stanley Park to rendezvous with Villano at False Creek, near GM Place. There was no mention of Elizabeth, but Sebastian hoped and prayed Villano had her, not Davey Jones.

Even as he resolved not to abandon his rescue attempt until he had definite proof that Elizabeth was no more, a loud, grinding collision threw him to the deck. Sebastian wondered what had happened now to cap this most eventful day. Picking himself up, bruised but unharmed, he rushed out of the cabin and found that the *Jana* had run aground on a sand bar off Spanish Banks, just outside Vancouver Harbour. He turned off the engine to prevent her from pushing herself any further up onto the bar and damaging her graceful bow.

"Ahoy!" It was Nelson nearby on the *Juliet*. "Where's the missus?"

Sebastian shook his head, the picture of loss. "She must be at GM Place."

"Need a water taxi?"

Sebastian had a wife to rescue—at least he desperately hoped he had a wife left alive to rescue—and a bomb plot to defuse, if Bill and Lester had not already succeeded in their task, so he quickly accepted the offer. It only took a few moments for the cabin cruiser *Juliet*, whose draft was shallower than the big-keeled sailboat, to come alongside the *Jana* and take Sebastian off.

"The Harbour Police are picking up those two buccaneers," Nelson reported. "If they haven't frozen to death."

"Good, but as Wordsworth said, there are still 'Wrongs unredressed, or insults unavenged.'"

"Off we go!" Nelson said, without even asking why, the game was afoot. He threw the throttles wide open and set a course for nearby False Creek.

Feeling piqued, Sebastian said, "Maybe you could just put me ashore and I'll call a cab." He had been at sea quite long enough for any lover of solid land. It seemed as if he had been at least three years before the mast.

"Get your head above the wind screen," Nelson ordered. "You'll be fine. You're an experienced sailor, now."

"Alright. 'Once more upon the waters! yet once more! And the waves bound beneath me as a steed That knows his rider.'"

In 10 minutes Nelson had put in at the False Creek Marina.

"Thanks for everything, Nelson," Sebastian said as he scrambled onto the wharf. He had never been happier to be back on dry wood. "Sorry about the bullet hole in the *Juliet*." His affection for the Shakespearean craft had half convinced him to start pronouncing the name of his favorite car, the Alfa Romeo, the same as the name of the bard's star-crossed young lover and not, as he had always done, like the last name of the actor, Cesar Romero, but without the second "r", as in row-may-oh.

"I doubt the owner will even notice after I putty it over," Nelson said. "I better get her back before he notices she's gone."

"She's not yours?" Sebastian asked, stunned.

"I'm a retired janitor. I could never afford this beauty. I do odd jobs around the marina for a little extra cash."

"Do you know a custodial engineer named Lester Means?"

"Nope; different union. Why?"

"I should introduce you. With advice from him, you could afford the *Queen Mary*."

Chapter 39

Outside the new global Mecca of round ball, Lester and Bill sat, shoulders slumped, eyes downcast, on the steps overlooking False Creek. Lester was frantically making calls on his cell, while Bill, hand-rolled cigarette in mouth, was idly playing with a rapier when Sebastian sprinted up the steps to GM Place.

"You're waterlogged," Bill observed, stating the obvious in lieu of a greeting.

"Better than being a dead head," Sebastian replied.

Bill asked, "Where's Elizabeth?"

"She wasn't on the boat. Villano may have her or, if he doesn't, he'll know where she is. Why aren't you inside?"

"Lester failed us," Bill said sadly, profound disappointment mixed with the utmost disbelief in his voice.

"I've called everyone I know and no luck," Lester wailed. "Security is tighter than for the Asia-Pacific Summit."

"You got into the summit?" Bill asked.

"I didn't. My cousin's best buddy wanted to meet the Prime Minister of Japan. It was the least I could do, considering."

"Considering what?" Bill asked.

"We don't have time for this," Sebastian warned.

"Considering said cousin's best buddy worked at a gas station," Lester said as he glanced through his electronic phone book. "I give up. I've called everyone with the faintest connection to GM Place, the Grizzlies, basketball, the media or sports in general. I can't get us in. I even called in a bomb threat, but the cops said they already have two inspectors inside investigating a bomb threat."

"What's a gas station got to do with meeting the Prime Minister of Japan?" Bill asked, persisting in his quest for an explanation from Lester.

Sebastian tapped his sodden shoe, making a squishy sound that failed to convey his growing irritation at the direction of the conversation, which was drifting dangerously off course.

"Nothing whatsoever," Lester replied.

"Then why did you arrange for your cousin's best buddy to meet the Prime Minister of Japan?" Bill asked, wandering deeper into the maze of Lester's business dealings, which even Internal Revenue Canada had given up even attempting to begin to investigate, let alone understand.

"That's enough!" Sebastian snapped. The dunking in Burrard Inlet, being shot at, reaching the verge of seasickness several times, and being worried sick over his missing wife, had done nothing but darken his mood and shorten his patience. He had, in short, had enough. "Give me that," he barked and grabbed the rapier from Bill. "Let's go."

Leaving wet, salty shoeprints, Sebastian led the way up the steps followed by a curious Lester and an offended Bill, who still wanted to discover the relationship between Lester, his cousin's buddy, a gas station and the Prime Minister of Japan. Rapier at the ready, Sebastian stalked up to a security guard at one of the arena's doors. The guard failed to suppress a smirk at the soggy apparition standing before him.

"Can I help you, sir?"

"I have reason to believe there's a bomb in a basketball in the arena and the villain who did it kidnapped my wife," Sebastian stated, deciding to cut to the quick, even if it drew blood in the form of disbelief.

"A basketball bomb?" The guard's smirk deepened.

"Exactly."

"I'm sorry, sir, but I can't let you in," the guard said, folding his beefy arms across his ample chest.

Sebastian, his temper short and wet, decided that *audace, toujour audace* was the order of the day. He whipped the rapier up and stopped it an inch below the 6-foot-4-inch guard's chin. The move was impressive, although less so to Sebastian who had hoped to stop the blade an inch below the guard's prominent proboscis.

"Open the door," Sebastian ordered the now white-faced rent-a-cop.

Holding his head steady and aloof in order to avoid the rapier like a debutante-to-be balancing a book on her head, the guard reached back and pushed open the door.

"Keep him occupied, Lester," Sebastian ordered, handing Lester the guard's riot baton—being Canada, he had not been armed with a gun—to keep the guard civil.

Sebastian ran across the concourse with Bill close behind. They bounded down the bleacher stairs to the basketball court, where the Grizzlies practiced for their next game against the Chicago Bulls, who needed another Michael Jordan or three to stand even the remotest chance of taming the Grizzlies.

Outside, the dark-haired man who drove the rented red sedan approached Lester and the guard, who were already discussing a possible deal to trade tickets to an upcoming concert for a new home theater system. The stranger asked for Sebastian and was visibly distressed when he was told once again he had just missed the elusive professor. The dark-haired man was on the point of giving up on this particular job, when he started to talk to Lester, who could help anyone solve any problem.

Inside the Grizzly Den, as GM Place had been nicknamed by Vancouver's preeminent sportswriter, Neil Williams, only to have credit for the name appropriated by a *Sports Illustrated* reporter, Sebastian spied a profusion of basketball players and, worse, balls. The whole team was there; "Dead-Eye" Polotnik, his good eye focused on the basket as he practiced shooting three-pointers from mid-court; Eddie "3-Point" Anderson, dribbling up and down the court as he recovered from a strained instep muscle suffered during a drunken croquet game; and the twin Hills, Jack and Gill, working with basket-rim-scraping Bertram Reginald

"Roddy" Windsor on their soon-to-be patented in the form of a video game, Bear Bite Defense. But, most distressing for Sebastian, there was no sign of Elizabeth or Villano.

With the rescue mission apparently on hold, the bomb took precedence and Sebastian knew what he must do. He flew into the practice session wielding his rapier with a verve and spirit rarely seen in Grizzly opponents of late. Coming in on Dead-Eye from his blind side, Sebastian had impaled the basketball the star was about to shoot before the phenom even knew he was under assault. The ball went poof and deflated. Not having found the bomb, Sebastian raced after 3-Point Anderson as the guard sped up court, dribbling. Anderson chose that moment to change direction and Sebastian, his shoes as moist as the Pacific, slid past him but not before he connected with a slashing attack with his rapier. Anderson was mystified to find no ball returning to his hand. Looking back and down, he saw the two halves of the ball he had been dribbling dying a slow and wobbly death on the boards.

Sebastian had already picked himself up, leaving a rather large wet streak on the hardwood. He raced down court, his shoes squelching, toward the remainder of the starting five as they practiced at the other end of the court.

Adderly and Short, viewing all this from the first-row balcony where they had managed to hide themselves after claiming they were investigating a bomb plot, were already racing up the stairs. They sprinted across the concourse and downstairs to the court to apprehend the rapier-wielding, basketball-deflating Dr. Gianninni. The good doctor, however, had time before the imminent arrival of the inspectors and he used every millisecond. The Hills and Roddy Windsor decided a tactical retreat was in order since their Bear Bite Defense had never run into a competing Rapier Offense. Dropping the basketball he was holding, Roddy Windsor retreated toward the stands even as the Hills decided to make themselves scarce behind the basket support. Sebastian was left free to cleave the basketball in half; again, nothing.

"Sebastian!" Bill yelled from the sidelines. "Was that wise?!"

Looking around for any other basketballs, Sebastian yelled back, "What do you mean?!" He panted to catch his breath, for a moment pausing in his quest for the right bomb-laden basketball.

"If any of those had been the bomb, would the roof still be on this place?"

Luckily Bill pointed out the error of Sebastian's methods when he did, for Sebastian was, even then, racing for the ball cart on the far sideline. As Adderly and Short reached the main concourse and ran down between the seats to the court, Sebastian revised his technique and started picking up and testing the weight of each of the balls in the cart.

"Hold it right there!" Short yelled as he and Adderly, 9 mm pistols drawn—Mounties, unlike security guards, carried guns—reached courtside.

Sebastian was holding a basketball gingerly as far from his body as his short arms allowed.

"Don't move!" Adderly shouted, stopping his charge 10 feet from Sebastian, his pistol aimed at the English professor's damp chest.

"This basketball is a bomb," Sebastian announced, holding the ball carefully and gingerly like the newborn baby of an overprotective Grizzly mother.

"Yeah," Adderly said, "and we're all basketball hoops."

"It *is* a bomb."

"I suggest you listen to my nephew," Bill began, walking toward the triangle of tense men on the far side of the court.

"Stay out of this, old man," Adderly barked, his classes on police-civilian relations forgotten.

Bill decided he may as well retreat into the stands, hopefully out of range of any impending explosion. If the basketball was a bomb and it went off, he would be glad to identify the remains of one uncommonly rude Mountie.

Sebastian held the ball in one hand and reached back with his rapier in the other.

"Freeze!" Short yelled.

Bill ducked behind the nineteenth row of seats while he calculated the odds of surviving an explosion in that particular position relative to where the basketball was then being held by his nephew. He need not have bothered.

In light of Bill's comment, Sebastian reconsidered attacking this particular basketball with his rapier. Sebastian stuck the blade in his belt and, basketball held high, he turned and sprinted up an aisle behind him. Adderly and Short set off in pursuit. After a few dozen steps it became a hot pursuit as the two inspectors, long on paper work and short on physical fitness, were soon sweating, both experiencing near-death experiences. Either inspector would have loved to have just shot their suspect so they could stop running, but Sebastian had not threatened them directly and an Internal Affairs investigation of an OIS (Officer Involved Shooting) was the last thing either inspector desired. It devoured time off like a second job. Worse, it would nix both their applications to participate in the world-famous RCMP Musical Ride the following year. The ladies went wild for the red-coated riders and neither inspector wanted to risk losing out on that splendid opportunity for female companionship.

When Sebastian reached the concourse he headed straight for a snoozing guard atop a metal chair.

"I've got a bomb! Open the door!" It was a rather dramatic way to ask to have the door opened, but he thought it would do the trick. It did.

Once outside, Sebastian saw he was on the city side of the arena with nothing but pedestrians, cars and office buildings for miles before him. As Adderly and Short burst out of GM Place behind him, Sebastian recalled his fondness for a certain body of water as a location for the disposal of bombs. Water-cooled by his soaked suit, Sebastian led the way, basketball held high, around the arena toward False Creek.

Sebastian would have made it to the water and, very probably, would have safely disposed of the suspected basketball bomb had it not been for his right sole. Made by a less gifted artisan than the tailor who had stitched his jacket, the dunking in Burrard Inlet had loosened it. As Sebastian sprinted toward the broad stairs that led from GM Place down toward the parking lot and Pacific Boulevard, which skirted False Creek, the sole came loose. It flapped open, caught on the cement and Sebastian fell if he had tripped on a Leprechaun's clothesline. Sprawling face first, he tried to hang onto the basketball but, his hands wet and still a pale blue from his swim, as well as nearing exhaustion from his day's triathlon of swimming, fencing and running, he lost hold of the basketball.

Slammed into the cement, the air knocked out of his lungs, Sebastian watched as the basketball bounced once, twice and then disappeared down the steps ahead of him. He buried his head in his arms, awaiting the explosion.

"You're under arrest," Short barked as Adderly snapped handcuffs on Sebastian and hauled him to his sodden shoes.

"You don't understand," Sebastian protested. "The ball was a bomb."

He gestured with his nose, since his hands were occupied by the handcuffs, at the basketball as it bounced on its merry way down the steps and out into the empty parking lot.

"Right," Adderly said, "and my gun's a 24-ounce steak."

Adderly and Short turned to take Sebastian back to their car when an explosion slammed them down to the cement. Hogarth had set the basketball bomb to explode after 36 dribbles. This, he and Villano had hoped, would ensure the basketball exploded right in the middle of the Grizzly practice, not when some ball-boy bounced the ball once or twice before practice. The ball had just bounced for its 36th and final time. The ground shook. Chunks of asphalt rained down on the steps just behind them. The world seemed to be the center of a Wagnerian *Gottdomerung*.

As the noise, debris and smoke dissipated, Sebastian, lying between the inspectors, looked over at Adderly and said, "I know a chef who's got a wonderful secret sauce for steak that just might make your gun a tad more edible."

Chapter 40

More hours later than he cared to remember, Sebastian stepped out of the downtown RCMP station. He was still damp, his body ached and he realized that unlike his father who had hunted bears, wrestled steers and broken horses in Alberta well into his sixties, the active life was not for him. He had told his story a dozen times, signed a volume of reports, statements, waivers, and a dozen other forms that he had given up reading after the first three sentences of legalese. Now, finally, he was free to go. And he had been the witness, not the felon. How much paperwork did a criminal have to fill out? It probably took longer to fill out the paperwork than to serve the prison sentence.

Short and Adderly had the airport, port and border blanketed with men looking for Villano and Elizabeth. With only a slight tinge of guilt, Sebastian neglected to mention Hogarth's role in the conspiracy. Hogarth had given Sebastian the information that had enabled him to find the basketball bomb and save the Grizzlies. Even if the young man was an international terrorist, Sebastian would not be the one to finger him. If Hogarth went straight, fine. If he continued fighting for his New Luddite Revolution and was arrested, then it would not be on Sebastian's head. Sebastian liked to think, even if it was a Shakespeare quote, that 'The quality of mercy is not strain'd' in one Sebastian LeClerc Gianninni. He had foiled the plot; the police could worry about punishing the perpetrators. Sebastian's part in the matter would now be restricted to finding his wife. Unfortunately, the two inspectors had interrogated the thugs fished out of the harbour to no avail; Villano had not shared the secret of where he was keeping Elizabeth with either of them.

Outside the station, Bill and Lester waited for Sebastian in Bill's Cadillac. Bill tried to reassure Sebastian by saying, "They'll find her."

Sebastian nodded, far from reassured as they climbed into the Caddy.

"Any leads?" Lester asked.

"None."

Bill started the car and said, "Let's go home."

"They let you keep that?" Lester asked.

"Yeah," Sebastian said, holding his rapier fondly. "They took pictures of it, but figured it wasn't instrumental to the case. I thought it played a crucial role in the day's events."

"I still don't understand why you risked blowing us all up by attacking the basketballs with that thing," Bill said as they started south for Blaine.

"I needed the fastest way to find the bomb," Sebastian explained from the back seat. "I didn't know if the bomb was set to go off at any minute, so I figured a rapier through the ball would remove all doubts about which were real balls and which were bombs."

"It didn't occur to you that a bomb might react rather negatively to a sword going through it?" Bill asked, wondering if his nephew had fallen far from the family genetic apple tree, which generally produced relatively sane, intelligent apples.

"I didn't think the bomb would be set to explode if a sword hit it," Sebastian said, his words coming with difficulty as weariness enveloped him. "The suitcase didn't explode when it hit the water and, besides, who would design a bomb with a rapier in mind?"

In the depths of despair over Elizabeth, Sebastian stared dejectedly out the window as they drove past GM Place.

"There's the crater from the basketball bomb," Bill said, pointing at the 36-foot hole in the parking lot. Crews were filling in the unplanned excavation and preparing to resurface the lot for that evening's game. They would need the parking spaces. As usual, the game was sold out.

Bill swung south past the end of False Creek and Sebastian looked over at the Pacific Central Station. An ornate, beaux arts edifice built in 1910, it was a symbol of an earlier, genteel age of travel, when rail ruled the world—or at least the land portion of it.

"The railroad!" Sebastian exclaimed, sitting upright as if someone had jammed him in the backside with an epee.

"Yeah," Lester began, "one of my first jobs was with the Canadian National Railway—"

"Adderly and Short said they were covering the border, the airport and the port," Sebastian interrupted, "but not the railway."

"But if Villano takes a train, he'll have to cross the border to get out of the country," Bill said.

"Only if he goes south. Turn around! Go back to the station. He may have Elizabeth with him and, if he doesn't, I'll make him tell me where she is, if it's the last thing I ever do."

"I still don't see," Bill began, even as he waited for a break in the oncoming traffic to swing the enormous Cadillac around.

"Villano can take a train east across Canada with Elizabeth," Sebastian explained, "Then he can take a boat from a port on the east coast."

"A police alert for them must have gone out all across the country," Lester said, familiar with the workings of the police given his many dealings with them regarding the ownership of various and sundry, and not so sundry, goods.

"If it takes Villano four or five days to take the train to the east coast, it'll give him ample time to change his appearance, and by then the cops will have relaxed their vigilance."

"And the police will be focusing on the west coast, not the east coast," Bill said, warming to the idea.

Bill swung his yellow convertible around to a cacophony of horns and curses from other drivers, before turning into the Pacific Central Station parking lot. Trusty rapier in hand, Sebastian leapt out, ignoring the screams of his bruised and battered body, and sprinted for the entrance. Bill and Lester followed their leader inside.

"I'll talk to a ticket agent I know," Lester said, peeling off from the others. "He might be able to tell me if Villano or anyone answering his description bought a ticket today."

"Ask if anyone saw Elizabeth, too," Sebastian urged the custodial engineer.

"I'll call Adderly and Short," Bill said, heading for a bank of telephones as he dug in his pockets for change.

Sebastian ran through the doors and out onto an expanse of platforms that stood under metal canopies to shield travelers from the famous and persistent Vancouver rain. Unlike during the height of train travel when the Canadian National Railway built the station, most of the platforms and tracks were empty. Only two passenger trains sat awaiting the signal to chug away for points across North America. Sebastian sprinted up to a porter.

"Where are these trains going?" Sebastian asked, fighting to get his breathing back to normal after the dash from the parking lot.

The porter sniffed at the appearance of the dirty, middle-aged man dressed in wrinkled clothes that appeared to have been laundered in dirty harbour water. Even so, he politely replied, "Track 3 is destined for Banff, Jasper, Edmonton, Hay River and, via ferry, Yellowknife. Track 4 is the Transcontinental Line, destined for Hope, Spuzzum, Calgary, Regina, Winnipeg, Thunder Bay, Sudbury, Toronto, Montreal, Quebec City, Fredericton, Antigonish, and Halifax."

Yellowknife was difficult to use as a starting point to go anywhere, so Sebastian rushed over to Track 4. He jumped up to peer in the window of the first car: no Villano or Elizabeth. He checked the second car. No one looked like Villano or Elizabeth, even in disguise. Sebastian rushed on to check the third car. He was near giving up hope when, in a gap between curtains drawn across a compartment, Sebastian caught a glimpse of part of the back of a woman's head. He would have recognized that head anywhere: it was Elizabeth's.

Villano spotted Sebastian jumping up and down outside his cabin's window. It was not difficult to do since everyone on the platform was looking at the man who appeared to be a hobo doing his imitation of a rapier-armed jack rabbit. As Sebastian rushed toward one end of the car to gain entry, Villano, unseen by his pursuer, went the other way to exit from the opposite end of the car. His plan should have worked. He would have exited the car from the front, just as Sebastian entered from the rear. Villano, however, did not count on the presence of a studious ticket porter.

"Your ticket, please, sir," the elderly porter asked when Sebastian reached the car's rear steps.

"I don't have a ticket," Sebastian replied.

"I'm sorry, but you can't board without a ticket."

"I don't want to take the train. My wife was kidnapped and is being held in this car."

"Kidnapped? On one of our trains? You must be mistaken, sir."

"I am most definitely not."

"In any case, I am sorry," the porter began again, but was cut short as Sebastian, assuming his stunt with the GM Place guard would be equally successful on a Via Rail ticket porter, whipped his rapier up to the porter's chin and demanded admittance. Ungentlemanly behavior, true, but these were desperate times.

The porter had seen it all; if not rapiers, then at least knives, blackjacks and the occasional gun. Without a second's hesitation, he grabbed the rapier with his white-gloved hand and thrust it back at Sebastian like an unwanted advance by a seedy lady of the night.

"I am sorry, sir," the porter said, keeping his manner courteous even in the face of a most uncouth act, "you cannot board."

Dismayed at the failure of his stratagem, Sebastian was about to plead his case, when he spotted Villano sprinting up the platform toward the terminal. Sebastian raced after him, leaving the porter to regret the dark line left on his white glove by the encounter with the tire-rubber-stained rapier, as well as the decline in the class of passengers the railway was attracting these days.

"Stand and fight, you cur!" Sebastian yelled, scattering passengers left and right as he brandished his rapier.

Villano drew a revolver from his coat pocket, stopped and aimed at Sebastian, who darted behind a metal column. Villano fired. The bullet whined off the metal girder inches from Sebastian's nose. Villano turned and rushed for the door. He probably would have made good his escape if it was not for the terminal door. Many people have had difficult encounters with doors. A door may have a plaque that says 'push' and they pull, or vice versa. At normal walking speed the encounter involves a sudden stop, mild embarrassment, and then reassessment of the situation and an adjustment of the direction in which one's hand is applying pressure to the door handle.

Villano encountered this phenomenon at full speed and with his head turned back to keep an eye on the rapidly approaching Sebastian and his rapier. Villano grabbed the polished brass door handle and pushed. He would have been through the door in one smooth motion if the door had opened into the terminal. It did not. He was stopped as suddenly and as assuredly as if he had run into a wall made of the finest brick and stickiest mortar. His chest, left arm and temple struck the resisting door with a force similar to that provided by the right upper cut of the middle-weight champion of the world, not just a single-belt holder, but the real champion who has consolidated all of the many and varied championship belts. Villano collapsed like a marionette whose strings some uncouth child has snipped with their mother's sewing scissors.

When Sebastian arrived, he found Villano motionless on the floor. Sebastian scooped up the revolver Villano had dropped and slid it, safety on, into his jacket pocket.

"Is he dead?" an onlooker asked fearfully, having heard the impact of Villano's head with the unyielding door all the way across the platform. The impact had sounded ominously similar to a coconut hitting the pavement after being dropped from a twelfth-floor balcony.

Sebastian kneeled and felt for a pulse. "No, he's alive."

"I'll call an ambulance," a bystander said and hurried into the terminal.

Villano opened his eyes and groaned.

"The police and an ambulance are on their way," Sebastian said, hoping Bill had contacted Adderly and Short and convinced them to high-tail it to the station.

"The truth be told, I don't think I was ever cut out for a life of crime."

"You really need to start young," Lester advised as he arrived. "All the greats do."

"Lester, good of you to come," Villano said, still lying on the platform. "It's fitting that you're in on this little adventure at the end, since you were in on it at the beginning."

"Give me your ticket and the key to your compartment," Sebastian ordered Villano, who complied. "Watch him," Sebastian ordered Lester, handing him Villano's gun. Sebastian sprinted back to the third rail car.

After using Villano's key, Sebastian flung open the door to Villano's sleeping cabin to behold his Elizabeth, reading the *Wall Street Journal* and sipping chamomile tea.

"Sebastian!"

"Elizabeth!"

"I feared never to hear your voice again; 'The devil hath not, in all his quiver's choice, An arrow for the heart like a sweet voice.' Your sweet voice, Elizabeth."

They hugged and kissed.

"'I had no earthly hope,'" Elizabeth said, reciting a line from one of Sebastian's favorite poems, Byron's "The Prisoner of Chillon."

"'With what a deep devotedness of woe I wept thy absence— o'er and o'er again / Thinking of thee, still thee, til thought grew pain, / And memory, like a drop that, night and day, / Falls cold and ceaseless, wore my heart away!'"

"Keats?"

"Thomas Moore."

"Lovely. How did you ever find me?"

Sebastian gave a Cliff Notes version of his day and then Elizabeth filled him in on her day. She rose early to behold a sunny and newly romantic world. She found Sebastian sound asleep after the night's activities, terrorist and otherwise. She had fetched the *Wall Street Journal* from the front lawn, happy to see her Mercedes recently delivered from the garage in the driveway, and re-treated to the bench in the back garden to read her paper and admire her new birdbath. She was surprised when two men in coveralls skulked around the corner of the house. One carried a small tool chest and the other a canvas sack. They were facing the house and behaving in a most secretive and sneaky fashion. She jumped to a conclusion: a totally wrong conclusion, but a conclusion nonetheless.

"If you installed it wrong, you don't have to sneak back at such an early hour to fix it," she said.

The men spun around as if they had been caught with pockets bulging with coins in the National Mint. Both looked as confused and dumbfounded as Sebastian looked when she discussed how she had diversified their retirement accounts by asset, sector, risk, term, time horizon, and nationality.

Thinking the men had not heard her, Elizabeth tried again. "I said, if you installed it wrong, you could have come back during normal business hours to fix it. What's wrong with it anyway?"

"With what?" one of the men asked, as confused as any man has been in the presence of a female, which is to say, supremely confused.

"The bird bath, of course."

The two men looked at each other. The taller one nodded and, as if as one, they lunged at Elizabeth. In a moment, she was tied up, gagged and jammed into the canvas sack in a most undignified and uncomfortable position. Her cries, muffled by the gag and the sack, barely reached beyond her dark, confined canvas world. She was hustled around the house and stuffed into her car's trunk. The thugs drove her Mercedes across the border. They even used one of Sebastian's novels as a decoy to sell to the border guard and distract his attention from inspecting the car, especially the trunk, which had been turned into a steerage compartment for Elizabeth and the explosive suitcase. Luckily for them, the thugs ran into a border guard who was married to a romance aficionado, or maybe it was an aficionadress. Once in Vancouver, the thugs had delivered Elizabeth to Villano, who then took her along to plant his bomb before they boarded the train to make good his escape.

Sebastian asked, "Did Villano harm you, my love?"

"Of course not. He was a perfect gentleman."

Arm in arm, Elizabeth and Sebastian strolled back to where Villano still lay, nursing his bruised brain.

"Are you alright?" Sebastian asked.

"I fear so, but only to face a lifetime in prison."

"I understand all the network stuff and the link to the Grizzlies," Sebastian said, "but why'd you do it? You're a tenured, full professor with a beautiful wife, a nice house, a boat. Why risk it all?"

"It was a lot of money," Villano said with a grin. "If I succeeded, then like Pistol, 'Why, then the world's mine oyster, / Which I with sword will open.'"

"What would you do with a pile of cash?" Sebastian asked.

"I still have dreams and 'We are such stuff as dreams are made off.'"

"But why?"

"'When beggars die there are no comets seen.'"

"Quit quoting Shakespeare and answer my question!" Sebastian demanded, losing patience with his colleague.

Villano hesitated and then, realizing the final whistle had blown, confessed, "So I could leave my wife."

Sebastian, Elizabeth and Lester stared down at Villano in shock.

"She and I have been drifting apart for years," Villano explained, gingerly probing his bruised head. "When we met, though, it was love at second sight."

"Second sight?" Sebastian asked.

"The first time we met I was working for her father on a research project with a looming deadline. I hadn't shaved in three days, my hair was long and I looked like a tramp, sort of like you, today," Villano said, gesturing at the rumpled, sea-washed Sebastian. "The second time though, I had cleaned myself up to meet her father at their house to discuss our next project. She answered the door and I thought she was the most beautiful woman in the world. She filled my eyes and, besides her incomparable looks, she was fascinating. Everything she said and everything she had done seemed like she had come from another world from mine.

I was enthralled. I asked her for a date and we were married six months later."

"Sounds idyllic," Elizabeth said wistfully.

Villano managed to sit up. "It was, for years. I got her flowers for no reason other than that I loved her. I wrote her little love notes regularly. I complimented how she looked, bought her nice dresses and planned romantic trips, evenings of steaming baths on cold winter nights, and succulent dinners in bed. It was bliss."

Elizabeth asked, "What happened?"

"She got busy with her career, as I did with mine. We began to take each other for granted. I lost count of the times I prepared a wonderful breakfast in bed and she had an early morning meeting and barely had time for a mouthful."

Elizabeth looked down at her shoes.

"I would try to initiate intimate evenings and she would say it was too late, she was too tired or suggest we could take the following night off. Then the next night, something else would come up. It was not all her, of course. I was busy facing the-publish-or-perish challenge to get tenure. I wrote articles and went to conferences, leaving her for weekend after weekend, or spent weekends working. I loved my work—we both did—and we drifted apart. When I finally woke up to the state of our marriage and tried to reconnect with her, it was too late."

"It's never too late," Elizabeth asserted, grasping Sebastian's free hand. His other hand held the rapier in Villano's direction.

"Sometimes it is," Villano said. "I tried to rekindle the romance, but we were both nervous. We would plan an evening, but it would be so routine, as if we had done it all before. I tried to be creative, but we were both set in our ways. It was not like it had been. We knew each other too well. It was like we were fulfilling an obligation, not doing what would make each other feel loved."

A silence fell on the group, saddened by the story of faded love.

"I still love her dearly, but I can't stand to live with her and not have the romance and intimacy we once treasured," Villano confessed. "I knew she was as unhappy as I was, since she at times tried and failed to rekindle the flames, too. I decided it would be best to separate. I wanted to leave her the house, the cars and even the boat, so she would have the income and security she deserves, but I needed money to set up my own life. The network would pay me enough to allow me to leave my Jana comfortable here and set up a new life for me overseas. I would have a chance to meet someone else and experience a romance like Jana and I once enjoyed, and she would have the same opportunity."

"You must feel wretched," Elizabeth said.

"'What's gone and what's past help *should* be past grief,'" Villano quoted. "I fear the Bard was right: should be past grief, but is not."

A gloomy silence fell on the group like a shroud.

Bill ambled up to the group, attempting to roll a cigarette. "The police are on their way," he commented as if he were mentioning when the next race was set to parade to post. "Hi, Elizabeth. Great to see you. Are you well?"

"Yes, fine. Thanks for asking."

"As Lear said, 'Come, let's away to prison,'" Villano said, resigned to a long future spent indoors. He started unsteadily to rise.

"Lear was mad when he said that," Sebastian commented, his eyes focused on some distant, faraway place. Lowering his rapier from Villano to his side, he said, "No."

"No?" Bill asked, halting in his construction of a cigarette just as he was about to lick the paper closed. "No, what?"

"No, Dr. Villano is not going to prison."

"He's not?" Bill asked in disbelief.

"No," Sebastian repeated, 'stung by the splendor of a sudden thought.' "Dr. Villano's bombs killed no one. He will pay for the damage to the parking lot at GM Place, while I will cover the expense of the basketballs I punctured." Sebastian did not know the first bomb had sunk the *Unsinkable Molly Brown* nor did he know the lawyers aboard the sunk unsinkable *Ms. Brown* had insurance that would soon build a new boat, christened the *Truly Unsinkable Molly Brown*.

Sebastian outlined his idea.

"Villano should be punished," Bill asserted.

"He's a terrorist," Lester stated.

With newly restored loyalty, Elizabeth supported her husband wholeheartedly. "Sebastian's right, he didn't hurt anyone."

"There's more to a man than the worst thing he has ever done," Sebastian said.

"How can you forgive him? He almost killed you with that basketball bomb," Bill said. "He kidnapped Elizabeth."

"As Shelley wrote, 'Revenge is the naked idol of the worship of a semi-barbarous age.'"

"Have you watched the news recently?" Lester asked. "We live in a semi-, if not completely barbarous age; wars, brutality and barbarity are everywhere. You can't just let him go. He's been our—your enemy."

"'It is easier to forgive an enemy than to forgive a friend,'" Sebastian recited.

"Sounds like something an effeminate poet would say," Bill said, disgusted.

"Blake was not only a poet, he was a printer and a painter, too."

"Well, being a poet and a painter definitely makes him a real man, then," Bill said.

"We don't have time for this," Sebastian said. "My testimony would be crucial to convicting Dr. Villano and I will not provide it."

"Me neither," Elizabeth stated.

"Will you help me or not?" Sebastian asked the others.

Bill and Lester hesitated.

"It'll make a fascinating story for your racetrack cronies, Bill," Sebastian said. "You can probably get a free dinner out of the telling of it, Lester, at Le Crab."

After a pause, Bill and Lester looked at each other and grudgingly nodded.

"The police will be here soon," Sebastian said. "We must act fast. Lester, do you know a place where we can hide Dr. Villano until nightfall?"

"Sure," Lester said, as if he had been asked if there was a fast food restaurant nearby.

"Lester, take Villano in a cab to your hiding place," Sebastian ordered. "Bill, go to Spanish Banks and get the *Jana* off the sand bar."

"Why's my boat on a sand bar?"

Sebastian ignored Villano's question. Time was against them. "Get the *Jana* to Lions Bay Marina by 11 tonight. Lester, you get Villano to Lions Bay right at 11 tonight."

"But there's a Grizzly game tonight," Lester said, sounding like a whining five year old.

"Some things are more important than a game," Sebastian stated.

Lester and Bill stared at him in shock, stunned beyond belief by Sebastian's blasphemous statement.

"What are you going to do?" Elizabeth asked as she and Lester helped Villano to his unsteady feet.

"I'm going to try to give love a second chance."

"It won't work," Villano lamented.

Sebastian said, "You should know that 'The course of true love never did run smooth.'"

Villano said, "I fear this is not a midsummer night, nor is it a dream."

"We might be able to make it a midsummer night and turn this misadventure into a dream," Sebastian asserted. "Now, get going everyone."

It was a hectic day for Sebastian. He had to deal with Adderly and Short, who arrived just after Bill, Lester and Villano slipped out of the station through the repair yard. Lester knew one of the railway engineers. Sebastian dispatched Elizabeth to her office to work on certain legal documents, so he was left to face the inspectors alone. He explained to the Mounties that he had thought Villano might take the train, but had been proved wrong. He also explained with a plausible degree of reluctance that Villano did not have Elizabeth. She had merely hid out at a girlfriend's after a spousal spat. Short and Adderly did not give Sebastian a hard time. They rushed out of the station as fast as they could to return to the police station, where they could watch the Grizzlies-Bulls game on television. Tip-off was mere minutes away.

Attracting the attention of everyone in sight, Sebastian whipped his rapier in a few practice flourishes as he left the railway station. He had so hoped for a dashing, death-defying sword fight on the roof of a moving train, but it was not to be. Villano had no sword and, besides, Sebastian's loose sole, held together with elastic bands from the police station would have seriously impeded his fencing style, especially on the roof of a moving train.

The dark-haired man in the rented red sedan drove toward Sebastian as the English professor waited for a cab in front of the station. Sebastian recognized the car and, deciding Uncle Bill just might be right when he said someone had been following them, sprinted away from the car along the front of the terminal.

"Dr. Gianninni!" The man yelled, even as Sebastian spotted an open cab.

Sebastian piled into the taxi and, waving a $20 bill, urged the cabby to the utmost speed. The driver stomped on the gas pedal. The abrupt acceleration flung Sebastian onto his side on the floor,. By the time he picked himself up, the red sedan was far behind. Sebastian was relieved to have made good his escape, since he had important business to attend to.

The cab took Sebastian to Villano's house, where he found Jana Villano. After an initial shock, Jana grasped the situation fully. Elizabeth arrived with the papers she had drafted after consultation with her company's in-house attorney, which would give Sebastian the power to liquidate all of the Villano's assets in Vancouver. Jana was hesitant to sign but, with a scribbled note from her husband, which Sebastian had taken the precaution of asking Villano to write before his swift departure with Lester, she signed.

At the appointed hour that night, Bill and Captain Nelson Fish, whom Sebastian had recommended to help Bill in easing the *Jana* off the sand bar, arrived at Lions Bay Marina by sea, followed soon after by Lester and Dr. Villano by land. Sebastian had obtained provisions and, the *Jana* fully stocked, Dr. Villano sailed into the night for his distant rendezvous with romance. Before setting sail, he thanked them all profusely and Sebastian most of all.

Days later, Jana Villano and her prized pair of canines, a Scottish terrier, Haggis, and a Keeshond, Hero, after Shakespeare's heroine, flew to a distant isle and rendezvoused with her husband in the most romantic of ways: a certain restaurant overlooking the beach; a red boutonniere in the button hole; and code words to confirm identity, although none were really needed.

Dr. Kratz, the president of City College, also was soon thanking Sebastian, albeit against his will. Although Sebastian had been unable to identify the restroom stall wall graffiti artist, the graffiti soon ceased. Kratz would have to await another Herculean task to delegate to Sebastian so the English professor would fail and Kratz could then justify transferring Sebastian to the athletics department. Little did Kratz know that Sebastian had not only identified, but had confronted the author of the bathroom stall wall dissertations.

"I know you did it, Professor-Uncle Bill," Sebastian said one day as they sat in Bill's office. "Stop it or I'll have to inform Kratz."

"Who, me?" Bill asked, as if bending, let alone, breaking any rule, law or ordinance was beyond his ken, even as he smoked his latest misshapen cigarette. His small fan blew the incriminating and illegal smoke out the drilled holes in his window.

"Yes, you."

"How do you know it was me? The eloquent style?"

"No."

"The brilliant arguments?"

"No."

"The references to all manner of greater and lesser philosophers, thinkers and writers?"

"No."

"Well, then maybe arguments in favor of liberty and against bureaucracy?"

"No."

"Then what was it?"

"The cigarette butts you left on the floor. They were hand rolled. No one rolls their own cigarettes anymore, except you."

Bill raised his tobacco-stained hands in surrender. "Okay, okay, guilty as charged."

"Will you stop?"

Bill considered the proposal. "Only if you talk to the editors of *The Free Spirit* and ask them to publish my essays now and then. They censored my articles after I argued for students learning more by experience rather than just from lectures."

"That doesn't sound like something they'd censor."

"I merely argued that those studying criminal law might try breaking some laws."

Sebastian frowned but said, "I'll speak with them." He would suggest to the editors, whom he advised, that they put Bill's columns under the heading, "Modest Proposals," after Swift's essay suggesting eating Irish children as a means of ending the dual problems of famine and overpopulation. He made it clear to Bill, however, that his suggestion would in no way be construed as an order. Even so, Bill was soon a regular columnist in *The Free Spirit* and his work no longer appeared on bathroom stall walls. Luckily, Kratz read more bathroom stall walls than student journals, so he never noticed the similarity between Bill's columns and the anonymous bathroom stall wall dissertations.

Sebastian told the police about the shadowy man in the rented red sedan, but with no license plate number, there was little they could do. Sebastian faced a situation so aptly described by Coleridge; "Like one, that on a lonesome road / Doth walk in fear and dread, / And having once turned round, walks on, / And turns no more his head; / Because he knows a frightful fiend / Doth close behind him tread."

Days later in a hall at City College, the dark-haired man with the rental car finally cornered Sebastian as the English professor emerged from a lecture. In a sea of students, the man approached. Sebastian feared his life was about to end at the hands of a fiendish assassin hired by the foiled television network.

"I'm James Sterling and I'd like to have a word with you, Dr. Gianninni, if I might."

Sebastian hesitated, wondering if hit men normally introduce themselves to their victims. The assassin bore little resemblance to anyone's conception of Coleridge's 'frightful fiend.'

Sebastian swallowed, steeled his resolve and followed the dark-haired man to an alcove. The man turned. Sebastian glanced around. Few potential witnesses were in sight, but at least there would be a few to identify his body and, possibly, pick out the assassin from a Mountie lineup. In any case, he was tired of running, tired of scanning every room for a potential killer, tired of feeling hunted all the time. If this was to be the last seconds of his life, so be it, he would die thinking of his beloved Elizabeth.

"I'm a senior editor at Glencoe, Culloden and Cumberland, the New York publishing house."

Sterling had a sister who worked as a border guard at the Peace Arch border crossing. She had alerted him to some splendid manuscripts she had just purchased from Sebastian LeClerc Gianninni. After receiving copies, the editor took the first available flight to Seattle and after driving to Blaine had been trying to catch up with Sebastian ever since.

"I love your novels," Sterling explained with barely bridled enthusiasm. "They're in the grand tradition of satiric renditions of romantic literature."

"Satiric?" Sebastian asked, suddenly extremely worried, but not about being assassinated.

"Yes, in the same vein as Lovelace's 'The Rape of the Lock' and Cervantes' *Don Quixote*."

"My novels are *not* satires," Sebastian exclaimed, appalled. "I will not have them advertised and sold as such." What would his students and colleagues think when, after years of defending romantic novels as valid and serious literature, he published what were portrayed as satiric romantic novels?

The editor offered a substantial advance, but Sebastian would not yield, at least until Elizabeth heard about the number of zeros in the advance. A compromise was struck. Although he still railed against the fact that romance novels rarely appeared with a male name under the title, Elizabeth got the advance for the Gianninni family coffers and Sebastian's good name was saved through the use of a pen name; his once-again adoring wife's maiden name, Elizabeth Lee.

AFTERWARD

by

Sebastian LeClerc Gianninni, PhD

All these years later, Elizabeth and I still talk of those golden days in April when our lives were full of excitement and purpose. The Grizzly's 2000-2001 record season has faded from memory and vanished from the record books. With the failure of the bomb plot, Lester later told me, the network decided to destroy the team so much that they would never ever be world champions.

The bad news came fast in the summer of 2001. The discovery that Bertram Reginald "Roddy" Windsor had taken substantial doses of steroids as a child to counteract a rare degenerative disorder that led to dwarfism, disqualified him from playing in the NBA. Eddie "Three-Point" Anderson's relationship with Lester Means was discovered amidst a point-adding scandal. Anderson was banned from the sport. I still hear rumors he plays pick-up games, and regularly wins, in courts all over the Yukon, Nunavut and Keewatin, the former Northwest Territories. The brothers Hill, the backbone of the Grizzly Bear Bite Defense, it turned out, were not really brothers. They were illegal immigrants from Switzerland, who had snuck into Canada in hopes of getting into the lucrative miniature cuckoo clock manufacturing business. Their big hands barred them from this precise profession, so they turned to basketball. Having led the Grizzlies to a 94 percent winning percentage for the season, their illegal status was discovered and they were shipped back to Zurich economy class.

With such a plethora of scandals, the NBA ruled that the entire Grizzly season was invalid and ordered their record reevaluated in light of their squad of questionable players. This led to their glorious season going from near perfect to being ruled a 23 and 59 season, a pitiable 28 percent. They would not even get to play in the playoffs. The Grizzlies were extinct, at least in Vancouver. They moved to Memphis for the 2001-2002 season to put their soiled history behind them, although it did little to restore them to glory. They were also 23 and 59 their first year in Memphis. Apparently Grizzlies do not thrive in the wilds of Tennessee.

Although my Lord Byron wrote, "Nor florid prose, nor honied lies of rhyme, / Can blazon evil deeds, or consecrate a crime," I cannot say that I am sad I allowed Hogarth and Dr. Villano to escape. Hogarth is now a successful businessman. He owns So You Want to be a Spy. He takes wannabe spies on international trips in pursuit of all manner of government secrets. It is all make believe, of course, and the profits are also rather unbelievable. There are battalions of 007 wannabes out there. He now attends minor league baseball games with his son, games that have no delays for television commercial breaks.

Dr. Villano is a full professor now at the tiny university on his chosen island paradise, with his loving Jana at his side. She is now CEO of an Internet company that markets romantic aides. She made millions when her company went public, but she still works out of their home to be close to her husband. Elizabeth and I often visit them on romantic excursions now that our lives have to a certain degree returned to some form of normalcy. Villano and I still debate the merits of the Romantic Poets and the demerits of Shakespeare at the Villano beach house, which overlooks a serene, azure bay. I believe the Romantics are ahead by a comfortable margin in the ongoing debate, although Dr. Villano would undoubtedly beg to differ. Whatever the score, I am glad the Villano's journey, as happened in Mr. Shakespeare's *Twelfth Night*, "ended in lovers meeting."

The Grizzly Extinction Plot was only one of the many exciting episodes in my long life with Elizabeth. If my often accurate and always attentive biographer, Liam Shay, should wish to wile away a wet winter evening in Blaine with my lovely Elizabeth and me listening to the tales of our life together before a crackling fire, with hot cider near at hand and my faithful hounds, MacDuff and Allegra, curled up at our feet, then he may find time to put fingers to keyboard and tap out another tale. I have so many, maybe he would know which one to relate next....

The End

About the Author

The Grizzly Extinction Plot is Liam Shay's first novel. He has contributed to two edited volumes and his work has appeared in several magazines. Born to a Gaelic family, storytelling has always been a significant part of his life.

About Kerrera House Press

Kerrera House Press is an independent press dedicated to producing the books you keep. Visit us at KerreraHousePress.com for more information about our authors and our latest books.

Reader Resources

For a reader's guide, character bios, information about sports teams that have deserted their cities, and more about the writing of *The Grizzly Extinction Plot*, please visit KerreraHousePress.com.